THE SEVEN LEAGUE BOOTS

ALBERT MURRAY

THE

SEVEN LEAGUE BOOTS

A Novel

Pantheon Books
New York

All rights reserved under International and Pan-American Copyright
Conventions. Published in the United States by Pantheon Books,
a division of Random House, Inc., New York, and simultaneously
in Canada by Random House of Canada Limited, Toronto.

Library of Congress Cataloging-in-Publication Data

Murray, Albert.
The seven league boots / Albert Murray.
p.   cm.
ISBN 0-679-43986-2
1. Jazz musicians—United States—Fiction.   2. Young men—United
States—Fiction.   3. Afro-American musicians—Fiction.   4. Afro-
American men—Fiction.   I. Title.   II. Title: 7 league boots.
PS3563.U764S48   1995
813'.54—dc20   95-2622
CIP

Book design by M. Kristen Bearse

Manufactured in the United States of America

First Edition

2 4 6 8 9 7 5 3 1

*For
Mozelle
and
Michele*

CONTENTS

The castle hill was hidden, veiled in mist and darkness, nor was there even a glimmer of light to show that a castle was there.

—Franz Kafka

One

THE APPRENTICE

I

When road band buses used to go west by way of Memphis and Little Rock in those days you picked up Route 66 on the other side of Oklahoma City. Then six hours later you were through Amarillo and the Texas Panhandle country and on your way toward Tucumcari and across New Mexico with a short service stop in Albuquerque and a layover in Gallup, which was thirty-two miles beyond the Continental Divide and not more than thirty minutes from the Arizona state line.

Then early the next morning there would be Holbrook and the Petrified Forest and the Painted Desert stretching away in the distance and as you pulled on through Flagstaff and headed for Kingman and Yucca, it was California here I come. *And I said I come from Alabama and so did Joe States, who by that time had been crisscrossing the country from border to border and coast to coast by rail and by bus as a full time professional band musician for almost twelve years.*

I said I come from Alabama, and he said me and you schoolboy me and you. Which he had been winking and repeating ever since the day I came to Cincinnati as a temporary replacement for the bass player a year and that many months ago. What he had also said then was So you from down in the Beel, well I'm old Joe States from up in the Ham. Then he had gone on to say now let me tell you something, young fellow. Anybody come asking you some old stuff about where your banjo, you tell them what I tell them. You tell them I got your goddamn banjo swinging down you know where.

When I came on board the bus the first time that Monday morning and found that my assigned seat was directly across the aisle from his he said, Like I said Schoolboy me and you my man me and you and the one right back there behind you will be Otis Sheppard, Ole Cool Papa Spodee Odee the box picker.

That's the rhythm section minus the bossman because he'll be up in seat num-
ber two right behind old Milo the Navigator. Everybody gets a double seat in
this organization.

They were en route to New York. But from Cincinnati, they were
swinging down into Kentucky for dance dates in Lexington and Louisville,
and then turning back north to Indianapolis for two nights before heading
across Ohio by way of Dayton and Columbus to Wheeling, West Virginia, and
so on through Pittsburgh and Philadelphia.

Now there's somebody that actually did go down into Louisiana with a
sure enough country-ass banjo. But he don't come from no Aladambama. He
come from outside of Memphis, Tennessee, in other words Missippi. So anyway
once he got down to New Orleans, he heard something that made him trade
it in for a guitar. He went down there seeking his fortune and that was it, and
didn't nobody have to tell him.

Right 'Sippi? he said, and Otis Sheppard, who was as used to being
called 'Sippi as Cool Papa, grunted without opening his eyes, and that was
when Joe States said, Now me I am the one that can tell you something about
coming from Alabama playing music, and I am talking about playing music
for a living.

I'm talking about I'm the one that hit the trail out of Birmingham with
my trap set in a goddamn cotton sack, and I'm talking about laboring on the
L and goddamn N Railroad. And whenever I decided to stop off somewhere for
a few days I'd hide my sack in the thickets down by the railroad until I found
myself a little gig to pick up enough change to move on.

So you tell them I got their banjo, Schoolboy, he said. And before I could
say what I was going to say about how old Luzana Cholly used to snag freight
trains out of Gasoline Point with his twelve string guitar slung over his shoul-
der like a rifle, he said, What I had was a pedal contraption for my bass drum
and ride cymbal, a folding stand for my snare, a couple of sets of sticks, a set of
brushes and mallets and that was my trap set as we used to call them in those
days. And then when I got with the bossman and we started this thing he got
now I had to keep adding all this other stuff to keep up because he was always
coming up with something he wanted to try out. So when we went over to
Paris that first time, and all these French cats kept coming up to me talking

about vuzet the battery I said goddamn right I'm the goddamn cotton picking dynamo of this outfit.

I didn't get around to mentioning Luzana Cholly until several days later when we were on our way across eastern Ohio. Somebody started talking about the cities on and near our route that people from places down home went north to settle in back during the boom days of the nineteen twenties and I could have named families who had kinfolks who had moved to Ohio during the same time when Willie Marlowe, who was the first scootabout playmate I ever had, left Mobile for Detroit, Michigan. Which was also when Roger and Eddie Parker left elementary school because they were moving to Pittsburgh. But I said the one I always thought about when I thought about Youngstown was Luzana Cholly, who had also been just about everywhere but had never settled anywhere.

I said he had hoboed on just about every railroad line in every section of the country and he always took his guitar with him and Joe States said, Now see there, me and you again Schoolboy. Leadbelly, Blind Lemon Jefferson, Big Bill, Robert Johnson, and the one and only Mr. Luzana Goddamn Cholly. That's right he did used to spend a lot of time around the outskirts of the Beel. Now I first met him out on the road. Not on the circuit. Just on the road hittin' the tonks. I used to have to hit a few of them myself but me I was always headed for the circuits.

So you come up knowing old Luzana Cholly. Goddamn, Schoolboy, he said. And then he said, But talking about Mobile I played the Pike Theater out on Davis Avenue when I was on the southeastern territory circuit, and I also remember playing some dances in the Gomez Auditorium right down the street from the Pike.

So you know I know Papa Gladstone, he said. Old Papa Stone was always my meal ticket when I got stranded down there a few times. Old Papa Glad. He's been running dance bands in that town longer than anybody and also putting the marchingest band in the Mardi Gras parade every year. Man, I went down to Mobile looking for a gig one Mardi Gras and old Papa Glad had three outfits working dances somewhere after the parade every night; and afterward I cut out on the GM&N and beat my way on up through Missippi to Memphis and points up the Big Muddy.

Me and you Schoolboy, he said once more that afternoon as the bus zoomed across Arizona toward Needles and the Mojave that many months later on what was, at long last, my first trip all the way out to the Pacific coast. And I gave him the highball sign, thinking about how I used to dream of going to Los Angeles as I sat in my secret spyglass place in the chinaberry tree.

Every time somebody else left Gasoline Point for that part of the country the talk, around the fireplace if it was a winter night or on the swing porch in the summertime, was always about how you took the southbound Pan American Express on the L & N down to New Orleans and changed to the Sunset Limited westbound on the Southern Pacific for the Texas plains and the desert and cactus horizons of New Mexico and Arizona.

Then when you finally reached the end of the line and came out of the Union station in Los Angeles that many days later, everywhere you looked there would be palm trees and blooming canna lilies and bougainvillea plants and also buildings with Spanish arches and terra cotta roofing. And when you came to the station exit you'd be at the foot of Sunset Boulevard. And somewhere not far away in the pineapple golden distance beyond the blue Pacific coast horizon was a paradise island of Santa Catalina and the town of Avalon.

That was the way it always used to be when you heard what you used to hear back even before Cousin Bird, whose given name was Roberta, left on the Pan American for a month's visit that time and came back and went back six months later to stay. It was always Los Angeles and not yet Hollywood and Beverly Hills until I began reading movie magazines, especially *Screen Land* and *Photoplay*, when I was in junior high school.

When I reached senior high school, moving pictures and movie stars had become a part of what you read about and thought about as never before, but by that time the main thing for me had become college. So even as I still kept up with not only all of the current movies but also with the fan magazine features about life in Hollywood and Beverly Hills, the place above all others that I wanted to visit was Paris by way of New York and London; and then there would be Rome and all of Europe, the Mediterranean and the Aegean.

But I said what I said because as conscious as I was of what it meant for me of all people to be on my way with the band I was with to play at the Palladium followed by a week in a nightclub on the Strip and three days in a recording studio, the closer we came to arriving, the more I felt as if I had come directly from Mobile on the old Sunset Limited after all.

When the bus rolled on through Topock and came on down to the bridge across that part of the Colorado River, you were at the state line; and you were also leaving the Mountain Time zone for Pacific Time, and in a matter of not as much as thirty more minutes you would be pulling on up the steep grade from the old Indian and Mexican trading town of Needles, beyond which there would be the gray and purple sagebrush and dry lakes of the Mojave, with one cluster of mountains after another in the distance on both sides of the mostly flat desert route all the way to Barstow.

I said California. I said Hey California. And Joe States said, One more time Schoolboy. One more go round for the old Alabama jackrabbit.

Then when we came to San Bernardino and the freeway and there were only sixty more miles to go, he looked over at me again and said, I can clue you in on a few things about these people in this man's town, statemate; and I'm talking about things that will be useful to you whether you decide to stay in this music business or not.

II

They were already on the bandstand warming up when I got there that morning. You could hear them as soon as the taxi pulled up to the curb, and I also saw the bus in the alley leading to the backstage loading ramp. Then there was the sound echoing in the empty auditorium as you hear it on your way past the publicity pictures and placards in the entrance lobby.

I came on into the auditorium and stood looking at them. The stands with the bossman's name on them were all set up in place, and the five members of the reed section were already seated in the front row, but each one was studying his own score and blowing as if whispering to himself. The three trombone players were standing in a triangle off to stage left working on ensemble riff passages exactly as I had always imagined the hocknet figures had been worked out in Ellington's "Bragging in Brass."

Upstage off to the left each of the four trumpet players was walking in his own private circle doing his own lip and finger exercises. Some dance band trumpet players walked with a stylishly deliberate slouch, but these four held their shoulders as erect as you were required to do in school marching bands.

The guitar player and the bass man were strumming and thumping softly in time with each other, but drummer was still unpacking and assembling his setup. He took his time and examined each piece of equipment as he took it out of the big charcoal gray traveling case with the bossman's name stenciled on it. As he put each piece into place he kept testing it and his stool until he was satisfied.

There was nobody at the piano yet. I didn't see the bossman himself and I wondered if he were backstage in the dressing room that he was going to be using for the next three nights. But I also knew that sometimes he was the first one to arrive, and that sometimes he came along on the bus with everybody else, and other times he would not come in until later on and then would stay on working by himself after everyone was gone except the caretakers.

The club had a long rectangular dance area with tables bordering each side and booths along each wall, and there was a roped off reserved section down front next to the footlights. The floor had already been cleaned and freshly sprinkled with wax flakes, and most of the chairs were stacked upside down on the tables.

I wondered if the purple and gold stage drapery stood for anything in particular. The walls were gray with a shoulder high purple and gold border design. The gabled ceiling was white. But the exposed rafters and beams were black; and there was also a hanging globe of mirror glass mosaics like the one that always used to revolve above the junior/senior prom decorations at Mobile County Training School every spring no matter what the theme for the occasion was.

The cleaning crew had opened all of the shuttered windows, and there was a fresh midmorning breeze from the moist late springtime Ohio weather outside, but there was the not unpleasant nightclub aroma about the place even so. I went inside the roped off area and took a chair down and sat at a table about ten feet from the solo microphone.

I had my fingers crossed, but I felt fine. I had spent the whole night in a day coach from Montgomery, but once I checked in at the hotel and took a shower and shaved and changed, I was ready to do whatever I had to do. So when the desk clerk told me about rehearsal and said nobody would be coming back until mid or late afternoon, I took the cab to the club to report in and get that part over with.

Each section went on working on its own for a while longer. Then the clarinet player, who also doubled on alto and soprano and who was known as The Pro and the Old Pro as in old resident professional or expert because as number one assistant arranger and straw boss (or concertmaster) he was the one who was next to the Bossman

Himself, stood up and went over to the piano and waited for everyone else to move into place.

He sat at the keyboard with a pencil in one hand looking at the long master sheet spread out on the rack in front of him and waited until the drummer tapped the shaft of the high hat cymbal. Then he called out the first piece, not by name but by number, and put the pencil behind his ear and played the comp chords all the way through and came back and began a vamp. And on the fourth bar he nodded to the drummer.

I knew what to expect because I had been present at one of their rehearsals before. That had happened back down in central Alabama eight months earlier. I had been in the group of students waiting on the sidewalk in front of the campus guesthouse when the band bus arrived that morning, and when I found out that they were going out to the club right after lunch to get set up and also to run through some new material, I cut all of my afternoon classes to be there.

The Bossman Himself was there from the very beginning that time. The club owner, whose name was Giles Cunningham, had pulled up to the front entrance and let him out of the black Cadillac while the bus was still being unloaded at the stage door, and he headed straight for the piano and before anybody else could unpack and start tuning up, he was already making changes on the score sheets that he brought with him.

What they had begun with that time was something he was still working on, and first wanted to hear how the trumpets, trombones, and reeds sounded separately and then together, but without the piano part and with the rest of the rhythm section also laying out for the time being. Then as he went on pulling out other scores and calling for passage after passage in no particular order that I could figure out but that they skipped to without any confusion whatsoever, I realized that they were not there because they were trying to put the finishing touches on something special for that night. What they were doing was a part of their weekly routine.

Everything they did that afternoon in Giles Cunningham's ballroom was just fine with me because after all of the years I had spent listening to them on records and the radio, there they were in person and there I was that close to them, and to the Bossman Himself making it all happen almost as if as much for my benefit as for his own.

I didn't leave until it was all over, and after the dance that night I went backstage to his crowded dressing room and touched his elbow and said how great it all was, but I didn't actually meet him person to person or even novice to maestro until two days later when Hortense Hightower did what she did and said what she said. And that was when he said what he said and I couldn't believe my ears. And she said, What did I tell you. She said, I know what I hear when I hear something. And he said, That ain't no news to me. But I still didn't know what to think, and then that many months later the telegram came and she said, See there. And Giles Cunningham said, Like I told you before when it comes to stuff like this she's just like old Art Tatum's left hand playing stride. She don't never miss, my man. She don't never miss. Not on something like that.

As they went on working through the first two numbers that first morning in Cincinnati, I kept waiting for the Bossman Himself to walk in any minute. And either slide onto the piano seat beside the clarinet player, or take a chair off to one side, or out in the auditorium. When they stopped for a break forty-five minutes later there was still no sign of him.

When the signal came, the four trumpet players went back through the center exit laughing and talking among themselves. The clarinet player stayed at the keyboard making changes on the master sheets, and the bass and guitar players moved over and stood looking over his shoulder. Two of the trombone players and one of the tenor men moved off into the wings on the left. But the third trombone player stood up and stretched and sat back down, and so did the other tenor man.

The alto player lit a pipe and opened up a magazine, and at first the drummer sat talking to the other reed men about something on a sports page of the *Cincinnati Inquirer* that he had handed them. Then when they passed the paper on along to the third trombone player and started running exercises on their horns again, the drummer made several more adjustments on his equipment, stood up, lit a cigarette, and came to the apron of the bandstand and stood with his legs apart and one hand in his back pocket, looking out into the auditorium.

He was wearing sunglasses, a white nylon baseball cap, a blue short sleeve polo shirt with hard-finished tailor shop perfect gray slacks, and his shoes were gray suede wing tips with very thin leather soles and low heels. I already knew that his clothes were always as natty as his drumming was fly. And I also knew that he was from Birmingham and that his band name was not his real name, which was Jonathan Wesley Gayles, not Joe States. But he was everybody's statemate, because he knew how to make himself at home everywhere, and he could also have called himself the band's elder statesman.

Say now hey there, States, he said, waving and stepping down onto the dance floor and heading toward me. So what say there, my man. And I said, Nothing to me man. And he said, Me neither, my man. I'm just up there trying to keep enough flesh and blood mustered up to drive the man's twenty mule team the way he wants it to go; and, man, sometimes these fifteen mule headed road band scobes can make your job a whole lot harder than a sure enough twenty mule team and a half.

Then he said, Hey I'm old chicken butt Joe States. And I said, Hey man you couldn't deny it if you wanted to. I had you tabbed, man. And, man, you're some mule skinner for my money. And he said, Who me? Man I'm just up there faking. And I said, Some faking, man. You and Sonny Greer, you and Jo Jones. And I also thought about old funny-eyed Dike Spivens, who cut out from Papa Gladstone and Mobile for New Orleans and then worked his way to New York by way of the Southwest Territory circuit.

So what's been happening since we came through here the last time? he said. And I said, Hey man, I'm green on this one, man. And he said, Yeah? Damn man, I was counting on you to put me next to something new. And I said, Not me, man. I just pulled in for the first time this morning. And he said, No stuff. And I handed him the telegram from Milo the Navigator, and he said, Hey Goddamn, man. You're old Shag's replacement. And I said, Temporary replacement, but he let that pass and said, Hey Shag, here he is. And the bass player, whose name was Shelton Philips, turned from the piano and looked out toward us and said, Is that him? And Joe States said, Yeah man, here this schoolboy the bossman been telling us about.

Everybody was looking at me then, and the clarinet player said, Well bring him on up here, Joe. And Shag Philips met us at the foot-lights and we shook hands, and then the trumpet players came back and we were all gathered around the piano; I already knew all of them by their proper names as well as their nicknames because I had been keeping track of all the changes in the lineup over the years.

The trumpet players were Ike Ellis, Osceola Menefee, Scully Pittman, and Elmore Wilkins. The trombones were Wayman Ridge-way, Malachi Moberly, and Fred Gilchrist, who was no less important for being the single section man who seldom took solos. The two tenors were Old Pro (as needed) and Herman Kemble, who was also known in the band as Big Bloop. The alto was Alan Meadows and the baritone was Ted Chandler. Then there were Joe States, Shag Philips, and Otis Sheppard with the Bossman Himself. I said my name, but they had already picked up the cue from Joe States and were calling me Schoolboy as they were to do from then on; and I didn't mind at all. Not then or at any other time later on, because they always said it just right, even when some of them shortened it to Schoolie and some oth-ers said School or Schoo which after all was also short for Scooter.

If somebody had started some of that old what-say-professor or what-say-young-'fess stuff, I just might have turned right around and walked out of there. Not that I myself ever had anything at all against teachers. Not me with my brand new college degree. I just didn't have any intention of tolerating any wisecracks that implied that there was anything either ridiculous or unrealistic about education.

But there was none of that. The way they said it made you feel the way you used to feel when people around the fire circle and on the swing porch used to look at you the way they always looked at you when somebody said what they used to say about taking to school and your books so that you could bring more credit to your people some-day whatever line of work you chose to follow.

So by the time I was through shaking hands snatching palms and slapping shoulders with everybody, I was already looking forward to the time when, as much for my ongoing development as for their own technical benefit, some of them were going to begin saying things like, Let's see what the schoolboy has to say about this. Hey, maybe the schoolboy been reading up on this. Hey, maybe the schoolboy dug something about this stuff in some footnotes somewhere. Hey, let's get the schoolboy to put his slide rule on this.

While everybody was getting settled back in place to go on with what they were working on the clarinet player took me aside and told me that Bossman Himself was in New York negotiating a recording contract and was not due in town until the next afternoon. In the meantime, he said, you just relax and start checking these cats out at close range. And don't worry about nothing. And I mean ever. Don't never ever, he said, smiling his Old Pro smile as he gave me a pat on the shoulder that made me feel as only old pros can make you feel about your possibilities. Then he also said, And by the way, you might as well call me Old Pro like the rest of them, Schoolboy.

III

Back at the hotel later on that first Wednesday afternoon, Joe States and Shag Philips invited me to come along with them; and after hamburgers at a lunch counter down the block, we checked by the poolroom where they left messages for a couple of local friends. Then we went on to the early evening showing of the current Clark Gable movie, and afterward they took me to one of the eating places where the local musicians, entertainers, and athletes used to hang out in those days.

We made our way along the counter slapping shoulders and exchanging jive greetings and gestures and took a booth from which you could see out onto the street; and that was where Joe States began telling me what he was to tell me about who was who and what was what in the band and about how much I was going to enjoy getting to be a part of it.

But first Shag Philips said what he had been waiting to say. As soon as the waitress had taken our orders, he held up his hand and said, I just want you to hear this directly from me, Schoolboy. Man I sure do hate to have to be cutting out all these old jiveass thugs in this old homemade road band, and only reason I'm doing it is the situation back home.

Which he said was such that he was the one who had to be right there on the spot to take care of and there was no telling how long he was going to have to run things himself before he would be able to leave somebody else in charge and hit the road again.

Look Joe, he said, I'm just trying to make this young man realize how lucky he is to be coming in with a bunch of fellows like this. He already know that there ain't no better band out there anywhere. So I just want him to know that there ain't no better cats to work with and there ain't no better bossman to work for. If you can call it work. Like the bossman always says, when it comes to music you practice and then when you get on the job you *play*.

He reached across the table and patted my hand, and then he just sat looking down at his place mat because he couldn't say anything more. And Joe States said, Ain't nothing else in the world like this out-fit you coming into, Schoolboy, because ain't nobody else in the world like the bossman. Because the thing about it when it comes to him is that it ain't never just about cutting them dots. With him it's always as much a personal thing as it is a technical musical thing.

That's exactly what I'm talking about, Shag Philips said, not minding the sound of his voice or the moisture in his eyes. Man that's what gets you and that's how come I already know it don't matter where I am and what I might be doing, I'm always going to feel like I'm a member of this band, just like I feel like a member of my flesh and blood family.

And when I said what I said about alma mater he said, Hey dig it, man.

The waitress came back with our orders then, and as we ate, Joe States said, You going to like it, Schoolboy. I can tell. You just wait until Friday night. You just wait until you start getting to know these cats up close on a day to day basis from town to town. And speaking of the devil, he said, there's two of them just walked in. And I looked and saw Ike Ellis and Herman Kemble.

Shag Philips stood up and waved for them to come on over, and when they got there, he gave them his side of the booth and excused himself to go back to the hotel because he was expecting a long distance call.

So you all starting right in trying to teach this college boy bad habits already I see, Ike Ellis said winking at me. And Herman Kemble said, You better watch 'em, Schoolboy. And Joe States said, Who me man? Come on man. Ain't much these college boys ain't already been into these days. Both of y'all know that.

But sure enough now Joe, Ike Ellis said. What you cats up to for later on? And before Joe States could get halfway through saying Ain't nothing happening, Herman Kemble said, Man don't come trying to hand me none of that old hype. You rhythm section thugs been the chick chasingest cunt hounds in this band since in the beginning was the word and the word was you know what.

So come on, man, Ike Ellis said, What you timekeepers got on the line? And Herman Kemble said, It may be a big grizzly bear but she's always out there somewhere, everywhere we stop. One horse town, tank town, any old crossroad, Schoolboy.

I know good and well that you all got something in Cincinnati for this schoolboy to get next to, he said. And Joe States said, Come on, Bloop, does this schoolboy look like he needs somebody to fix him up with anything? Man, what this cat's going to need is somebody to help him fight them off.

I already knew that Herman Kemble's nickname was Bloop and that sometimes he was also called Big Bloop and I was also to find out that when the bossman wanted a certain kind of tenor sax solo he called him the Bishop. He got everybody all revved up and rocking and shouting and when they came to the solo chorus he would say, And now, the Bishop. Or say, You tell them, Bishop. Or say, Go tell them, Bishop.

Plenty of time for the trillies, Bloop, Joe States said. First things first, man. We were just about to give him a quick inside rundown on the bossman. And Ike Ellis shook his head in mock sadness watching me out of the corner of his eye and said, You'll need it, Schoolboy. And Herman Kemble said, Lord, will he evermore need it.

But I knew they were just signifying because they couldn't really disguise the mischief in their eyes or in their voices. So I pretended to be alarmed, but I couldn't hide the twinkle in my eyes either. So we all ended up laughing at ourselves. And then Joe States looked at me and started.

Now the first thing, he said, is that the goddamn man is a goddamn musician. And I'm talking about first, last, and always. And I'm not talking about somebody that folks call a musician just because he can play some kind of instrument because he learned it from a book and can run down something you hand him on a sheet of paper. That's not what I'm talking about and I'm not talking about calling somebody a musician because he can get a job playing music. Ain't never no time when it's really a job to that man, Schoolboy.

And Ike Ellis said, He sure telling you right about that, Schoolboy. Ain't never been no time like that for that man.

That's because it's the man's life, Schoolboy, Herman Kemble said. When something is your life, man, that makes all the difference in the world; and that's why that somitch ain't never shucking and jiving. Don't care what kind of place we been booked into and how few of any kind of people turn out to hear us.

Tell him, Joe, he said. And that's when Joe States said, The thing about that is it don't make no difference who else you booked in there to play for, you always playing for him. It's like he's the goddamn microphone and then he sends it all out through the amplifiers and speakers and he don't never want to have to be sitting there hearing some old half-ass bullshit. And just remember most of the time the stuff you playing is his, and the rest of the time it's something he picked out because he wants you to do it his way.

Which brings me to another thing, Ike Ellis said. You know, a lot of times when something is somebody's whole life like that, the somich is subject to become a goddamn fanatic or maniac or something. You know what I mean? And Joe States said, Like that somitch I saw in a goddamn movie a long goddamn time ago. You remember that old movie that old John Barrymore did? I think it was called *The Sea Beast* or something like that. And old John Barrymore was this peglegged schooner captain and his whole thing in life was hunting down this goddamn tigertoothed whale all over the seven seas.

Hey yeah I remember seeing that, Ike Ellis said. Now that was one more tormented cat. Man, seem to me like I can still see old John Barrymore glaring like he's out to tangle with the devil himself, and I swear I can still hear that pegleg bumping back and forth on the captain's deck—and man, unless I'm mistaken that goddamn movie came out way back before there was even Vitaphone.

But you see now that's just the thing about our bossman, School-boy, Joe States said. You ain't never going to catch him up there, in there or out there anywhere acting like everybody else got to put up with some crazy ass shit from him because he's the one that's the mad genius.

Not him, Herman Kemble said. You never met a more regular cat than that stud, Schoolboy. I'm telling you. Ain't nobody in this band can put him the shade when it comes to partying. And Joe States said, Look you're talking about the champ because he can be out there balling till the swallows came back to Capistrano, and then be the first one up the next morning just like ain't nothing happened but counting sheep.

Inking in some more dots, man, Ike Ellis said. Ain't nothing ever going to get in the way of that. And Joe States said, Inking them dots. Inking them dots. The first thing he heads for every morning (sometimes even before he goes to the bathroom) is the nearest piano and there are all them little scribbles on all them little scraps of paper in his pockets he's got to deal with.

That was when I asked about Old Pro and about how soon he was usually called in when something new was in the work, and Joe States said sometimes right at the beginning but mainly because Old Pro just happened to be there at the time. But most of the time the first to be called in was always somebody or whichever section he had in mind for some particular passage he was working out.

Sometimes he would pass out fragments of the manuscript and make changes as he listened to the run-through. And other times he was just as likely to compose directly on the horns by dictating the notes to each instrumentalist, by humming them, by name or by sounding the tones on the piano. Then he would make his first draft of the score from the playback.

As a matter of fact, Joe States said, Old Pro might not get to see how the whole thing is laid out until it is ready for the first run-through by everybody together. All he knows up to then is his part in the reed section.

Now me, I'm just about always the last one to see what's actually written down, he said. And Ike Ellis said, Yeah but let me tell you something about that, Schoolboy. He don't even need to see it then and probably ain't never going to look at it no more. Tell him, Bloop, he said. And Herman Kemble said, It's the goddamnedest thing you ever saw, Schoolboy. After all the years they been playing together Old Joe's so tight on the bossman's case that when the bossman's nose itches, he can always count on Old Joe to be ready to sneeze even before he himself realizes that he wants to.

You hear this stuff, Schoolboy, Joe States said. Now that's these horn blowers for you. All I'm doing is just doing my goddamn job and here they come signifying some hocus pocus bullshit.

Yeah but you just wait till you see the stuff, Schoolboy, Ike Ellis said. And Herman Kemble said, Man, it's uncanny. And Joe States said, You hear this stuff. Man, all you all talking about is plain old experience. When you got enough experience, you might not know exactly where somebody is going, but it don't take much time to figure out which way he's headed.

They went on drinking what they were drinking, signifying at each other for my benefit; and then on the way back to the hotel Joe States locked arms with me and said, Me and you, Schoolboy. Me and you. Ain't nothing for you to worry about, because the bossman handpicked you himself and that means that he knows that you can already do exactly what he wants you to do. So anything else you need, get to me fast.

IV

When I finally made it back to my room that first night in Cincinnati, I lay awake in the dark going over what I had been hearing about the bossman. Then even as I began to think about what I was going to have to say to him the next day, I was already remembering what had happened when he came into the club to catch Hortense Hightower's one o'clock show that Saturday morning that many months ago.

I didn't find out that Hortense Hightower had set it all up, until she called me that next afternoon to tell me what he had told her. *All she had said that night was, Well look who just came in. And what I saw was him being led to a table right down front, and I knew that the one who came along with him was Milo the Navigator, his road manager; and all I thought was that they were there mainly for a late night snack and also because Hortense Hightower and Giles Cunningham were among the many longtime friends he had made in towns all across the country over the years.*

But it was really her doing, and I didn't have any idea of what was really going on. Even when she left us playing instrumentals for the rest of the set and went down joined them and sipped her usual ginger ale, while he and Milo the Navigator had their fried chicken, potato salad, and beer. I just thought that, being the official hostess as well as an old personal friend, she was out there to help lay on the good old special down home brownskin service.

So when he got up and followed her when she came back on stage for the last set, I just thought he had talked her into letting him back her for a couple of numbers so that he could listen to her from his usual position at the keyboard. Then when he stayed on up there jamming with us until closing time, I just thought he was probably doing something he liked to do from time to time to unwind before turning in; and when he said what he said afterward, it occurred to me that sitting in like that was also one of his most direct and practical ways of keeping in touch with (and ahead of) whatever was happening among local musicians in all sections of the country the band traveled through on its swing around the coast to coast circuit every year.

That was very nice, very nice, very nice, he said, looking back from the front seat as Giles Cunningham headed for the campus to drop him at the guesthouse and me at the dormitory. Milo the Navigator had already left after Hortense Hightower's last number. They were pulling out that next morning en route to New Orleans for a theater date at the beginning of the next week.

How did you come by stuff like that? he said. And I told him I guessed that I had just picked up here and there, more from listening to the whole group than from practicing the bass fiddle because I'm still in my first year of trying to do that. And he said, That may be so but you've been a musician all of your life, my man.

I can tell one when I hear one, he said. It's my job, he said. I don't know what the hell else you do, and I bet you're damn good at whatever it is, but you've also been a musician all of your born days, if you know what I mean. Some people think you're a musician if you can play anything they put in front of you but to me a musician is somebody who makes his instrument say something even if he can play in only one key and can't name that.

Then he asked me where I was from, and when I told him he said, I wondered about that. I thought that was what I heard in there. That's old Gladstone's town. So you're one of old Gladstone's boys. And when I said in a way I guess but not really because I never ever even touched an instrument in Papa Gladstone's presence, he said, That's all right about that, if you grew up down there that's who you grew up hearing.

And I said, Beginning with Mardi Gras and at baseball games and picnics way before I was old enough to know what dance halls and dance bands were really all about. And even as I spoke it occurred to me that I couldn't remember when I didn't already know what honkytonks and juke joints like Joe Locket's in the Bottom were all about.

Old Papa Gladness, he said. And I said, Then later on when I was in junior high school I used to go all the way into town to listen to Papa Gladstone rehearsing a band just as I also used to go by the assembly room to hear the Mobile County Training School Musical Demons add new numbers to its dance book, which I already memorized cover to cover, note for note by ear.

So it looks like I had you tabbed right away, he said. And I said, You sure did. And he said, That's old Papa Gladness for you. He's got as many children forever turning up somewhere as old Uncle Bud in that old bone knocking rhyme, Giles; and not just children he might have forgotten after all these years, but a whole slew of others like this young fella here that he didn't even know was one of his in the first place.

Then he said, If you're from down there, you must also know something about an old barrelhouse piano player named Doodlebug McMeans. And when I said, By name, reputation, and riff quotations only (because he always played in a place way down on the other side of town), he said, Now let's see now, I guess old Riverboat Shorty was before your time because hell he was getting on up there when I first met him; but he was the one that used to tangle with old Jelly Roll Morton when old Jelly used to come up to Mobile from New Orleans.

He was still around when I left, I said; but he wasn't playing very much anymore. I used to see him out at baseball games getting on up there but still sharp in his peg top pants and silk shirts and either a straw katie or a Panama with the brim turned down all around and you couldn't miss those rings, that cigar holder and that watch chain and fob which is why he always wore one of his fancy vests even when he wasn't wearing a coat.

That's Riverboat all right, he said. This boy knows something, Giles, he said. And then he said, What about the one they call Red Bird and another one known as King Velvet? And what about singers? What about Velma Mackie, Cleo Quitman, and the one and only Miss Big Money Watkins, who used to be out there on the trail making some of the same rounds as Ma Rainey and Bessie and all the rest of them red hot Smith mamas.

And I said, Now you're talking about some of the places I was beginning to be able to get into by the time I was at the end of my first year of high school. (By which time I had also begun memorizing all of the records I liked—and some I didn't—without even thinking about it. Somebody would just walk up and say, Hey Scooter what about when old so and so said, and either hum or whistle the solo passage and also the background including grunts for the rhythm; and if you had heard it you always joined in to prove that you had picked up on it too.)

We went on talking about Mobile all the way to the campus, and when Giles Cunningham pulled up behind where the band bus was parked in front of the guesthouse, I said I would walk from there and got out and took the bass from the trunk and waited until the two of them decided what time the bus would circle by the Pit to pick up the box lunches on its way out of town the next morning.

They shook hands and after Giles Cunningham headed back toward the main gate, the two of us stood there on the sidewalk under the elms talking a little while longer with him asking if I knew Pensacola Slim, who was the one who had begun by taking him to places in the Grove and out on Chinchula Road back when he first brought his band to the Pike Theater years ago; and I remembered Pensacola Slim as a man about town whom I knew only by sight, by automobile and reputation.

Which was also the case with the Yates brothers and their well to do family who were the TOBA circuit people in Mobile as well as the owners of the Davis Avenue ball park and the sponsors of the Mobile Black Bears baseball team. For me they were no less legendary when you saw them in person than they were in the stories you heard about them and about Cleve Huddleson The Contractor, not only around the fireside and in Papa Gumbo Willie's barbershop but also in some of Mr. B. Franklin Fisher's morning assembly talks.

But to him they were people he had done business with and also had fun with during brief stopovers in Mobile, and he mentioned going with them down to their summer house and fishing camp at Coden, a place everybody knew about because Booker T. Washington once spent a vacation there with them. I didn't mention it but I also knew Coden by sight, because it was only about two miles from Bayou la Batre and about eight from the picnic beach at Mon Louis Island.

Pushing the fiddle case along the tree lined avenue to the upper end of the campus and the dormitory, I could still see the Mobile people and places he had mentioned, and then I also began to think about what it was like to be a full time big league road musician. Your headquarters would be in New York but your home would be nowhere in particular and everywhere in general which is to say anywhere at all.

Anywhere you parked your bus. Anywhere you unpacked your bags. I said anywhere I hang my hat. Anywhere I park my feet, remembering myself all the way back to the me I used to be when my best of all possible running buddies was Little Buddy Marshall who said, Hey shit I reckon and set out for the seven seas and the seven wonders, ready or not, compass, spyglass, maps, and mileage charts or no compass, maps, or even mileage charts.

My good old best of all possible roommates, who reckoned always in terms of calculable probabilities, contingencies, and comprehensive implications would have said, Yea verily. But only after having carefully estimated, however casually, the risks and having given due consideration to the alternatives.

On the subject of road musicians he would also have reminded me of all our conversations about the Chansons de Geste of the troubadours in medieval France and the improvisations of the commedia dell'arte during the early

years of the Italian Renaissance; and he would have pointed out the connection
of what he used to call the ineluctable mordality of the picaresque (because all
yarns like all tunes actually begin and end with and, as in: And it came to pass
and so it went) and the ultimate rootlessness that is the perpetual condition
humaine.

As for what had been said about how I played that night, I couldn't
help thinking about it again once I stood the instrument in its rack in
the corner and sat on the bed taking off my clothes but I also knew that
the best way to take it was as very nice words of very generous encour-
agement from a famous professional to an eager to please beginner. In
any case, since I didn't think of myself as being a musician, not even a
part time one, or even a potential one, what it really meant was that I
hadn't messed up. And I could always say I got through the whole session with the Bossman Himself without being told to lay out. It never
once crossed my mind that anything else would ever come of it, certainly not within the next twelve months.

Not that I had actually forgotten what I had heard over the years
about how the great personal sound of his band was based on the fact
that he was so good at turning beginners into the expert sidemen and
soloists that his always very special arrangements and compositions
required. Somebody was always talking about that, and I never questioned it. I just didn't think it would ever have anything to do with me.

V

He finally came into Cincinnati from New York that Friday morning, but he was not at rehearsal that afternoon; so I didn't see him until Joe States took me to him when we got to the club that night.

In that band in those days you were always due on the scene an hour before opening time, and he was already there when we came backstage. The door to his dressing room was open, and he was talking to Old Pro. He saw us and held up his hand and said, Hey there you are. Come on in. And Old Pro said, See you later. I got to go get pretty; and as he passed me he said, You know how it is, Schoolboy. Even when I don't take solos I'm sitting right up there on that front line where people can even see my goddamn socks. And Joe States said, Me and you, Pro. Me and you. I just popped by to bring you our school-boy, bossman. Me and you later, Schoolboy. Anything you need, get to me fast. Well, look like you done it again, bossman. All I got to say is when it comes to that you got a knack second to none.

So then there was only the two of us for the first time since that last night on the campus that many months ago. And he said, How was your trip? And I said, Fine just fine thanks. And he said, I sure am glad you're taking me up on this. I've been thinking about you, and I believe I might just be on to a little something for you before long. We'll see. Meanwhile, Pro tells me that he and Shag and Joe and Otis have already started getting you clued in on the book; and they all say you're a very quick study. And I said, Well so far it's been more like fun than work. And he said, No wonder you've made such a good impression on everybody just like I knew you would.

He also said, Just pace yourself and keep your eyes and ears open and let things soak in and you don't have to worry about anything, because that's really how you become a part of us. If you know what I mean. And I said I thought I did. But the best part was what everybody had already said about him never asking you to do anything that he didn't already know you could do whether you yourself knew it yet or not.

Through the open door I saw Osceola Menefee and Scully Pittman coming toward us, and he said, Stick around. They're just checking in. First they let Milo know they're here because he's the timekeeper. Then they see Pro because he's in charge of the book, and they just kind of look in on me in case I might have worked up some little something different that I might want to drop in there somewhere during the evening.

So I was also there when everybody else came by that first night, and they all gave me a pat on the shoulder, and sometimes also an avuncular wink like the hometown baseball team going onto the field from the dugout and as if to say what somebody in log carriage crew at the Buckshaw sawmill always used to chant when the one o'clock back to work whistle blew.

When all of them had come and said what they had to say and left, he said, So here you are on board as we weigh anchor and head seaward. Which to me whose first scoot buddy was Little Buddy Marshall meant seven-seaward. And I said, Aye aye Sir and snapped to, not with my first year roommate's sidelong glance of conspiracy but with the grin you couldn't ever really repress when Miss Lexine Metcalf or Mr. B. Franklin Fisher designated you with their blackboard pointers.

It was curtain time then, and everybody was standing in the wings and he said, Okay, now for the time being, there's a chair for you right next to the piano. I want you to just sit there and get used to hearing how everybody sounds when you're that close to me and Joe and Otis.

That caught me by surprise, because until then I had been picturing myself spending the first few nights in a chair in the wings off the rhythm section side of the bandstand. But there was nothing to do but to nod okay, okay, okay, if you say so, it's all right with me. Then when we heard Milo the Navigator give the all on, all on call, he gave me a pat on the shoulder and said, So there you go. See you in a minute. And I left him rolling his shoulders and dangling his fingers.

There was a very important difference in the way the band sounded when you were listening from where I was sitting. Everything was there and it was all together exactly as it had been rehearsed to be. But as Joe States was to point out when I said what I said later on: Everybody on the baseball team is in on all the action and they all respond to every pitch and every swing and crack of the bat and they all call the play by the same name, but no two of them ever see it from the same point of view, if you know what I mean. Just like the reed section is down there from us like the infield and there's a trombone section and the trumpet section, and you also got the rhythm section like the battery.

When you sat listening from where my chair was, you also felt you were already a part of the team effort. So much so that I found myself actually trying to help the other sections push the notes out into the auditorium. But when everybody stood up to take a bow at the end of the first set, I stayed put in my chair and applauded along with the audience before following Joe States backstage.

That was the way the Bossman Himself wanted me to spend the band's opening night in Cincinnati, and every now and then he would look at me and wink; and sometimes he would name the progression he was playing, and at other times he would name the changes and variations that Shag Philips was running. The second night started out the same way. But when we came back from the first intermission, he said, well how about it?

He was already noodling and doodling at the piano before the rest of us started filing back on stage, and at first I thought it was just a little something to go with the glass-clinking, table-hopping intermission atmosphere. But then I realized that he was really playing for himself and that what he was fooling around with was either something new or a new treatment for something already in the book. You couldn't really tell because he kept going back over it again and again, as if he were only vamping until everybody was back on stage and in place and ready.

I listened expecting him to weave in a figure that would be the signal for the band to find the score sheets for the next number, but before he did that he looked at me and winked again and said what he said. And when I said, If you say so, he went on vamping and I scooted into the wings and was back in place with my bass before he finished another chorus and he said, yeah and went into one note per measure and Joe States came riding in on the high hat cymbal going chickachee chickachee chickachee chickachee, like whispering locomotive steam over a steady driving four/four on what he called his boom boom pedal.

Then when Otis Sheppard strummed the first two bars of the changes I took the second two as a fill and also as if in a quick response to his call and when he repeated as soon as I also repeated, Joe States brought the whole ensemble in shouting like batting hell for leather. So I did what I did because nobody had to tell you that we were going to be highballing it until the bell and flag sign came from the bossman's piano.

Meanwhile Osceola Menefee, Big Bloop and Old Pro would have done their jive time lying, signifying and tall tale telling and retelling in the number of choruses the bossman wanted from the trumpet, tenor and clarinet before sending old Malachi Moberly out with his dirty toned trombone to take it up to the bridge before the outchorus.

That was how I got to make my first bow into the applause along with the rest of the band, and just before they sat back down, Alan Meadows said, Shame on all of you old thugs. This is this young fellow's first time up here with us, and you all got him out there chomping all through this stuff like he got on boomman's hip boots or something. And Joe States said, Well he showed you didn't he? And Ted Chandler said, Yeah he did. And Wayman Ridgeway said, You bet he did. And Osceola Menefee said, Ain't nobody said he didn't. And that was when Scully Pittman said, Hey Boots, Yeah Boots what about Seven League Boots? That's a pretty good one, bossman.

The Bossman Himself was also smiling and he looked at me and winked again and as the audience settled back down he began the next vamp and he kept me going for the rest of the set. But when he brought in the arrangement of what we had played, he called it "Outbound Express" because it was a turnaround on "Alabamy Bound" and he also kept in the "Banjo on My Knee" licks that Joe States and I had sneaked in.

VI

S hag Philips left at the end of my second week, because by that time Old Pro and Joe States had taken me through almost all of the arrangements in the folders the band was using on that tour; and they said I was ready to take over full time. And Otis Sheppard, who always sat in with us whenever Old Pro wanted him there, also said what he said about the only other thing I needed was the experience of holding the job down on my own.

So the Bossman Himself said okay and that Shag Philips didn't have to worry about leaving him in a bind. And that very next morning he himself began talking to me and Old Pro about some of the notions he already had in mind for me to start getting ready for two of the numbers we were going to record when we made it into New York at the end of the month.

You ain't got a thing in the world to worry about, Schoolboy, Joe States kept saying on the way back from seeing Shag Philips off on the train to Florida that second Sunday night. Like I say, you were handpicked by the Bossman Himself in the first place, and I mean right off the bat; and he don't ever do that unless you got something he been looking for. You might not ever find out exactly what it is, but if he sent for you, that means you got it, poppa. And you got me and on top of that you got Old Pro.

Old Pro, he said. Old Pro—and if you didn't know it already you been around here long enough to find out for yourself that we call him that because that's exactly what he is in this mammy-made outfit. And when I said what I said about what I had already heard about Old Pro's reputation as one of the best straw bosses in the business, he said, Not one of the best, the best. Barring none, Schoolboy, barring none that ever did it.

Old Pro, he said again. When the bossman want to set the quails up to flip and put the house in an uproar all he got to do is sic the gold dust twins on them, referring to the in-house nickname that had finally been settled on for Ike Ellis and Scully Pittman because of the way their trumpets alternated and then came together on the verse to the band's special arrangement of "Stardust."

We also got that big one-two tenor solo punch of Old Pro's setup coming after Wayman Ridgeway's alto getaway and followed by Big Bloop in the cleanup position or vice versa; and when he want to make sure everybody still going to be out in the alley for the next go-round, here he come with old Malachi Moberly taking a couple of nasty-talking trombone choruses.

Talking out of school, I cut in to say, and under nice folks' clothes. And he said, They're the ones you're going to be hearing people talking about and calling for just about everywhere we go. But it takes more than a string of knockout solos to add up to the kind of music this band plays, and that's where Old Pro comes in again. Because he is the bossman's A-number-one musician's musician.

In the first place, he said, the somitch can play any instrument in the band. This band or any other band or any other kind of band not leaving out a string band. And I don't mean just to show off enough to prove some chickenshit point. I'm talking about cutting some dots to get a sheepskin from a conservatory. Because that's what he did, and he also used to be a school bandmaster. And you know what that means, don't you, Schoolboy, he said. And I said, It means you have to know how to show everybody how to hold his mouth and/or fingers and how to start out being letter perfect.

That's exactly my point, he said. And it also means he can read anything you put in front of him, and he can write anything he can hear. Then in the third place, he is also a pro when it comes to dealing with all the different kinds of people you got to deal with in this trade, not just musicians but this whole entertainment business thing out here. Man, Old Pro can step in for Milo the Navigator bright and early tomorrow morning without missing a beat. Old Pro is a pistol, my man. He don't go around looking like a high priced dentist for nothing.

Joe States was also the one who said, Get Old Pro to tell you about him and the bossman back in the old days when they used to knock around Harlem together. Ask him about all them old stride time piano sharks like Willie the Lion Smith and Luckey Roberts and James P. Johnson, and just wait until he gets going on some of those old master musicians like Will Marion Cook and Harry T. Burleigh; and you'll find out about a lot of heavy historical stuff that's behind this band that people don't realize is there.

Everybody's always carrying on about how hip and out front this band has always been; but, man, this stuff we play is also *historical*. Everything this band plays is connected with some kind of story about something that is flesh and blood and history, he said. And then he said, Old Pro is going to see to it that everybody is cutting them dots, but that's just a convenience like a map. It's always that little story that counts with him and the bossman.

And I said, I can see that. I can hear that. Because I will always remember what my roommate during my first year in college used to say about the best way to get to the meaning of a poem was to see it as a part of an ongoing conversation.

Get to Old Pro, Schoolboy, he said. All you got to do is just catch him when he got a little spare time. Because I know him just like I know the bossman, and I'm telling you it'll mean a lot to him. Because you're a college boy. Because to him and the bossman all the flesh and blood and history in this music they got this band playing makes it just as classical as them preludes and études and sonatas, cantatas, and fugues and all the rest of that symphony hall jive. Because if you can give people them deep itching goose pimples you're doing your job as a musician.

He said, Just watch your chance and get to Old Pro. And I said I would and one day during the week I was in New York that first time I did. *When I came out of the movie that afternoon it was raining and I stopped in at the Peacock and the first one I saw was him sitting by himself at a table for two by the window smoking a cigar and sipping what I knew by that time was bourbon on the rocks in an oversized Old Fashion glass as he turned through* The New York Times *folded the long way.*

There were also several other daily newspapers and current magazines at his elbow next to the window; and along with the tall glass of water chaser in front of him there was also a dish of ice cubes. He waved me over to him and it was a good time to get him started and I did, and he said, I thought I already knew something about music. I was from Atlanta and my folks had always sent me to the best teachers and I went for smart. I had won every contest and scholarship I ever tried for, and I was making straight A's at the conservatory.

Several of us were down from Boston between semesters, and this particular night I had come uptown with some friends I was staying with down in Greenwich Village, and we were making the rounds with some guys I had known since they were in Atlanta at Morehouse, and that's when it happened. I'm sitting up there listening to stuff I had been hearing and liking and taking for granted all of my life, and all of a sudden it was as if it was all brand new and something had happened to me. And when I looked around there was this one special very fly and together-looking cat smiling at me at the next table as if he had been watching me all along and could actually see what was going on inside me. That was really the beginning of me and bossman.

Because he said, Hey fella you look like somebody who has just heard the word and seen the light. And I said, Amen. Man, this stuff is something and I mean really something. And somehow he knew that as good as the performance was, what I was talking about was the music as such because he said, Ain't nothing better. Not to my ears.

We kept nodding and shaking our heads at each other through the next three numbers, and at the end of the set he introduced himself, and I told him where I was in town from, and he invited me and my friends to come along with him to a couple of other spots. And who was in the first? Nobody but old Willie the Lion all by himself except for that cigar and derby hat but what he was doing on that piano made you think about things you could do with a whole band.

Then at the next and last stop for that night there was old James P. wearing no hat but lolling his cigar about with his teeth, tongue, and lips as if getting your fingers to do what you wanted depended on knowing how to hold your mouth exactly right. That was some night, Schoolboy. Man, every time I hear him taking off on old Edgar Sampson's "If Dreams Come True" it all comes back to me like yesterday. Man, you bull fiddlers got to love cats that stride like The Lion and James P.

Anyway that was the night I met the bossman and from then on, it was me and him every time I could make it down from Boston. I don't want to go into all of that now. I'll just say he was already looking forward to the day when he could make a full band out of the pickup group he was just beginning to gig around town and the nearby sticks with on a catch-as-catch-can basis, whereas for my part I had never thought of playing that kind of music for a living. Not that I hadn't always liked it. But when you went to the conservatory in those days, that meant that you were preparing yourself to follow in the footsteps of Harry T. Burleigh, Clarence Cameron White, and R. Nathaniel Dett and such like. So what I was looking forward to was a job as bandmaster and maybe head of the music department at a big city central high school or college one day so that I would have time to compose and train enough student musicians to organize my own concert orchestra.

So I went on and got my degree all right. But in the meantime there was this thing the bossman and I had going, and through him I had come

*under the influence of Will Marion Cook and Royal Highness. Remind me
to tell you about me and the bossman and Dad Cook sometime. I'm pretty
sure the Bossman Himself is going to take you by to meet Papa Royal before
we leave town.*

*Well as I was about to say I went on out there and started doing what I
did in Kentucky for three terms, and it was not really a bad job at all. But my
whole outlook was different by then and when the bossman got in touch and said
he was ready to go for a full contingent, I came on board as first mate, and I'm
still here because we've got something going and it's getting better every day.*

It was still raining, and we went on talking until it was time to
meet Milo the Navigator and Joe States in the Braddock Bar at the
corner of Eighth Avenue and 126th Street, one of the main spots musicians and entertainers working in the current shows at the Apollo Theatre used to pop in and out of in those days. And when we got there
Old Pro said, You were right Joe somebody has been schooling this
schoolboy from way back and we do have a lot to talk about. And Joe
States looked at me and said, Temporary replacement. Some stuff. And
Old Pro said, We'll have to see about that, won't we Joe?

VII

By the time I got around to catching Old Pro with enough free
time to spend telling me what he told me about himself and
the bossman as we sat looking out at the traffic splashing along 125th
Street in uptown Manhattan that rainy afternoon, Joe States had
already told me something about the personal background of every-

body else including Milo the Navigator, whose real name was Miles Standish Barlow. Milo was from Columbus, Georgia, the pleasure town of Fort Benning, where he was given his start in the business end of show business by Pa and Ma Rainey, who took him on the road as an errand boy while he was still in knee pants. When he struck out on his own he worked his way up to an advance man on the Toby circuit and began dreaming of the day when he would own his own theater or maybe even a string of theaters and maybe also a baseball park and his own team that would challenge the Kansas City Monarchs, the Pittsburgh Homestead Grays, and so on. But when he met the Bossman Himself, it was as if being the honcho for the greatest band in the world was the very thing he had been preparing for all of his life.

Me and you, Schoolboy, Joe States said patting the spare seat beside him as the bus hummed on out to the open countryside en route from Cincinnati to a string of one night stands that would take me through Pittsburgh and to New York for the first time. Then after that there would be New England, from which we would head south along the Atlantic Seaboard.

Like I said, Schoolboy, he said. And I said, If you say so, Unka Joe. And he smiled because he knew all the uncles I meant. And he said, I do say so, Schoolboy, I do say so, which means get to me fast. He patted his seat, pointed his finger at me, and jerked his thumb.

So I sat with him for the rest of that morning and that is also what I was to do for a few hours every day during the week that it took us to work our way on out of the Midwest and into Pennsylvania. And while he was talking about Otis Sheppard we saw one of the trumpet players reach up and put something in the overhead rack and that was why the next one he told me about was Osceola Menefee, who had straight black maybe part Creek or maybe part Seminole hair and sometimes was also called the Kid from the Okefenokee, because the region of Florida where he was born was as close to the Georgia state line where that particular swamp was as to the national park that commemorates the same chief he was named for. (It was also only a few miles from the Sewanee River, but the only thing that had been made of that so far was a riff pattern that the bossman had woven in behind the trumpet solo in his variation on Louis Armstrong's "Lazy River"). He had gone to elementary school in Jacksonville and high school in Charleston, South Carolina, which was where he became so good on his instrument that he dropped out of school to go with his first road band.

Now you see old Scully Pittman up there calling them hogs already, he also went on to say that first morning on the road. Well, he ain't got no Indian in his blood, but he's the one that grew up around what was left of all them tribes and nations that got resettled in the old Oklahoma Territory, because his family moved out there from somewhere in East Tennessee somewhere near Chattanooga when he was still in his diapers. Now he can tell you something about Indians from firsthand and fireside and everyday neighborhood facts of life. Just like somebody like you from down in your part of Alabama when somebody asks you about Creoles and Cajuns. He don't go around trying to claim no family connections or anything like that, but anytime we come across any Indians in any part of the country and you want to know something about them, get to Scully Pittman. He can run it down for you, cousin. Beginning back before Pocahontas and not skipping from the last of the Mohicans to the last of the Apaches.

But now when it comes to that trumpet, you can tell he grew up listening to the old Blue Devils band that used to range from Oklahoma City all through the southwest territory. And there is some U.S. Cavalry mixed in there, too, and I'm not just talking about "Bugle Call Stomp" and stuff like that. I'm talking about for a while back when he was growing up, he used to dream about running away and going up to Fort Riley, Kansas, and enlisting as a bugle boy.

That's what he told me, Joe States said. And then he said, Hey did you all know about the 9th and 10th Cavalry down Mobile way? And I said, We did but not as much as about the 24th Infantry over at Fort Benning, Georgia. And then I said that I had always thought of trumpet players as having the most military bandstand posture. And he said, And trombone players. From all them John Philip Sousa marches and them school bands. I think I know how come the reeds get farther away from holding their shoulders like that than the brass. But later for that.

But it ain't never later for him when it comes to the ponies, he said looking out at the network of neat white rail fences and mostly flat Kentucky bluegrass pastureland, and I knew that as we rolled on toward the next settlement I would soon be seeing the manor houses and private stables and training tracks such as I had seen only in movies until now.

Him and Mojo Wilkins. And there's our man Otis. Not that they're the only ones. They're just the regular ones. Because when we are spending a few days in certain towns where they're running, you're going to find quite a few of the rest of us out there trying to pick them too.

And that includes me too, Schoolboy, he said. And sometimes you might even see Old Pro and the Bossman Himself out there studying them forms, placing them bets, and hanging on the rails, especially and the big ones like Belmont Park when we have enough time in New York. And out on the Coast it's Hollywood Park and Santa Anita and down in Miami it's Hialeah.

But don't get me wrong, he said. Quite a few of us like to go for the old two-dollar window from time to time, but this is really a baseball band. Man, some of these clowns are almost ready to come to blows about their favorite big league baseball teams, especially between Labor Day and the World Series.

Baseball and big time boxing, he said. Hey man, this goddamn band hauls our softball gear around everywhere we go just like all the rest of our stuff. Which brings us to old Malachi Moberly, he said, because he's the one that almost went on the road as a shortstop. And he could have made it on up to the Kansas City Monarchs or the Homestead Grays and such like. But we came through Bogalusa and the bossman heard him playing trombone one night and told him he could be a big league musician and play twelve months a year for the rest of his life.

You take me myself now, he said. I used to go for a jackleg tailor back in The Ham; and I guess I can still get by at it if push comes to shove. But music is my natural hustle, Schoolboy, and I wouldn't change what I do for the bossman with somebody managing money for J. P. Morgan.

Of course, it's always a good thing to be able to do something else along with being a musician, he said. And then he said, Now when it comes to any kind of gadget the one to get to is Old Plug. And I knew he was talking about Alan Meadows and I said, Didn't I hear somebody call him Juice the other night? And he said, Ted Chandler. That's what Ted Chandler calls him because he's always tinkering around with something plugged into electricity.

And when I said there was a cat back on the campus that we all used to call Juice because of all of the cans of grapefruit juice he used to spike with chem lab alcohol, he said, you want to watch that stuff, man. That stuff will drive you crazy and make you blind to boot. And I said, Not me. I said, This guy was in organic chemistry. And Joe States said, Me I want to see them when they break the seal.

Then he said, When it comes to drinking, old Wayman Ridgeway got everybody in this band beat cold and I don't mean just drinking. That clown can drink it and then carry it. Hell, if you don't smell it on him—and you can't even do that most of the time—you don't even know he's been anywhere near any. Be sitting up there steady sipping on that nickel-plated flask and playing as much music as anybody that ever picked up a trombone. Ask Malachi. Ask the Pard. Somitch play that slide horn like it's got keys on it. Battle a trumpet in a minute. But after all, he came up on old Louis too. And believe it or not, so did the Pard, he said, referring to Fred Gilchrist, also known as the silent partner.

I looked back at Wayman Ridgeway across the aisle from Osceola Menefee, sleeping with his head on a pillow against the window, his patent leather sheen hairdo held in place with a tight fitting baseball cap. And when I asked about his hometown and Joe States said Chillicothe I said, I thought maybe you all called him Big Sip because he was from Mississippi like Otis Sheppard. And Joe States said, Chillicothe,

Ohio, out of Roanoke, Virginia; and that leather gut somitch ain't never missed sipping nothing.

And another leather gut in this band is old Ike Ellis up there wearing that stocking cap. Ike ain't no steady drinker, but if he's somewhere among a bunch of lushes putting it away, he can put as much of it down the hatch as the next one and wipe his mouth and walk on out of there like it was lemonade or coffee or something. You probably already know that he's from Little Rock, Arkansas. But did you know that the bossman just about kidnapped him out of a machine shop down there? Old Ike's daddy wanted him to be a master mechanic or engineer or something like that. But his uncle came along and gave him a start in music. You see that cornet he doubles on sometime? His uncle used to blow that same horn with the old Sunset Royals down in Florida.

When I said What about Herman Kemble? as we went on with my orientation session that morning en route from Louisville to Indianapolis before heading east to Dayton and Columbus, he said, Who the Bishop? That's the Bishop, Schoolboy. I don't know. I think maybe if they had let that big butt bastard stay in school, maybe he might have turned out to be a lawyer or something. Maybe he really would have turned out to be a bishop. But they kicked him out of the eleventh grade for knocking up a girl and wouldn't marry her, and all he been doing ever since is just blowing that old blooping foghorn, which is what he had started doing with a little hotshot local semipro crew as soon as he was big enough to start sneaking into the joints.

Houston, he said. And then he said, Beaumont, Dallas, Oak City. We got him from Ross Evans in Wichita. We happened through there on our way out to Denver, and they were trying to hustle their way back to Houston; and the bossman hired him and let Ross hold enough cash to haul the rest of them home. Old Bloop had just one change of threads to his name and just about the raggediest ass tenor you ever saw in your goddamn life. But boy was he ready. He was evermore ready, Schoolboy. Challenge any of them. Battle to a fare-thee-well, and then blow ashes to ashes over them. That's where that bishop stuff comes from. We mostly call him Bloop, but one night at a jam session somewhere somebody called him the Presiding Elder and after a while it got changed to the Bishop. So we call him Bloop but sometimes when we are talking about him he's the Bishop.

Don't let him fake you out now, Schoolboy, he said as I turned to look down the aisle to where Herman Kemble lay stretched out across the backseat. He might get a little juiced every now and then, but don't be surprised when he start asking you a lot of deep questions about stuff. Because in a way he's still a schoolboy too. And I'm not just talking about somebody getting his lessons and winning prizes. I'm talking about genuine curiosity right on across the board. Man, the first thing he could have been was a mathematician, but his grade school math teacher was also his first music teacher and the school bandmaster.

The morning I asked him about Elmore Wilkins and Ted Chandler, he said, Frederick Douglass Chandler from Richmond, Virginia, and Elmore Lincoln Wilkins from outside of Nashville by way of Detroit, Michigan. But just let me get back to old Sporty Otis for a minute. When he slung that old country sounding banjo over his shoulder and snagged a freight for the Crescent City, the one that turned him into a guitar player and made a road musician out of him was old Choctaw Cheney. Old Choctaw must have come through Mobile with them twelve strings and that diamond stickpin and them railroad and work camp blues and swamp hollers. It was old Choctaw Cheney that hooked him up with one of the greatest piano players that ever tore up a jam session. Old Blind Baltimore Livingston. That was in St. Louis, and old Baltimore with a drummer named Plug Willis and a bass player calling himself Bull Montana, was swinging down through that territory to Galveston and back around the Gulf states to Florida; and when the bossman, Shag Philips, and I went to check old Baltimore out one night in Chicago, they had come up the Atlantic Seaboard and barnstormed the mining towns; and we all agreed that Otis on guitar was just what we wanted.

Get old Otis to tell you about what a hell of a musician old Baltimore is, he said. Then he went on to say that Ted Chandler was the son of a Richmond doctor and that his mother, who was a graduate of the Oberlin Conservatory of Music and a former concert pianist, was a music teacher. There was an older brother who was a surgeon and one sister who was the older sister was a nurse and another who was a school supervisor.

Everybody in the family and the neighborhood had expected the youngest Chandler to be a dentist. But at the end of his second year in Washington as a premed student he decided that the musicians you heard at the old Howard Theater in those days were much more important to him than what he was supposed to be doing on the Howard University campus. So he told his mother that he had decided to go up to New York and become a professional musician.

He left it up to her to make everything right with the old man, Joe States said closing one eye and touching his temple with two fingers, which she did even though she knew he wasn't going to any conservatory because he knew she had all the confidence in the world in what he would do with all of that practicing in all of them hard keys she brought him up doing every day. And when the bossman and I ran across him he could blow the hell out of anything with a reed in it. And the bossman promised him if he took the baritone chair he'd see to it that he would have plenty of chances to double on anything else he wanted to.

Now old Jomo with the mojos, he said finally nodding toward Elmore Wilkins. I don't have to tell you about nobody got nothing on him when it comes to that plunger and any of them mutes and any kind of derby fanning. Our other name for him is Mucho Moola, Big Money because he can be rich anytime he want to. His family is well off up there in Detroit. His old man came up to work for General Motors and saved his money and set himself up in business and hit the pay dirt. And that's what he was trying to bring old Jomo up to take over but the trumpet changed all that. As a well off kid he was started out on the best piano and violin lessons money could buy in Detroit, because his family could afford it. And they could also afford the best instruments, and before long the violin was getting him more attention

at summer camp than his athletic ability. Until one year when some little fat kid named Fatgut Gus Something Something turned up from
somewhere down home with a trumpet and started stomping and scatting and shouting some up tempo blues and took the spotlight.

But just for that one year. Because when they came back that next
summer, old Jomo had gone straight home and got himself a trumpet
and he was ready for old Fatgut Gus. Not just because he could play all
them notes on the trumpet he was used to hearing on the violin but
even more because of all that signifying he could already do with his
plunger and about five different mutes, plus a plastic, an aluminum,
and a felt derby, which he called his mojo tools.

That's how he first got to be known as the Jomo man, and then
Jomo with the mojos; and when we came to Detroit a few years later
and heard him, and he heard what the bossman was doing with old
Malachi and Bloop, he agreed that he belonged in here with us, and
that's where he's been ever since.

So much for the family business, Joe States said pulling his cap
over his eyes and letting his seat back. But what the hell, you might as
well do what you really want to do with your life. And Jomo Wilkins
can afford it, Schoolboy. You see him up there curled up in them two
bus seats like he's lucky to be in out of the weather? Man, with what he
going to have coming in automatically from his old man's side, he can
live on easy street, and I mean in high style without ever hitting a lick
at a snake again. Look at him. Shout you some blues, too, when you
need him to. As you well know. Low down dirty or otherwise. Clown
you some novelty with capers. Croon you some jive-sweet when the
Bossman don't want to sic old Osceola Menefee on the trillies. Or
when you want him to either join or follow some of old Ocie's mellow
come-on stuff.

VIII

We had pulled into New York on Sunday night, but we were not due in the recording studio until Wednesday morning. So Monday was a free day, and we spent all of Tuesday in a rehearsal hall uptown on 131st Street off Seventh Avenue around the corner from the old Lafayette Theatre; and on the lunch break we all went around to Big John's, and the treat was on Milo the Navigator.

There was all of the new material the bossman had been working up during the tour, and as usual he had also made changes in several of the old arrangements that he wanted to record again. Not as a matter of updating in terms of the going fashion of the moment but rather because to him some compositions were like the canvases some painters keep putting back on the easel not because there's anything wrong with them but because they like them so much that they have to go on playing around with new touches here and there.

It was also already pretty clear to me that when you rehearsed with that band you were never really working to get the score as such letter perfect. Usually that was only the beginning, because most of the tricky passages and special problems of execution were almost always worked out and double-checked by Old Pro beforehand. So the main thing was not whether you could execute what was on the music stand but how close you could come to the feeling being signaled from the piano. What mattered was what the bossman wanted to hear, sometimes for the time being and sometimes maybe from then on.

When we finished the last run-through, it was six o'clock. And Joe States said, What did I tell you? Didn't I tell you? You see what I'm talking about? Been in here rolling like a bunch of cotton wharf dockhands since this morning and still blowing like they trying to make the lineup and get a letter sweater or something. And the man ain't crack-ing no whip. He just punching some chickenbutt piano keys.

But what can I tell you, Schoolboy, he said as he started breaking down and packing his setup. This man has got himself one hell of a crew of musicians, and they ready to tear this stuff up down there tomorrow. Hell, I'm kind of ready my goddamn self. Hell, we'll blow the goddamn *Encyclopaedia Britannica* for him, all it takes is a quick lit-tle segue not even a vamp.

You already know what happened when he starts laying down them extended vamps, he said. And I said, I sure do, remembering how he brought me on that night in Cincinnati. And Joe States said, I been in this band since forever, and the somitch can still raise big fat goose pimples on my hidebound behind anytime he really wants to; and that's when I'm subject to drive the rest of these thugs right on into the jaws like them six hundred troopers in that poem.

Milo the Navigator told everybody to be downtown at the studio before nine o'clock. He printed the address, the studio number, and the bus and subway numbers on a portable blackboard for those who would not be taking the band bus down Seventh Avenue from the Woodside at 7:45 with a stop at Hotel Theresa at the corner of 125th Street.

There were several questions about the new uniforms that we were supposed to be measured for before leaving town, and then Old Pro began collecting the folders section by section and when he came to me he said the bossman was in the office on the phone at the moment but wanted me to stick around. So I told Joe States not to wait for me.

Old Pro sat at the piano and started checking through each folder. I waited on a high stool by the window from which in those days you could look out across the rooftops of that part of Harlem to the ridge that stretched south to Morningside Heights and Columbia and north to CCNY and Hamilton Terrace.

When the bossman came back in, I stayed where I was until he finished looking over the sheets Old Pro showed him, and then he held

up his hand to let me know he was ready to leave; and when I joined
him on the way out I found that I was in for a double surprise.

I was wondering if you'd like to run with me for a while tonight,
he said; and all I could get myself together to say was, You're the bossman. You're on. Because I could hardly believe my ears and he said, I
mean beginning as of right now. No change necessary. And I said, I'm
with you, bossman. I'm with you.

We came on downstairs and out onto the sidewalk, and he said,
Well good but now are you sure that this is not cutting in on something you already had up for the evening? And I said, Absolutely. I said,
Nothing special and nothing definite. I was just going to look around
up here a little more and turn in early for tomorrow. And he said, This
won't keep you out late at all.

He flagged a cab heading up Seventh Avenue, and when he got in
he gave the driver the street number and settled back and said, I'm
going up to see Daddy Royal, and I thought you might like to come
along and meet him.

And I said, Not Royal Highness.

And he said, Ain't but the one, Schoolboy, ain't but the one.

And I said, Grant Simpson.

And he said, Ulysses Grant Simpson.

At that time Royal Highness, the contemporary peer and sometime
nemesis of such legendary show stopping dancers, vaudeville entertainers, and musical comedy headliners as Ernest Hogan, Williams and
Walker, Miller and Lyles, Slow Kid Thompson, King Rastus Brown,
and Bojangles, was living in a penthouse up at 555 Edgecombe, across
155th Street and north of the main part of Sugar Hill and also overlooking Coogan's Bluff and the Polo Grounds, which was the home park of
the New York Giants National League baseball team in those days.

In the lobby there was a woman's voice on the intercom responding to the buzzer, but when we came off the elevator upstairs, Royal
Highness himself was waiting for us in the open door. He was around

five feet nine and he looked as if he were just about the age his father must have been in the publicity pictures of him that I remembered from the *Pittsburgh Courier*, the *Chicago Defender*, and the *Baltimore Afro-American* back in Mobile County Training School. And his smooth medium brown skin was exactly the shade I had always thought it was, although all of the photographs of him that I had ever seen had been black and white.

Here's my bandleader, he said. Back in town from another go round. What say there, maestro. You all come on in here. And the bossman bowed, making a flourish with his hat, and said, Daddy Royal. Ain't but the one. And we stepped inside and they stood holding each other at arm's length and the bossman said, You looking fine, Daddy Royal. You're looking great. And then he said, This is the new bass player I was telling you about.

So I did my little bow, and he patted me on the shoulder with a warm down-home grandfatherly twinkle in his eyes and said, You're already welcome in the band, so you're automatically welcome up here young soldier. I make it a practice not to shake hands with finger musicians. Hell, their goddamn hands are too valuable for any and everybody to be coming up and grabbing and wringing and twisting them all the time. Hell, people ought to remember that's your goddamn bread and butter and also the keys to your soul bank they putting all of that extra wear and tear on.

Then the first thing he said after we helped ourselves to drinks from the sideboard and sat down was, Boy you thought I was dead didn't you? A lot of them think old Royal is dead. Boy, I ain't near 'bout dead yet. I might not be getting around much anymore like I used to, but I'm here and I'll be here after a lot of them check out. Right up here watching to see what you young splibs got going to deal with them jaspers.

But now don't get me wrong, young soldier. Let me get this straight right now. Don't you ever let nobody tell you that you were put here on God's earth to spend your life worrying and bellyaching about some old jaspers. Excuse my language, but fuck that shit, young soldier.

I'm starting right in on you like this, he said. But I ain't never bellyached to no jaspers in my life. Because the notion I was brought up on down home was that you just go out there and show the somitches. Do whatever the hell you do and let them get to that. Some of them are always going to be looking for ways to deny you your talent. Hell, that's the game of life, young soldier. You ever played any game in which there wasn't somebody trying to deny you something? Boy, now this is exactly what gets me. Don't nobody love tangling in baseball, football, basketball more than splibs—and don't mention boxing. So how can any honest to goodness splib turn around and start bellyaching because some jaspers are out there doing the same thing? Like I say that's life and it's also life that there's always some others out there that will invest in any promise that you might show—and it don't take but one when it's the right one. Look at Irving Mills. Look at Joe Glaser. Now what I want you to remember always is that everything else I say about splibs and jaspers comes down to this. So now just make yourself at home.

The first thing he wanted to hear about from the bossman was how the band was getting along financially; and the bossman said fine better than ever in that the new recording contract looked very good. They started talking about agents and details of the entertainment business then and I was not really listening anymore. So I picked up my drink and started looking at the multiple rows of photographs that lined the walls and shelves and also the top of the ivory white grand piano.

There were glossy blowups of familiar sports page portraits and prize ring action shots of Jack Johnson, Joe Gans, Sam Langford, Harry Wills, and the young still up and coming Joe Louis, all personally inscribed to Royal Highness—as were those of Rube Foster in his warmup sweater, Satchel Paige following through on the mound, and Josh Gibson in his catcher's gear with the grandstand in the background.

As I moved on to the panel of entertainers and musicians, there were copies of some of the same promotion portraits that I had first seen as a little boy waiting my turn in Papa Gumbo Willie McWorthy's barbershop next door to Stranahan's General Merchandise Store. There were also some that reminded me of myself as I was when as a teenager I first started stopping by Shade's Bon Ton Barbershop and Shoe Shine Parlor across from Boommen's Union Hall Ball Room on Green's Avenue.

Then there was a special gallery of autographed originals of entertainment page sketches and caricatures of Royal Highness himself, usually sporting a coronet at a jaunty angle (something he had never actually done). In some of the snapshots he was wearing a top hat and tails, and in others a homburg with gamble striped pants, or a derby along with patent leather shoes and spats. In still others he wore no hat at all so as to show off his widely imitated footlight glossy hairdo.

To keep out of range of the conversation I skipped the end of the room where the mantelpiece, the piano, and the big console record player were and crossed directly over to the opposite wall where contemporary paintings, mostly from Paris, were hung along with various tribal masks, shields, and spears from the Benin, Senufo, and Yoruba areas of West Africa.

When you came to the next wall, you were at the door to the terrace, from which there was a view of the after dark Manhattan skyline that brought back the way I used to feel about New York not only when I saw such scenes in cops and robbers movies in the Saenger Theater in downtown Mobile, but also whenever I used to hear Cab Calloway either on record or radio singing about Creole girls in a revue tune called "Underneath the Harlem Moon," back when I was still in junior high school and had not yet read Alain Locke's book *The New Negro* and found out about the so-called Harlem Renaissance.

After that many years I could still whistle the melody to "Creole babies walkin' 'long with rhythm in their thighs . . ." note for note as I used to do. But even as I began to do so, what I found myself thinking about again after that many years, was how at first like just about everybody else around Gasoline Point I didn't pay very much attention to what the lyrics were really about, and when I did I hated them because they were about highbrows going slumming whereas what I had always pictured to myself as I whistled was a panorama of frizzly headed copper colored girls all dressed up and strutting their stuff along Lenox Avenue at twilight with the midtown skyscrapers twinkling in the distance.

What remembering all that also brought to mind was an old James P. Johnson ragtime piano roll titled "If You've Never Been Vamped by a Brownskin, You've Never Been Vamped at All"; and at the very instant that I realized that such was the sort of tune that both Royal Highness and the bossman would be pleased to reminisce about there was the bossman's voice at the door telling me that something was about to be served.

So I came back inside and the three of us went into the dining room, and that is where I met Stewart Anderson, who was much better known as Stewmeat Anderson (as in Pigmeat Markham), because he was once half of an old vaudeville comedy team billed as Stewmeat and Small Change (Small Change Flint, formerly Skin Flint because his real name was Glenn Aldridge Flint).

Over the years the stage name Stewmeat had been shortened to Stew (for stew chef as in sous-chef), because when bookings became scarce during the Depression the act broke up and he started a hole-in-the-wall eating place on 132nd Street between Seventh and Lenox avenues with himself as chief short order cook and bottle washer; and with two-thirds backing from Royal Highness, an old hometown boy from Norfolk, Virginia, he expanded into a neighborhood hangout on 134th Street between Lenox and Fifth avenues where the most popular special was not a stew of beef and root vegetables but down-home pork neckbones and rice.

It was his wife's voice that we had heard on the intercom in the lobby. The two of them were sharing the large apartment and keeping house for Royal Highness, who had been married three times but had no children and no close relatives and so not long after his last divorce had invited them to move into the north wing to keep him company.

By that time all three of them were in retirement, but they were also still business associates because they had held on to part ownership of the restaurant, which now under new management was paying off better than ever.

In the publicity pictures of Stewmeat and Small Change in costume Stewmeat always wore a very gaudy vest padded to look like a bay window. In the amusement page snapshots of him in street clothes he looked as much like a stylishly tailored athlete as like an entertainer, and at dinner the night I met him, you could have mistaken him for a retired prizefighter who treated himself to regular massages, facials, and manicures and still dropped by his favorite Lenox Avenue barbershop to check through the sports pages of the daily papers while having his shoes shined.

His wife whose name was Cherry Lee from Cherie Bontemps a cafe au lait Creole former dancer from New Orleans had worked in the chorus line at the Cotton Club, at the Apollo, and at Small's Paradise before marrying him and helping him run the original hole-in-the-wall restaurant.

After saying the blessing Royal Highness, who had pointed me to the first place on his left, went on with the tête-à-tête conversation he had going with the bossman, who was sitting on his right directly across from me. Then as he turned in my direction he said, So this young fella is all set for his first recording session in the morning. And the bossman nodded and winked at me, and I said, I hope so. And Royal Highness said, You just go on down there and play that bull fiddle. Them jaspers down there in that studio ain't got no stuff for you.

Boy, any time you can play music to suit the bossman and Old Pro, you can forget about them jaspers down there twisting them knobs and watching them dials. Hell, a lot of them jaspers don't know anywhere near as much about them highfalutin studio gimcracks as you might think. Let alone splib music. They're doing what they're doing and you're doing what you're doing. Hell, I know a lot of people that can talk your head off about Mozart and Bozart and don't know the first thing about the kind of Mose art that band can put goose pimples on anybody's behind with. He told you about them goose pimples, didn't he?

He turned back toward the bossman again then, and they went on talking as before but on the way back into the parlor he left the bossman with Stewmeat Anderson and guided me into his huge dressing room and showed me a double row of handmade shoes that he had been ordering since the mid-1920s from a London cobbler recommended by the Prince of Wales and he said, You know what I want to do? When them records you all going to start making tomorrow come out, I want to put on one of my favorite pairs of old hoofing boots and just sit in my old rocking chair in there just listening and snapping my fingers and wiggling a toe every now and then.

Don't worry about it, he said again. But watch yourself. And watch out for them bright lights.

And I said, I'm trying to. And he said, I'm talking about not losing sight on the world like some I've seen. I'm talking about when you see what you see and hear what you hear you really going to find out that a lot of this stuff up here ain't nothing but some of the same old jive all wrapped up in a big city package. I'm thinking about how some folks come up here all wide eyed, and when them bright lights from them tall buildings hit them, they think the first thing they better do is get rid of the good old tried and true down-home stuff that got them all the way up here in the first place.

Boy, don't you ever let nothing make you forget that what's always out there waiting to rip your drawers is that same old bear you been tussling with all your life, and man that somitch is just as grizzly in the city as he is in the swamps. Boy, it's just exactly like what the old folks always used to tell me it was; the bear comes in any and every shape, form, and fashion, and sometimes in no shape, form, and fashion that you can really describe. Just like you can't describe the goddamn blues, even when they got the mug on you like ugly.

When we came out into the hallway the bossman and Stewmeat

Anderson were standing by the sideboard where the drinks were. Royal Highness told me to serve myself, and I chose seltzer and he made himself a bourbon on the rocks. Then we all followed him on back to the living room where he sat in the high back Scandinavian rocking chair and lit a cigar and took a long puff followed by a sip of bourbon and said, So now tell me, Emp, is this young fella going to take You Know Which What in that cool booted seven league stride you been telling me about? Or should I say Miss You Know Which's What. And the bossman said, Joe thinks so. And Royal Highness took another puff from his cigar and winked at me and held up his glass and said, A good word from Joe States goes a long way with me, young fella.

What I'm talking about now, son, he said, is when them dazzling bright lights twinkling at you happen to be the blue eyes of some of them mane tossing ponies prancing around with all that ofay enthusiasm for flesh and blood and nitty gritty. Boy, the stuff you got to deal with in the circles you moving into now is totally different from tipping on the Q.T. with Miss Ann down yonder.

Boy, sometimes I wonder, he said. As I took a quick look at the bossman and realized that what Royal Highness was saying was as much a part of what the visit was about as anything else. Boy, sometimes I wonder. Boy, I'm not sure. But sometimes I do wonder if the admiration of some of them people don't screw up more splibs' heads than just plain old segregation as such ever did. If you know what I mean.

I mean all that bad taste some of the classiest jaspers I ever met sometimes go for. I mean how some of the very jaspers that supposed to know so much about everything, can turn around and excuse splibs of some old half assed shit that ain't no other splib would ever let you get away with. So I'm also talking about how you always got to be on the watch out for the kind of ponies that will make you feel that you're already God's gift to women and don't need to change a thing.

As he went on talking, you got the impression that you were being warned against an occupational hazard that was every bit as dangerous as alcohol and narcotics. But what he was to say when he brought it up again during my third visit was: Don't worry about it. All you got to do is just remember that they're supposed to be able to put you next to something else besides what's between her legs, and even in her pocketbook.

You see all of this fine stuff all around this apartment? I didn't hustle it, son. I'm not talking about playing them. I'm talking about handling yourself out there in that same classy world you went to college to qualify for.

So now look here, young soldier, he said, when the bossman and I stood up to take our leave that first time, I know you got all your spare time booked solid with things you want to find out about New York all by yourself. But when you come back in another time, you know where to find me. Hell, we didn't get around to talking about old Gladstone yet. Hell, I know Papa Gladness down there on the Bay, just like I know Fess Whatley in Birmingham and Willis James down at Bama State.

Then the bossman and I shook hands and held shoulders with him at the door, and at the elevator we turned and waved again. And he said, Where the hell is that goddamn Joe Ass States? Tell him I say he better get his skinny butt self on up here with all them new lies he always saving up to add to my private stock. Tell him I say don't lighten up on that high hat, but get to me fast.

IX

In the cab rolling south along St. Nicholas Avenue toward 125th Street, the bossman told me that it was Royal Highness who had insisted that he begin building his full band when he did, and that Royal Highness had also helped him get its first bookings and had helped to underwrite its first tour. But it was Royal Highness himself who was to fill me in on how their very special relationship got started.

Me and your bossman go back a little ways, Schoolboy, he said at one point when I went back up to see him the next time the band had several free days in New York, I'm the one told him he was on the way to become The Emperor of Syncopation. I said, With the stuff you putting in the game, if you just keep on charting enough of the territory you heading into you can stake your claim to a whole empire, and that means you'll be the Emperor. If he told you I was one of the ones back there that helped fan a blaze under his young behind, all I can say is the spark was already there and there was plenty fuel everywhere.

But now don't get me wrong, he also said. I'm not really talking about just plain old everyday egotistical competition. What I'm talking about is what can result from just trying to do the best you can, whatever it is you do, no matter who else is also trying to do it. Because when it comes to musical competition, even when you turn out to be better than every living and swinging somitch in sight, what about all them others who may be out of sight but not out of earshot, like Bach, Mozart, and Beethoven? They still right there in the music store while a whole lot of others have come and gone.

That's what I told him right at the outset. I said, You get to be the kind of Emperor I'm talking about not because you're out to wipe out everybody else. I'm talking about doing what you're doing in a way that commands everybody else's respect. I told him, I'm not going to knock the money and popularity that hype can bring you. But it's the genuine respect you command that makes you the goddamn boss.

The first time he came backstage to see me, I asked him if he wanted to be another jackleg dancer, and he said he was a musician. He was already on his way as an after hours piano player and he was also doing pretty good gigging around catch as catch can with his own sextet. There was something about him that really impressed me right away. He was good looking enough not to have any kind of trouble getting with the quails. His threads were fly, and he carried himself with cool class. But the main thing for me was the expression in his eyes when he got going about music and about music and life experience.

When he said what he said about music and dance, I said, goddamn, boy. You know something don't many people know. I said, Don't many people realize the meaning of what you're talking about. Because, he said, Some people say dance is about music so dancers need musicians. But to me music is about dance because the way I hear it dance actually came before music, and that's why we measure music in dance time. So musicians should be trying to dance whatever instrument they play.

I was working down on Broadway in one of the headline live variety acts being featured with a big first run movie. We were doing five shows a day between the film feature, and when you were not on, you could just stay around backstage and have visitors or you could go and hang out somewhere in Tin Pan Alley. Or visit backstage with friends who happened to be playing at other Broadway theaters at the same time.

He caught the act that first time, and I told him to come back to see me and I told him to just come on back to the stage entrance and ask for me next time.

That's how it began and he would drop by from time to time. And then one day he brought me a piece of music he said he had written, and when I asked him what it was about he said it was about me and for me. So I took him over to the piano back there and made him sit right down and play it over, and I couldn't believe my ears. That young fool had me coming out of that piano, comping for me with one hand and doing me with the other. He was mostly just hinting and half kidding, but he had me, young fella. I knew exactly where he was going with it, and I also knew he was a born musician. And you can bet a fat man that old Daddy Royal knows one when he hears one. He told me it wasn't really filled in yet but he just wanted me to hear it at this stage. And I said, You got it going all right. But, boy, what you need for your kind of music is a full band. I said, Boy, your true instrument is them eighty-eight keys in a fourteen to sixteen or eighteen piece orchestra.

I took him around and put him in touch with some master musician friends of mine, and when they heard him they all said the same thing, which was the same thing I had told him. I'm talking about solid professional writers and arrangers like Will Vodery and Ford Dabney and I'm pretty sure that a college boy like yourself knows about old Will Marion Cook and Harry T. Burleigh.

And I said I sure do and told him that Cook's "Swingalong" and Burleigh's "Deep River" were school glee club songs just as J. Rosamond and James Weldon Johnson's "Lift Every Voice" was the general assembly period anthem along with "My Country 'Tis of Thee" and "The Star-Spangled Banner." Then as he went on talking, the other tunes that came to mind were "Sweet and Low," "East of the Sun and West of the Moon," "California, Here I Come," "Avalon," "The World Is Waiting for the Sunrise," and the mock church testification song that went: "Oh Yes, Oh Yes and When You Die . . ." because the sound of that kind of music was also a part of the atmosphere that Mr. B. Franklin Fisher brought to Mobile County Training School along with Miss Lexine Metcalf.

People forget what kind of musicians these men were, he said. Everybody knows that some of them wrote hit tunes and could play some fingerbusting stride piano. But I'm talking about something that goes all the way back before the old Clef Club down in Hotel Marshall at Seventh Avenue at 54th Street. When you're talking about people like the ones I'm talking about you're talking about masters of all kinds of harmonics for ensembles of just about any kind of instrumental combination or voice mixture you can come up with.

I'm talking about people with solid experience of being not just arrangers and composers but musical directors to boot. So anyway, they all heard what I heard and told the young fella he was not just a born musician but a born composer just exactly like I said. And they all still got their ears cocked and he knows it. Jimmy Johnson, Willie the Lion, Will Vodery, Old Will Marion. We all dropped it on him. We were the ones that told him to forget about all of the hotshot all-stars and pick his own sidemen one by one because they fit in with what he was trying to do as a composer. Because what I realized as soon as he played that little sketch for me was that he needed a full band that he could play just like he played the piano.

He came backstage to see me because I was supposed to be The Great Royal Me and I as much as told him that's all right about me. I said now it's your turn to do what you can do about being the Almighty Imperial you.

Now, he was to say at one point when I went back up to see him again the day after the band came back to town the time after that, Let me tell you a little something about how old Daddy Royal started out in this racket. Maybe you've heard about it or read something about it, but I want you to get it directly from me. Boy, I got my goddamn start as a blackface minstrel comedian in one of them fly by night circus tent medicine shows—or maybe I should say one after another of them. And then one day I said to myself I said, Hell, I ain't cut out to be no two-bit tent show clown. I'm a goddamn dancer with enough stuff to be a class act. And I got on out of there and I worked my way on up into vaudeville.

Back then when a road show hit town and there was somebody in it doing something, and you figure you could beat him doing it, you could challenge him and battle him right then and there. Of course now if you were not ready, shame on you. But if you really had something, you also had yourself a job, sometimes maybe even his job.

This was in Savannah, and I started woofing and stuck my fish and he decided to teach me a lesson. So he dared me to come up on the stage, and *boy!* I was *up* there before he could get the words out of his mouth. Because I knew I was ready, and I low more scandalized him. Man, I didn't just put him in the dozens, I put his butt in the wind.

They started calling me Kid Stomp the Royal High Stepper and stuff like that, and I battled my way on down through Atlanta, Mobile, and New Orleans to Beaumont and Houston and all the way out to Los Angeles and San Francisco and then all the way back across to Kansas City, St. Louis, and I worked out of Chicago for a while. And when I say battle I mean you never could tell when the next local tiger was going to try to ambush you.

So when I hit New York that first time I figured I was ready. I was already being billed as Kid Royal the King of the Stompers, and when I made the scene to pay my respects to the joints along Lenox and Seventh, I would be wearing one of my homburgs or derbies and my chesterfield or my alpaca with the maestro fur collar. I was dressing the part as if to say Who says I ain't? It didn't take but just a few days for the word to get out that there was this young hotshot in town, and when I made it to the Hoofers Club later on that week they were expecting me as I knew they would be. Well, they didn't run me out of there, Schoolboy, because I wasn't jiving. I was laying some stuff down and everybody knew it. But I did find out that I had to go and come again. Which I did, and when I got to be one of the top dogs around there, I promoted myself to Royal Highness.

At one point during another visit later on that year he was to remind me of how much territory his stomping grounds had covered. It not only stretched beyond Harlem and Broadway to most of the four star showcase theaters from Boston all the way across to San Francisco and Los Angeles but also took in a string of the choice music halls in western Europe.

In my heyday I was billed and booked as Royal Highness all over that part of the world too, Schoolboy, he said when he came back into

the living room from the study where Stewmeat Anderson had called
him to the phone and saw me standing in front of the panel of framed
foreign language placards and marquee displays. Boy, you should have
seen me over there moving among them hereditary royal dogs. Man,
me and them and them and me.

Them trying to get with old Mose and old Mose trying to get
with all that gold plated castle and palace routine. All that confetti,
spaghetti, and filigree stuff. And of course you know I had to get next
to some of that royal intrigue poontang, me being an old triggerman
ever since I found out what it was made for. So talk about tipping on
the Q.T., me and them pedigreed stone foxes, some of them grandma-
mas, and them and me. Boy, ain't nothing like hearing your name whispered close up in one of them European accents early in the morning
just about the break of day, sometimes in a wing of one of them old
rambling castles or while you're all bogged up in silk and downy pillows in one of them forty acre flats with garden terraces overlooking
some world famous boulevard or other.

Hey, what you talkin' 'bout, young fella! he said and took a long pull
on his cigar, his eyes twinkling not only because he was remembering
how it was but also as if he knew that the way he said talking 'bout
would evoke all of the old yarn spinning and lie swapping places in my
down-home boyhood.

Another thing me and old Jack Johnson used to talk about, he said
taking another sip of cognac and another pull on his cigar. Boy, one of
the main things about the people I'm talking about is the sporting life,
and that was just like putting old Br'er Rabbit in the briar patch. Anytime you start carrying on about handling horses and hunting dogs and
wing shooting and deer and bear tracking, and stuff like that you just
bring out the down-home stuff I was bred and born to. Boy, I fished all
the way from the crawfish pond to the Gulf Stream, and I used to hunt
cheechees with a slingshot, possums with a forked stick, and rabbits
and squirrels with lightwood knots. *Whatyoutalkinbout!*

Every now and then old Jack Johnson used to come up and whisper something about the whereabouts of my royal skids, because once
when I had a show in Zurich, Switzerland, I went up in the mountains

with a bunch of them and decided to get on a pair of skis, something I'd never done before in my life. But, hell, I was a dancer, and I had also skipped along the top of quite a few boxcars in my young hoboing days. So I got with that too, for one afternoon. Then the people backing the tour moved in and called a halt to that egotistical bullshit as if to say "It may be your ass but it's our goddamn money."

Every time old Jack Johnson used to bring that up, I would always say, Hey, just look who's talking. Ain't you the same Jack Li'l Arthur Johnson that woofed himself into the Plaza de Torros to go bare knuckles against the horns of a goddamn Miura bull?

Boy, you tell them young splibs I say Old Daddy Royal is still here, he was to say when it was time for me to head back down to Seventh Avenue again. You tell them old Daddy Royal say old rocking chair ain't quite got me yet. Tell them I say if they don't know what to make of what I'm all about, shame on them. Because I'm a goddamn fact, and when you deny me you denying history. And that's just like trying to deny the law of gravity. You tell them I say even when I'm dead and gone I'm still subject to be a fact for some time to come.

X

Sometimes when we left town late at night, everybody would already be curled up and asleep even before the bus made it out beyond the outskirts and settled into that cozy soporific open country hum again, and unless there was an early morning relief stop at a service station or at some wayside inn or crossroads general merchandise store, you wouldn't hear another word from anybody until we pulled up in front of the next hotel or boarding house.

But there were also times when you could wake up and tell where you were even before you opened your eyes because all you had to do was listen, and somebody would start calling off and repeating either the place name, like an old time railroad conductor, or start signifying about some street name, building, or other identifying landmark as Ike Ellis did for my benefit on the next morning of my first trip south from New York by way of the Atlantic Seaboard states.

Well, there's old man Johnny Jim Crow, Schoolboy, he said just loud enough not to disturb anybody else. And I knew that we had recrossed the line and were back in the section of the country that had been a part of the old Confederacy and that we had stopped for a traffic light in a courthouse square that had a gray monument of either a CSA officer on horseback, or a pack bearing rifleman, facing north.

Still up there, Ike Ellis said; and Alan Meadows said, Still up there trying to make out like them people didn't get the living dooky kicked out of them. And Ike Ellis said, Man, did they ever mo. Man once them Yankees got all of their stuff together and got them gunboats rolling down the Mississippi and then cut across Tennessee to Georgia and the sea, kicking every living and swinging ass until times got tolerable, I'm telling you, mister.

Grant and Sherman, Joe States said. Old Grant and old Sherman, and I'm not forgetting Mr. Sheridan and old Chickamauga Thomas either. These people had old Stonewall Jackson, but the Union had the rock of Chickamauga. Him and Sheridan are my boys too, and old Admiral Farragut down in your neck of the woods, Schoolboy. And Otis Sheppard said, Hell, I know something about that one. Damn the torpedoes, full speed ahead.

Hey, but wait a minute, Joe States said. Here's what I'm talking about now. I'm talking about once old Abe got rid of that simple ass McClellan and turned things over to old Grant, and Grant teamed up with old Sherman, and they got that one-two punch going, it was all over for these people. Fare-thee-well, land of cotton, jump for joy.

McClellan, Malachi Moberly said. Man, goddamn. Where the hell did they get that McClellan from? They say he was a badass somitch on the drill field and on maneuvers. But all he ever did on the battlefield was make Robert E. Lee look good in the newspapers. Man, that clown made Lee look good even when Lee was having to retreat because he had gotten his ass in a bind. But now when they put Grant on old Lee's case it was like stink on doodoo all the way to Richmond.

Man, Joe States said, Old Sherman told them at the very outset. Old Sherman was from up north but he was working in a military school down in Louisiana when they first started talking all that old loudmouth secession jive. He told them. He said, Personally I like you all, I really do. He said, Some of the best friends I made up at West Point come from down here. But when you all start talking some old stuff about messing with the Union, I'm sorry, you all don't know what you all are letting yourself in for. That's what he told them, and when that didn't do any good he showed them.

Oh but did he show them, Ted Chandler said. So much for the Seesesh. Don't care how mad these old peckerwoods anywhere down here get about any-thing, the one thing you don't ever hear any of them ever talking about no more is secession. They wave their flag and give that old rebel yell but that's as far as it goes, buddy.

These people, Wayman Ridgeway said. These people and all this old hype, and they keep on passing it on from generation to generation. That's one of the main things I can't understand about this whole situation. Look, Schoolboy, what about this shit. Now they put the badmouth on old Benedict Arnold for whatever it was he did, and then they turn right around and let these people get away with all this old stuff. And I'm not talking about the denying us our birthrights, I'm talking about glorifying old Jeff Davis and Lee and Stonewall and them, even old Nathan Bedford Forrest.

Man, that's right, Ike Ellis said. Man, they ruined Benedict Arnold's reputation forever, and here these people down here still putting up all these old monuments and hanging out all these old Dixie banners all over the place on holidays, national holidays.

Then he also said, Look, you all I'm talking about the Constitution. Wasn't no Constitution when Benedict Arnold came along. Man, old raw-boned, frozen face Jeff Davis flat out told them. He said, Look, these are my niggers just like these are my livestock, and if you all don't let me have my way about how I run my business I'm going to tear up this piece of paper because that's all it is to me.

What about all this old stuff, Schoolboy, Osceola Menefee said, What did them college profs say about all this old historical hype? And I said, As far as my profs were concerned the greatest Civil War monument is not some piece of stone or bronze sculpture up on a pedestal anywhere, not even the Lincoln Memorial on the Washington Mall, Grant's Tomb above Riverside Drive, or Sherman facing south in the Grand Army Plaza. The way they see it the Civil War memorial that really counts for us and for the whole country, north and south, east and west is that little statement that Lincoln read from a page of a scratch pad up at Gettysburg, Pennsylvania, on the nineteenth of November almost a year and a half before the war was over.

I could have gone on to say that all colleges like the one I went to were Civil War memorials, but I didn't because I just wanted to go on listening to them; and also because Ted Chandler was already saying, Hey well all right, Schoolboy. And then he said, Hey you all hear this deep stuff our schoolboy is laying down for us? And Ike Ellis said, Them college profs sure did school him right on that one. And Alan Meadows said, Because they want him to be dedicated to the proposition. And that was also what he was to go on talking about that afternoon when he came into the Snack Shack across the street from the auditorium and sat at the counter with Joe States and me.

Say now look here, Schoolboy, he said. That was some heavy stuff we were getting into this morning. Man, by the time you hit the ninth grade, everybody in our school already knew that address by heart. You had to commit it to memory word for word and get up before an audience and recite it with the same feeling that was always there when you heard "Lift Every Voice."

Heavy, Joe States said. Man, you talking about something heavy as church. And Alan Meadows said, In church it was the Lord's Prayer and the Lord Is My Shepherd, and in school it was I Pledge Allegiance and Four Score and Seven. And Joe States said, You know something? Until I hit the road and started to get to know some of our folks up north, I didn't realize that they didn't do all that up there like down the way.

Man, what we really talking about now is the old folks and the old land-

marks, Alan Meadows said. And Joe States said, God bless them both. And then he said, Let me say this again because I can't say it too often. When it comes to education, the old folks have always been on the case.

I'm talking about like way back before Emancipation. If you found a way to learn to read and write and figure it was like outfitting yourself with a pair of them seven league boots, that somebody—who was it?—mentioned the other day, for the Underground Railroad. Then after Surrender, every time somebody put up a new school they saw it as another Amen to Appomattox.

And said as much, I said. And he said, You know it too? And I said, To them it is still as if every good mark you make on your grade school report card is like another bullet to help bring about old Stonewall Jackson's final Waterloo.

But schoolboy that I still was (and still am) I also knew that you should never forget that there were also those who did not listen to the old folks because sometimes they acted as if what they scoffed at as "book learning" was a bigger threat to their well being than segregation. So much so that some of them not only pulled for poor students against good students, but were also very likely to insist that good students' achievements were the result not of conscientious application and integrity but of luck, hype, trickery, or favoritism. Not that they really thought of schoolboys as being more dishonest than anybody else but that book learning and everyday common sense and the practicality that added up to success didn't go together. So to them schoolboy was a term of contempt.

On the way out to the West Coast that first time it was Elmore Wilkins who started signifying about landmarks of another kind; and as soon as the others began joining in, you could tell that they were saying what they were saying not only because there was a schoolboy along this time, but also because it was something they had been doing among themselves from time to time over the years.

One more time, Elmore Wilkins said looking out across the plains at the mountains against the sky in the distance. One more once, Schoolboy, he said. Now, you know what I always have to think about every time we head out this way? Them folks making this trip back in the old days of the covered wagons. And Joe States said, Man, I know what you mean, but what about them cats that were all out through here way back before that? What about all of them Spanish studs tramping and camping all out through here looking for gold? Man, do you realize that they came all the way across the Atlantic Ocean from the old country and left them ships anchored back somewhere on the coast, and didn't even have any maps to go by?

Maps? Osceola Menefee said. Man, them cats were making themselves a map as they went along. Man, what can I tell you? Man, don't forget you're talking about the same somitches that navigated their way all the way across the wide open seas. And Joe States said, Them cats were making history. Man, them cats had history in their blood.

And passed it on to the ones that became the early settlers and the forefathers that turned all of this part of the hemisphere into one nation under one flag, Ike Ellis said. And Malachi Moberly stood up and stretched and put his magazine in the overhead rack and said, Man, what about that goddamn trip your forefathers made in the bottom of that cattle boat? And Ike Ellis said, Aw man, don't nobody feel like playing no dozens today. And Malachi Moberly came and sat beside him and said, Man, ain't nobody trying to put nobody in some old dozens.

Damn, man, he said putting his seat in a reclining position and stretching his legs, They're my forefathers too. Come on, man, you're talking about making history and making the flag. Man, there's a whole lot of doodoo all mixed up with all that other stuff they come up with to stick them stars and stripes together with. Man, all that old coonskin and log cabin jive is all right with me but man, history is all in the way you look at it.

Now me, he said to the bus at large, What I can't help thinking about every time we head out this way is Indian history. Man, them folks messed around and lost everything to these people. And when Ted Chandler said, Yeah Jack, but them goddamn Indians went down swinging, Jack, he said, but Jack, them goddamn Indians ain't swinging no goddamn more, Jack. Man, that's exactly what Indian history comes down to, and that's what I'm talking about. Man, me, I don't intend for us to go down at all. Man, look out the goddamn window and see what they left these folks with. Man, how you going to ever swing anymore when you ain't got doodly squat to swing with? Man, ain't nobody in history ever got themselves faked further out of position than these folks. Which just goes to show you that it takes a whole lot more than being brave or even making people scared of you. Ask Scully.

Well thank goodness Old Mose has played it smarter than these folks, Joe States said. And Ike Ellis said, So far, man, so far. Which is a goddamn miracle when you stop to think about how loud and wrong some of our people can sometimes be. Scully knows this.

We rolled on westward and I was following the route on the road map and mileage chart, and nobody said anything else above the ongoing sound of the bus. So I nodded off thinking about the Continental Divide, and the next voice I heard was Osceola Menefee saying, Now you know what this kind of country put me in the mind of, Schoolboy? Science, man. Science.

And I opened my eyes and saw that we were less than a mile away from the foothills of the Rocky Mountains. I was wide awake and I opened the map and mileage chart again.

Man, Osceola went on saying, What Joe and you all were talking back there a while ago was history. But man, this kind of stuff we pulling deeper and deeper into now was out here even before history. Man, you start thinking about what you looking at in this kind of country the next thing you know you also thinking about not just mineral deposits and wildlife and livestock on the open range, and all that but also glaciers and volcanoes and earthquakes and planets. Man, you're going to see more telescopes and stuff like that out this way than in any other place I ever been in the whole United States of America.

As soon as he had mentioned science, it was as if you were back at Mobile County Training School where you had studied animate and inanimate specimens in the room with the long laboratory table and on the wall above Mr. Troupe C. Hodges's desk there was the Periodic

Table of Elements that you would be using when you came to study physics and chemistry the following year and the year after that.

I would have used the word primordial instead of before history or prehistoric, but since I didn't want to sound academic all I said was that he and I were thinking along the same lines. And Wayman Ridgeway said, Hey Scully, you hear who up there going all whatchmacalogical on the schoolboy? And Scully Pittman said, Man, I'm listening to this stuff. And Wayman Ridgeway said, Hey Bloop, you been knowing this cat for a long time. Where's he getting all this new jive from? And Herman Kemble said, Man, don't be looking at me. Man, I wouldn't know. Maybe that's some of what he's been getting from some of all of them little Miss Goldilocks he been bagging and heading for the shed with *all by his goddamn self* these past few years. And Alan Meadows said, Well, if that's where he's getting it he sure got a funny way of getting it. And everybody was laughing then, not because what Alan Meadows said was hilarious but because they were pretending that they had heard something questionable about Osceola Menefee's manhood.

Hey what's happening back there? Milo the Navigator said from the front seat, pretending that he hadn't been listening all along. And Osceola Menefee said, Man, nothing but the same old sixty-six. Here's somebody trying to use some intelligence about man and the environment, and here they come in the goddamn gutter. And Scully Pittman said, Man, All I said was you sure have a funny way getting what you getting from them college girls.

Okay, man, Osceola Menefee said shaking his head and laughing along with everybody else. Okay, he said, and then he said, You see there, Schoolboy. These are your folks, man. How you ever going to get their head out of the goddamn gutter long enough to make some kind of progress? Them other people trying every way they can to qualify, and all you can really count on your folks to do is come up with another way to signify about some ofay poontang.

Yeah, Herman Kemble said not long after everybody had settled back down into the ongoing sound of the California bound bus again.

Yeah, but don't let any of this fake you out of anything along that line of action, Schoolboy. Because, man, as far as I'm concerned all of that bright-eyed and bushy-tailed curiosity is as much a part of my birthright as anything else out here.

Especially seeing as how you can just about always count on so many of them being stacked so fine, Otis Sheppard said. And Ike Ellis said, With them bass clef calves and treble tipping toes and insteps. And Herman Kemble said, And all I ever seen any of them looking for is some meaningful experience as they call it, to help them get themselves together for life. And ain't never stingy about nothing that really matters to me.

You tell him, Joe, he said. Am I fakking or just yakking? And Joe States with his seat still reclined as far back as it would go and with his baseball cap still pulled down over his eyes said, You ain't yakking, Bloop. You fakking and cadillakking. But you ain't telling our college boy nothing he ain't already hip to.

Then he said, Of course now, me myself, now speaking of birthrights, every time another one of them latch on to me and start hitting me with all them questions about the beat and syncopation and blue notes and, oh boy, improvisation, improvisation, improvisation that gives me a very solid notion that they feel that I am as much a part of their birthright as old Unka Remus used to be. Yeah, Unka Remus, he said. Because if you believe that Unka Remus was some old harness mender all bent over with rheumatism sitting around spinning yarns for some little old shaggy-headed boy from the Big House, you talking about them people's Unka Remus. Not my Unka Remus.

XI

I n those days you left Route 66 at the junction with the San
Bernardino Freeway, which came all the way into the downtown Los Angeles interchange at Civic Center, and that was where you
picked up the Hollywood Freeway. Then you came on past Western
Avenue and turned off and circled back on to the overpass and you
were on Sunset Boulevard.

Well, here's this old two-by-four factory workers' town, Schoolboy, Joe States said as we came on by the local broadcast studios on
both sides of that part of the street. And Otis Sheppard said, Don't pay
no attention to that kind of old talk, Schoolboy. He's just as glad to be
coming back out here for the umpteenth time as you're glad you're
finally making it for the first time.

And Joe States said, Yeah glad. Who said I wasn't? Not me. This
is one of my most favorite side hustle towns in the U.S.A. You damn
right I'm glad. The way I rake in these people's ready money for a little hot jive piecework here and there in this town is a sin and a shame.
That's exactly what I'm talking about. Everybody knows about the big
fat world famous studios, because that's all a part of the Hollywood
glamor mill hype. But, man, it's that network of subcontracts that most
of these pretty houses and this good living come from.

We rode on past a long Paramount Pictures building and a
Columbia Pictures headquarters was in the next block. Then there was
CBS followed by Music City; and we came onto Highland Avenue and
La Brea, and I saw the Screen Actors' Guild and the Screen Directors'
Guild and after we passed Fairfax Avenue and stopped at a traffic light
near Schwab's Drug Store, we came on past Villa Frascati and I saw the
huge plastic statue of a blond drum majorette wearing a white cowboy

hat and tasseled white boots, revolving on a pole advertising Las Vegas as the place for Beverly Hills people to go for fun and games.

The bossman and Old Pro got out at the Château Neuf, which was in the same neighborhood as the Garden of Allah; and we headed back along Sunset and took La Brea across to Hollywood Boulevard and came on along past Grauman's Chinese Theatre, Max Factor's makeup headquarters, and the Pickwick Bookstore to Vine Street and pulled up the hill to the Vineyard Motel.

Last stop. Last stop. All out and everything off but my tools and the music stands, Joe States said standing up. And then he said, Get to me fast, Schoolboy.

So when I found my room I just left everything there and came back out to the courtyard, and he and Otis Sheppard and I walked back down the hill past the Capitol Records tower to Hody's and I had my first Hollywood hamburger and malted milk.

We went for a short walk beyond the Pantages Theater then and came back up the hill again, and when I finished my shower and got into bed, it was almost two o'clock, and as I was falling off to sleep I heard Herman Kemble opening his door across the hall and saying, Don't nobody be bothering me about nothing in the morning, and I mean nothing under a hundred dollars coming this way. Don't nobody call my name before twelve o'clock. Anybody see me up and about before 2:00 P.M., you can bet a fat man I'm walking in my goddamn sleep.

I found my way around Hollywood on my own that next morning, and in the afternoon I went out to Beverly Hills and walked all the way across Rodeo Drive to Wilshire Boulevard. Then that night Ross Peterkin the disc jockey, local man about town and longtime cutbuddy of Joe States, came by in his Roadmaster convertible, and Joe States and Herman Kemble and I rode across town to West Los Angeles with him. That is where I met Gaynelle Whitlow.

We were standing at the bar in The Home Plate, and she came in and sat in the stall next to the jukebox while Ross Peterkin was ordering our drinks, and when I asked him who she was, he said, Hey, that's somebody I want you to meet. Hey, Joe, this schoolboy got good eyes to go with his good ears. And Joe States, who was talking trash to the cashier said, Who you telling? That's my states from down in The Beel.

Ross Peterkin waved, and she smiled back and he took me over and introduced me; and she said, Well, hello there, Mr. College Boy. And Ross Peterkin said, How about showing this down-home boy some big city fun? And she moved over to make room for me beside her and winked at him and said, I thought you just said he was a big-time college boy. And Ross Peterkin said, So what? Right now he is a brand new road musician on his first trip out here to glamor town. And one thing for sure, this college boy got three legs just like the rest of the thugs in that band.

Joe States and Herman Kemble were there then, and Joe States leaned over and put his arms around her and kissed her on both cheeks, smacking his lips and sighing and rolling his eyes in exaggerated blissfulness saying, All this fine brown, mellow frame and her own eight cylinder rolling stock to haul it all about in.

And she said, I thought maybe you were not speaking tonight. I was wondering if you'd decided to pass or something. And when Herman Kemble said, Pass for what? she said, I don't know. But you know how some of you old big-time musicians can sometimes get, from having all them people running after you. And Joe States said, You looking so good, baby, I had to hold back and get up some nerve. And she said, You hear this stuff, Bloop. And Herman Kemble said, Baby, he's just trying to tell you like it is. And she said, You guys. Especially you guys in that band. Every last one of you, trying to be just as bad as that man himself.

So look here, Ross Peterkin said then as the three of them bowed and backed on back toward the bar, Maybe we'll run across you all later on, maybe at the Five Four or somewhere. And she said, We'll see. And then she said, So you're Shag Philips's replacement. People out here keep tabs on that band just like other places. So tell me why they call you Schoolboy. And I said, Well it's not really just Schoolboy. It's also Scooterboy and also Scootboy and also Scooboy.

Then when she asked me about college I also went on to tell her something about Mobile County Training School; and that was what we were still talking about when we came outside and drove along West Adams to the Rumpus Room, where she left a note for somebody with one of the bartenders. After that we came on past the University of Southern California, Exposition Park, and the Los Angeles Coliseum; and shortly after we crossed the Harbor Freeway and turned right, she said, I'm sure you've been long hearing tell of Central Avenue. And I said, Ever since I first started hanging round the barbershop. And she said, Well here it is.

She said, They say everybody from down home had at least one cousin over in here somewhere. And I said, And somewhere on the South Side of Chicago and above 110th Street in Manhattan and in the Black Bottom section of Detroit and so on depending on the part of the old country you hail from.

We stopped at the Crossroads Tavern, and she introduced me to Ford Shelby, whose place she said it was; and as soon as she told him that I was with the band he rapped on the bar to get attention and said, Hey folks, I just want you to know that a brand new celebrity just walked in. And everybody wanted to buy me a drink, but he said everything I ordered was on the house. Then he said, How's the bossman? And I said, Still rolling.

And still the best that ever did it, he said. Tell him I'll be out there tomorrow night.

They started reminiscing about the band as they had known it over the years then, rehashing tales that I had already heard on similar occasions in town after town from coast to coast, about what Joe States said to somebody somewhere one night and somewhere else on another night, and about how from the very beginning anytime anybody from the band walked in anywhere the music always picked up. Not because they had come to challenge anybody in a cutting session, which none of them ever did anymore. But because along with everything else hearing blues music was supposed to do for you, the boss-man's band had also always been the one that represented that special class (or easy high style and elegant or swinging manner) that always made you feel that however well you already did whatever you did, you should try to do it better.

When you dance to that music, somebody said, It is not just a matter of going out there and doing something to show that you can get down with the latest do. You feel something deep inside yourself when you hear that music.

That's exactly what I've always said, somebody else said. And sometimes that is also what puts you on the spot. Because if I'm out there dancing I feel like I'm missing something up on the bandstand. And if I'm just standing down front looking and listening I feel like I should be back on the floor doing something to go with the way the music makes you feel.

Then a voice down at the other end of the bar cut in and said, Hey I got a question I want you to answer, young fella. And I said I would if I could. And he said, Is the bossman really the one that thinks up all that stuff can't nobody else play but you all? And somebody at the opposite end of the bar said, Well there's old Govan for you. Always coming up with some old back-fence signifying jive. And the one called Govan said, Man, didn't nobody ask you nothing. I'm talk-ing to this cat here. He the one in the band. You ain't in nothing.

I said, Naturally the bossman is always the main one. That's why he's the bossman. And he said, What about Old Pro? And I said, He's the straw boss, and he writes some few things too. And he said, The way I heard it, the man ain't got nothing on Old Pro. Of course, me myself all I can say is Old Pro is supposed to be the one that went to the goddamn Boston Conservatory of Music.

And Ford Shelby said, Don't make no goddamn difference who went the hell where, when you hear that band playing something, it always sounds exactly like the bossman wants it to sound, don't give a damn if Shakespeare wrote it. Then he turned to me and said, You tell him I said I'll be over there tomorrow night. You tell him Ford Shelby.

He knows me. You tell him old Ford is still out here fighting that bear and dodging cold weather.

We made it to the Twilight Lounge just before the second show began, and that's where I met Silas Renfroe. He was leading a five piece combo that night, playing tenor, alto, clarinet, and flute himself, with Eddie Sinclair on piano, Jamison McLemore on bass, Nelson Scott on trumpet, and Fred Stokes, better known as Red Folks, on drums.

Our table was right next to the stage, and at the end of the set all of them came and spent the whole break sitting on the knee high apron of the crescent bandstand talking to us. And when I told Silas Renfroe that I had heard the bossman telling Old Pro something that he liked about one of the combo's recordings, Eddie Sinclair said, What did I tell you. I told you that man don't miss much, and don't forget nothing. And Silas Renfroe said, You sure did, but it's still hard to believe.

Jamison McLemore said, Of course, don't nobody have to tell you that you got the best bull fiddle gig in the world. And I said, talking about hard to believe, man, I keep expecting to wake up and find out that I fell asleep listening to records and have been dreaming that I was doing Blanton and Oscar Pettiford rolled into one.

When it was time to go back on the stand, Silas Renfroe gave me his phone number and said, Anytime you're out here and have some time off give me a buzz, and I'll pick you up and we can have some Mexican food at my house, and maybe some Sunday we can drive down to TJ to the bullfights. And Red Folks said, You tell that Joe Ass States I said he could at least get sick or take some time off and go to Hawaii while the band is out this way, at least once in a while.

When we pulled up to the Five Four there was a crowd outside, and when we got upstairs there was elbow room only. But we did get to dance two times before the end of the set, and we stayed long enough to hear old Decatur Wilcox play some barrelhouse piano and sing three lowdown way down-home blues numbers. Then we went on to the Safari and sat in an alcove and sipped sour mash, and she told me about leaving Gulfport, Mississippi, and living in Chicago and Detroit before coming to Los Angeles.

Then she said, Now I'm going to take you to get some of the best barbecued spareribs I ever tasted anywhere on this side of the Rocky Mountains. So our next stop was the Wagon Shed, and when she put in our order, she said, I know you're a big boy and all that, but you just got to try some of this lemonade, and when I took a sip I said, I see what you mean. This is the real stuff, right off of the down-home church picnic grounds and hey, ain't no flies on this potato salad either.

From our booth in the dining room you could hear the jukebox in the bar, and somebody kept playing "9:20 Special" all during the time we were eating, and when we left she was humming it and snapping her fingers, and when I joined in she said, Do you guys ever play that? And I said, Sometimes, thinking about how Count Basie's band, whose tune and recording it was, played it like a transcontinental express train batting hell for leather across the wide open spaces en route to or from the Pacific or the Atlantic coasts. Whereas the bossman had us doing it sometimes somewhat slower and sometimes not but always more like an East Coast limited reverberating along the cuts and fills and against the urban density of Washington, Baltimore, Philadelphia, New York, and Boston.

I always did like that number, she said. And I said, Me too. And when she said, You know how some pieces make you feel good in a very special way, I said I'd tell the bossman that there was a very heavy request for it tomorrow night. But I didn't tell her that in our current arrangement the bossman and I had a piano and bass spot just before the out chorus.

You took the Imperial Highway across to the Harbor Freeway and there was no inbound traffic and only a very light premorning fog, and she drove on humming "9:20 Special" with me drumming bass time on the dashboard, and we were turning up the slope to the Vineyard Motel in fifteen minutes.

Then before I could decide which magic words to try first she said, What time is it? Which was all the vamp I needed, and I said, Just about that time. And she said, Well we better get on in here and do this thing and get some sleep. You got to work tomorrow you know or is it already today?

When we woke up it was almost two o'clock that next afternoon, and as she headed for the shower I said, Breakfast, brunch, or lunch? And she said, Make mine just plain old ham and eggs and grits and black coffee. So I put the order in to room service and joined her in the tub and by the time we got back into our underwear the trays were delivered.

She said, Call me sometime. And I said, When? And she said, Sometime when you get back around to the likes of me. And when I said, What about tonight? she said, I'll be there and I'll be listening for my number, but don't look for me. She said, I don't care what you say, I know good and well ain't no Alabama cutie pie out here on his first trip really want to hook up with no old down-home broad before looking over this crop of mane tossing ponies this town is so famous for.

Outside on our way through the patio we waved at Ted Chandler and Osceola Menefee, who were sipping beer at a table in the shade of a big California bright beach umbrella. Malachi Moberly was in the telephone booth, and Milo the Navigator nodded at us from where he stood in the office door talking to somebody inside.

So, you just go ahead and help yourself to some of all that eager pink stuff that's out here waiting for you, she said stopping me at the entrance. Then when you get back east you can tell them about how it was with somebody in the movies. Then when you come back out here sometimes and get a little homesick for some down-home cooking, that's when you might really want to give your new brownskin kissing cousin a buzz, and we'll see how you follow up on that nice little lick and a promise.

She gave me a lotsabrownskinmama hug and kiss and patdown-there then, and then she winked and turned and did that fine brown cake walking babies strut all the way to her parking space. Then she turned and waved and winked again.

It was not until we had finished our West Coast tour and were back beyond the Rockies heading for a string of one-nighters leading into Chicago that Joe States told me how Gaynelle Whitlow came to be my first date in Los Angeles. The bossman himself had set it all up and left the rest to Joe States and Ross Peterkin. Everybody else in the band knew about it because that was the way things were on the road with the band in those days. But the Bossman Himself was the only one who never mentioned Gaynelle Whitlow.

XII

At the Palladium that next night everybody except the Bossman Himself was backstage even earlier than the usual forty-five minutes before curtain time. At least half of the lineup was already there when Joe States and I came in with Old Pro just ahead of the others and when I got dressed and started tuning my instrument, we still had thirty minutes in which to warm up, primp, and woof at each other.

You knew that the bossman was also somewhere on the premises, but I hadn't yet seen him when Old Pro gave the all on whistle, and he was still nowhere in sight when Old Pro gave the downbeat for the first number. So I figured he was checking us out and also getting a sense of the audience from somewhere out in the middle or back of the auditorium, and when I looked over into the wings as we hit the out chorus of the third tune and saw him looking at us with his eyes stretched in mock astonishment, I was not at all surprised.

He stood with one leg dropped back and his forward foot pointed inward, his body erect but with one shoulder ever so slightly lower than the other, both rotating ever so gently, his arms hanging relaxed and his fingers dangling as if fresh from the manicurist; and when we did a repeat on the tag, he nodded to Old Pro and waited for the applause to fade. Then he made his entrance, doing that thin soled imperial patent leather sporty limp, wide legged stride, saying, Thank you thank you thank you and now.

The applause started up again as he reached the microphone and it was for him this time and it was an ovation, into which he bowed smiling and saying, Thank you thank you thank you again, as he backed away and moved over to the piano. He sat waiting for the crowd to settle back down once more, and the next time he said, And now, and now, he began the vamp to our theme song, and when he raised both hands, and Joe States brought us in, it must have sounded as if we had been playing the first three numbers behind a scrim.

We did two repeats on the out chorus then instead of following up with a bright getaway jump tune so that Scully Pittman could call out the dancers with a high register trumpet solo, and Big Bloop could pile on the goose pimples, he made a fast segue into the new twelve bar riff tune in C natural designed for theaters and concerts and called "Showcase," because it had enough space for as many solo spots as he chose to use.

Everybody had a four bar solo spot that night, and we took it out with Ike Ellis and Scully Pittman blowing at each other from opposite sides of the stage as if from coast to coast; and when the applause and the thank you thank you thank you died down, we took our concert stage routine bows, one by one, section by section, beginning with the trumpets, followed by the reeds and the trombones and then Joe States, Otis Sheppard, and finally me. And Otis Sheppard said, I always did like this town. And Joe States said, Now let's lay some stuff on the natives. I ain't showing nobody no mercy at all tonight, Schoolboy. When we walk into that after party I want them trillies waving some trimming at me.

That was the night I met Eric Threadcraft. He was among the first people who came backstage during intermission. Joe States and Otis Sheppard and I were standing by the sprinkler control unit, and I saw him waving at us as he worked his way through the crowd, and I thought he was somebody from the entertainment section of one of the newspapers or magazines and I was pretty certain that he was coming to talk to Joe States not me; and I didn't want to have to listen to any more of the same old questions about what jazz really is and where it came from and where it's going and who is taking it where. So I said I'm going over here a minute. I'll be right back.

But Joe States said, Hey, wait a minute, I want to introduce you to this cat. I want you to meet this cat because I want you to have some business connections in this town. You always need to know somebody like this in a town like this. This is one of the cats I was talking about. I'm already set to do some Q.T. stuff for this cat next week.

Eric Threadcraft was there then and he said, Hi, fella. And I said, What say, man. And Joe States said, I know you already started picking up on what we putting down on the bull fiddle these days. And Eric Threadcraft squinted shaking his head saying, I can't really believe it yet. And Joe States said, Man, ain't nothing you can do but believe this stuff because it makes your bones remember.

He was talking with his arm around my shoulder, and I wondered how much Eric Threadcraft's ofay background prepared him to know about Uncle Bud, Uncle Doc, Uncles Ned and Remus—or really Uncle Bud-Doc-Ned-Remus; and I decided that he had probably heard of Uncle Remus just as most fay boys had heard of Uncle Tom (not of Harriet Beecher Stowe but of the ever so black political rhetoricians) but his Uncle Remus was probably only old Joel Chandler Harris's good old arthritic darky harness mender and spinner of backyard yarns for towheaded down-home boys from the Big House. But my Uncle Remus (or Bud or Doc or Ned) was another avuncular proposition altogether. *But Joe States was his unka Remus even so.*

As Eric Threadcraft and I shook hands, Joe States began telling him about how the bossman had heard me during the fall of my senior year and had decided to try to entice me to come in as a second bass player (after graduation, of course) even before he had to realize that family circumstances were going to cause Shag Philips to give notice.

So, we got ourselves a blue ribbon college boy, he said; and then he said, And I didn't say conservatory. I'm talking about that deep classical and philosophical and diapirical economical psychological scene, man. That's what he got a degree in, man; and that's what we're working on because he still got to realize that he's supposed to be a full time musician. He still thinks he just lucked into a new side hustle that will bring him in enough loot to get him to and maybe through some graduate school or something. Man, we keep telling him ain't no university ready for this stuff yet. This stuff belongs out here in the everyday world that this band is all about. Like where we at right now and will be tomorrow.

What can I say, my man, Eric Threadcraft said. I just heard you out there and I take my man Joe's word on you even if I hadn't.

At that time he thought of himself as an apprentice arranger-conductor, and his main occupation was making records. Most of his jobs were with pop singers, and most of his scores were written for big studio bands that included strings and such symphonic woodwinds as flutes, piccolos, oboes, and bassoons. He also used a certain number of instrumentalists who played our kind of music, and he always used our kind of rhythm section even when he also had the whole percussion section of the regular studio orchestra on hand. That was how he and Joe States had been brought together, and they had been friends for about three years when I came along.

I really get a big kick out of working for this cat, Joe States said, slipping his other arm around Eric Threadcraft's shoulder. All of them sugar coated saw fiddles and wine stained reeds, and me in there in the middle of all them opera tools! Of course I'm just taking his money for doing next to nothing. Man, all I have to do is just sit in there and pat my feet and twiddle my sticks and stir and flap my brushes and be ready to boot all that mess up every now and then when my old good buddy here points that teacher stick at me.

And Eric Threadcraft said, That's doing plenty, fellow, believe me. It's money well spent. And Joe States said, See what I'm talking about? That's what I like about working for this cat.

And that was when Eric Threadcraft turned to me again and said, I'm already all set with a bass player for next week. But you can count on something with me the next time you're out here, if you're interested. And I said, I'm interested all right. And he said, A fellow with all the stuff you got going can always make a good living in this town. Man, there's no telling how much Joe States could make if he stayed out here for a while. Just freelancing. And I don't doubt that you can do the same thing.

It was time for the rhythm section to be getting back in place for the second set then. So we shook hands and he said, Next time. You can count on it. And I said, I'm game. And as he headed away waving he said, That's good enough for me. It's a deal. And as Joe States and I came on into the wings, Otis Sheppard, who was waiting for us, said, Man, some of these gray boys sure got a lot going for them in this town.

And Joe States said, Especially that one. You keep in touch with him, Schoolboy. And I said I would and he said, You two are going to get along just great. Hell, you can even talk some of all of them deep thoughts back at him. He'll like that.

That was also the night I met Felix Lovejoy. During the second intermission I was on my way upstairs to look at the dance floor from the balcony, and as I came on to the landing, somebody tapped me on the shoulder and said, There's that man. How's the new bass champion?

And I said, That's not me, man. You got me mixed up with somebody else. And he said, Hey man, I've been in this business long enough to trust my ears, and I call them as I hear them.

He introduced himself then and told me about his radio program and invited me over to his table to have a drink and say hello to his friends. And that is how I also happened to meet Shirley Comingore the same night. She was talking to another Scandinavian looking blonde who, like her, had long legs with the kind of shapely calves I always spot right off and who also gave me a smiling squint and a nose wrinkle as she said, Hi there.

What are you doing afterward? Felix Lovejoy asked me. And I said there's a party or something up in the hills somewhere. And he said, Well let's talk business right now then. I want you for my record show the day after tomorrow afternoon, and I'm also inviting you to my jam session at The Key Sunday afternoon. I know the band's policy against sitting in, but I just thought you'd like to dig the scene as my guest.

Somebody cut in on us at that point and he excused himself and stood up and stepped aside for a minute, and when he turned back to me he took a business card from his wallet, wrote a figure on it, and handed it to me and said, How's that for the day after tomorrow? And I said it looks pretty good to me, man. And he said, There's more and there's fun. This is a money town and a fun town. And I said, That's okay by me too, man.

As I was leaving, Shirley Comingore invited me to get to The Key in time for her vocal set. And I did and that was when she said what she said about getting in touch with me the next time the band was in town, because she was thinking about some changes and working up some new things that she wanted to run through with me. But as things turned out we didn't see each other again until over a year later.

XIII

When Joe States and Ross Peterkin and I got there the after party was in full swing. You could hear the music and the noisy chatter and laughter as soon as you came along the curving drive to the parking area. We came on up the wide flagstone steps to the main yard, and I saw the big rambling house, and there were people moving about on the long cantilevered balcony where the lanterns were, and others clustered about the tables on the patio around the swimming pool.

The three of us came on past the couples sitting and strolling about in the darkness of the palms, and suddenly the cool moist breeze reminded me of how close I now was to the Pacific Ocean. *And I said, California. I said, Hey California. I said, Here I am from Alabam. Me and my expectations and my obligations and now my speculations.* And I crossed my fingers.

They were dancing in the drawing room. There was a trio (piano, bass, and drums) from Central Avenue playing after hours gin mill blues extensions, and as we circled around the edge of the floor, I saw Osceola Menefee dancing with a sandy maned Texas looking woman. For some reason I guessed (correctly) that she was a successful booking agent who had once been an extra and a starlet. She was dancing in her stocking feet with her eyes closed, and old Osceola Menefee was looking all nonchalant and doing an old down-home barrelhouse bump and roll on the sly.

We passed Ike Ellis talking to two very pretty brunettes who looked like chorus girls and also looked like old fans of his; and I saw Scully Pittman and Wayman Ridgeway going to the sliding doors that opened on to the patio. I didn't see the bossman, but when we got to the bar there was Old Pro. He was sitting on a high stool talking to a silver gray man and two elegant women who did not look like entertainers, and I could tell that one of them was French by the way her lips moved.

Among those who either said hello or shook hands and said their names or waved or gave us a smiling nod of recognition as we moved on around from one room to the next, there were more good looking women of all ages than I had ever seen at one party before. There were no flies on the guys either, not in Hollywood. But you were not really going to have to compete with them that night. Not only because there were so many more women present, but also because more than enough of them were mainly fans of the band in first place.

When we got to the bar and tasted our drinks I said, Man, the stuff is here just like you said. I said, Man, everywhere you turn. And Joe States sipped his drink and said, Cool it, School. Man, ain't no rush. Man, let's eat first. Man, I know what's going to happen. Man, if we don't grab us something to eat right goddamn now before we start meeting folks we subject to never get another chance at it. I don't know about you, but I'm hungry. I been driving this mule train. Man, I'm the goddamn pick and shovel of this goddamn aggregation, remember?

Then he said, Man, you see all them pink pussycats out there licking their chops? Man, I ain't about to tangle with any of that overeager stuff on no empty stomach after what we laid on them down there this evening. They expect something special after that, and I got my goddamn reputation to keep up. So first, I'm going to get something under my belt, and then I'm going to jive around until my system's settled back down, and then in the cool calm of the wee wee hours I'll be ready to take care of some business.

The food was being served out on the west terrace and we ate looking out over the patio and the garden. The fog had not begun to roll in yet and you could see beyond the nearby hills to the distant network of sparkling lights spreading away across the Los Angeles basin toward where the Pacific shoreline, which I had not actually seen yet, was supposed to be.

Ross Peterkin and I served ourselves from the seafood smorgasbord and the salad table, but Joe States said, To each his own, School-boy, to each his own, and headed straight to the corner where the charcoal grills were; and when he came back to the table we had taken he said, Treble clef for you, bass clef for me. Like I said, Schoolboy, I'm vamping for heavy duty.

When we finished, the two of them went down the steps into the patio. They went along the edge of the pool to the table where Herman Kemble and Malachi Moberly sat with nearly twice as many single women as couples sprawled at their feet. I came back into the drawing room. I wanted to look around before joining in the festivities. It was my first chance to see what the inside of a Beverly Hills mansion was like.

The Bossman Himself was there then and they had him surrounded. I saw him standing as if stashed on one of his favorite mainstem corners once more, ever so relaxed, but missing nothing, kidding
about music with the fellows, and talking trash with the ladies at the
same time. I didn't stop to listen because by that time I was as familiar
with the current chitchat line for local variation as I was with the
themes in the current bandbook. *Oh that was mainly some of our leftover
last year's stuff. Wait till you hear some of our this year's stuff, which also
includes some of our year before last stuff mixed in with a preaudition of some
of our next year's stuff. Oh hello, Miss Excitement. The outrageously beautiful people are over here. They stand back there only as long as it takes for us
to click on our shields against the radiation. In your case we'd still be taking a
chance if you stood back there all night. So you've heard about the misinfor-
mation they've been passing out about you. Gross distortion. Scandalous mis-
representation. Because do you know what they said? They said that you were
very pretty, but they didn't say that you were going to be this pretty.*

I made my way across the floor and came up the steps to the level
where the library was. The door was open, and the lights were on. So
I stepped inside and saw that the bookshelves were on one side of the
room and that the opposite wall was a gallery of paintings, watercolors,
drawings, and sketches, among which, thanks to the influence of the
roommate of my first two years in college, I was able to identify those
by Monet, Matisse, Picasso, Paul Klee, John Marin, Stuart Davis, and
Charles Sheeler.

There was a long conference table in the center of the room, but
the main desk was at the other end facing a glass wall of sliding doors
that opened out onto a balcony beyond which you could see across the
valley and Los Angeles to the Pacific Coast darkness once more. I
checked the time on the wrist watch that was my commencement
present from Miss Slick McGinnis when I graduated from Mobile
County Training School, thinking: *This many miles from Gasoline Point.
This many miles from Dodge Mill Road.*

Then just before I turned to start back down to the drawing room,
I realized that someone had stepped in from the hallway and was about

to say something. I could tell that it was a woman before I looked around, and I hoped she was somebody from this part of town, and she was. And she had the diction I wanted to hear and the sailboat tan to go with it, and she said, Golden Boy, and introduced herself as Morgana.

But not before what she said about some of the paintings. Do you like the Tamayos? That was what she was already saying as I looked around. And when I said, Very much, she said, Well good for you and good for Rufino. The next time I see him I must tell him that I found a bass player in a library looking at two of his pieces while a big Beverly Hills party was going on downstairs.

It so happened that as few examples of Rufino Tamayo's work that I had seen up to that time (mostly in book, catalog, and magazine reproductions) I was already much more taken with his work than with what I had seen by Diego Rivera, Orozco, and Siqueiros, who were much more famous. Yet even so the Mexican artist that I was most familiar with in those days was Miguel Covarrubias, because of his drawings and caricatures in *Vanity Fair, Vogue,* and *The New Yorker* magazines, and also because he had published a book of caricatures called *Negro Drawings.*

I didn't say anything about any of that however because I didn't think she really wanted to go on talking about art, and I knew I didn't. So I waited to see what else she would say, and she said, You were followed, Golden Boy. You were spotted, stalked, tracked, and now stand bearded. That makes you mine, Golden Boy. So let's play games.

And I said, I never argue with beautiful women after midnight. And she led the way back down through the drawing room and across the patio, and fifteen minutes later we were dancing naked in the dark in her house in Bel-Air, where it was as if the music came floating in on the breeze along with the fragrance of the subtropical flowers outside.

She said, When I saw you up there on that bandstand holding that warm brown female shaped thing against your left thigh and shoulder and making it respond to the deft manipulation of your fingers like that as if you were Gaston Lachaise playing around with auditory putty, I knew you were the one for me so I went to the party and waited, and when the three of you came in I've had a bead on you ever since.

As she spoke she put my hands where she wanted them and we danced down the hall to a door and she backed through it clicking on the lights, and we were in the bedroom, and you could see us everywhere you looked, because there were mirrors on all of the walls and also overhead.

From then on I was so busy doing what we were doing that there was hardly any time to look around and check things out, but you couldn't miss the way the streamlined design of the room itself, along with the functional Scandinavian furniture, set off the period piece chaise longue and dressing table with matching chair and old silver and ivory accessories.

You couldn't miss the Picasso drawings of nudes and satyrs and the Matisse studies for odalisques, but I didn't see the Braque painting of an artist and model until it was time for me to go back into the living room and gather up my clothes the next morning. And that was also when I saw the wall of shelves where books and records were, but there was no time to find out what was there. So I didn't even mention it.

When I said Morgana Who, Morgana Which, Morgana What, Morgana Question Mark, she said, Morgana Period. She said, Morgana Exclamation Point. She said, That's my name for myself after dark, Golden Boy, especially from midnight to daybreak.

It doesn't make anything any less real, Golden Boy, she said propping herself up with three pillows against the headboard of the rumpled silk garden flower patterned ever so subtly perfumed bed. It only makes things less literal. Or somewhat less literal in any case.

She then lit her first cigarette since the one she finished in the car on the way from the party. But she took only several pulls on it before putting it aside to start teasing me again, saying, Let's see now where were we? Saying, How about right about here? And how about this? Followed by this which brings us to such as this. And when I said, If you say so, she said, I do say so, Golden Boy. I most certainly do.

And so hithering and thithering on we went, doing the also and also required for the also and also she desired. And what came after what she said what she said about that, could only have been a very brief nap because when she said what she said next, it was as if I had just closed my eyes.

She said, And now I've got to get you home and be back in place before seven. She said, I turn back into the daytime me on the final stroke of seven. She said, No more Miss Night Creature until after dark. And only sometimes even then, she said, such as when Golden Boys from fairy tales materialize in an atmosphere as earthy as that at the Palladium last night.

I got dressed in the not yet warm Palmolive green dampness of Bel-Air in the early morning thinking, *A sunkissed missy don't be late. Thinking California, hey, California.* And schoolboy that I still was, also thinking: *Your smile, eyes, nose, and your tutti frutti et cetera.*

Then outside we came winding back toward the main residential section of Beverly Hills not in the convertible but in the station wagon that I guessed she used mostly to go to the marina and the stables, and there were willows and olive shrubs and date and banana palms all along the sidewalk just as there were in the lush Estate Gardens and that was also when I found out that the tree you saw most often along all of the streets everywhere in Los Angeles was called the black acacia.

When we turned left on Sunset Boulevard at 5:45 radio news time and I saw that the traffic was already building up I remembered what Joe States had said about Hollywood being a factory town, where headline stars and their supporting casts had to get to work almost as early as the technical crews, including the makeup and wardrobe experts. That was when I realized that I hadn't asked Joe States about how all of those unemployed and mostly broke people hoping to be picked as extras in crowd scenes got to and from studios as far out as Burbank and Culver City.

I looked over at my very intriguing hostess at the steering wheel, and she smiled and nudged me with her elbow without taking her eyes from the traffic, but neither of us said anything. But when the music that came back on following the weather report turned out to be a set of four of the recordings the band had made on my first trip to New York, she looked at me and nodded and began rubbing her palm against my left thigh in time with the figures I was playing on the bass and kept it up all the way to the corner of Vine Street.

Then when we pulled up to the motel entrance she said, We must do this again sometime. We really must. And I said, If you say so. And she said, I do say so. But she didn't give me her telephone number and I didn't ask her for it. I said, Whenever. And as I got out, she said, I'll let you know. And I stood on the curb watching as she made a U-turn and waved and headed back down the slope and across the smoggy dimness of Hollywood Boulevard.

When Ross Peterkin drove by and picked Joe States and me up again that afternoon, the first thing he said as we headed across town was, Hey Joe, how about that fine fay fish I saw our college boy cutting out with last night. And Joe States said, And didn't get in till daylight this morning either. And Ross Peterkin said, Fay Morgan. That's some big league and bass clef stuff there, Schoolboy.

Then when he said, How did that action go, man? And I said, Fine man, great man. But when he said, She's somebody that can really make it worth the time and energy, I missed the point. Which I realized as soon as I said what I said when he asked what he asked next.

Because when he said, So what kind of righteous response did she lay on you, my man and I said, Nothing really weird or anything like that, my man, just solid box with a few nice frills, he looked at me and looked back at the traffic and said, Box? Come on, man, you know I ain't talking about no box. Hell, it's all among friends. What kind of loot did she lay on you for a start? And when I said that I hadn't even thought of any deal like that at all because I was just out to have myself some fun and that I had enjoyed myself and that was that as far as I was concerned, he said, Hey Joe we got to school this schoolboy some more.

He didn't say anything else until we crossed Melrose and came on by the Wilshire Country Club, but I could feel him looking over at me and then back at the street. And then he said, Yeah Joe, we got to clue this young fellow in on a few more facts about life in this neck of the woods.

Look boy, he said, patting me on the knee, in the first place, you don't ever want to be going around talking about how much you enjoyed fucking no rich white barracuda, don't care how good looking she is. Man, I know you ain't hard up for none. So how the hell you going to enjoy wrestling with some tough ass horse riding, tennis playing, sailboat bitch you don't even know?

And that's when he said, Hey Joe, let's circle over by my pad for a minute. I want to show our young friend here something.

He had taken Vine and Rossmore to Wilshire Boulevard, and at the next corner he turned right and came along Crenshaw to West Adams and on across to Baldwin Hills. And when we came into his deluxe bachelor apartment, what surprised me was not all of the custom made furniture and state of the art electronic gadgets. All of that was completely in keeping with the range and quality of his wardrobe and the style of his two automobiles. And I had also expected all of the personally inscribed photographs of sports stars, entertainers, and musicians, many grinning into the camera alongside him, some taken in the room where they now hung. And I would have been disappointed if his record collection hadn't turned out to be one of the most comprehensive (what with all the European issues) that I had ever seen up to that time.

What I had not foreseen was a wall of books that he guided me straight toward so that I could see that along with all of the detective and Western stories and novels of adventure and intrigue and all of the nonfiction about music, science, and current topics; there was also a six-foot shelf of histories of families such as the Astors, Biddles, Mellons, Rockefellers, and Vanderbilts, among others, and about such men as August Belmont, Diamond Jim Brady, Jim Fisk, J. P. Morgan, Leland Stanford, Stanford White, and so on and on including the top people in the movie industry up to then.

Now here's my point, my man, he said. I just want you to realize that when you start messing around with the class of stuff you cut out of that party with last night, you got to check it out just like everything else you learn about in college.

He moved over to the coffee table and picked up the current issue of *Town and Country* from a spread of magazines that included *Vogue, Harper's Bazaar, Vanity Fair,* and *The Diplomat,* and when he found the page he was looking for he held it up to show me a full page closeup and a facing page of action snapshots and said I just wanted you to know who you spent the night with last night.

Man, he also said, When you rubbing up against somebody like this you ought to know what you're doing. Because on the one hand you could have yourself the next best thing to old Aladdin's magic lantern but on the other hand she could be just another rich white babe out to slum on you like it's her natural due. If you don't know any better than to let her, he said. And I could have said, Hey man, she's doing what she's doing, and I'm doing what I'm doing. But I didn't. All I did was nod my head and say, Hey we can't have that. So that's some more stuff I've got to watch.

All during the time Ross Peterkin and I were talking, Joe States stayed carefully out of earshot and didn't join in at all: But back outside, as we stood waiting for Ross Peterkin to finish answering a telephone call, he put his arm around my shoulder and said, Everything is cool, statemate. You ain't scandalized nobody. That's just his way of cluing you in on the Bel-Air neck of the swamp. He can tell you a whole lot about them people, because he started out as a backyard boy, you might say. Because his folks came out here from somewhere near Bluefield, West Virginia, to work on the household staff of one of them big estates in Santa Barbara back when Hollywood was still just getting started. Remind me to fill you in on old Ross and all them rich kids he used to play with before they went east to school and over to Europe.

When Ross Peterkin rejoined us a few minutes later, he also gave me a playful hug and a mock left jab and said, No sweat, Schoolboy. No sweat, my man. And that was also when he said, It's just that the first kind of box that came to my mind when you said Fay Morgan laid it on you is the fancy gift wrapped kind that comes from Hermès and A. Sulka.

XIV

I spent the next Monday morning riding around with Osceola Menefee, who had the use of somebody's Oldsmobile convertible for several days. The weather was fair, and along with the warm mild breeze there was the aroma of freshly trimmed shrubbery and lawn grass and yard blossoms. There was also some gray blue haze in the near distance but the Los Angeles Basin smog was not as thick and bothersome in those days as it was to become a few years later.

I said, California. I said Hey, California. I said, Me and my postbaccalaureate contingencies. I said, All the way from the spyglass tree and dog fennel meadows and the L & N canebrakes and Hog Bayou. I said, This many miles from Chickasabogue Swamp and Three Mile Creek Bridge.

We turned off Vine onto Bellamy Boulevard, which we took to La Cienega and came all the way through Restaurant Row to Wilshire and cruised along the Miracle Mile shopping district in the busy traffic of the forenoon bargain hunters. But instead of going all the way into Civic Center, we turned and came back to the La Brea Tar Pits and found a parking area and spent the rest of the morning in the Farmers Market.

Osceola Menefee bought California souvenirs to mail to female fans in six cities, while I was deciding on something for one very special person who like me also had what amounted to ancestral expectations and obligations to fulfill before becoming formally engaged to take on the personal responsibilities of marriage and parenthood.

That was also where we ate lunch that day. Then it was time to head back to Hollywood, and we took Fairfax Avenue, and at three o'clock we were in Studio 2B, 7000 Santa Monica Boulevard, and I was all tuned up and ready for my first West Coast recording session to begin.

Milo the Navigator passed out the music in the sequence that it was stacked on the table by the piano, and as Old Pro took each section through its revised passages and then had us all run the whole arrangement down together except for solo parts, the Bossman Himself sat in the glassed-in control booth checking the balance and sometimes dictating further revisions over the speaker system.

Then when he was ready to take over, he whistled into the microphone and held up his hand and said, So now that everybody else seems to know what is supposed to happen, let's see what our first chair keyboard man has to say about it. If he can't take care of his awesome executive responsibilities, this session is in big trouble and believe me he will be docked.

He stood up and came down out of the control booth walking his crotch-airing, knee-loosening, back-straightening, shoulder-adjusting sporty limp walk and took his place in the center of the studio rigged setup facing the reed section on the floor level, with me and Joe States and Otis Sheppard on his left. The brass section was on a split-level platform behind him, the trombones up one step, the trumpets up two.

And now, he said as he began a vamp that he kept going until he was absolutely sure that he had everybody worked up to hit the groove he wanted. Then as he went on repeating the progression as if only for himself, he said, Hey trombones just remember that all your stuff is supposed to be jive time fanfare. Everything. Foreground and background.

And all the trumpet stuff is monkey business, he said. You come leapfrogging in and everything you do is acrobatic like jugglers, tumblers, and trapeze artists. Solos, riffs, every phrase should be like a jive quotation from the signifying monkey. And the reed section growls and roars and it can slither and twitter and also thunder like a herd.

So Joe, that makes you the cage boss this time around, he said. And then he also said, Old Clyde Beatty himself with a stool and a whip and a pistol. And with a set of spurs, too. Because this thing has got to come on with cymbals streaking and flashing and clashing like lightning even before the fanfare blows away the thunderclouds like parting the curtain for the acrobats.

He was looking at me then, and he said, Elephant boy. He said, Bull fiddle, I want you to walk those goddamn elephants right up through the middle of all this stuff like you don't even know it's there. Or better still, just like you wouldn't give a good goddamn if you did know it was there. Like, What the hell is this? Because you are en route to your next camping site out on safari at a steady pace that will get you there before sundown.

He set the tempo again then and dictated the bass line by naming the notes as he played them for me on the piano and when I started thumping and got it right, he said, keep it right there. He went on through the progression again and nodded to Old Pro and held up his hand and stretched his eyes toward the control booth and said, Let's do it up flashy like Ringling Brothers and Barnum & Bailey.

But before bringing his hand down for take one, he said, Maybe something like "Nonstop to the Big Top." Or maybe "Flipping the Flop in the Big Top." Or even maybe something like "Three Rings Three." Or what about something as simple as "Elephant Walk" as in "Camel Walk," and "Cakewalk," with the circus show time atmosphere speaking for itself?

Then he said, Name to come. Just remember this is my Hollywood open air carnival stuff. Don't be confusing this with my Broadway footlight stuff. My Broadway stuff is something else. That's my midtown stuff that I compounded from the uptown stuff that we brought back from the road in the early days. This is my California stuff.

He also said, Don't be getting this stuff mixed up with my other pit band stuff. That's our black tie stuff and our white tie and tails stuff. This is our out here stuff that I got from our tank town and our showboat on the river stuff. But what the hell, just don't forget the hot dogs and hamburgers and the peanuts and popcorn and Cracker Jack and cotton candy. Which made me remember a poem my roommate and I used to read about the Emperor of Ice Cream. *The only emperor is the Emperor of Ice Cream.* What would old Daddy Royal make of that?

We took a break at six o'clock, and when we came back at seven-thirty the studio audience had grown from the cluster of local musicians, entertainment page reporters, and Hollywood hipsters who had been looking on from the corner by the door to the control booth during the afternoon to a double row of chairs that Milo the Navigator had arranged to have set up along the wall between the main entrance and the table where the refreshments were.

When Osceola Menefee's date came in, he told me that her very pretty early thirtyish-looking blue-eyed brunette friend had come along to meet the bass player. So during the next playback I went over with him to where they were and found out that her name was Enid Metzger and that she was a staff designer in the costume department at MGM, and also that her shade of olive skin made freckles invisible until you were close enough to shake hands.

I said, I hope you don't mind having to sit through all this repetition. And she said, Are you kidding? I just hope we're not in the way or anything. And I said, Not at all. I said, The bossman likes to have a general public audience in the studio when we're recording, because that way we're playing for people not microphones and mixers. And Osceola Menefee said, How you going to be in the way when you so much a part of what's happening? And when his date, whose name was Beryl Boyd, said what she said about divided attention he said, Let me tell you something about these musicians in this band, baby. The bossman couldn't be happier than to see you all in here like this because he know good and well these thugs ain't never going to mess up his music in front of this many pretty women.

This is really something, Enid Metzger said when we went back over during the next playback. And Osceola Menefee said, I guess I know what you mean. But to tell the truth, baby, me I'm just up there trying to make myself a living. Another day, another dollar. And she said exactly what he expected her to say. She said, That's not the way it sounds at all. It sounds wonderful. It sounds simply marvelous. And he said, Well, that's because you and my inspiration are here.

On the next break I said, You never know. We might be here for quite a while longer. And she said, Mox nix. I'm only sorry we couldn't get here earlier. So when the bossman finally called it a day, I said, You're invited to the private party. And she said, How private? And I said, Very. I said, I will be the party of the first part and you will be the party of the second part. Or vice versa. And she said, That requires some serious deliberation. Yes. And we followed Osceola Menefee and Beryl Boyd on out to the convertible. But when he came to the final stoplight before turning left onto Vine, I told him to let us out and we shopped at the old Ranch Market and took a taxi on up the hill.

There was nobody in the patio of the Vineyard when we came through it with two chicken salad sandwiches and two cartons of hot tea with lemon in the takeout bag I was carrying and an assortment of California fruit and nuts in the small tourist packet she had; and as we came on along the hallway, she clutched my free hand and fell in step and said, Is this another kind of elephant stride? And I said, Not really.

I said, I think of an elephant stride as being a lumbering gait, just as a lion or a tiger has a stalking gait. And at another time I probably would have gone on to tell her that the circus piece should not be confused with program music, because rather than being intended as a more or less literal imitation of specific sounds as such, it is a matter of making music by playing around with sounds that obviously go with the festive atmosphere of circuses. But that would have broken the spell of what had gotten under way during the ride from the studio.

So I said, No I guess you could call this a Harlem stride of sorts. I said, Let's call it the swinging patent leather avenue gait of the after hours creeper en route from the last gin mill to some action that brings more satisfaction than can ever be reduced to a powder or put into a bottle of whatever proof or vintage. And she said, What about strutting as in strutting one's stuff and strutting with some barbecue?

But we were there then, and I opened the door and clicked on the light and said, See, nobody here but the very best people. Like you and me. Then I said, Remember who you came with now. I said, Or better still, no cutting in. And she said, Don't turn on the radio. She said, I can still hear the band. She said, All I have to do is close my eyes for a minute so don't turn off the light either.

She had to leave early the next morning because her production unit was getting its kits assembled to be shipped to the shooting location in Europe that she was scheduled to leave for in three days. But she said she would be the party of the fourth part that night if invited by the party of the third part. And I said, Consider yourself not nearly so much invited as beseeched. And she said, See you here. Then she also said, My treat this time.

She's fine people, Schoolboy, Osceola Menefee said when I got to the studio that afternoon. Man, you're going to be thanking me for a long time for putting you next to some people as special as Enid Metzger. Now that's something with some follow-up the next time we swing out this way. And the thing about her is that she could have made it out here just on her looks and being stacked so fine. But she never traded on that, because she's just as deep as she is good looking; and what she's really deep into is not some entertainment and jive but all of that historical and geographical costume stuff that I'm sure you all going to have a lot of fun talking about between the rounds. Man, wait till you see that nice place of hers. Man, she's keen on all of the same kind of things you see when some of them hip globe trotting Ivy League profs throw parties for members of the band.

There were three professional photographers at the session on assignment that afternoon and evening, and I also saw a big bushy bearded weatherbeaten man sitting off in a corner by himself working with his huge sketch pad against an easel shaped like a lyre.

One of the photographers was so preoccupied with the Bossman Himself that it was almost as if everything else were incidental. The other two moved from section to section framing individuals and groups in various clusters and from various angles, one of them using three Nikons, the other alternating between a Contax and a Hasselblad, the one zeroing in on the bossman with two Leicas on neck straps and with another Leica and a Rolliflex on tripods set up in the curve of the piano.

The three photographers worked so smoothly that you could hardly tell them from the studio sound crew. They did all of their shooting while we were rehearsing. Then during the actual takes they moved back to the wall and stood looking on and listening along with the reporters and other visitors.

The big man with the sketch pad sat patting his feet as he worked away at his easel, and as I kept checking him out from time to time I got the very strong impression that whatever he was painting was more involved with what he was hearing than with what he was seeing. Because the only thing he was really looking at was what was on the easel. Every time he raised his head from that he closed his eyes.

He was wearing thick-soled rawhide sandals and a pair of baggy khaki safari shorts, with his faded blue denim shirt open like a bush jacket, exposing his shaggy chest and stomach; and when Otis Sheppard saw how I was keeping an eye on all of the squirming and frowning and leg pumping and smiles and sighs of release and relief he said, Man, what can you do about a cat like that, Schoolboy? All this stuff we're here laying down all these years and that somitch over there still missing the goddamn beat. And man, forget about the groove.

He would have gone on but Joe States cut in then and said, Hey Spode, you didn't tell him who that is. That's Django the artiste, Schoolboy, and if he ever heard anybody in this band saying what Spode was just saying it would wreck his whole frigging life. Man, old Django's whole thing is that his kind of painting is exactly the same as our kind of music. You see that design of that easel, don't you? Man, sometimes you see him over there using his brushes just like me. I mean using two goddamn paintbrushes just like me with my wires. And don't get him started on us and Africa for God's sake. Man, when he gets going on about being the paleface missionary from Shango, he can make it sound like you just got off the boat straight from the paradise lost land of gumbo and barbecue.

You know what old Joe told him one time, Schoolboy, Otis Sheppard said. Old Joe said, Hey Django, man, my family is from a long line of highly distinguished zebra jockeys just like all them Kentucky Derby winners beginning back with Oliver Lewis and coming on through Willie Walker, Isaac Murphy, who was the greatest that ever did it, Soup Perkins, Willie Simms, and Jimmy Winkfield.

But Joe States said, That's all right about what I told him, Schoolboy. Every time you see old Django rip off another one of them sheets that's another umpteen thousand dollars.

XV

When I made the trip all the way out to the West Coast with the band the first time, my status had already been changed from stopgap temporary to extended indefinite, because I had already said what I said to the bossman about staying on for a while longer when I talked with him that morning that many months earlier down in Bay City, Florida, on our way around the Gulf Coast.

I had talked to Joe States the night before, and when he wanted to know what the bossman had said I said I hadn't been to see him about it yet but that I would do so the first thing in the morning. And I did. I found him working alone at the piano in the empty ballroom with a chrome coffeepot, a breakfast tray, and a package of cigarettes on a tête-à-tête-size ringside table in reach just beyond the bass clef end of the keyboard.

We were booked into the Bayshore Casino entertainment complex for the Labor Day weekend, and from where I was standing as we talked, you could see the pier leading out to the pavilion where we were to play open air matinees on Friday, Saturday, and Monday; and there was also the landing for the excursion boat. Off to the left there was the amusement park, and back to your right was a public beach and then the sand dunes curving away and the rolling whitecaps breaking out of the rising morning mist.

He was wearing slate gray slacks and a stone blue polo shirt and he still had on his silk stocking cap under his hat, a neutral brown porkpie with a navy blue band and with the brim turned up all around. And he was also still wearing his lounging slippers. He looked at his wrist watch, put his pencil behind his ear, lit a cigarette, and squinted through the smoke at the music rack in front of him. And said, I thought everybody else was sleeping late this morning. And I told him that Herman Kemble and Wayman Ridgeway had gotten up at five-thirty to go deep sea fishing with some local friends.

I'm the only other one up and about, I said. Except you, I said. And he said, We know about me, so what's your story morning glory? And when I told him and he said, So you changed your mind. I said, Somewhat. Only somewhat. Because what I had said when I agreed to meet him in Cincinnati the week after graduation, I did so not because it was the greatest break in the world for somebody who wanted to become a certified professional musician (something I had never thought about being). I had agreed because briarpatch scooterboy that I had always fancied myself as being and also felt you would always need to be, it was such a fabulously appropriate way to pick up additional ready cash you always needed to supplement the basic expenses covered by the fellowship I had won to do graduate work in the liberal arts. So I had said Labor Day and maybe also the fall semester. And he had said, So let me know around Labor Day. Don't worry about advance notice. Milo always has somebody on standby for emergencies. Anytime during Labor Day weekend will be fine.

Somewhat suits me just fine, he said looking at the empty Gulf Coast beach that would soon be teeming with people making the most of the last hot dry weekend of summer. Then, no doubt because he was no less aware than I was of the faint but unmistakable touch of early autumn in the late August weather along with the back-to-school shop windows and sports page items about football as well as the coming World Series, he said, But what about the university deal? And I told him it was still on.

Because I had found out that the award would still be valid that following year. So I had decided to go on working a while longer to build up a big enough cash reserve so that I could complete all of the requirements for both the M.A. and the Ph.D. in three consecutive years of residence and not have to take a year or more off to earn enough from the salary of an M.A. teaching somewhere.

I told him that I had not really changed anything fundamental. I said all I was doing was changing my schedule. But even as we went on talking I also began to realize that my ultimate career plans probably did not sound nearly so firm as my determination to earn graduate degrees may have suggested. Still it was not until later on that I could acknowledge to myself that for all the indoctrination in the ancestral imperatives as promulgated by Mr. B. Franklin Fisher at Mobile County Training School, I was really planning to go on into advanced training not because I knew what I wanted to become but because I still needed to find out more about the world at large before I could decide what I wanted to do in it.

Not that I still thought that there were any clear-cut answers. That was something my roommate and I had worked over in our after hours gab sessions during my first two years in college, and for him at that time it always used to come back to what Jake Barnes in Ernest Hemingway's *The Sun Also Rises* had to say one restless night in Paris: *All I wanted to know was how to live in it. Maybe if you found out how to live in it you learned from that what it was all about.* To which he used to say, Yea verily, much the same as Little Buddy Marshall back in Gasoline Point would have said, Hey, shit I reckon. But my roommate already knew that he wanted to be an architect, just as the bossman knew that being the kind of musician he had become was what he was really all about. And the same was true of Joe States and everybody else in the band.

Which brought me back to the proposition of being an answer to the old folks' prayers that I had already absorbed from talk around the fireside and on the swing porch even before Luzana Cholly all but took me by the nape of the neck to Miss Lexine Metcalf who in turn delivered me (which is not to say relinquished) to Mr. B. Franklin Fisher and the Early Birds of the Talented Tenth, which intentionally or not, brought me and Little Buddy Marshall (who acknowledged no obligation to anyone not even Luzana Cholly) to the parting of the ways. Because even as he was making up his mind to drop out of school because setting out for the seven seas was a matter of serendipity I was beginning to think of school bell time as Miss Lexine Metcalf's map

rack and globe and compass time along with her bulletin board windows on the world. So, by the time Little Buddy Marshall actually
skipped city on his own, I was not only on Mr. B. Franklin Fisher's pre-
first bell Early Bird schedule, but was also looking forward to college
(with its chime times and spyglass tree castles) to be followed by the
graduate school time required to earn what would be equivalent to the
seven league stride of the heroes in rocking chair story times.

So thank you again, I said looking out beyond him and the Bayshore
Casino ballroom piano to where the early shift caretakers and stall-
keepers were beginning to come to work along the beach. And he said,
No, let me thank you for bringing me some good news to go with all
this fine Spanish Main weather. And by the way, as things are shaping
up it looks like you'll still be with us when we go out to California and
the West Coast again before long.

Then when I apologized for the interruption he said, No sweat.
He had been sitting back from the piano with his legs crossed as he
sipped another cup of coffee and smoked another cigarette; and the
way he tilted his head with one eye closed against the upcurling smoke,
suddenly brought back to me once more how much he still reminded
me of Stagolee Dupas, *fils*, sometimes. Who sometimes used to like to
get up and go and play all by himself in the early morning emptiness of
the Gasoline Point jook joint known as Sodawater's. Old Sodawater
McMeans.

No sweat, he said. I'm just kind of fooling around with this little
thing I picked up somewhere. He bent forward and played the changes
ever so lightly in think-through tempo with only an offhand hint of the
rhythm. Then he uncrossed his legs and pulled his seat all the way up
to the keyboard again and put his cigarette on the ashtray and played
sixteen bars in the intended tempo, naming the instrumentation and
humming the part section by section and also saying, Ike, Bloop, Wayman, and so on.

All you got to do is drop it on us, I said. And he said, We'll see, we'll see. I just might spring it on Old Pro in a couple of days. Nothing special you understand. No big deal.

XVI

When we pulled out of Cleveland on the last leg of the trip back from the West Coast to New York for what was to be my first Broadway showcase theater date, Earlene Copeland, a local singer that the bossman and Old Pro had been trying for at least four or five years to add to the lineup, finally decided to put in with us for a while.

She's somebody very special, Schoolboy, Joe States said when he passed the word on to me as we came outside after breakfast and headed for the bus and the Pennsylvania state line that Monday morning. She finally made up her mind, he said. And I told him I was not really surprised at his news because I had guessed that something extra special was in the works as soon as I saw her at rehearsal that first day.

Even before I asked you who she was, I said. In fact, that's why I asked.

Not that I had guessed what he had just told me about. His news didn't surprise me because what I had guessed was how good she turned out to be, how smoothly she was going to fit in as our special feature soloist for that week in Cleveland. Which I was able to do because by that time I had covered enough territory to know that you could almost always count on hometown entertainers on our circuit living up to or maybe even exceeding their recommendations, no matter how downright legendary all of the frankly partisan pride and praise set them up to be. You could count on them coming through because such was the respect that people everywhere had for that band in those days that nobody would even mention any local hopefuls that might not pass Old Pro's preliminary standards and then bring some special stimulus to the bossman's imagination. You could always rely on that and in the case of Earlene Copeland there was also the example of Hortense Hightower, who had done what she had done for me, but whose own response for hitting the road again was, Not now, I'll tell you when.

We were all set up in the empty club on Euclid Avenue working on the new material that had to be ready for New York, and I was running down my parts with my eyes closed, because that way I could see the lead sheets that the bossman and Old Pro directed from, because I had memorized them verbatim exactly as I used to learn everybody else's lines and cues in the Dramatic Arts Club productions back in Mobile County Training School, a practice that was even more useful when you were playing in an orchestra than when you were acting in a play, especially if you were in the rhythm section with the Bossman Himself.

Sometimes I also kept my eyes closed and went on fingering my parts while the next selection was being chosen. That was why I missed seeing anybody come in. When I closed them nobody was out in the audience area, not even the cleaning crew. But when I opened them again, the first thing I saw was that a very stylish but casually dressed young woman with teacake tan skin, Afro-Asian slanted hazel eyes, and black naturally wavy very lightly oiled but firmly brushed hair, had come in and was sitting by herself at a table on the right side of the center aisle just three rows back.

You could tell that she was somebody who was not only expected but was also used to dropping by on a pop call on her own whenever the band was in town. My impression was that she was just about old enough to have finished college the year I became a freshman and I wondered how far she had actually gone in school. But before I could ask Joe States who she was, I saw the bossman acknowledging her presence by blowing kisses in her direction at the end of one of his short segues and I closed my eyes again.

But even as I went on thumping my part and memorizing everybody else's as before, I could still see her ivory ear loops barely dangle as she tilted her head ever so gently to the left on the afterbeat of the time we were playing in—and that she was keeping with first one foot and then the other—snapping her fingers so softly that there would have been no sound even if she had been standing at the solo microphone.

As the gray green mist outside turned into an intermittent drizzle I found myself remembering once more how it used to be when the weather would suddenly become too wet for my track and field workout and I would come into the assembly auditorium and sit listening as Carl Mike Thompson led the Musical Demons through his arrangements adapted from the Louis Armstrong recordings of "Sleepy Time Down South," "Lazy River," "Stardust," "Wrap Your Troubles in Dreams," and "He's a Son of the South." And also from such Ellington recordings as "Sophisticated Lady," "Rocking in Rhythm," "Mood Indigo," and "It Don't Mean a Thing if It Ain't Got That Swing."

There was also something about the cozy atmosphere of the bandstand that overcast morning in Cleveland that made me feel the way I used to feel when I settled all by myself at the table by the rubber plant in the corner of the main reading room of the library where I used to spend most of my forenoon free periods beginning the first week of my freshman year in college.

At such times it was as if you had the whole world at your fingertips. Which is why it was also as if the campus at large, which was only a little more than two hundred miles north by east of the chinaberry yard up the L & N beyond Chickasabogue Bridge, was the best of all spyglass places so far, exactly as Miss Lexine Metcalf and Mr. B. Franklin Fisher had obviously intended me to find it to be.

As a member of the band you knew that what you also had to have at your fingertips at all times as an ongoing everyday bread and butter matter of course wherever you were, was not only the bossman's entire repertory as such, but also as much of the world at large according to him as you could come by. So as aware of the striking newcomer as I continued to be, I still kept my eyes closed and my attention focused on the new material.

There were two more instrumentals to wrap up before moving on to the background charts for a set of pop vocals and uptempo blues features. The first instrumental was a jump number that was a Hollywood exit shout originally labeled "Checkout Time" and then "Wake Up Call" and finally "Rise and Shine." The piano vamp, which sounded to me so much like an early morning clock tower chime, had the instantaneous effect of arousing and bestirring the whole ensemble to three shouting choruses. Then Malachi Moberly did the trombone getaway solo, and Alan Meadows followed suit on alto. And that set up Ike Ellis for his centerpiece trumpet spot that Old Pro followed with a clarinet continuation the elegance of which was a signal for Ike Ellis to come back and take the out chorus up into the stratosphere. Meanwhile what Otis Sheppard and I had to do through it all was just go right on stomping the blues as if tomorrow were as certain as yesterday, while old Joe States rumbled his thunderbolts and crashed his cymbalic lightning as if clearing the eastern skyline for sunrise.

The other instrumental was called "Skipping City," but I thought of it as "The Mohawk Express" because the bossman had me laying in there like an upstate New York locomotive chugging the blues on the double from his piano intro to the tag, except for one eight bar modulation. Ike Ellis had three high register solo spots on that one, the first following Alan Meadows's alto setup, the next behind Big Bloop's evangelical centerpiece, and finally in the out chorus after the bell tinkling piano sequence.

There was hardly ever any real problems with jump numbers like those two. Putting the sheets for material like that in front of that band was like handing certain Hollywood studios a script for a Western or a gangster movie. It was a case of the rabbit in the briar patch from intro to coda, from breeze to fadeout and credits.

———

We went directly from the second instrumental to the first of the five background arrangements for the vocal set that was being worked up for New York. There was no coffee break. Everybody just turned to the next sheet on the stand and listened to the variations the bossman noodled and doodled as he vamped his way to the downbeat. So I wondered if we were giving the good looking woman out front an overview because she was the guest singer, or if we were being taken through a preliminary for our own benefit while we waited for the guest singer to arrive.

As he almost always did when we were getting background charts ready for guest singers, Joe States filled in the vocal lines, sometimes stage whispering the actual lyrics, sometimes humming them, and sometimes scatting them while mugging like who else but Louis Armstrong himself. Mostly he made it seem as it he were doing so because he was working out his drum and cymbal accents, but it didn't take many guest singers long to realize that not even Old Pro could give them a better demonstration of how the bossman wanted the lyrics voiced against the band's special background treatments.

Joe States, who was forever making eyes and pretending to pine and sigh on sweet groove instrumentals, and who was always likely to become a one man amen corner any time we got a straightaway blues set, vocal or instrumental, going in any tempo, was also a great one for setting riffs verbally. He would come up with some significant catchphrase (usually from some figure the bossman would sneak in on the piano) and start saying it over and over flashing his heads-up signal at the trumpets or the trombones or the reeds or even the whole band when what the bossman wanted was a unison shout.

Such verbalized cues or mnemonics might sound somewhat like anything from an old work chant or an old field or swamp holler or some old saying, slogan, or motto or some current wisecrack or brand new jive line. There was no big mystery about it. As soon as I saw Joe States looking the way he looked at the section he had in mind when he began an offhand repetition of something like, *Say now hey pretty mama, let's get it on;* or *Well let's go Big Shorty let's go, let's go;* or *All night long,* as he did the very first time I ever went to watch the band rehearse.

But you could also tell that what was now happening was strictly a spur of the moment thing between the bossman and Joe States, and that not even Old Pro knew when it was coming until it was already happening. Which is also why everybody knew that there was no use complaining when Joe States suddenly started cracking the whip as if the band were dragging when it was already in high gear. All anybody was going to get was what Herman Kemble got that time when he forgot himself and shook his head on the way back from the solo mike as if to say, Man, what you trying to do?

The first thing he got when the set ended was an answer, Man, don't be shaking your head at me. Man, don't even be looking at me. Man, I'm just doing my goddamn job. I'm giving the bossman what he wants. Man, I'm just sneezing by the numbers, and if you can't get with it shame on you. But hell, Bloop, you did cut them dots, and look at the big ovation you got.

We ran right through the five background charts for the vocal set plus one encore, and then it was break time, and I let myself check out our good looking visitor again. I saw her stand up as the bossman made his way toward her with his arms already outstretched. They hugged and kissed and stood talking with their arms still around each other, and then he brought her back to the stand and everybody gathered around sighing and signifying.

She knew everybody and she greeted them one by one, signifying right back at the best jive passes they could come up with. I was the only one she didn't know, so when she got to me she said, So we got ourselves a brand new bass man. And the bossman said, This is our very clean, keen, and ultraspecial schoolboy, with a college degree no less. And she shook my hand giving me a very genuine smile and said How about that—and kind of cute to boot!

She also said, I was listening to you just now, and I also have the new records and have been catching some of the broadcasts, and I think I know exactly why they picked you for Shag Philips's replacement in this band.

Then as the bossman steered her on over to the piano and we headed backstage Old Pro said, No stuff, Schoolboy, she's so right for this band it gives me goose pimples to think about it. Wait till you hear what she does with this stuff tonight. Wait till you hear her shout some blues. Wait till you hear that lovely creature sing any goddamn thing.

Private stock, Schoolboy, Joe States said as I handed him a mug of coffee. Man, every band on the road is after that honey tree, but we saw her first; and we've been bringing her up to our own specifications every chance we've had. Hell tell him Pro. Like I say private stock. Tell him about all that stuff you and the bossman sketch up and don't put in the book until we come back through Cleveland because it's for her.

One of these days, Old Pro said, one of these days. One of these days, she's going to give in and do some records with us and that's going to bother a whole lot of people. Mark my words. But now let's get this straight now because I'm not trying to predict that she's going to become an overnight jukebox sensation. What I'm talking about is somebody who's going to put her stamp on everything she touches, and I'm saying that's going to turn a whole lot of people around.

When we came back on the bandstand she was still sitting on the piano bench with the bossman and that was where she stayed during the rest of the rehearsal, and the two of them were still there when the rest of us left for the hotel. So the first time I got to hear her strut her stuff was when she came on in the guest spot that night.

And strut her stuff is exactly what she did. She had it and she knew precisely what to do with it. As soon as she came on, it was as if she had been working with us every night. Her timing was perfect. Her beat was exactly where it was supposed to be, and her intonation was as natural to the band as the bossman's uniquely voiced brass and reed sections were.

I can still see her at the microphone as I did from my position in the rhythm section with the jampacked, spellbound crowd in the dimness beyond the footlights. She was wearing a strapless black sheath dress that did to a T what it was designed to do for the rubbery elegance of her not quite café au lait tan, size ten body. And she had her own way of standing and moving and doing that cold stroking walk off routine all the way into the wings and pausing before coming back doing an upbeat one-sided strut, almost like posting on a right diagonal. As we riffed an old off time vaudeville shout theme above the applause.

You have to be there and see as well as hear the band on a night like that. Everything is right and everybody is ready; and before you know it you're in the middle of something you'll never forget. The Bossman Himself can't really explain what is really happening on a night like that and he doesn't ever try to. He just sits there working with it, making the most of it as only he can.

That was the way things got going that first night, and the next night just picked up where we left off and kept going, and the same thing happened the night after that and night after that and after that.

XVII

She'll be catching up with us in the Apple, Schoolboy, Joe States said when he saw me looking for her because everybody else was in place, and the bus was getting ready to pull off on schedule. Then he pushed his seat into the reclining position and said, Actually she didn't make up her mind and give the word until after the last show. So she needs a little time to take care of a few things before cutting out.

We were booked for two nights in a ballroom in Pittsburgh, and then we would be en route via Harrisburg, Lancaster, and Philadelphia to New York for one open date and two rehearsal afternoons in Harlem before opening down in the midtown theater district as a headline feature in the stage variety show on the same program with what was billed as a major first run movie production.

That's the deal, Schoolboy, he said. So we finally got ourselves the singer we've been waiting and wishing for. And not because of the Broadway thing either. Not really. I'm not going to say that Broadway didn't have anything at all to do with it. But I will say it didn't have as much to do with it as the recording deal, and if you want to know the truth, I really don't think that had but so much to do with it either. I think the main thing was that she just decided that the time was right. And what did that was the stuff we laid on her this past week. I think that's what swung the record thing. I really do. Because she knew about the Broadway gig before we came, and there was always a guaranteed recording proposition. But, boy, when the time came for us to break camp this go round she realized that she was just not ready to say good-bye like before. Not yet. Not with all the stuff that was still building up. So she said okay if you still want me I'll give it a try and see if I'm up to it.

So what you think about it all, my man? he said as the bus worked its way toward the suburb and the route to Pittsburgh by way of Youngstown. Did you ever get a chance to have a get acquainted chat on your own?

And I said, Hey man. I said, Yeah man. I said, Hey she's all right with me man. And he said, Hey we're not just talking about a hell of a singer that's getting better and better every go round. I'm also talking about the fact that she's such special people. And I said, Hey man I could tell that as soon as I laid eyes on her and that was when I told him about what happened when I was window shopping my way along Euclid Avenue near Terminal Towers that Thursday afternoon.

I'm going your way she said, and I looked and there she was about to step into the driver's door of an Oldsmobile Eighty-eight parked at the curb; and when I said, Now just let somebody try to tell me I haven't been living right, she said, I don't know about that and I wouldn't bet on it since you're a member of that band of old rounders and reprobates but you sure have been playing right.

Then she said, I haven't had a chance to thank you for that fine and mellow bass line you've been laying down back there. The more I hear it the more I realize why I like it so much. It makes me feel that I'm back among family folks. Not just hometown folks, which is fantastic enough, but family bosom folks.

Which made me think about how beginning back during the fall of the year I left Gasoline Point for college, every time I hear Louis Armstrong playing "When It's Sleepy Time Down South" it takes me back to the family bosom coziness of the tell-me-tale-times around the fireplace and on the chinaberry yard swing porch with the fireflies in the distance above dog fennel meadows.

But what I said was, I sure am glad to hear you say that it comes out that way, because I know that you know what it means to be up there trying to keep up with the likes of Joe States and Otis Sheppard, not to mention the Bossman Himself.

And she said, I do know and I also know enough about that band to know that you've got them trying to outdo themselves every time around. Hey I think it's just great and so do Uncle Joe, Uncle Bloop, Uncle Ike, and all the rest of them.

And bossdaddy couldn't be happier, she said. And I said, Who always has something else for you to get to. I said, Talking about different strokes for different folks and not because he's always trying to find something new either. Not at all. Novelty is not what he's after. Absolutely not. Not him. With him it is not a matter of updating as such but of making music that is suitable to the situation. So you always have to be ready for changes in accent and shading here and there, to say nothing of extensions that come from his just about perfect sense of how the local response is shaping up.

You're sure right about that, she said. If there's such a thing as absolute audience pitch, he's got it. And I'm sure you know all about him adjusting the sound of the band to fit the variations in acoustics from one auditorium to another.

Oh yes, I said, so far as he is concerned that is as much a part of the game as tuning up the band in the first place. That was one of the first things Joe States told me.

Incidentally it was also Joe States who had confirmed the old tale I had heard in college about the time when two arrangements had to be adjusted to utilize a studio feedback noise because the recording technicians couldn't get it cleared up before the end of the session, and the band couldn't come back the next day because it was pulling out of town first thing in the morning.

Then when she said, So where are you headed? And I said, Nowhere in particular, just feeling my way around, trying to get the hang of things, she said, Well come on, get in and I'll give you a quick zip around just to get you started with a picture of how all this stuff is laid out.

Trust me, she said as we pulled out into the traffic. I know how much fun it is to find your way around in a new town on your own, and I promise that this won't spoil any of that. It's just that I've got these wheels and you don't have but so much time.

And I said, Spoil? Lady how could you spoil anything? And she said, Well you know how it is with down-home welcome do. Ain't nothing like it. But when it gets in the way it's a real drag. I mean really. Like a millstone.

She said, I was born up here but my folks are all from down there. So that's the way I was brought up, and I've also spent some time with my grand-folks down in Anniston and Gadsden, Alabama, and Rome, Georgia, back when I was just a tot. I haven't been back down that way since but when they used to come up here from time to time, they always expected to see the result of all the old landmark teachings. She pointed out the sights along Euclid Avenue, and as we cruised on toward Eighty-ninth Street she asked me if I had ever heard of the Karamu Playhouse. And I told her how I had found out about it from the director of the campus little theater during the fall of my freshman year. So even before we came to the curve that led to the grounds of Western Reserve University she had already started asking about what cam-pus life was like in a small college town in central Alabama. And as we drove by the main academic buildings and circled past the Museum of Natural History, the Museum of Art, the Garden Center, and the Historical Society I went on to tell her about my first roommate, whose self initiated research projects were as important to me as the course of study that led to my degree.

I could tell that she liked hearing about college life and that being a college graduate made me somewhat special in her eyes, but I didn't go on with any more details because we were coming to other landmarks and also because I wanted her to have something to ask me about when we ran into each other again.

The rest of the quick spin included a turn through Rockefeller Park that brought us to Lakefront and along Memorial Shoreway and then back to the Terminal Tower, from which she pointed out that Cleveland was a city of heights stretching away from Lake Erie. I had heard of Cleveland Heights, University Heights, and Shaker Heights but not Garfield, Maple, or Bedford Heights, and so on. When she dropped me off at the hotel, she said, So that's it for a start for the schoolboy. Meanwhile for the road musician's Cleveland I leave you in the capable hands of a certain drummer and a whole crew of the smoothest thugs that ever hit this town in my day. See you backstage. And hey, thanks again for what you're laying down back there.

She's very special people, Schoolboy, Joe States said sitting up to look out and check landmarks and mileage markers and then settling back down again as we zoomed on toward Youngstown, East Liverpool, and our Pittsburgh stopover.

Very special people, he said again, pulling his cap back down over his eyes once more. So she took time out for a little hometown hospitality. That's her all right. She's got class and she knows class when she sees it. I knew I could count on her to find time to begin to form her own personal opinion of our college boy. Man, I didn't even have to think once let alone twice about it.

She don't miss much, Schoolboy, he said. Especially when it comes to what's happening in this band. She knows good and well that we're a bunch of thugs. But that don't keep her from also knowing that we got ourselves a band with class second to none. And class is what she's about. You don't need to put on no airs when you've got what she's got, Schoolboy.

No two ways about it, statemate, he said turning toward the window and curling himself into his open country sleeping position. The only thing about it is I don't know how long we're going be able to keep her out here.

XVIII

When we opened on Broadway the following week, it was as if she had been a regular member of the band all along. You had to be there to appreciate how smoothly everything she did fell into place. And the audience liked her as soon as they saw her, and she came right on down front and justified their first impression with the same ease with which she had responded to the completely partisan hometown enthusiasm back out in Cleveland. And was called back for an encore at the end of each set.

The reviewers and show biz chitchat tidbit columnists not only singled her out for special mention, but most of them also made a point of saying that she was a first rate newcomer with a very bright future as a headliner in her own right. Some went on to compare her with Ethel Waters in her glamor days, Adelaide Hall, Valaida Snow, and Nina Mae McKinney. Even the jazz reporters who had come mainly for the band's instrumentals decided that she was not just a pragmatic concession to show biz commercialism but was an excellent in-house vehicle for the bossman's songwriting genius. Which was second to none.

It was the kind of opening you hoped for, and everything got better as the first week moved on along and we really settled in. Mean-

while it also turned out that our new singer could take the daylong
schedule in stride, as if doing that many shows between midmorning
and 1:00 A.M. were the most natural routine in the world.

All I can say, she said, brushing questions about it aside with an
echo if not a riff on an old work holler that I used to hear the sawmill
hands down at Blue Rock on the Chickasabogue give when the afternoon back to work whistle used to blow. All I could say, she said, is the
work ain't hard and the bossman ain't got a mean bone in his body.

To the entertainment page interviewer who came backstage the
second afternoon to find out how she had managed to seem so unfazed
by the fact that she was making her debut in one of the biggest theaters
on Broadway, she said, Of course you know good and well where you
are, but believe it or not, it actually didn't make all that much difference. Because you're really doing what you're doing for the bossman
wherever you are. When that piano calls you out there you go, and
when you get there it's like having him cradling you in his arms. And
with all of my uncles back there supplying everything the bossman even
hints at wanting, you don't even think about confidence. You go with
the feeling that nobody else in the world can give you like this band.

That was also when she brought up the old one about the bossman and the New York telephone directory, which I had first heard
somebody passing on as a bunch of us sat listening to the radio in
Shade's Barbershop back when I was still in my first year of senior high
school.

No question about it, she said. Not in my mind. If he decides to
make jump arrangement on it in any key in any tempo, the band will
swing it and the minute it starts to swing it, I will know exactly how I'm
supposed to sing it. Sometimes this band comes up with things that
sound weird to a lot of other people, but you know something? It
always sounds perfectly natural to me.

Because that's the way she was brought up, Joe States said. Talking about somebody being earmarked. We've got it right here in the
flesh and blood. And if the bossman wants her to sing the goddamn
Milwaukee, Wisconsin, telephone book she'll make all of them w-i-c-

z's and c-z-y-k's sound just as red, white, and blue as Jones, Smith, and Ben Franklin on the Fourth of July—and like she said in any key, any rhythm, any tempo.

As for how it was for me, the main thing was that the bossman was so pleased and so was the band. Not that he said so in so many words and neither did the band. Not even Joe States. Everybody just gave me the same nods and winks they usually give you when things are clicking even better than usual on a one night stand out on the road some-where. Nobody mentioned anything at all about the fact that I was opening on Broadway for the first time.

My guess is that the reason the reviewers who singled me out for special comment made no mention of my debut either, was that they were familiar with the recordings I made with the band by then and so already thought of me as a regular part of the lineup. In any case it all added up to the impression that I was doing better than just good enough.

So from the very outset I was free to make the most of being in midtown Manhattan all day every day, and as soon as I found out exactly how much time you could actually count on having to yourself between all-on calls, the first thing I did was to make my way over to Brentano's on Fifth Avenue between 47th and 48th streets and buy the copy of the guide to New York City that I've kept all these years. And from then on, break time was not only old movie catch-up time and nearby theater playgoing time, but also New York Public Library or Museum of Modern Art or Metropolitan Museum of Art or Madison Avenue and 57th Street gallery time. And that was also when I started browsing and shopping at the Gotham Book Mart on 47th Street in the diamond district.

We were extended for an extra week. Then after one day off we spent the next three afternoons in a midtown studio recording Earlene

Copeland. That was all the time we needed for two solid takes on each number on the contract, plus three extra instrumentals that the boss-man and Old Pro had worked up just in case there was any session time to spare, which there was.

Following that, as usually happened before you went back out on the road again after a Broadway run in those days, there was a sold-out week up on 125th Street at the Apollo Theatre, where the audience would be made up mainly of Harlem people, among whom there would be many from down home and also of another of other people from elsewhere in and around the city some of whom had already been to see us on Broadway, some more than once.

The two main hangouts for musicians and entertainers between shows at the Apollo at that time were the bar in the Braddock Hotel on Eighth Avenue and 126th Street and the one off the main entrance to the Hotel Theresa on Seventh Avenue at 125th Street, which was not only the favorite shucking and jiving stand for the ever so hip or fly uptown cats and chicks (as they were then known as) but also the most strategic checkpoint for sportswriters, gossip columnists, political reporters and commentators, and various hype artists and feather merchants as well.

Playing at the Apollo Theatre and also at the Savoy Ballroom up the east side of Lenox Avenue between 141st and 142nd streets was a very special New York experience in those days. Because as soon as you came on cracking and popping the audience response made you feel as if you were a member of a very popular baseball team taking the field in your hometown park. So much so that every time somebody else come out to the solo microphone it was like a local boy stepping into the batter's box and having everybody from the grandstand all the way out to the center field bleachers pulling for you to ride one out of sight. They even picked up on section riffs, ensemble obligatos, and solo call and section and ensemble response exchanges as if they were matters not unlike running bases and executing double plays, squeeze plays, and so on.

That was the way it was uptown during those years not only for us but also for any band with the right stuff, which at the time also used to be called the righteous stuff and also the mellow stuff. It was a matter of having the stuff that hit the right groove, which was the one that took them down home to tell-me-tale times around the fireplace and on the swing porch once more, wherever you were from.

Not that such an audience response was unique to Harlem. It also happened elsewhere. Because as my old college roommate would have said, recordings and the radio and the jukebox had made the band no less a part of their mythosphere than of their atmosphere, which made your live performance in a sense the experience of the fable become flesh. Hence their sense of kinship. They were part and parcel of the down-home flesh from which the fables came.

Down in midtown I had been eating most of my meals at a Chock Full o'Nuts counter and in the Automat in Times Square. But the Apollo was only a few blocks away from Stewmeat Anderson's hole in the wall. So I had to go by there a couple of times to keep in touch with Royal Highness. And you also had to stop in at Big John's place up on Seventh not only for the special that one of Fletcher Henderson's brother Horace's jump tune was set to celebrate, but also to spend some time in the company of the people who used to hang out there in those days.

Incidentally one of the things about eating in Harlem during my first week long gig at the Apollo was that there were Chinese restaurants everywhere you turned, and that most of the meals delivered backstage seemed to be Chinese. Before that time I had no idea that so much chop suey, chow mein, and egg foo yung was eaten in uptown Manhattan. That came as a big surprise and another surprise was the rice. Unlike the best down-home rice, which is cooked so that each grain is as freestanding as it is moist, the rice served in Chinese restaurants was downright *gummy!* So much for something I had wondered about for a long time. Chinese would have one hell of a time trying to eat properly cooked down-home rice with chopsticks.

XIX

R *olling, rolling, rolling,* I repeated to myself as we zoomed on along from the Blue Ridge Mountains of Virginia in the early morning mist, because what I woke up remembering again was how much my old roommate used to love to chant the opening lines of Rilke's "Cornet": *"Riding, riding, riding, through the day, through the night, through the day. Riding, riding, riding. And courage is grown so weary, and longing so great. There are no hills anymore, hardly a tree. Nothing dares stand up. Alien huts crouch thirstily by mired springs. Nowhere a tower . . ."*

We were circling back down into the southeast again on a string of one-nighters and weekend specials that would take us across the Carolinas and over to Knoxville and Chattanooga before entering Georgia by way of Dalton. Then after Atlanta, Macon, and Savannah there would be the Florida resorts along the oceanfront all the way to Miami, from which we would head for New Orleans by way of the Gulf Coast route north from Sarasota and west through Pensacola, Mobile (in the wee hours), and Gulfport.

There was a very good turnout everywhere we played, just as Milo the Navigator had promised, sometimes even better than he had estimated. And I also liked going back through as much of the territory as I had already covered with the band, because that was the way you became more familiar with key landmarks and also more intimate with new acquaintances, and so acquired another part of the seasoning that made the difference between being an ever so promising apprentice and a fully qualified professional road musician in every sense of the word.

But even so and even with our new vocalist not only on board but also spending as much time as she spent sitting with me as I checked

through my maps, mileage charts, and regional guidebooks every time
we got ready to pull out for the next scheduled stop on the first half of
our itinerary I couldn't keep myself from thinking about how far away
Chicago still was, and about what a long and roundabout way I was
having to take to get there for the first time.

 Commodious vicus of recirculation indeed. Until we left Miami we
were always rolling on and on in the opposite direction, even as the
scheduled time of arrival became shorter and shorter. Then when we
finally hit the trail northbound from New Orleans on the way out of
the bayou and delta country, with a sold-out stopover in Memphis,
going to Chicago in city-skipping four/four hell for leather time was
what everybody had in mind, including old Milo the Navigator himself, who was always supposed to be at least five towns ahead of all the
rest of us, including Old Pro and the Bossman Himself.

 I was the only member of the band who had never been to
Chicago before even on a visit. But that was only one of the reasons
that I was so much more eager than probably anybody else to get
there and get settled into the routine of work for which we had been
booked into the Regal Theater. Going up to Chicago, Illinois, and
also up to Detroit, Michigan, not unlike going out to Kansas City and
California Here I Come, was already a part of what skipping town for
the seven seas was all about. Some years before all of the souvenirs
brought back to Mobile County Training School from the Century of
Progress Exposition by Mr. B. Franklin Fisher, who had taken the top
three prizewinning seniors of the Talented Tenth Early Bird program
of that year up to see it when I was in the ninth grade, there were the
Windows on the World bulletin board pictures of the Hub City of the
North Central states and the railroad center of the nation as a whole.
And long before that, there were almost as much fireside and swing
porch tale spinning and lie swapping about Chicago as about anywhere else. Along with all of which and everything else over the years
there were all of the times that Chicago had been featured in the
movies.

 Added to all of which was also the fact that Chicago was also the
hometown although not the birthplace of my good old very best of all

possible roommates. Not that I thought that I would be able to look him up, or that he might turn up backstage one night. There was hardly a chance of that, because the last letter from him was post-marked Mexico City, where he had gone to serve an apprenticeship after graduating from the Yale School of Architecture. And from there he planned to go on down to Brazil where he hoped to be hired as a journeyman with Oscar Niemeyer, whom he had met while at Yale when Niemeyer came to New York to help design a pavilion for the New York World's Fair in Flushing Meadows.

In his letters there were always references to and quotations from books and magazine articles that he hoped I would find time to look into, which I always did and which also made me miss our after lights out exchanges in Atelier 359 more than anything else about college because I had graduated from college, but you never graduate from the likes of him.

As things turned out however I didn't really miss him very much while the band was in Chicago that time. I thought about him a lot all during the time we were there to be sure. But I was much too busy doing what by that time I was used to doing on my own to familiarize myself in a new town, to miss anybody—even him.

But even so sometimes no matter where I am, when something makes me realize how much I still do miss him, it is as if the first weeks of the fall semester of my freshman year were only yesterday: *when the dormitory cot, the chest of drawers, the desk with its own bookrack and straight-back chair were the only items of furniture on my side of the room, and the only thing on the wall was a school year calendar from the bookstore until I added maps from back issues of* National Geographic Magazine. *What with the library I really didn't think I needed much more than that for the time being.*

But what he had in mind for his side was an all-purpose studio, labora-tory, and workshop for the artist, craftsman, research technician, and engi-neer. So in addition to a drafting table and the sea captain's chair he had bought during the first week of class he also got permission to design and attach a seven-foot bookshelf along the wall beside his bed, because he wanted to have five feet of the great literary classics of the world and twenty-four inches of science and technology within easy reach at all times.

Which didn't surprise me at all, because I had already noticed that the first two items that he had taken from his overnight bag that first Thursday were a recent edition of The Odyssey *in a prose translation by T. E. Lawrence (under the name of T. E. Shaw), and* Technics and Civilization *by Lewis Mumford. Then when we picked up the packages that he and his uncle The Old Trooper had shipped ahead by parcel post, in addition to his drafting, surveying, mapping instruments and his camera and binoculars, there were also his own copies of* The Iliad, The Decameron, The Song of Roland, Gargantua and Pantagruel, Don Quixote, Candide, The Tragical History of Doctor Faustus, *and* The Three Musketeers, *which were at the end of the shelf nearest his pillow along with* The Testament *of* François Villon, Cyrano de Bergerac, A Study in Scarlet, The Sign of Four, *and Don Marquis's* archie and mehitabel.

There were also library copies of Sticks and Stones, The Golden Day, Frank Lloyd Wright on Architecture, *and Sheldon Cheney's* Primer of Modern Art, *which he kept with the textbooks lined up on the window ledge beyond the drafting table and which he would continue to renew until somebody else put in a request for them.*

He was very pleased that I intended to use my wall mainly for maps, but above the bookshelf on his side he tacked up a line of glossy magazine tear sheets of color reproductions of modern paintings beginning with Cézanne's "Landscape Near L'Estaque" and continuing with Picasso's "Nude Couple" and his "Jeune Fille à Mandoline"; Fernand Léger's "Paysage Anime: L'Homme au Chien," Lyonel Feininger's "Toc Turm," John Marin's "Lower Manhattan," and Charles Sheeler's "City Interior" and his "Classic Landscape."

There was no federal guide for the city of Chicago as there was for the city of New York, but there was a 115-page section on Chicago in the one for the state of Illinois, which I had bought before leaving New

York and studied en route along with Old Pro's copy of *Chicago, a Portrait* by Henry Justin Smith, illustrated by E. H. Suydam, whose sketches for books about New Orleans and Los Angeles I was familiar with also.

So I had my own orientation agenda worked pretty much by the time we arrived, and there were also the rounds that I had to make with Joe States, whose favorite book on Chicago, Herbert Asbury's *Gem of the Prairie*, I had also been reading on the bus. The only other Asbury books I knew about at that time were *The French Quarter* about New Orleans and *The Barbary Coast* about San Francisco.

Joe States took me to meet people who worked or hung out in places like Club DeLisa, the Grand Terrace, the Rum Boogie, and at least a dozen other clubs, bars, and lounges in the South Side area that included Garfield Avenue, State Street, Calumet Avenue, and South Parkway and environs. He also took the personal responsibility of cluing me in on the pimps and prostitutes in that part of town. The point, he said later, was not that he didn't think I could figure things out for myself but that Chicago was so different from New York and Hollywood and he wanted his young statemate to hit the scene copping what was popping from bar one.

On my own I started out at the Art Institute and went on along Michigan Avenue to the river, the Tribune Tower, the Wrigley and Daily News buildings. Then after familiarizing myself with the vastness of Merchandise Mart I went on out a few blocks farther along the shopping strip of Michigan Avenue before coming back to Randolph Street, the library, and the Loop.

The next day I started out at the Field Museum and came back to the library and the Loop and the day after that I spent the late morning looking around the campus of the University of Chicago before going on across 57th Street to the Museum of Science and Industry for most of the afternoon. Then for the rest of our stay I just took things as they came, which as usual included catching up on the new movies and also the reruns that happened to be showing while we were in town.

The band was always a big attraction in Chicago. And this time there were new and recent recordings in the music stores and being played on the radio throughout the day, every day; and there were also all of those longtime local fans who were eager to find out how Shag Philips's replacement on bass and the recently added vocalist came across in person. And who also made a special point of letting you know how keenly aware they were of the shadings that each instrument in the lineup represented.

Not that Chicago didn't have its own absolutely first rate world famous hometown band. Because there was Earl Hines and his by no means provincial Grand Terrace orchestra. And at that time Chicago was also still the functional hometown of Louis Armstrong himself. But even so our fans in Chicago, like so many others in most towns from border to border and coast to coast, identified with the bossman's music as if it belonged not one bit less to them than to the people of New York.

As for press coverage, Chicago was second to none. Along with a very enthusiastic arts and amusement section, reporters and reviewers of the dailies and their Sunday supplements, there were such national publications as *Down Beat* magazine and R. S. Abbott's *Chicago Defender*, and there was also *Esquire, the Magazine for Men*, whose elegance and prestige were comparable to that of such women's magazines as *Vogue, Harper's Bazaar*, and *Vanity Fair*.

Esquire's ongoing special interest in our kind of music was such that for a number of years it was one of the three top magazines covering the subject. The other two were *Down Beat* and *Metronome*, both of which were publications devoted exclusively to covering music. It also came to sponsor national popularity polls, annual achievement awards, and all-star concerts for a while.

The bossman, Old Pro, and Milo the Navigator, ever mindful of the connection between enthusiastic reporters and choice bookings and big advance sales, were always cooperative and charming in all of their contacts with journalists and disc jockeys. But nobody got a bigger kick out of kidding around with and manipulating so-called jazz critics than Joe States. He was forever sneaking some catchword or phrase into his backstage or ringside table interviews precisely because he knew that ever so hip reporters picked up on what you said and published it as their own special insight into the secret dynamics of the bossman's music.

This time around the subject was Earlene Copeland and the phrase was "torching in jive time," and they went for it just as others over the years seem to have gone for "blue note," "groove," "stride," "shout," "soul," "flatted fifth," "trumpet style piano" "walking bass," and so on. We were going along the alley from the stage door of the Regal and he looked at me with a poker face that meant that he was winking and rolling his eyes; and when I saw her the next day I said, Mark my words. By the time we get out to the Coast, the Hollywood disc jockeys will have audiences clamoring for at least two jive time torches and at least one encore in kind in every set.

XX

Back on the road again after Chicago, we headed for St. Louis and Kansas City, and from there we went on out to Topeka and down through Wichita and Oklahoma City to Dallas and Fort Worth before dipping farther south to San Antonio to make the long haul out of Texas north to Denver by way of El Paso, and then up through Albuquerque and Santa Fe.

Rolling, rolling, rolling, I began repeating to myself again as we cruised on across the Mississippi River Bridge from Illinois into Missouri that Tuesday before dark. Because I was thinking about my old roommate again. But this time the writer he brought to mind was not Rilke but Walt Whitman, about whom he had said in response to my letter about joining the band for a while: *Boy, what old footloose Whitman wouldn't have given to be able to traffic with the likes of that perpetually roving crew of festive but ultimately unfrivolous merrymakers.*

Song of the open road, yea verily. And also the also and also of it all. Hithering and thithering from here to there and from there to elsewhere after elsewhere. According to my old roommate, old Walt Whitman, barnstorming troubadour par excellence that he was, could only have been completely delighted with the interplay of aesthetic and pragmatic considerations evidenced in the maps and mileage charts and always tentative itineraries of Milo the Navigator of transcontinental as well as transoceanic meandertrails.

It was Ralph Waldo Emerson who spoke of "melodies that ascend and leap and pierce into the deeps of infinite time," my roommate also wrote, which, by the way, would make a very fine blurb for a Louis Armstrong solo such as the one on "Potato Head Blues." But, he went on, it was the old wayfaring bird of passage himself, whose "minstrels latent on the prairies" were counted among the pioneers "soon to be heard coming wobbling, soon to rise and tramp amid us."

Walt Whitman, to be sure, singing his specimen days "singing the great achievements of the present, singing the strong light works of engineers, our modern wonders (the antique . . . Seven outvied). In the Old world the east the Suez Canal / the New by its mighty railroads spanned / the seas inlaid with eloquent gentle wires." Yea verily. Or as little Buddy Marshall would have sucked his teeth two times and said, Hey shit I reckon, skebootie, hey shit I goddamn reckon.

None of which, my good old roommate was very careful to point out, was to imply that your position as a sideman in the bossman's far ranging road band was also like that of Ishmael on board the *Pequod* in Herman Melville's *Moby Dick*. Not at all. The bossman, as my old roommate knew as well as I did, was completely ordained and dedicated, to be sure; but not to the point of hell-fired obsession. So, very much unlike Ishmael, who had no options because he had signed on for the duration, you for all your junior apprenticeship status had the prerogative that, although it was completely unsanguinary, was no less authoritative than that of the all powerful Shahryar, the king to whom the tales of the Thousand Nights and a Night were told. Because all you had to do was give notice and pack your fiddle.

But wait, he went on to add as if you could hear his voice on the page and also see his sidelong glance across the dormitory room as he used to sit slouched in his captain's chair with his stocking feet propped against his bed. Leave us not forget the relevance of the three princes of Serendip (now known as Ceylon) to all the riffing and sundry improvisational carryings on, which I need not remind you, is no less personal than musical. Or should be.

Same old roommate, I wrote in reply, only more so. Picaresque by any other name were no less riff-style. The bossman's got your old commedia dell'arte swinging, old partner. And I do mean cracking and grooving as the occasion requires, whatever the occasion. Dance halls, roadside joints, clubs, vaudeville stages, picnics, outdoor jamborees, political rallies and barbecues, oom-pa-pa bandstands in city parks, Milo the Navigator books them and we play them, and I don't mean just knock them off. We play them barring none. No shucking allowed ever.

Stamping grounds and stopping places, I also wrote. Naturally there are some that you can't help becoming more excited about but there were none that you were ever allowed to discount. No lackadaisical nights in this man's outfit. The prestige of certain very special places did count for a lot, to be sure; and there was always a certain amount of special preparation. But the atmosphere and audience response mattered most even so. So much so that sometimes we were even better in some ramshackle roadside joint than on Broadway, in the Loop, or on the Strip and there are radio air checks to prove it.

So, a word more about those one thousand nights plus one, old pardner. Your point about my prerogative to cut out is well taken, but I'm really something of a very special case, because I'm still not sure of what I want to do with myself, whereas in point of fact, it is always the bossman who is Shahryar the headcutter. As everybody tells you when you show up for your first rehearsal, he's the one you have to make want to hear more tomorrow night.

You never knew when his next letter would come. Sometimes there would be one in a month or so but it was most likely to be more than six months between times. Because it was not so much a matter of keeping up to date as of keeping in touch in a random sort of way each on his own terms. And unless there was a question that called for an immediate answer you responded whenever you got around to it— sometimes as if picking up a conversation that had been interrupted by a telephone call three minutes ago, an old campus game we had begun playing with each other the day after reading that it was something that James Joyce did upon reencountering literary friends days, weeks, months, or even years later.

All I wrote about Chicago was that I had finally made it up there and had checked out most of the high points and found everything to be as advertised over the years. But right after my first trip to Boston I sent him an all but verbatim copy of the log I kept of my week of schoolboy explorations, which began with me finding my way along Tremont Avenue to Boston Common and Beacon Hill from the rooming house and eating place where most of the bands used to stay and hang out back during that time.

Then on my free time during the week that followed, I made my way from such downtown Revolutionary War era landmarks as old North Church, the Old State House, the Massacre Site, and Faneuil Hall among others (and also including the Augustus Saint-Gaudens Civil War memorial honoring Colonel Robert Gould Shaw and the Massachusetts 54th) over to Harvard and Radcliffe by the second day. I skipped Massachusetts Institute of Technology for the time being. So when I took off from Harvard Square late the next morning I took the Paul Revere route to Lexington, Bedford, and Concord; and by the time the bus pulled out of Boston and headed westward on the Old Post Road for one night stands in Springfield, Hartford, and New Haven, I had also been to see Walden Pond, the Concord Bridge, the Emerson, Alcott, and Hawthorne houses, and also the Bunker Hill Monument and *Old Ironsides*, which I had already seen and boarded as one of Mr. B. Franklin Fisher's Early Bird Explorers when it called at the port of Mobile and tied up at the foot of Government Street that time.

On the day that I had gotten around to going back over to Cambridge to see the Massachusetts Institute of Technology, I had actually spent most of the time revisiting the Fogg Museum of Art at Harvard. I also went to the Boston Museum of Fine Arts twice and the Isabella Stewart Gardner Museum, both in the Back Bay fens area.

Several months later my old roommate responded to my Boston notes by reminding me of Van Wyck Brooks's *The Flowering of New England*, which we had read during that second year because on his own he had been reading and rereading *Sticks and Stones* and *The Golden Day* by Lewis Mumford as background material for his course in architecture, and which had also led him (and then me) to read *American Humor, a Study of the National Character* by Constance Rourke, which is still one of my basic bibles on the subject of life and art in the United States.

The historic figure whom my references to the monument to Colonel Shaw and the Massachusetts 54th brought to my old roommate's mind was Frederick Douglass. We had read *A Narrative of the Life of Frederick Douglass, an American Slave, Written by Himself*, which he had checked out of the library during February of our freshman year. Since that time he had also read *My Bondage and My Freedom* and *The Life and Times of Frederick Douglass*. I had read *My Bondage and My Freedom* during the summer following my sophomore year but had not yet got around to *The Life and Times. . . .*

Frederick Douglass had been a very influential supporter of and also a highly successful recruiter for the Massachusetts 54th. But the main thing my old roommate had in mind this time was the world of the abolition movement, the fugitive slave, and the Underground Railroad, the point of which was to suggest that the itinerary of a road band probably took you to a lot of places that were once stations on the Underground Railroad. I got the point immediately and the first place that came to mind was Oberlin in Ohio, which I had not yet seen but which was already famous at Mobile County Training School as early on as I could remember, not only for its role in the antislavery movement and as the first coeducational as well as interracial college but also as a conservatory of music.

In fact I had already heard of Oberlin as a music conservatory even before I realized how many different kinds of junctions and lay-over spurs the Underground Railroad actually had. Come to think of it, Oberlin was probably the very first musical conservatory I ever heard of, because Miss Lucy Ariel Williams the concert pianist and daughter of Doctor Roger Williams of downtown Mobile had studied there, and so had R. Nathaniel Dett, the composer of "Listen to the Lambs"; and Will Marion Cook, who wrote the music for Paul Laurence Dunbar's "Clorindy, the Origin of the Cakewalk," and also created the Southern Syncopated Orchestra, was sent out there from Washington, D.C., as a student of the violin at the age of thirteen and had gone on to the Hochschule in Berlin to study with Joseph Joachim and had also taken lessons with Dvořák during the year Dvořák had spent in the United States circa 1893.

I knew about all of that before I went to college, not only because of what Mr. B. Franklin Fisher told us when he brought Miss Lucy Ariel Williams out to play "The Juba Dance" from R. Nathaniel Dett's "In the Bottoms Suite" during National Negro History Week that year, but also because Dett's "Listen to the Lambs" and Will Marion Cook's "Swing Along" were as much a part of the musical atmosphere of assembly room time as "Lift Every Voice and Sing."

Old Pro was the one to talk to about what for better or worse had been happening at Oberlin over the years. And incidently he was also somebody you could chat with about Will Marion Cook, whom he had come to know through the Bossman Himself, whose well-known apprenticeship to Cook had been arranged for by none other than Royal Highness, the only, who had also seen to it that the bossman got a chance to work under the direct supervision of Will Vodery.

At the time, my impression was that in recent years the reputation of the Oberlin Conservatory had been eclipsed by Juilliard, Berklee, and Eastman. But even so for me it was somewhere I looked forward to visiting, because its unequivocal commitment to the anti-slavery movement and its pioneering policies as an unsegregated and coeducational institution made it a hallowed and inspiring landmark that symbolized the Civil War and the Emancipation era much the same as Bunker Hill, Concord Bridge, and the Liberty Bell symbolized the period of the War for Independence and the principles articulated in the Declaration of Independence and the Constitution.

XXI

M eanwhile there was the also and also of me and Miss You-Know-Who, from what region of my mind, who was still a student down in central Alabama.

When I told her that I had decided to accept the bossman's invitation to come with the band for the summer, beginning the week after I graduated, we agreed that there should be at least one exchange of letters each week, and that I would make one Sunday morning telephone call every month, and that I would also send postcards whenever the itinerary took me somewhere that was of some personal or academic interest to either one of us. Souvenirs were a discreetly unmentioned option that I was only too happy to use to make such surprise and special occasional gifts as I could afford without violating my financial plan to supplement my graduate school fellowship grant.

The possibility of a short layoff time visit every now and then was not even considered until I changed my mind about staying on with the band beyond that first September. Then there was the all too obvious fact that the band always expected to be booked into some special spot during all holiday weeks and weekends the year round. So for the time being, we decided to wait and see how things turned out. As for

the likelihood of the band being brought back to town to play out at
the Dolomite again within the next year or so, no such luck.

*When I said what I said about the Mobile County Training School Doctrine
of the Ancestral Imperative, she said, So that's what they call it down there.
And I said, And also the obligation of the Talented Tenth and told her about
the Early Birds. And she shook her head smiling and said, Up my way you
were also earmarked by the time you reached the ninth grade, at which point
the question was whether you could qualify to be included in the Circle of
Young Achievers, who earned distinctive armbands much the same as first
team athletes earned letters and sleeve stripes, but which were worn only on
the school premises and when you were representing the school as a participant
on some formal public ceremonial occasion.*

*The first requirement was outstanding classwork. That was basic. But
excellent grades as such were not really enough. Along with being in the upper
ten percentile, you also had to exemplify that certain something that made not
only faculty members schoolwide but also civic leaders and church elders feel
that they had ample reason to expect you to become one in that precious number of the divinely chosen and endowed few who in answer to the prayers of old
folks long since gone would sally forth and so acquit themselves in the world at
large that generations yet unborn would arise and call them blessed.*

*In other words, I said, some Early Birds were specifically groomed and
charged to hit the open road of endless obstacles and opportunities in quest, if
not conquest, of whatever wherever forever, while others were no less carefully
counseled to "let down your bucket where you are," which meant that some in
that category were expected to go to college and come back into the Mobile and
Gulf states area as professionals, and that others would go directly from high
school graduation into the local workaday world either as inspired progress oriented apprentice artisans and business men and women, or by way of one of the
part time or full time technical courses recommended by the vocational guidance counselor.*

*But let me tell you something about that bucket jive, I said. Most people
I know don't know anything at all about the point Booker T. Washington was*

trying to make when he said what he said in that famous speech. They just take what he said at that point as a very wise old saying about not overlooking something valuable right under your nose so to speak. To them it goes right along with what old Booker T. also had to say about our people prospering in proportion as we learn to dignify and glorify labor and put brains and skill into the common occupations of life.

That's what it all adds up to for me too, I said, and I also knew a few other things about that historic speech in Atlanta. And I've also read the inscription directly from the monument at Tuskegee. But what Booker T.'s bucket always brings to my mind is a church song that goes as far back in my memory as the Sunday school shout that goes "Jesus wants me for a sunbeam. . . ."

And she said, Oh, I bet you I know that one, and said, Don't tell me, let me guess, and said, Oh, this is very easy. I bet you anything it's "Brighten the corner where you are," isn't it?

All I could do was open my mouth and stretch my eyes and nod my head and as we held each other and pressed cheeks, I thought about the difference between our obligations to our hometowns.

Hers was more specific and also more binding than mine. All I had to do was promise that I would always do my best and if I ever accomplished anything noteworthy it would be something that not only home folks but also others elsewhere could be proud. That was as far as the Early Bird program went. You earned your scholarship to college, and the rest was up to you. But in her case there was an ongoing relationship with her hometown sponsors. Unlike fellow Young Achievers whose training in medicine, dentistry, and law was being underwritten, she had not had to sign a commitment to come back and practice her (as yet unchosen) profession in her hometown for at least a certain term, but she had agreed to a sponsorship plan that included completing all residence requirements for a master's degree in the field of her choice one year after college. When she said, So that's my story and I said, So what about our story? and she said, Well I guess we're going to have to make that one up as we go along, won't we, I said, Touché said the big bad bull fiddle player-to-be, touché. And she squeezed my arm and brushed her lips against my cheeks and said, My Mister. Hello my Mister and got the Buster Brown blush that she knew Miss Tee's old riff and leitmotif was always good for. Then she said, I must say this. As much as I'm going to be missing you it's probably best that we're going to have to be separated for a while. I really think so.

And I said Me too, alas, me too. You didn't have to mention wedding bells as such on that campus during that time of year in those days. Because from wisteria blossom time on through the commencement season, few other rumors were more a part of the daily gossip than those about what graduating senior was getting engaged to marry whomever of whatever class level.

As for the next chapter (or following stanza, fit, canto, chorus, or sequence) of my own story, by the time my roommate and I said so long for now at the end of our sophomore year he (who referred to it as the Scooter Saga or Scooter Cycle to be) had made me aware as I never had been before of the fact that regardless of your career objectives your own story was something that you make up as you go along. Not that I was entirely unaware of it before. After all, as Early Bird conditioned as I was, I still had not settled on my career field.

And almost two years after his exit to the Yale School of Architecture, I still had not made up my mind except to continue my course of study in the Department of Liberal Arts with a major in literature. But my notions about my obligations to hometown expectations had undergone significant modification indeed. They had become more and more a matter of existential implication and less and less obviously a matter of personal social and political progress as such, without becoming any less pragmatic than direct involvement in concrete action as such, precisely because they were concerned with that upon which such action at its best must be predicated.

In any case, the closer I came to the bachelor's degree in liberal arts the easier it was for me to realize that what I really wanted to do next was to go on to a big university for graduate courses in the humanities. Because my personal preoccupations and concerns had far more to do with underlying assumptions, functional definitions, and basic issues than with direct hands-on professional involvement with the day to day operations of any programs and institutions as such, however prestigious.

Ancestral imperatives, yea verily, my brand new roommate had said as soon as I said what I said about Mr. B. Franklin Fisher and the Early Birds in response to what he had just told me about the support and implicitly heroic

but deliberately unspecific expectations of the great uncle, a former hard rid-
ing member of the 9th Cavalry regiment whom he sometimes referred to as
The Old Trooper and sometimes as Old Troop.

Ancestral imperatives, indeed, he said again then (and also time and
again later on), yea verily, who would gainsay that which so obviously goes
without saying? Forsooth not I, who am absolutely nothing if not ever mind-
ful of antecedents and derivations. But even so, he also said, but even so. But
even what most certainly does not go without saying and gainsaying is the
question of WHICH ancestors among which.

Which among which indeed, *I thought. It was not until sometime*
later that year that I suddenly realized how Luzana Cholly had eliminated
himself. But when I did, I also realized that the one I had always assumed he
retrieved me for was not the ever so pragmatic and no less comprehensive Mr.
B. Franklin Fisher himself with his primary emphasis on brown-skin
achievements in social and political service, education as such, business, and
public affairs, but to Miss Lexine Metcalf, who was to say Who if not you, my
splendid young man, my splendid young man, who if not you? And who was
also to say, Who knows but that you may have to travel far and wide to find
out what it is that you are called to do and be.

It was when I told my roommate about how I still felt about Miss Lex-
ine Metcalf that he vamped our after hours yak sessions into the first of a
string of riffs on what he called the actual, or in any case, the functional and
thus the true or real ancestors—opposed to the conventional flesh and blood
and thus official or legal ancestors.

Mind over matter, roommate, he said. Mind over matter, if you know
what I mean. Materiality is nothing without mythology. Your Mr. B.
Franklin Fisher himself was never talking about flesh and blood ancestors,
was he? Of course not. And nobody down there at that school of yours ever
thought he was. Everybody knew very well that he was talking about picking
and choosing, roommate, picking and choosing. As you pick and choose among
tools and weapons, roommate.

Then he said, Chacun selon sa faim, *roommate,* et après, peut-être,
selon son goût. *Then he also went on to say, I submit that necessity is the*
mother of fairy godmothers, roommate. And also of earthly godfathers and

Remus wise uncles of all shapes and fashions. So of course, Miss Lexine Metcalf, roommate. And but of course, Miss Lexine Metcalf. Who else if not she could carry on better for Miss Tee, my splendid young man, my splendid young man.

Eunice Townsend, Eunice Townsend, Eunice Townsend, I said as we sauntered arm in arm and cheek to cheek across the spring fresh tree lined campus thoroughfare with only that many more weeks before Commencement. And she said That's the official me of my birth certificate and also the make believe me of my aspirations, which according to you and the Snake also makes it the personal me, doesn't it?

By that time she had long since explained that Nona was a nickname that had nothing at all to do with her hometown identity. It came from the tune that Erskine Hawkins and the former 'Bama State Collegians had recorded and was given to her by members of the 'Bama State Hornets basketball team during an after game dance party at Alabama Normal.

We came on down the wide concrete steps and past the side entrance to the Dining Hall and found a park bench in an alcove of shrubbery of the Promenade Mall near the empty bandstand, and I said, First things first and she agreed and we held each other with our eyes closed for a while. Then when I said, So will you weave and reweave to keep the suitor wolves of Ithaca at bay, night and day? she couldn't resist putting her hands on her hips and mocking me with her eyes and saying, While the cat's away at play? And I said, Well not exactly. I said, More like while the self-styled Alabama jackrabbit is out somewhere trying to get from here to there in the road musicians' briar patch with his pelt if not untattered at least none the worst for fair wear and tear.

All the same, she also said on the day I left the campus to take the train to join the band in Cincinnati. All the same, there are so many occupational hazards out there in the world of music and entertainment I can just see crowds of good time people with all kinds of enticements lying in wait for their favorite bands in town after town all across the country.

But she didn't say if you can't be good be careful. She said, I'm satisfied that your Mobile upbringing will keep you on your p's and q's anytime you come anywhere near any women with a pigfoot and a bottle, mug or tankard of beer.

Then she also said, As for all of those good looking conjure women cleverly disguised as gay divorcées, who might sometimes sound so much like your Miss Lexine Metcalf, I'm sure I don't have to remind you that neither your Miss Metcalf herself nor your Mr. B. Franklin Fisher ever told you anything that would lead you to believe that there will ever be any shortcuts either to the Holy Grail or the Golden Fleece.

That was all she said on that subject, and I said, I know what you mean. I know exactly what you mean. And I couldn't keep from smiling and shaking my head as I blushed, because what she never could have gone on to say next was precisely what old Deke Whatley had already said earlier that same day when I stopped in to take my leave of the barbershop.

Say now look here, son, he said holding his clippers in one hand and his chomped on cigar in the other as I stepped back to salute and cut out, Now look here. Now you got your college degree and you're on your way to join up with the greatest musical aggregation that ever was and music ain't even your chosen profession. So that shows the kind of stuff you can lay down if you want to. But just one more detail—and I know good and well you already know this or you wouldn't have made it this far. But I'm going to say it again anyhow, son: That thing down there can get you into far more trouble than it can ever get you out of. It can get you into a lot of good places too. But how many bad places have you ever hear anybody say it got them out of.

Remember that now, he said and looka here. Send us a postcard every now and then, and let us know how you're doing up there in the big league. Hell we all betting on you my man. We're not just pulling for you, we're betting on you.

XXII

As the bus cruised on across North Dakota toward Montana en route to California by way of Idaho, Washington, and Oregon, Earlene Copeland came back to sit with me for a while; and Milo the Navigator followed her and slid in beside Joe States, and the two of them briefed us on the upcoming dance and theater dates in Spokane, Seattle, and Portland.

Then for the rest of the time between Fargo and Bismarck, she stayed on long enough to add something else to what she had been saying about what made that particular band so special. In her first interview back when she opened with the band on Broadway, she had said what she had said about singing and playing for the bossman even more than for the audience as such. Not that the audience was only incidental, she had added in another interview later on out in Chicago. Not at all. But in this band you always played to the audience through the bossman, even in your own hometown. Even then you didn't go out to the microphone as if to say, Hey here I am whom you've known since I was knee high to a duck, being featured by no less than the Bossman Himself. What the hometown folks actually heard you saying was This is the way my little part of our good old hometown stuff sounds to the bossman.

I've been thinking about this stuff, Schoolboy, she said, sounding almost exactly like one of the best looking and most popular senior class women on campus talking to an ever so self-centered but likable sophomore with a high grade point average. I've been giving it some more thought, especially since we came on farther west from places like Duluth and Minneapolis, and what I was trying to say to those reporters still goes, but there is also something else that goes along with it.

What I'm getting at is—well let me first say this: People in places like New York, Chicago, and out in L.A. and Hollywood, especially back in New York, always just take it for granted that they're the ones that get to hear all of the bands at their best, and I'm not going to try to say that they don't have a pretty good case, because the bossman always works up a lot of special stuff to spring on them. And naturally when that curtain opens and they have just come back off the road everybody is raring to tear up some stuff just to let everybody know who's back in town.

New York has got to be special, she said. And so is Chi-town and L.A. But you still can't really say that this band holds stuff back for the big city audiences. Not this band. Here we are way out here and just listen to this stuff we're putting down for these folks every night. Look, what I'm saying is this. If you heard this stuff on the radio you couldn't tell where we were or what kind of spot we're being picked up from. Not from the way this band is popping.

You sure couldn't, I said. Then I said, Hey what you're talking about is exactly why some of us in the dormitory used to spend so much after hours time in the darkened radio lounge fishing the airways. And now here I am out here as a part of this crew, and, like you say, just listen to what we're laying on these people like they're from somewhere down home.

But after all, I also said as we went on talking about the mainly German and Slavic backgrounds of the people you played for in this part of the country, but after all, that's radio and phonograph records for you. That's why Milo can come up with itineraries like this in the first place. These people may be way out here but they know exactly what to expect from us.

And that's exactly what the bossman never forgets and never lets you forget, she said. So come to think of it, that's why people who want to think that he holds back on the best stuff until we hit New York just might have things backward. I never really questioned it before, she said. But now that I'm out here with him I know better, and I'd say the new stuff has to get by these people out here on the road before he'll take it to New York.

That's how much respect he has for the people we play for all across the nation, she said. And that's when Joe States said what he said. He had been nodding ever since Milo the Navigator went back up front. But now he had been awake long enough to get the point we were trying to make. And he said, This is what I told myself about all of that a long time ago, not long after we started touring and I realized that there was never going to be any letup. I said, You know what this cat's really like? A master chef that don't never intend to serve nobody no bad meals anywhere ever. And that's what I still think. If it's your first gourmet meal he wants your first impression of his stuff to convert you to his way of cooking. And if you're already converted he wants to keep you coming back for more.

And another thing about him is that he never forgets about the people out there on a big special splurge that they've been saving up to treat themselves to. He wants them to wake up the next day feeling that what they had to scrimp and save to come and hear us was worth it. That's this man and that's this band, kiddies. Take it from Papa Joe.

When we came back on board after a snack stop in Bismarck, where I picked up a book about the Lewis and Clark Expedition and also one about Frederick Remington in a souvenir shop, Earlene Copeland took her seat up front behind Milo the Navigator and across from the bossman and Old Pro once more. So as we droned on and on along the four hundred mile stretch to Billings, I read about the adventures of buckskin explorers among the Mandan Indians until I dozed off, and when I woke up because we were making a comfort stop I checked the map and we were in Montana.

In the letter along with the souvenir postcards of Home Stake Pass through the northern Rockies that I mailed to Eunice Townsend, I mentioned that I had been reading about Sacajewea (or Sacagawea), the only woman serving as an Indian guide for the Lewis and Clark party. But as we came on from Butte toward Missoula and the narrow strip of northern Idaho I was thinking about my old roommate once again.

Because when I wrote about finding a copy of the Remington book, I also mentioned that on the very first day we met, my roommate had told me about the collection of original Remington paintings and sculpture in the Art Institute of Chicago while he was filling me in on his great uncle and benefactor, an ex-9th Cavalry man whom he referred to as The Old Trooper. And what that brought back to mind again was how she used to like to tease me about him from time to time, and then I was thinking about one time in particular.

When she said, *You and the Snake. You and the Snake. You and that snake doctor roommate you used to have.*

Then she said, It's just like him to have been here and gone by the time I came on the scene. So tell me, are you sure he was who (and what) he said he was? Anyway whoever named him snake doctor just might have been on to something. Because just about everything you've been telling me about him makes me wonder. To tell the truth if I didn't hear so much about him from so many other people I just might think he was somebody you made up. And as it is he still sounds like an updated disguise for old-you-know-who in English 322.

Are you sure that's not where you got him from? she said, looking at me with a mock pout that was as irresistible as it was mischievous. And I said, What I'm absolutely sure of is that he would have been no less impressed with such jolly good liberal arts talk like that as I am. Then I said, Because according to him making things up is the name of the game.

Indeed it was. As he made so unmistakably clear when we got back around to the matter of mothers and aunts and fathers and uncles during one of our after hours sessions near the end of that first September.

He remembered what I had told him about not being able to ask Miss Tee anything about the circumstance of my illegitimate birth, and he said, All she probably could have told you was something that she finally worked out for her own peace of mind when she could no longer deny that she had gotten herself into serious trouble.

That was pretty rough stuff, fellow, he said, and as for your father, she couldn't even tell you his name although she knew it.

Not after she had made that promise to Miss Melba all on her own, he said. And I told him that I realized that at the time, and I could also have said that I had not really been interested in any details that might change the family relationship I was already used to.

But I just let that go for the time being and he said, The name that really counts in this league or any other league from now on is the one you make for yourself and likewise the fathers that count are not necessarily the ones that begat us but the ones we choose for ourselves as we need them in certain situations and predicaments as we need and choose our own personal tools and weapons.

Then he clicked on a small flashlight that he had rigged up on his drafting board and sat up and opened his notebook, and as he wrote he said, Fathers comma, and then he said, Necessity as the Mother of. Which I guess was a new topic heading because he underlined it. Then he reached across the bunk to his bookshelf and took down his personal copy of The Odyssey, *saying, Telemachia, Telemachia, yea verily the Telemachus in us all, perceived or not, acknowledged or not.*

Then he said, Listen old pardner, one's mother is whoever is there and says she is, if she does what mothers do. To most practical interests and purposes, mother is verb as well as noun. Mother is if mother does. Mothers mother you. Like Miss Melba. But fathers are somewhat a trickier matter. Even when one bears the same legal name and is the spitting image of the man of the house. Or so I would have it.

Take Telemachus, he said. What he needs and goes looking for is somebody to help him rid the premises of all those rowdy and self-indulgent suitors camping and swarming all over the grounds and stinking up the goddamn place. He needs someone who is good at just the sort of cunning stratagems the ever clever Odysseus is past master of. As for Odysseus being his flesh and blood father as such, here is what Telemachus says right up front in Book One: "My mother says I am his son; for myself I do not know. Has any son of man yet been sure of his begetting?"

Pretty strong stuff, he said closing the book. But if you think he is putting himself in the dozens, you miss the point. Because as I see it, his most urgent concern is with the pragmatic function of fatherhood. In other words, old pardner, what this youngster named Telemachus hits the trail to find is an adequate father figure, or in still other words, someone whose manhood is worth emulating.

I said, I know what you mean, old pardner. Because I got the point about necessity and I also knew why he said what he said about the dozens. Not only because I already knew the story of the patient Penelope even before I found out it was part of The Odyssey but also because I had always known that those who play the game of insult called the dirty dozens place the main emphasis on the mother not the father. It is her virtue that counts. It is by implication taken to be no less sacred than that of, say, the Madonna. And any suggestion to the contrary is the ultimate offense, and is almost certain to lead to a violent showdown.

Because what is at issue is whether or not one is a son of a bitch, which is to say whether he was conceived as a result of his mother acting like a bitch or was in any case treated like one. A son of a bitch can never be certain of his father because his mother is a slut and if one's mother is a slut then her husband and one's official father is lacking in manhood and is either to be pitied or laughed at. But since he after all is not really one's father, it is still one's mother whose honor has been besmirched and must be defended.

In the game as I grew up knowing it, the dirty words as such were not actually spoken. In a sense, to play the dozens is to make insinuations that provoke one's adversary in a verbal duel to respond as if he has been called a son of a bitch outright. The insult is oblique. The allegations are signified or hinted at in an offhand and even seemingly playful manner. The game is over as soon as one of the players (i.e., verbal duelists) becomes angry, loses his composure, and begins using raw and direct epithets. Because from that point on, either might resort to physical violence.

The difference between playing the dozens and putting somebody in the dozens is in the manner. In both instances you're badmouthing somebody's family background by "talking about his mama." But in contrast to playing around (the point in playing the dozens), you can put somebody in the dozens as directly and crudely as you wish, depending on how eager you are to provoke a fight.

I said, But speaking of the plain old everyday facts that Telemachus was trying to find out about when he said what he said to old Nestor and also to Menelaus in the passages you just read. And he said, From Book Three and Book Four. And I said, Sometimes you think about that part of it too. So every now and then I used to wonder where my father actually was and what he did *for living and for fun and all of that. But most of the time it didn't even cross my mind. Not even I might have added, during those times when I used to have to think about how lucky I was that Mr. Paul Miles Boykin was not my father. He got married to Miss Tee but as far as I was concerned that didn't even make him my stepfather.*

Sounds to me as if to all practical intents and purposes, the identity of your, ahem, consubstantial father, has been mostly only a little matter of occasionally restimulated curiosity about some chickenshit gossip you once overheard and then overheard reminders of, old pardner, he said. And I said, Hey come to think of it. And he said, Whereas the Telemachus in us all is always a very urgent matter of fundamental necessity. Not curiosity, old pardner, not curiosity.

XXIII

It was at the end of the last week of my fourth trip to Hollywood that I decided that the time had come for me to leave the band. I hadn't planned things that way. I just woke up that morning and realized that as much as I still liked everything about being on the road with the Bossman Himself, I also wanted to stay around town as a freelance musician for a while.

Just like that. And also postponing graduate school once more as if the ever so obvious possibility of registering as a part time graduate degree candidate at the University of Southern California (across from the Coliseum) or at the University of California at Los Angeles (off Sunset Boulevard in Bel-Air) did not exist, not only because I had always thought of doing my graduate work on an Ivy League campus, but also because I still had not made up my mind about what I wanted my graduate degree to add up to as a profession.

Which, as I was finally beginning to admit to myself by that time, was also why I had decided not to leave the band at the end of that first summer. I had stayed on then not because I actually needed more money to supplement the fellowship grant for the year required to earn a Master of Arts degree. At the time I said what I said about sticking around for a while longer to accumulate a large enough nest egg to supplement on campus living expenses and incidentals straight on through the Ph.D. program. But the fact was that I had been having such a great time going where we went and becoming a part of things, that it was already past the registration deadline before I ever got around to thinking in any specific terms at all about any given course of study in any of the several catalogs that I had brought along.

And yet even as I woke up that morning thinking about sticking around to try my luck in Hollywood for a while, I was never more mindful of Miss Lexine Metcalf and her bulletin board windows on the world of peoples of many lands and her fairy tale castle towns. Because who else if not she (as if for Miss Tee) would say, Go where you will go and you will do what you will do as splendid young men have always found their own ways of doing, wherever they came to be, however they came to be there.

Miss Lexine Metcalf to be sure. But perhaps not Mr. B. Franklin Fisher, who after all was far more given to the statistical imperatives of social engineering than to such no less patent leather than blue steel avuncularities as were to be come by around the fireside, on the store-front, and in the barbershop.

So no perhaps (or ifs, ands, and buts) about it at all for such uncles as Bud, Doc, Ned, and Remus, for whom it was only a question of whether you were game enough to risk whatever you had to lose. Not that you were ever expected to take any risk that you had not calculated. No better for any fool who went around acting as if life were a dice game. *It may be a gamble young fella but it's a matter of much more than rolling them bones and snapping your fingers.*

As for what my old roommate had to say in response to my news about leaving the band to freelance around Hollywood for a while, I expected him to approve and he did. And then he also went on to bring me up to date on how he had come to feel about what his formally certified professional training as an architect was adding up to so far.

Shelter. By all means, he wrote at one point. Shelter. Yea verily. Still should not all basic architectural decisions be predicated upon fundamental assumptions about lifestyle, which is about nothing if not the whole human proposition as such? For what was ever more human than design as such? Shelter by all means indeed and also with every means and with whatever available material. But oh the ineluctable modality of it all, whether in caves or with sticks and stones or with Bedouin skins and fabrics or adobe and brick and so on to "I" beams and plate glass.

When he wrote like that, not only could you hear his voice and the way it went with his offhand manner and sidelong glance, you could also see him sitting in his sea captain's chair at his flattened out drafting board again, because the statement he was playing around with was as much an entry for his logbook as it was a part of what was already an ongoing dialogue with you.

Ancestral imperatives, to be sure, he was also to go on to write several weeks later. Ancestral imperatives, yes and again yes. That is not the question. As you know I've said so many times before. The question is which ancestors and what priority of which imperatives. Moreover as I've also maintained from the outset, even as the names that really matter when it comes to the determination of actual identity are the nicknames we choose for ourselves—or the ones we accept as appropriately definitive when suggested (sometimes even as a joke) by others, so it is with ancestors and their imperatives.

The point of which I already knew from a long string of riff sessions about the Telemachus factor of fatherhood and hence forefathers, beginning back during our very first month as roommates: That vocational choices and indeed the underlying assumptions of all vocational guidance programs as such, not only *could* but absolutely *should* be called into question or in any case reexamined as a matter of course from time to time. In view of inevitable modifications in our perception of the nature of the actuality as well as the implications of things.

Which was entirely consistent with what I somehow realized that Miss Lexine Metcalf wanted me to be prepared to take in stride when she used to say what she always used to say to me about journeys the ultimate destination of some of which could not be determined until you were already en route, and also about destinations that you might not be able to recognize as such until you got there.

And as for what Miss Lexine Metcalf may or may not have known about such ever so advanced seminar, laboratory, and field project subject matter as my old roommate and I were forever playing around with, she knew what fairy godmothers always know about what fables and fairy tales are fabricated to deposit in our consciousness as if on the dynamics of time-release capsules.

Nor come to think of it, was Mr. B. Franklin Fisher himself for all his messianic devotion to social engineering for community uplift as such ever really unmindful of such legends as made the point that the ultimate goal of many pioneers and trailblazers no less than that of explorers and discoverers was to find what there was to find.

XXIV

When I said what I said to Joe States at breakfast that morning, he said, Man, don't come trying to scare nobody with some old jiveass joke like that. Man, I ain't been up long enough to be dealing with no stuff like this you hitting me with. Man, I ain't even finished my first cup of coffee yet.

We were sitting in Hody's and from our booth you could see the traffic stopping and going through the intersection of Hollywood Boulevard and Vine Street. He was nursing his coffee while we waited for his ham and grits and eggs sunny side up and my waffle and sausage patties. I had finished my orange juice and was having a bowl of mixed California fruit.

Come on, man, he said, what kind of old henhouse do-do is this you putting down for me to squish my toes in this morning? And I said, Man, I'm trying to tell you. And he said, I know, man, but I just don't want to hear it. Then he said, Damn, man, you sure got some heavy stuff to lay on the bossman this morning.

And I said, Don't I know it though. I said, Man, do I know it. But man, this is one of those things. I said, Man, this is something I owe it to myself to check into. I owe it to myself to try to find out what this stuff is really like and if I can hack it on my own for a while. I don't know for how long but for a while.

That was when I told him about the recording dates that I had been asked to do with Radio Red for Decameron Records, and also about Felix Lovejoy; and when I said what I said about some of the things Eric Threadcraft wanted me to give him the go ahead to line up, he said, Like I told you that first night backstage, that's somebody on his way somewhere in this town. Hell, my man, that's your room and board right there and with some to spare. You can count on him for that already and he's just getting warmed up.

So at least I don't have to worry about you being stranded out here because you too proud to call the bossman and come back out on the trail, he said. And then he also said, I know how you feel. I really do. I'm telling you, man. I almost stayed out here myself some years ago. But man, me, I always been so much a part of this thing the boss-man's got going. And then too, I guess I got too much gypsy in my soul. After all, I first hit the trail riding the rails in what old W. C. Handy calls a sidedoor Pullman car.

When we came back outside and crossed Hollywood Boulevard, we were headed downgrade along Vine and we passed the Huntington Hartford Theater, and on the other side of the street was the Brown Derby Restaurant; and up ahead was the corner of Sunset and Vine. We then crossed Selma Avenue and came on along Sunset past the ABC Studio to Music City.

I followed him upstairs and he bought a new set of mallets, and we walked on over to the NBC KRCA building, and when I stopped at the door, he knew exactly what was on my mind. So he said, Hey I tell you what, I'm going in here and call the bossman myself and tell him and ask him what time you can come to see him yourself.

And I said, Come on man, you don't have to do that. I said, It's really my responsibility. I said, I'm just going to have to face him.

But I got his point, and I waited while he went inside and made the call; and when he came back he said, So, okay you ain't got nothing to worry about. You surprised me but not him. But hell that's another reason he's the boss. I told him you'd be coming over during the noon hour. So there you go. It's all in the family. I just told him you needed some time off on your own to check out a few things and he said why not, I'm pretty sure he knows his way around here by now and I trust his judgment.

Which goes for me too, he said. And all the rest of these thugs in this two-by-four outfit. So everything is going to be copasetic with them also. Because as important as all of us know this goddamn band is, and as pleased and amazed as everyone of us was at the way you just came right out of college and fell in with us and all this stuff, we all knew that you were going to have to move on after a while because there's so many other things you got to get together besides music. None of us know what it's going to turn out to be, but the way we figure it music is just a part of it.

It was ten minutes to ten and he had a recording session with a local pickup combo starting at a quarter after. So I threw him a jab, which he ducked and tied me up in a clinch. Then he gave me a shove and waltzed away as if to his corner of the boxing ring. And I went back across to Music City and found a booth and listened to six of Radio Red's latest blues releases. Then I sampled two batches of show tunes arranged and conducted by Eric Threadcraft until eleven-fifteen and then I came back outside and stood on the corner of Sunset and Vine and waited for a taxi.

When I got to his suite at the Château Neuf the bossman was listening to the transcriptions of the material we had done earlier that week. He was lying on the couch wearing one of his navy blue polo shirts under a stone blue V neck cashmere pullover, gray worsted slacks, and with fleece-lined slippers instead of the black loafer moccasins he wore to the studio. He was also wearing one of the fancy silk skullcaps that helped to give his always neatly dressed hair the special footlights sheen that was one of his sartorial trademarks.

As was also usual when he stretched out like that in his dressing room or somewhere backstage during a performance, he had his eyes covered with a neatly folded hand towel, which he did not remove to look at me when he extended his hand to greet me and point me to a seat by the window, and Milo the Navigator closed the door behind me and went back to the paperwork spread out on the table in the dining area.

Old Pro was operating the playback machine and also checking each bar against the lead sheet spread out on the music rack of the piano that was always a part of the bossman's furniture whenever the band was scheduled to be in any big town for three or more days. I had recognized which takes they were reviewing as soon as Milo the Navigator opened the door. It and the one that followed were two of the three we had made of a new piece called "Central Avenue Inbound," and from where I sat as I listened along with them, you could see down across that part of Sunset Boulevard to the Plush Pup Pet Shop, and on your right and across Havinghurst was the site of old legendary Garden of Allah motor court cottages, now replaced by a savings bank but once the setting for movietown off screen capers that the no less legendary movie magazine gossip columnists used to thrive on embellishing or even fabricating for people who used to be as preoccupied with the private scandals of movie celebrities as with the pictures they played in.

You could also look back up past Villa Frascati and Pandora's Box to the intersection where Schwab's Drug Store was. But Sunset Strip was out of sight around the bend in the other direction, and Beverly Hills was beyond that, and beyond Beverly Hills was Bel-Air, and then there was Westwood. Then if you turned left when you came to Wilshire Boulevard you could go all the way back to downtown Los Angeles by way of the Beverly Wilshire/Rodeo Drive shopping area and the Miracle Mile, then from the Civic Center interchange you could come down off of the Harbor Freeway and pick up Central Avenue outbound.

I didn't expect the bossman to ask me anything about what I had told him about staying in the band beyond that first summer to build up enough of a backlog for graduate school expenses, and he didn't. At the end of the second playback of "Central Avenue Inbound" he gave Old Pro the cutoff sign, but he didn't take the hand towel from his eyes. He hummed a riff phrase to himself so softly that you could hardly hear it and said, Hey let's try this, and hummed it again so that Old Pro could take it down.

Then after dictating three more phrases, what he said when he sat up and turned to me was, So you need to take some time off to follow up a few things on your own for a while. And I said, If we can work it out. And he said, We'll do everything we can as much as we hate to have you absent for any time at all. After all, you've been very nice about this whole thing of being out here with us this long without a break.

Old Pro and Milo the Navigator came over to where we were then, and Old Pro gave me a wink and hooked his arm into mine and said, You'll do just fine. And then he also said, Meanwhile how about that kid you liked in St. Louis? Scratch something or other from somewhere in Kansas. What about him, and who do you like out here that we can get on a short notice? And I said, Scratchy McFatrick in St.

Louis and Jamison McLemore out here. And Milo the Navigator said, With that house combo Silas Renfroe has at the Twilight Lounge and the bossman said, Right, now that you mention it.

Then he looked at me and said, So do you like him enough to recommend him as your fill-in? And I said, Definitely. I said, He's not just a good combo man, he also does a lot of studio orchestra work around town.

And when he said, Do you think he would like to play our kind of stuff? I said, I know he would. No question about it. He probably knows most of the book already. Like everybody else in that combo, I said, and he and Old Pro looked at each other.

I don't know how long you can count on him staying out on the road I said because he has a family here. But I do know that he'd like nothing better than a chance to play with this band at least for a while, in fact for as long as he can swing it.

So let me get right on this and see if this kid can go up the Bay Area with us next week, Milo the Navigator said leaving. And the bossman stretched back out on the couch and put the hand towel over his eyes again and said, Okay and get me some samples of his latest things with Silas and also a couple of the studio band things.

Then he was talking to me again and he said, So what do you like and think I might like about this Scratchy McWhathisname fellow in St. Louis? And I said, Fatrick, Scratchy McFatrick. Theodore Roosevelt McFatrick. Scratchy Mac. What I like about him is that sometimes when he really gets going he executes stuff on that full bull fiddle as if it's some little old toy saw fiddle tucked between his chin and shoulder.

As for his nickname I explained that it came from the fact that he had been a child prodigy, who had begun scratching out impossible riff figures on a hillbilly neighbor's saw fiddle in the Missouri Ozarks before his family moved up into Kansas when he was eight years old. Ever so hip jazz people tend to forget how nimble fingered some of those so-called hillbilly musicians sometimes are. Never mind how sad-assed so much of that kind of singing sounds to people who prefer music for stomping and shouting and tipping on the Q.T. as played by down-home and uptown musicians, when it comes to cutting a lot of dots in a hurry there are hillbilly fiddle, guitar, and banjo players who can get up and go with the best that ever did it.

I said, You know how the show biz part of the world of music is about clowns and acrobats. Well so far nobody seems to know what to do about all of that technical dexterity of Scratchy Mack except to use it mostly as a show stopping gimmick to be enjoyed as a trapeze or contortionist act. Which he is already good enough at to become a big time headline feature right now. But working for you in this band all of that virtuosity would always have to add up to music not just novelty.

He sat up again then and said, Hey Pro this sounds like something I can't afford not to look into. If this local boy is available we'll take him up into the Bay Area and also keep him for a while longer if he would like to stick with us. Meanwhile see if Milo can get this St. Louis wonder kid to meet us in Dallas. Hell, let's go for doubles on bulls for a while.

The doorbell rang then and he said, Hey there's lunch and your name is in the pot so stick around. And when the room service staff came in pushing the cart I guessed that the cuisine was Chinese and when the table was spread the main dish he had ordered for me was moo shu pork, which was my main choice in those days, and as always he also got a special kick out of suggesting which other selections you should try and file for future reference.

The only other thing he said that afternoon that had anything to do with the fact that I was staying behind in Hollywood for the time being was a question about how I had come to know about Scratchy McFatrick, and when I told him that Joe States had taken me to hear him, he said, Naturally, who else but?

That next morning we went back into the studio and after the second take of the revised version of "Central Avenue Inbound" he said, Hey these guys are wide awake already. These guys feel like playing some music this morning.

He started his new nightclub piano vamp, then stopped and gave the control booth the signal that he was ready to roll, then started again and kept noodling and doodling chorus after chorus with me and Joe States and Otis Sheppard until he decided which groove was exactly the one he wanted. Then when he pulled everybody else in he kept us going with one tune followed by another with only a modulation, a cue figure, and a segue in between for five numbers at the end of which he said, That's what I say about some people. They come by one day and tell you they got to split and then the very next day here they are in here playing your music like it's the main thing they were put on this earth to do. Not showboating to rub it in. Too much class for that. Just hipbone connected with the thighbone connected with the footbone stuff. So much the worse.

Then there was only time enough for one more. So he winked at everybody else and gave a signifying nod in my direction and began with a down-home meeting bell vamp as if to sic the whole band on me. Not to make me hustle and strut my stuff but in a medium church rocking bounce so that all I had to do was keep time and listen to the ensembles coming sometimes as if from the Amen corner and sometimes as if from the congregation at large and as if invoking and also responding to a big blooping tenor sax sermon by Herman Kemble, a short deaconlike baritone prayer by Ted Chandler followed by two thirty-two-bar choruses of very elegant riff shouting and carrying on after which the bossman, Joe States, and Wayman Ridgeway, got their little licks in before Scully Pittman took it up into the choir chancel from which Ike Ellis pushed it on out through the stained-glass windows and into orbit.

You guys, I said as we packed our instruments. You guys. And Joe States said, Not you guys. Us guys, every good-bye ain't gone, homeboy. Not for good.

The morning they pulled out for the Bay Area, there must have been at least twenty-five or thirty other people on hand to see them off. We were all in the patio of the Vineyard Motel, and when the bus rolled up at nine-thirty, I helped Joe States take his luggage out to the curb. And while they were loading, Ike Ellis started signifying about why I was staying in Hollywood. And Scully Pittman said, Now come on old buddy, you don't have to jive the Skull. And Moe said, If he want to get in the movies, that's his business. And Ike Ellis said, Maybe so. But only up to a point. After that, it's all our business. I'm talking about don't be letting them have you up there beating out no hot jazz with no shoeshine rag. And don't be letting them pull off all them fly clothes and smearing no jungle Vaseline on your brown velvet skin and don't be hopping no bells in no tap shoes. And don't be flipping no flapjacks like the goddamn stove is Joe States's drum set.

There was a circle of people around us laughing and nudging each other then, and Herman Kemble said, Boy, if I ever see you up there talking about Yassir Mr. Charlie and rolling your eyes and flashing your pearly teeth your natural ass is going to be my personal shit stomping ground. And when Malachi Moberly said, Hey Bloop, man, you talking to a college boy. Man, you don't have to worry about no college boy pulling no burnt cork stuff like that on his people, Wayman Ridgeway said, Hey I don't know about that. Don't be too sure. Look at what they had old Paul Robeson up there doing, and he went to more and bigger colleges than our schoolboy and on top of that he's always somewhere bragging about how radical he is and don't care who know it.

So see there, Herman Kemble said. That's why I'm telling you, Schoolboy. And I said, Ain't never going to be no days like that, Bloop. Forget it man. And Joe States said, College or no college, that's my statemate. Don't worry yourself about him when it comes to some old tired ass hockey like that. You ain't never seen this boy do anything that wasn't a credit and you never will. The bossman and Old Pro whose luggage was already on the bus pulled up in some Hollywood friend's chauffeured limousine and while Old Pro was talking to Jamison McLemore the bossman made the rounds shaking hands and chatting and kissing all of the women good-bye. Then he called me and I followed him to his seat on the bus, and he said, I know how you feel about all of this. And when I said, I don't really feel so good right now, he said, I'm not talking about that, you'll get over that. I'm talking about taking on a town like this all by yourself. I'm talking about being game and having the kind of guts you had to have to come on the road with us straight off the campus in the first place.

Milo the Navigator came in then and took his seat across the aisle and opened his briefcase and winked at me and handed him a check for me and as I stood up to go, he waited until I slapped palms with Old Pro in the seat behind him, and then he said, I know I don't really have to tell you this, but I'll just say it anyway. Out here you get Arabian nights not just every night of the year but also twenty-four hours of every day. So the special thing to remember about this town is that the fun out here is always better when you're also working. Always remember that, especially when you have to tear yourself away from something just before it gets to be as good as you think it can be if you stick around.

Everybody was in place and they were ready to roll then and I stepped back onto the curb, and as the motor idled I came back along the sidewalk to the window where Joe States sat with Jameson McLemore beside him. And when the motor revved up and the door closed, Jameson McLemore said, Man, I just got to say it again. Man, thanks for remembering me. Man, because of you I can die happy.

And as the bus pulled away all old Joe States could do was look at me and wave ever so tentatively and shake his head, not in disapproval or in bewilderment or even with any last minute misgivings as such, but only as if to say, And so it goes young fellow and so it goes in this business. I almost forgot.

When I opened the envelope on my way back through the patio, I found that the whole band had chipped in to add a substantial bonus to the already generous paycheck, and there was also a note stating that I could always draw an advance against my return any time I gave notice that I wanted to do so.

Two

THE JOURNEYMAN

XXV

I had been on my own in Hollywood for six weeks when I was approached by Jewel Templeton as I stood on the sidewalk outside the Keynote Lounge that Sunday night. I was waiting for a taxi and behind me the fairyland cobweb red and purple neon sign blinked as its yellow border flowed, and you could still hear the music of the ongoing jam session back inside in spite of the sound of the horns and motors and tire treads of the extra heavy weekend traffic both inbound and outbound along that part of Sunset Boulevard at that always busy time of the evening.

You could see who she was as soon as the Rolls-Royce pulled up to the curb and stopped directly under the streetlight. She was driving and she was alone, and I guessed that she was about to say something because she leaned toward me smiling; and since I assumed that she knew who I was because she had probably seen me with the band, I thought she was going to ask me something about the bossman, and maybe also about why I was no longer with the band. But when I stepped forward and she said what she said, I realized that whatever else she wanted to talk to me about she was also there because she had decided that I myself was somebody she wanted to talk to.

So, here you are. Mr. Bass Master himself, she said smiling somewhat more like an infrequent backstage visitor than a movie star. And I said, Not quite. I said, Accidental apprentice at best, who may or may not be ready to become a side hustle journeyman of sorts. And she said, Some journeyman. Radio Red. Eric Threadcraft and also that many recordings with his Imperial Highness himself to begin with. Some apprenticeship. Some journeyman I must say.

The Sunday afternoon jam sessions for which the Keynote Lounge was so well known in those days began at four o'clock, and I had played until seven and picked up my check and promised to come back the next Friday night at nine. Then I had put on my light London Fog trench coat and zelin cloth porkpie hat and stepped out into the not quite chilly Southern California after dark breeze and was on my way back to my room to drop off my instrument and change clothes before heading across town. I hadn't been along Western Avenue to West Adams and then to Crenshaw in two weeks. I hadn't been on Central Avenue in almost a month.

I had seen her inside. She had been there three nights in a row, and she had come by herself each time and had sat in the same alcove sipping what looked like the same tall cold drink that I was pretty certain was only a seltzer and lime, and tapping her fingers ever so tentatively on the napkin. You couldn't see and judge how she kept time with her feet, but every now and then she would tilt her head to one side as we accented here and there.

In those days the Keynote Lounge was the kind of place whose regular patrons were always more interested in music and musicians than in movie stars, and so it attracted a significant number of movie stars, who came because they had a special interest in the music as such and also because it was a place where they could enjoy being out just for the fun of it without being preyed upon by overenthusiastic admirers and autograph seekers. In the Keynote Lounge it was the music fans, especially the record collectors (among whom were a number of movie celebrities), who were the seekers of autographs.

That was why the only reason I was somewhat surprised when I saw Jewel Templeton that Friday night was not because I had expected her to like music. It never occurred to me that she was someone that wouldn't like it. What impressed me and made me curious was that her interest was so obviously that of a serious newcomer, and I wondered whether it was professional or a matter of personal development—or maybe both; and I decided that it was not a matter of casual or frivolous exploration whatever it was.

When she came in that Friday night wearing a blue sheath and a single strand of pearls and carrying a silver fox stole, I speculated that she was dropping by on her way home from a recital or maybe a ballet or modern dance concert, and you could also tell that she had made a reservation and was expected not because she was a regular patron but because she was who she was.

She came back Saturday night for the ten o'clock show, wearing an outfit that suggested she had spent the day, and perhaps had also had dinner at some nearby place out of town, probably some place I had not yet seen but had read about in the movie magazines back in high school—or so I found myself free-associating as she was led to the same alcove as the night before.

On that Sunday she came in at 6:20, just as we were about half way into the six choruses we ended up jamming on "Royal Garden Blues"; and as soon as I saw the slacks and blouse she was wearing with a blue blazer draped over her shoulders I assumed that she had come directly from home this time and probably intended to go directly back there afterward because she was either studying a new script or was in the process of choosing one, probably about a nightclub entertainer or hostess, I found myself speculating again, or maybe a detective story with a pop or torch singer in it.

She was that close to the bandstand again then and you couldn't help being aware that she was there even when you were not looking out beyond the footlights, and suddenly I was sorry that I hadn't decided to stay on for the whole session. Not only because she was who she was but also because I always get a great kick out of playing for people who listen the way she did. I like to think of the sophistication of such people as being so cosmopolitan that they can be frankly curious or even downright square but who regard their inability to connect with something unconventional not as a question of ignorance or barbarism but simply as a matter of specific idiomatic orientation.

When I finished my last set and took my bows I smiled as I turned in that direction without actually looking at her or anybody else, but as I made my exit I did look back that way because I wanted to see her that close once more, just in case she did not show up again that next week. Then hoping that she would, I decided to sign on for every set Friday through the Sunday late show.

She said what she said as she pulled up to the curb where I was, and I answered as I did; and the next thing she said was exactly what you couldn't admit you hoped for until it happened, and I crossed my fingers. She said, If you're not waiting for anyone in particular you always need a lift in this town. And I said, Now that you mention it, I guess I do at that. And when she said, Well then, I opened the door and braced my instrument on the backseat, and as I got in beside her and gave her my address I made a little weak crack about rolling stock.

I said, Here I am all the way out here on the western frontier without my own pony and packhorse. I'm going to have to fix that very soon. And she said, I'm sure you will, because my guess is that you're going to be a very busy fellow around these parts.

Then she turned the headlights back on and got ready to move out into the traffic, but with her foot still on the brake pedal she said, Meanwhile if you're not really in a terrible hurry because people are waiting for you somewhere, I wondered if you would mind talking with me a bit about this fascinating world of very special and wonderful music that I've been only superficially aware of all these years.

So close and yet so far, she also mumbled to herself as we waited for the light to turn green, and when I said I was not in any particular hurry to get anywhere I either promised or was expected to be, she said, Well then in that case. And when the light changed she pulled into the traffic going in the opposite direction from Vine Street.

You stopped playing early tonight, she said as we rolled on along the Strip toward the Interlude, the Crescendo, and the awnings and tables on the terrace of a place that was called Pupi's in those days.

My time was up, I said. I got started early. And when she said how sorry she was that by the time she got around to calling in to check the Sunday schedule the first session was already under way. And when I told her that she hadn't missed anything that was really special, she said she thought that what she caught of the session the night before was very special.

Especially those two friends of yours, she said then, the ones that kept playing back and forth at each other. They made a lot of difference. Their sheer delight in just playing around with the musical possibilities in each tune like that was instantaneously contagious. Where were they tonight? Are they somebody that even someone who is as uninitiated as I am is expected to know about already?

The trumpet player is Sonny Craig, I said, and the alto man is Jay Wheeler. Tonight they're working their way back east by way of the southeast rhythm and blues route (which Joe States used to call the back alley circuit). They're somebody not many people may have heard very much about if anything at all yet, but the general public just might be very much aware of them before long. Not necessarily as a team. Probably each on his own. But as kindred spirits.

The three of you really had something going up there, she said. And when I said, We did have fun, she said, The way you kept looking at each other with mock frowns and stretching your eyes and smiling each to himself as well as at each other as if you were swapping previously unrecounted anecdotes and episodes of some old yarn the outlines of which you all shared a common recollection to begin with. That was terribly intriguing and it was just fascinating to be that close to such informal but precisely controlled and relentless, yes, relentless indeed, improvisation.

I was completely taken with the fun and games elegance of it all, she said as we settled into the tempo of the traffic and came on beyond The Seven Chefs and around the bend from Hamburg Hamlet. But I also had the feeling that I was missing something because I really didn't know enough about what it was about. I could tell that something was being said very well indeed, but I didn't know what it was.

That's good enough for me, I said. So long as you have been taken with it. And that was when she said, All the same I hope you don't mind talking to me about such idiomatic things as that, because I just love to have you tell me what I should do about it sometime. Sometime when we get to know each other well enough to ask about things without feeling that I'm sounding like a tourist, if you know what I mean, she said looking at me and smiling again and I had to squint and press my lips together to keep from grinning from ear to ear.

I might as well tell you, she said, I've been doing some homework on that special world of music you work in. For personal not professional reasons, she said. Very personal reasons and by that I don't mean personal hobby rather than current production project, although I don't rule out the possibility of finding a role as an eventual consequence. I mean personal in the sense that my books and art pieces are personal. My garden is a hobby, cooking is a hobby, if you know what I mean. Anyway, what I must begin by telling you is that I know who you are because it was while I was doing my homework that I came across an item about His Imperial Highness leaving town with a local musician filling in for his regular bass player who was staying behind to work on several projects around town for the time being.

And when I said, But that was only a teeny weeny squib in a pop music rag, she said, you get used to picking up all kinds of little details like that in this town. There are people out here who make their living getting things like that put into show biz news tidbit columns for clients. And there are others whose livelihood depends on picking up on what is barely mentioned in passing and also spotting names that are merely mentioned for the first time.

Mainly I've been reading things and buying recordings, she said. And I would like to find out what you think about what I have. And I said okay and that records were the main things for getting it all together if you listened to enough of the best. Even if you were already pretty certain about what you preferred, a wide sampling of records was the best way to relate your special interests to the rest of it. Because with records you could have some of the best of all of it right at your fingertips long before you could get around to hearing enough of it live.

So I've been led to assume, she said. And that is why I would like to have your opinion of what I've come by so far. And I said, Anytime you say. And she said, What about tonight? Or do you have an early call in the morning? Maybe you could at least take a quick look-see and give me your general impression for starters. Would you mind doing that for me?

Not at all, I said. And when I also said, Tonight is fine with me, she said, Oh, wonderful. And does that mean that maybe we could listen to a few of them, too? Would you mind terribly? And when I said not at all, she said, Are you really sure it's not a bother, a presumptuous imposition? I said, Absolutely. I said, Absolutely not. I said, I would absolutely love to. And the pleasure would be mine. And she said, No angel, mine, mine, mine.

We were that far beyond the Beverly Hills Hotel then and she turned off Sunset to the right and when she had come on through the tree-lined residential streets and began winding and climbing up toward where the hillside began there was no other traffic either coming or going. So, for the time being there was only the two of us alone together in the softly purring vehicle which she steered with all of the expert ease that I had taken for granted she would.

Neither of us said anything for a while and then you could tell that there was not much farther to go as soon as she looked over at me and said what she said next.

I hope you really don't mind this, she said. I hope this is not going to be too boring for you. I'm very much aware of the indulgence I'm asking for on such a short notice. After all what I'm so newly excited about must be such old stuff to a top flight professional like yourself.

And when I said, Not all that old and not so topflight professional as all that either, if at all, she said, All the same what I'm talking about is kindergarten stuff as you well know, and I can't tell you how pleased I am that you agreed to run the risk of spending the evening having to respond to a lot of dumb questions. And when I said, We'll see about that I was thinking Jewel Templeton, Jewel Templeton, Jewel Templeton. On some level of consciousness or subconsciousness people who have earned that level of international esteem know very well that they can afford to be as square or naive-seeming as they need to be in order to find out what they think they need to know about. In fact sometimes when it suits their purpose they may even go so far as to invite condescension in order to make sure that they are adequately drilled on the fundamentals of whatever it is they're trying to get at.

No, the ones most likely to be a downright drag are almost always those ever so persistently friendly ones dead set on impressing you with how much inside stuff they already know about the music (and "the musical life" as well) as a natural result of their intimate association with other performers young and old, local and nationwide over the years.

I said, I absolutely cannot imagine you being boring about anything whatsoever, and certainly not about music. You never get away from fundamentals in music. And when it comes to the way we play what we play, I said, thinking about Eric Threadcraft, curiosity about idiomatic details comes under the heading of fundamentals.

To which she said, How nice of you to put it like that. But all the same I'd just as soon not turn out to be somebody who comes across as being all but hopelessly unfamiliar with too many things that should have been an intimate part of my life all along.

Then she said, Well, in all events, here we go. And when we leveled off again we were there and I could see the house and the trees and the dark grounds with the other hillside house shapes above the sparkling valley and the lights of that part of Hollywood reflecting against the sky. We came on through the archway and along the upcurving drive to the carport above which were servants' quarters, and I saw that she also had two other automobiles and a station wagon.

I followed her along the breezeway to the shallow steps and into the wide entrance hall, and the split level drawing-dining room opened out into the patio, the pool, and the view across the dim valley to the distant hills. Nearby, you could also see another wing of the house with a second story sundeck and steps leading down to the poolside, which I suddenly remembered having already seen in movie magazine photographs over the years.

———

The recordings in her collection of the great European composers, musical comedy scores, and popular standards were on the same waist-high to eye-level shelves of the white built-in, wall-length floor-to-ceiling bookcases along with the art books and portfolios of sketches for fashion, costumes, and set designs. There were no shelves from waist-level to the floor, only closed-in cabinets and drawers in which she stored back issues of magazines and some of her less important shooting scripts and a few souvenir props of early films in which she had bit parts.

Most of the recent purchases that she wanted me to spot-check and react to were on a long limed oak bench near the ultra deluxe sound system. But there were also quite a few others stacked on the rectangular glass top coffee table in front of the long tuxedo style linen covered lounge.

Just pick out something you yourself would like to hear, she said heading toward the one step up to the dining area level where the bar stood near the door to the patio and the pool. That's how I would like to begin if it's all right with you, she said. Not something for me, just anything that happens to strike your fancy. Let's start that way and then later on or maybe even some other time we can get around to some of those that I have had in mind to ask somebody about.

So when she came back pushing a highly polished brass serving cart outfitted as a portable bar I had decided to begin with the Kansas City bands, piano players, and singers, because I still enjoyed the ones I picked out as much as I did when I first heard them during my sophomore year in college, and also because having her responding to them along with me at the outset would make it easy for her to appreciate the notions that I was pretty sure I was going to try to get across about the nature and function of the traditional down-home blues in jazz improvisation and composition.

She clicked on the turntable and I handed her the first record and she adjusted the volume and came back to the cart and said, Help yourself or name your poison. And I helped myself to one jigger of bourbon over three ice cubes in a sparkling crystal glass for Old-Fashioneds and

added water from the silver pitcher, and she said, Me too, and made
her own and held up her glass to be touched and said, Well then so
here we are. So nice of you to come. Oh, this is great fun already. Then
after one ceremonial sip along with me, she said, I'll be listening
upstairs as I slip into something more homelike and I'll be right back
down. Meanwhile, do *faites comme chez vous*, as they say. To which I
made a stage bow with my glass extended and as she turned and headed
on up to the mezzanine landing I took another sip and moved back
over to the bookcase again where, as I had expected, there were more
novels, short stories, and plays than anything else. But in addition to
the tall art books there were also some about the history of the theater,
stagecraft, the history of music, and the lives of the great European
composers. Biographies also outnumbered volumes dealing with special historical periods and general historical surveys.

That didn't surprise me either because I guess I had always
assumed that movie people were more concerned with the daily texture of life in given time periods and places than with political and
social issues or even military problems as such. After all, the characters
you were cast to play might turn out to be on the side of an issue you
personally opposed. Such characters had to be made as believable as
the ones on the side of the issue you supported.

When I came to the section of books on travel I was not surprised
that it was not very large, because I had already assumed that she kept
her collection of tour guides and foreign language manuals along with
her maps, atlases, and other basic reference materials in a special inner
sanctum workroom somewhere upstairs, which was also where I
guessed that she kept most of her books and artifacts related to American history and culture as such.

There were also travel books in the collection of international
cookbooks on the shelves lining the short corridor between the dining
area and kitchen. That was some few years before Samuel Chamber-
lain came to write and illustrate *Bouquets de France* and *Italian Bouquet*,
which Waverley Root followed with *The Food of France* and *The Food of
Italy*, but Jewel Templeton's kitchen library, which is a story in itself,

had evolved from the same emphasis on the interrelationship of food
and travel.

When she came back downstairs wearing a pale blue silk smock with
off white raw silk slacks and patent leather flats, she had also combed
her hair so that it was shoulder length, and she looked more like the
famous screen and fan magazine personality than the no less glamorous but somehow somewhat less familiar woman who had just
brought me home with her.

The woman I had met less than an hour ago outside the Keynote
had in effect been a familiar all but improbably friendly stranger with
whom I had instantly become involved in a very cordial person to person relationship that was as yet undefined. Now suddenly she was the
Jewel Templeton you had come to know so intimately from all of the
closer than life closeups, special camera angles, and sound effects that
you felt that you could not only read the way her eyes and lips and nos-
trils reacted in a whole range of intimate situations but also how her
breath already sounded before the words came.

She put her empty glass on the serving cart and stood with her left
hand behind her neck, her cheek against her forearm, her hair falling
around her raised elbow; and when she saw that I was following my shot
of bourbon with a tall glass of seltzer she helped herself to the same, and
after her second sip she said, Oh say, if you worked from the first set
you've not had anything to eat since lunchtime, or midafternoon at the
latest. So how about something to eat? And suddenly remembering that
all I had eaten since breakfast was a hamburger with a vanilla malted in
the midafternoon I said, Well, now that you bring it up.

Which was when she slapped her forehead and said, Oh my God,
there is dinner! I had completely forgotten all about it. Now that's
really something, I mean really. You have no idea. Not that I have a
huge appetite. But mealtime is not something that often skips my
mind. Unless I'm deeply absorbed in some special undertaking. So I
guess I must be even more excited about all this than I realized.

The help had left at six, she told me as she beckoned for me to follow her up to the dining area, where she set two plates, but except for a few little personal finishing touches that she always insisted on adding, everything was ready and waiting.

Then I also followed along as she went on into the kitchen, and when she saw how curious I was about all of the special equipment and utensils, she said, I have accumulated all these fancy gadgets because I myself am something of a fancy cook. You have no idea what a special thing this food thing is with me, in spite of all the concern about staying thin that the mere mention of Hollywood brings to mind. I actually designed this kitchen along with my first husband, who as you probably know was a set designer and also something of an architect—or in any case a collaborating architect.

As for the size of the kitchen library, she had been given her first guide to French food and a handbook of French wines in preparation for her first trip to Europe when she was eighteen and had begun adding new and old titles before the trip was over, and before long food and wine books had become a very special enthusiasm. Her taste was basically French, but she also was almost as taken with Italian cuisine, and then came German, Polish, Scandinavian, and other European dishes; and her menu might include Spanish, Portuguese, and Latin American specialties any day of the week.

Not unlike many other people along the Pacific Coast she also ate a lot of Polynesian, Chinese, and Japanese food, but with so many outstanding Far Eastern restaurants and caterers so readily available, she had never felt the urge to try out any Far Eastern recipes at home except when among the gift packages that she received from fans from many lands there were Far Eastern food items with recipes included.

Among her special food loving friends there were, to be sure, also a number of winemakers, those in France and Italy predating those in northern California, who had in due course come to outnumber them by a considerable margin. Some of these also belonged to a special circle of "mushroom friends," many of whom also grew their own herbs and spices.

———

The main dish that night was neither strictly French nor Italian. She called it Escallops in Short Order and explained each step as she zipped along. The pieces of veal were already cut and dusted in flour so all she had to do was sauté them quickly in olive oil and splash in the right amount of dry vermouth and beef stock, let the gravy thicken slightly, and then sprinkle in already prepared fresh rosemary, chopped scallion, and parsley and wafer thin slices of lemon. And *voilà*, in less time than it took to play through three selections of approximately three minutes each.

She made a salad dressing of olive oil, fresh lemon juice, and sea salt in which she tossed Bibb lettuce and sliced plum tomatoes in a wooden bowl rubbed with a half clove of garlic. She said that there was a choice of a red wine, a chilled white wine, or both but that the red would go better with the cheese course. So that's how I came to have my first taste of Barolo and the cheese was gorgonzola and for bread you had a choice of crusty French or Italian rolls or you could either cut or break the French ficelles to suit yourself.

Meanwhile the records I had chosen included "Six Twenty-seven Stomp" (as in Musicians Local 627), with Pete Johnson on piano with a seven piece group of Kansas City all stars; "Piney Brown Blues," with Joe Turner singing along with Pete Johnson and several of the same all stars; "Baby Dear" and "Harmony Blues," with Mary Lou Williams on piano with her Kansas City Seven (from Andy Kirk's band); "The Count" and "Twelfth Street Rag" by Andy Kirk and the Twelve Clouds of Joy, with Mary Lou Williams on piano; "Good Morning Blues" (with Jimmy Rushing on vocal) and "Doggin' Around" by Count Basie; and "Moten Swing" and "I Want a Little Girl" by a group led by Eddie Durham, trombone player, a pioneer electric guitar player and key arranger for the late Bennie Moten and the early Count Basie orchestra.

We skipped dessert and coffee and brought the leftover wine back to the main part of the drawing room, where she curled up in what was obviously her favorite overstuffed chair and I took over the operation of the sound system; and when I said, You can go either way from Kansas City, south to the blues and New Orleans and Louis Armstrong and all of that, or east to stride time in Harlem and Duke Ellington and all of that, she said, Whatever you say, maestro. So I said, Why don't we just stick with what we already have going? And she said, Why don't we indeed?

Then she also said, May I take that to mean that you approve of what you have found so far? And when I said, No question about it and said, I can't get over finding so much of this stuff up here in these elegant hills, that was when she told me that she had been shopping from a list prepared for her by a newfound friend in St. Moritz last winter.

Believe it or not, she said, that was really the first time I ever stopped and listened to the blues as you listen to what is called serious music. I must tell you all about that because that is really what all this goes back to: the Marquis de Chaumienne, my favorite twentieth century human being. He is an extremely handsome sixty-seven-year-old French diplomat, sportsman, and patron of the arts, whose family involvement with America goes all the way back to the time of De Tocqueville, and whose knowledge of the things that make America American is absolutely staggering, especially to somebody with my conventional midwestern upbringing.

Oh I really must tell you about what happened when I finally got to meet and become friends with him over there last winter. I most definitely must and now that I think of it, I can hardly wait. But not tonight. He himself would not have me interrupt this music for that.

So we went on playing the records I had set aside. And in answer to questions that she would signal for a pause to ask from time to time, I said what I said about the infinite flexibility of Kansas City four/four, riffs, and riff chorus compositions, about stomps, jumps, and shouts, about voicings, timbre, mutes, plungers, aluminum, plastic, and felt derbies and also about how the old Kansas City jam sessions were said to be similar to and different from the ones in the Keynote.

Then to call attention to how late it was getting to be I said, And now for an example or so of the after hours groove if the time will allow. And she said, Oh by all means. And when I began with Count

Basie on piano with his rhythm section of Walter Page on bass, Jo Jones on drums, and Freddie Green on guitar playing "The Dirty Dozen" from the stack that also included "How Long Blues," The Fives," "Hey Lordy, Mama" "Boogie-Woogie" and "Oh Red," and she said, Perfect, just simply precious. I can't wait to tell the marquis about this. Oh I don't believe this really.

Your choices are among his favorite examples of what he calls the functional and therefore truly authentic American chamber music, she said. According to the marquis, whose explorations in the United States also included the back alley honky-tonks, jook joints, and barrelhouses, it was in the gin mills, cocktail lounges, and small intimate after hours hole in the wall joints that you found the twentieth century equivalent to the music you heard in the elegant European chambers of the old castles and châteaus of yesteryear.

She stood up and began moving around the room doing dance studio warmup stretches and she dimmed the lights. Then when I put the Eddie Durham octet version of "Moten Swing" on again, she came striding back in my direction with her back ever so statuesque, her shoulders square, her legs and thighs moving like a Busby Berkeley chorus girl and I began snapping my fingers and tilting my head on the diagonal.

We were facing each other like that for the first time then, and as she opened her arms she also stepped out of her flats saying, Do you know what this shoe thing is about? And when I said, What kind of old shoe thing? she said, This barefoot thing some of us have. There's supposed to be some big symbolic something about it. There are these friends of mine who insist that there is something about this kind of music that all but literally undresses them, that makes them respond as if they are or should be naked.

I don't know about that, I said, as we stood vamping in time, in place. But hey, I'm all for it in some situations that I can think of. To which she said, I hear that twinkle in your voice, young man. We stepped off and did a very nice trot and she also took her first spin very well, but when I tried to take her from a soft stomp to a cozier and

groovier shuffle, she missed a beat and became somewhat self conscious, but as soon as I began snapping my fingers she picked right up
and relaxed and smiled and said, I don't know. Those girls out in those
places along Central Avenue seem to have their own special way of
handling all this. I don't know. Some marvelous way of stylizing it
without destroying the truth of it. Some way of controlling and even
enhancing it in the very process of giving themselves to it.

I said, That's all right about them, lady. What you do just being
yourself will do just fine. And she said, Well thank you, gracious sir.
Thank you for being so consistent with the impression that I've had of
you from first sight.

Then she said, I was watching you. Friday night, last night, and
tonight. Did you realize you were under surveillance? and I said, Not
really. I said, I could tell that you were listening to what I was playing.
I was pretty sure of that, and I began to play around with certain little
things just because somebody special was out there paying attention.

Well thank you again, sir, she said. I had no way of knowing that,
of course, but I did like everything you played, as if with such nonchalant elegance, and I might add incidentally that I kinda like what you're
doing at this very moment. And also that I am absolutely certain that
I'm going to like what it is all leading up to.

XXVI

That next morning I remembered where I was and what day of
the week it was as soon as I heard the shower running and
realized that I was awake and who was in the bathroom. So when I saw

how early it still was, I closed my eyes again and settled back into the pillow, and when I woke up again it was half past nine.

When you rolled over and sat up with your feet on the floor, you were facing a wide picture window through which you could see the houses on the nearby hillsides and the sky fading from bright to silvery gray as it stretched away beyond Hollywood toward downtown Los Angeles. The temperature was seventy-five degrees, and there was a breeze that made the fluffy pink and metallic gray bedroom smell as blossom fresh as it was cozy.

On your left beyond the foot of the wide bed there was a glass paneled door that opened out onto the sun deck, and when I pulled on my shirt and slacks and stepped into the terry cloth slides that had been left along with the hapi jacket for me and came outside and looked down into the patio I saw Jewel Templeton in broad daylight for the first time. And I think that was probably the first time I ever crossed my fingers after the fact.

She was sitting in a deck chair by the swimming pool wearing a black bathing suit, and she had on white rimmed sunglasses and a white gondolier style straw hat with a wide red band, and on the low table at her elbow I saw a wicker basket full of mail. There were also several new books and a stack of new magazines along with two spring binders that I took to be screenplays under consideration.

When she looked up and saw me and waved I said, Movie stars sure do get up early. And she said, Old studio habits. As a rule they also turn in early.

Musicians sleep late, I said. And when she said, So I see, I said, When they can, which is not all that often, but there is always the bus and the ever so soporific open road. And before I could say what I was going to say about how early the Bossman Himself often got up, she said, Soporific is not what I've ever found any dressing room to be, not in the studio, not on a remote back lot, and not on location.

So all I said was that I imagined that directors were somewhat like bandleaders such as the Bossman Himself when it came to the hours they kept. And she said, I would not be at all surprised. After all they have everybody's part in the whole cast or band bouncing around in their consciousness. It's a wonder they ever get any sleep. But then it may well be that the difference between sleeping and waking is not the same for them as for people like myself.

Then she said, Tell Maurice what you want for breakfast and tell him to serve it out here. Meanwhile why don't you come on out and take a dip. There are trunks and clogs. Esther will bring them up.

You could hear the midmorning radio music downstairs and also the cook and the maid moving about. I looked around the airy bedroom again and peeked into the workroom, and then I looked outside again, and beyond the pool there were wide steps leading down to the level where the two tennis courts were, the white chalk lines sharp against the clean red clay, the chain-link fence interlaced with splotched ivy, the gate framed with bougainvillea. I could also see the greenhouse and a low red brick garden wall beyond which there were beds of flowers and a plot of kitchen herbs.

Somewhere nearby somebody was operating a power mower, which you could hear beyond the radio and the voices downstairs. And you could also smell the freshly cut grass and the lawn chemicals in the breeze and see the hillsides in that direction and that part of the sky getting clearer and clearer as the valley mist became thinner and thinner. *California, hey California.*

The water was just right and I swam half of the first lap under the surface and finished with the Australian crawl and paused and came back showing off my three beat American crawl. Then I did a racing turn and a few rolls and a few backstrokes and breaststrokes and climbed out and dried myself and draped the towel around my neck and came along the poolside to where she sat smiling and holding out her hand.

We touched cheeks backstage style, and she stood up and came with me to the table under the umbrella where Maurice, a graying pale tan Creole from Louisiana, served me a glass of orange juice and a bowl of Polynesian fruit to be followed by a two-egg ham-filled omelette and toast. All she had was a cup of tea with lemon, and when I finished we came back to the deck chairs, and that was when she told me about being between pictures.

From the gossip columns I already knew that she had been between husbands for the past five years and that she was also between regular escorts. Her last divorce was number three. Her last publicized romance had ended before she flew to Europe in the late autumn of the past year to spend time on the Côte d'Azur and Provence before going on by way of Paris to Switzerland for the winter season.

She had not decided on a next movie script yet. She was not in a hurry, because in the meanwhile she had become involved with a very special personal project that had grown out of a friendship she had come to have with the Marquis de Chaumienne, who had given her a new insight not only into her profession but also into herself as an American and as a twentieth century person.

I told her about the deal I had with Eric Threadcraft, and we talked about Felix Lovejoy; and she wanted to know about all of the clubs that I had been working in around town. Then she asked about the records I had played on with the band, and that was when I started telling her about how I came to be in the band instead of graduate school and about Joe States and Old Pro; and when I came to the Boss-man Himself she said that she had always known that he and Louis Armstrong were in a class above and beyond everybody else but that it was not until recently that she had begun to understand why.

That was all she said about that at that time, and then she began to tell me about some of the things that had happened back during her early days in show business, and as she settled back recalling the names of faces and places it was not long before you realized that she was reminiscing perhaps as much for her own benefit as for the ever so casual orientation of an acquaintance of less than twenty-four hours.

Because what she was not only recalling and relating to me but also in effect if not intent sharing with me was not at all the usual movie magazine personality profile platitudes about how you pick up on the tricks of your trade on the road to fame and fortune. What she had begun remembering herself back into was her innermost sense of the texture of the existential quest for your personal definition, for which public recognition is often mistaken perhaps by most people and certainly by press agents.

As I sat listening to what she went on to tell me about how the stock companies used to make their way across the country, I was also thinking about Milo the Navigator, who when he used to say "fifty roads to town" also as often as not meant fifty roads to fifty towns, all of which were only way stations en route to the castle town that was your ultimate personal destination.

Which is why when she finished what she was telling me and patted me on the thigh before turning back to her mail and magazines, what I closed my eyes and nodded off thinking about was the Bossman Himself, whose castle town destinations were exactly the same matter of the same maps and mileage charts as those of Milo the Navigator, to be sure, but who even so would also have been described by my good old best of all possible freshman and sophomore roommates in terms of the barnstorming troubadours of the yesteryears of storybook times.

When I realized that I was awake again and that I could hear the horns and motors in the distance because the sound of the nearby power mower was gone, I could tell that the sun was now directly overhead even before I opened my eyes. You didn't have to open your eyes to know that you were still in Southern California either, but even so there was something about the hillside breeze and the smell of the freshly cut lawns and freshly trimmed shrubbery that made me feel the way I used to feel every time I walked across the campus during the first term of my freshman year.

I said, California, hey California. But I didn't make any sound or move my lips because I knew that I was being looked at. I kept my eyes closed a little longer and then opened them and saw her smiling at me and wondered if I myself had been smiling without realizing it so I tried to wink but all I could do was squint and grin, and that was when she reached out and meshed her fingers in mine and said, Well then, shall we go back upstairs for a while?

———

We didn't come down for lunch until the middle of the afternoon. It was a chicken salad lunch with Bibb lettuce a platter of fruit and a napkin covered wicker serving basket of warm French rolls. The wine was Pouilly-Fuissé, and when she held up the bottle and I pronounced the name to her satisfaction she smiled and touched my arm and said that my musical ear stood my school book French in good stead. And that was also when she promised to have me sample such lighter weight red wines of the Beaujolais region as Fleurie, Moulin-à-Vent, and Juliénas before moving on to the vintage Burgundies and Bordeaux.

After lunch we settled down in the living room area and went on playing the records left over from the night before, and for a while she closed her eyes and kept her own time. But when I looked again she was taking her clues from my foot tapping and finger snapping, so I began naming dance steps that went with the rhythm, tempo, and the beat of each number; and when we came to Jimmie Lunceford's "I Wanna Hear Swing Songs" she stood up for me to show her how to do the Florida Off Time, after which she was also up for the steady four/four velocity of "Time's Awasting" but not for the all out killer diller clip of "Swinging on C."

She led me over to the deep tuxedo couch then and sat in the corner facing me with her finely shaped and carefully tanned calves and ankles tucked under her, and after lighting a cigarette she told me what she decided about us.

I do hope you will take this in the way that it is certainly most sincerely intended, she said, because I was never more serious about anything in my life. So here goes. I've decided that there is something about you that I would not like to treat as a pleasant but brief encounter.

I must have said something in response, and I can think of a lot of things that I could have said; but I don't remember anything at all about what I actually said or what I did. I don't remember that I was really surprised. So I think that I must have felt the way you feel when you're playing a game (or doing anything for that matter) and you become so taken up with doing what you're doing that you forget that there is any prize or reward involved. Anyway, the next thing I remember her saying was what she said about my eyes.

Maybe it's the way they always shine, she said. And curiosity and sincerity are only the beginning of it. There is humor and patience that add up to a precocious wisdom. Then she also said, I'll just bet you something. I'll bet you were always everybody's little bright-eyed boy back in your hometown. Whether they liked you or not, she said. I can just tell about things like that. After all, who was I if not little Miss Sparkle-eyed Goldilocks of Small Ridge, Wisconsin?

That was that Monday afternoon. I moved my things into the studio apartment above the garage that night.

XXVII

That Tuesday morning she went down and came back with the breakfast trays and we ate in bed and sat propped against the pillows talking, and that was when she told me about the Marquis de Chaumienne. She described him as having classic Gallic features, a deep almost leathery ski-slopes-and-shipboard tan, neatly clipped iron gray hair, and a military mustache. He was of medium height, trim, elegant, his bearing casually correct, his presence magnetic; and as soon as you heard him speak you could tell that he retained his charm and authority in many languages. He spoke nine fluently and not only was he at ease (and among acquaintances) in most of the capitals of the world, he also knew his way around the countryside, the back country, and the back alleys.

She had finally met him that fateful night last winter in Saint-Moritz. The American born wife of an Italian film executive had introduced them during a gala in the grand ballroom of the Palace Hotel. He had bowed from the waist and kissed her hand and held it smiling, and she still couldn't get over what followed. He had already known who she was. Not only that but he had taken her in tow immediately and had started telling her all about herself as a screen actress, naming her roles and discussing them in a way that made her want to rush out and see them all over and over again.

When she laughed and told him that she was quite certain that none of her producers and directors had ever been seriously concerned about or even remotely conscious of most of the implications, overtones, and relevancies he was suggesting, he had only smiled and folded her hands in his, kissed her again on both cheeks, and said, Of course of course, producers were in the business of manufacturing for the general public but that it was precisely in the process of turning out clichés, popular romances, and pulp adventure yarns, things of that sort, that they sometimes wrought far better than they ever really intended. But there were, after all, many truly gifted craftsmen in the film industry, and they sometimes went beyond their immediate popular commercial orientation and became literary artists without ever really intending to do anything except the same old thing a little better, or maybe only a little sleeker.

The two of them strolled arm in arm along the edge of the dance floor and left the ballroom and made their way to the bar, where he seated her in a quiet corner and ordered whiskey. Then looking at her again, the mature approval of his knowledgeable eyes suddenly reminding her of the producer who had chosen her for her first starring role, that warmly personal way he had of putting you at ease so that you could function at your best. He talked about the marvelous and marvelously curious American girls in the stories of Henry James; and he told her that she herself was another one of what Henry James had called "the heiress of all the ages," in a sense perhaps even Henry James himself had not visualized. Certainly she projected a dimension of earthiness that he didn't find in James's ever so inquisitive and adventuresome American princesses. Also, whatever her studio press agents really meant by their glib characterization of her as a sex symbol, she was in effect an American-born heiress of all female fundamentalities from Eve to James Joyce's Anna Livia Plurabelle.

She forgot all about what was happening in the grand ballroom, and they spent the rest of the evening in the bar talking about what he called the archetypal plurabilities of the all-American Anna Livia Plurabelle. *Which is why back in her room she had dreamed of playing two-handed then four-handed piano duets with Henry James for James Joyce who suddenly looked like Abraham Lincoln, Henry James playing the right hand keys, herself playing the left.*

The next morning he had taken her skiing, and they had eaten lunch on the sunlit terrace looking out across the town and the scattered settlements along the wooded valley of the upper Engadine. There was a usual elaborate buffet and they helped themselves to soup and shellfish salad and sat sipping champagne until the middle of the afternoon, the conversation ranging from the Alpine terrain before them to his boyhood fascination with the romance of the Rocky Mountains and life in the old American West, which had also led him to his longstanding special interest in American horse breeding. He was especially interested in that all-American circus performer, cow pony, and fourth of a mile racer known as the quarter horse. He still scheduled occasional trips to California to coincide with the quarter horse racing season.

He also talked about the western railroad lines that he had come to know in his youth, and when he told her about his several visits to Indian ceremonials near Gallup, New Mexico, he had promised to take her to see the priceless kachina dolls in the private collection of a literary friend of his the next time he and she were in Paris at the same time. He himself had begun by collecting firearms, traps, and tools of the old fur trappers, traders, and mountain men. Then it was the hardware and equipment of the range and cattle trail.

So when she went to dinner at his chalet two nights later she was not surprised by the number of western objects in evidence, but she was absolutely amazed at how by displaying them on the walls and about the drawing room as he did, he had transformed such homespun workaday nineteenth century American ranch items as branding irons, corkscrew horse-tethering pins, bits, rowels, stirrups, bullwhips, lariats, and various strands of barbed wire into artifacts with a patina that was both prehistorical and *dernier cri*. The collection of branding irons and tethering pins was especially impressive and eye opening. In fact she was already reacting to them as art objects before she suddenly realized what they had actually been designed for.

She was also immediately impressed with the Marquise de Chaumienne, a stunning soft spoken woman in her early fifties, whose tawny hair was streaked with silver and whose clothes made you conscious all over again of the kind of elegant women who produced so many great French and Italian fashion designers.

There were two other dinner guests, a young Italian contessa whose family manufactured musical instruments and parking meters; and a Danish baron who had once competed in Olympic ski events. The marquise had not been at the gala. She and the contessa, who was also her houseguest, had just returned from Amalfi by way of Milan that morning.

When she thought about it on the way back to her hotel afterward she realized that she would not have been surprised if the food had been chuck wagon chili or pigs' feet, black eyed peas, collard greens, and corn bread or red beans and rice. But what the menu really featured was the cook's special dish of game birds and a fine red wine from the marquis's vineyard in Médoc. But after the cheese course the marquis had led them into another room promising her that along with coffee and Armagnac there would be some delightful messages from the United States to the world at large.

The first thing you noticed was the screen, so you looked for the projector but then you also saw the recording and playback system. So when he turned the sound on she had thought that he was tuning in on some special American broadcast over one of the State Department shortwave radio channels that European diplomats and foreign correspondents listened to and she had not known whether to expect a spe-

cial news roundup or some new high level policy statement. So much
for my estimate of the situation, she said.

What came out of those huge high powered speakers was the
absolutely startling downbeat of a jazz orchestra, which broke into
something that sounded like the blues and a war dance at the same
time, the trombones hoarse and rowdy, the saxophones moaning, the
trumpets shouting and screaming, the rhythm pounding as much like
the beat of a transcontinental American express train as the beat of
movie soundtrack tom-toms.

She was flabbergasted. It was as if the whole evening had suddenly become some kind of carefully prepared European joke about
American jukebox culture or something or other. She closed her eyes
and held on to herself and made up her mind to be amused. But what
she saw when she stole a look around the room was the baron patting
his feet in all seriousness, the young contessa moving her head from
side to side and snapping her fingers soundlessly but confidently. The
marquise sat smiling, rubbing her palms along the arms of her chair,
her eyes twinkling with excitement. And as for the marquis, himself, he
was pacing back and forth tapping his stomach with the flat of his
hand. She settled back relieved. But before she could get her attention
focused on the music as such again, the first selection was over and
they all had turned toward her smiling and applauding.

Since that night she had been spending as much time trying to
learn all she could about American music as she spent trying to find a
new screenplay. She had passed all the next afternoon at the chalet listening to recordings, air checks, and transcriptions, and asking questions. And on her way back to Hollywood she had stopped off in New
York for fifteen days shopping for the selections on the list the marquis
had made up for her and also making the rounds on all of the
nightspots he had mapped out for her.

I called him last night she said. While you were picking up your things,
she said, getting out of bed and standing on her fine tan legs and

insteps with only the transparent shorty shorts between me and her and the window. It was eleven o'clock and she wanted to swim and spend some time in the sun and eat lunch on the patio before going down into Hollywood to keep several appointments. I was going to spend the afternoon practicing and then I was going to take a long nap before getting dressed and taking the Ford runabout that she called her auto incognito to meet Eric Threadcraft at Hotel Watkins across town on West Adams. She went into the dressing room and came back wearing a very brief black two piece outfit from the Côte d'Azur. All I had to do was step out of my pajama shorts and into the swim trunks.

He's at his place in Médoc, she said. He's back from some mission in the Far East. We talked about you. He never ceases to amaze me. He knows exactly who you are, and thinks you're awfully good. He has those last things you did with the band. He gets advance promotion copies of everything along with the reviewers and disc jockeys. You didn't tell me you had an original piece coming out.

I haven't heard any evidence of it, I said. I know we made some tapes, but you never know what they're going to use. Anyway it's not really all mine. It's just one of my riffs that the Bossman Himself told me and Old Pro to set up for the band.

He says you have true talent for thinking in terms of the whole band, she said. He says the contours of your musical personality are already becoming distinctive. And I must also tell you that he's especially pleased that my first jazz musician friend is as he puts it bass clef.

Did I tell you what he said about me and the bass clef that first night? she said. He said what he said about me and Daisy Miller and then he said but as great as Henry James was, he was a trifle treble for the likes of me. He also said I had ragtime in my ways, blues in my bones, and spirituals somewhere deep down in my soul.

Then later as he was driving me back to my hotel in the sleigh, there I was all wrapped up in my most elegant mink and wearing my most sparkling Cartier carats and the most expensive coiffure that money can buy in Saint-Moritz and he calls me one of Ma Rainey's children, one of the sparkling daughters from the muddy waters of the upper Mississippi. The blue-eyed first cousin to Bessie, Mamie, and Trixie Smith.

And I said, The Big Muddy. Hey, Wisconsin is on the upper Big Muddy as is Davenport, Iowa. I'll take you over Bix Beiderbecke any day.

XXVIII

During my first months in Hollywood, Eric Threadcraft and I did most of our work in the canyon view hillside apartment that he always referred to as his old air conditioned woodshed with drafting tools. We hardly ever went down to the recording studio to rehearse anything either then or later on until he was satisfied that all of the parts of whatever we were working up arrangements on were ready for a full band run-through just before the first official takes.

In the beginning we actually spent most of the time talking about what he liked so much about the Bossman Himself and his band, which he said was always one and the same thing with his music in much the same sense as Picasso and his palette and easel were the same as his painting. When you said Picasso you meant the paintings. When you said the Bossman Himself you meant the music.

It was also during that time that he used to like to come along every now and then when I made the rounds to the spots across town along and off West Adams and along and off Central Avenue. And nothing pleased him more than being invited to sit in on piano on occasion here and there. To which he always responded not with a solo but by vamping and comping not only to avoid making himself a target in a cutting session but mainly because that way he would go on listening as the arranger-composer and conductor that he was (but admitted only to an apprenticeship to).

Hey fellow, if only I had grown up having to earn my way into sessions like those, he always said afterward. Hey wow! Man, there's no telling. Because so much of this wonderful stuff depends on nuance and scruple. The idiomatic nuances one absorbs growing up and the scruples peculiar to the convention from which your definitive aesthetic judgments are derived. Hey fellow, I'm talking about growing up learning how to break the proper rules properly and mispronounce the right words correctly because you are not so much taught as conditioned to know that something goes not like that but like this.

But the main thing during those first weeks and months was what I could tell him about being as close as I had been to the Bossman Himself. Tell me. Tell me. Tell me, my man, he started saying at the very outset, and as much like an ever so enthusiastic amateur as he almost always must have sounded to some people, as soon as you stepped into his picture perfect streamlined workshop, you could see that his collection of recordings, band equipment, and memorabilia and his files of articles and photographs were those of a professional whose dedication to his métier was longstanding and comprehensive.

Naturally I'm already pretty much clued in on the vital statistics, he said. Man, just wait till you see some of the background stuff I've been picking up from the Washington and Baltimore of his boyhood days and the years of his apprenticeship. Hey fellow, it turns out that there were fantastic piano players all over that Potomac and Chesapeake area in those days. Some with formal training from the conservatories and others who could play anything by ear as soon as they heard it and run variations on it for an encore. And then there were those TOBA showcase theaters featuring all of those headliners from New York and everywhere else. Man, don't let anybody try to give you the impression that there was anything provincial about that Washington and Baltimore scene of those days.

And don't forget how those Washington people felt about their schools and colleges, he also said. And then he said, okay, so I know that our man didn't go to college and I also know that it turns out that there was no college and certainly no conservatory for him to go to. But I would like to talk to you sometime about music in those colleges. I know about the choirs, the so-called jubilee singers and the groups singing spirituals, but what about our kind of musicians? I really hope we can get into that sometime.

Anytime, I said, anytime at all. So let me just say this about it now. There were college dance bands as well as marching bands for parades and ceremonies. But what has always counted with the dance bands is not the music department but the road bands: what you heard them doing in person, on broadcasts, and on records was what you had to contend with no matter what was happening in formal courses in the music department.

There you go, fellow, he said. Man, that tells me a lot already because it's just like what happened in painting and literature. Contemporary painting didn't come from any of those Paris academies but from people like Cézanne. And current fiction didn't come from what was being taught in the universities but from people like Joyce and Proust and so on. Oh say but this is going to be just great. And great fun in the process.

Things got under way before the end of that same week. He agreed to orchestrate a portfolio of twenty musical comedy hit tunes for one of the several recording studio bands he worked with from time to time, a thirty-five-piece all-purpose outfit that included the string section of violins, cellos, and also a harp. He was also going to conduct and I was going to be his main man in the rhythm section.

As special assistant to the arranger-conductor, my job was to go by his apartment and listen to what he had in mind and supply the bass line and also make suggestions about the overall treatment that he came up with for each selection. The main thing he wanted from me this time around was the beat. He was gearing everything to that he said, and not even the band itself would know what was getting to them. And that was also when he said that it was what I could do for his left hand that would make me his right hand man in the studio.

So, here we go, fellow, he said on the phone when I checked in with him that morning. It's not the World Series, but it's not bush league either. And I said, Hey man, I'm a rookie in this stuff. Man, I need all the spring training and exhibition workouts that I can come by in this league.

Look, fellow, this could very well be the beginning of one hell of a team, he said. I hope so, because that way I could also count on having you there to save me from any obvious ofayisms. Among a few other things, he said. And when I said, Come on, man, he said, I know what you're going to say, but I want your ear on this stuff all the same. I'm talking about nuance and scruple, man, remember?

All I said when he said what he said the next time around was what I've been saying for as long as I can remember. He said, The only question is how long you can stand to be involved with this much of this kind of stuff. *And I said, As far as I'm concerned it all goes with the territory, my man. Always did and always will. No less than newsprint, fashion magazines, run of the mill movies with popcorn. I said, also remembering myself window shopping along Dauphin and then Royal Street in downtown Mobile, Alabama, and how the current songs you heard not only from the mechanical megaphone in front of Jesse French Music Company but also in the department stores always went with the gas fumes and the sound of the traffic and the latest styles on display in the haberdasheries and sporting goods show windows and with the blue steel fairy tale glitter and smell of drugstore counters and soda fountains.*

If you know what I mean, I said. And he said, I do. I do, my man, I do. In other words pop stuff is really urban folk stuff. That's precisely what Tin Pan Alley has always been about. City stuff, all the way from the street corner and the hole in the wall and after hour joints to vaudeville, the road shows and the palatial showcases during the days of the annual Follies, Scandals, and Vanities and so on to the Hit Parade charts.

Two weeks later we were ready to start recording, and when I signed in at the studio that Monday morning he was already there, and so were most of the band members. They were laughing and talking as they settled into place and got ready for the sound check, and he was in the control booth reading the *Los Angeles Times* with Felix Lovejoy, the popular local radio host and record producer who was now working his way into the movie business, peering over his shoulder.

When Eric Threadcraft looked up and saw that I had found my place and was all set up, he raised his baton and waved for me to join them, and the three of us slapped palms and went through our new buddy-buddy greeting routine and he said, So let's drop it on them, teammate. And I said, If you say so, maestro. And when Felix Lovejoy, whose nickname was Felix the Cat as in the old funny paper and silent movie cartoons, said what he said, shortening maestro to mice as Ernest Hemingway had done in an article I had read in *Esquire* magazine back during the fall term of my freshman year in college, Eric Threadcraft said, Me with my Cat with the Golden Paw on the one hand and my Cat with the Golden Fiddle on the other.

Then as he and I came on back out to the bandstand, he hooked his arm in mine and we went over and slapped palms with Ted Ripley, who was the drummer on that session and who had only recently come back into town after four weeks in Las Vegas. Then before heading for the podium he said, Mice yeah mice, hey mice. So let the Cat get to plucking away and just listen to how the mice will play.

Every section was tuned and waiting then and he opened the first score and called out the folio sequence number and raised his baton, and from the very first rundown, everything went along so well that by break time we were ahead of schedule. He stabbed the baton at me playfully and turned and almost ran to the control booth for the playback. Everybody else headed outside to the rest rooms, the telephones, the vending machines and/or snack bar.

Ted Ripley overtook me on the way to the newsstand in the snack bar, and started telling me about the job he had just finished in Las Vegas. And as he talked lowering his voice and cutting his eyes about him, screwing up his face and holding his stomach as if the memory itself were enough to knock him out all over again, I remembered meeting him the night the band opened at the Palladium on my first trip to town.

He had come backstage to talk with Joe States after every set, and I had also spotted him in the second row at every concert we played in Southern California that time around, his lips moving, his head bobbing, his eyes never leaving the stage. He owned every recording that Joe States ever played on, and he knew each arrangement note for note. He had the same drum set as Joe States, some of it once owned by Joe States himself; and when he played he moved his elbows like Joe States, holding his head at the same angle, his ears cocked, his eyes narrow, even when he was smiling his stage smile, even when he was being nonchalant. Sometimes on upbeat numbers he would forget and close his eyes and hum to himself as if gritting his teeth, but even so he kept his tempos as steady as a metronome and he was always right there with something to go with anything you tried.

So how do you like it in there this morning? he said as we moved from the newsstand to the Coca-Cola machine. And when I said, Pretty smooth hustle so far, he said, Man, like why not? With the stuff we're laying down for them. But I also mean what do you really think of this kind of gig? he said making a face suggesting a mild cringe. And when I said, It's all right. It's fun, it's interesting, he said, Hollywood stuff, man, and looked as if he could taste it. Cocktail lounge sonatas, soda fountain concertos, plush after hours joint whiskey sipping *études*. Man, you can shuck your way through all that stuff. Then he said, But what the hell I'm a pro and I do have eyes for the kind of checks that come from this scene.

And that was when I told him that I liked that kind of music for what it was. Because I did and I still do. I don't have anything against cocktail lounge music. On the contrary, I liked the idea of hearing myself on the sound systems not only in swanky cocktail lounges but also department stores, lunch counters, and all of the other places of the workaday world. And then there were also all of those homes of all kinds that kept the pop music radio stations tuned in almost all day, almost every day.

Speaking of being a pro, I said, to me this is just another dimension of the trade. And he said, Hey that's cool with me, man. I can see you know what's happening. And that's what I like about that Eric. Hey that Eric knows what he's doing. That helps, if you know what I mean. He's not kidding himself. That's the difference. He knows exactly where it all goes. That's why in my book he's the greatest thing out here. I mean really. I mean you've got to hand it to him. He's got it all working. I mean like he can hear from blues to bop, and he can chart them from heads to Bach, Beethoven, and Brahms. From twelve bars to twelve tones. Hey and he knows who to get help him swing them.

By six o'clock that evening we had completed all the takes and retakes, and after the others had packed up and gone, Eric Threadcraft, Felix Lovejoy, and I sat together in the control room and listened to the retakes of the first three tunes again and decided that they were as good as we had hoped. Then the three of us came outside into the still early twilight brightness of that time of year in Hollywood, and I stashed my instrument in the auto incognito and as we headed down the north side of the sloping sidewalk, Felix Lovejoy said, It's my news so it's my treat.

He took us to a place across from the Vine Street Brown Derby, and outside the window where we were seated you could also see the Huntington Hartford Theater and beyond Selma Avenue there was the local American Broadcasting Company station. And farther on up along Sunset Boulevard you would come to the Palladium, where the two of them had first heard me play in person.

The waiter who had seated us came back and took our orders and as he turned and started for the bar, Eric Threadcraft said, And now the news. And I leaned forward and cupped both my hands to my ears and that was when they told me that the contract that they had been negotiating for a full length feature movie score was finally in the bag.

In this bag, my man, Felix Lovejoy said, and opened his briefcase and took out two movie scripts and Eric Threadcraft took one and pushed the other toward me as Felix Lovejoy went on to say that all we had to do was read the story and think about it and then go back through it scene by scene and knock together something that would put the audience in the groove that the director was going for. And Eric Threadcraft said, We're going to give them a different kick to get on, and the thing is to get them on it before they realize what's happening. Of course we could put out a manifesto and dare the smart set not to be up to date, but you don't have to do that with the kind of music we've got.

I said, I know what you mean, man. And I did, but as he and Felix Lovejoy went on talking about the actualities of feature film production all I did was look at the title and studio logo. I didn't even try to skim the first page. I didn't want to start thinking about the actual work until I could settle down by myself. I was not even going to mention anything about it to Jewel Templeton until I had done that.

You could tell that Eric Threadcraft was already familiar with what the project was about (and perhaps also with earlier drafts) by the way he flipped through his copy of the script while Felix Lovejoy made scratch pad notes from several documents in his briefcase. *I took another sip of the tall drink and looked outside at that part of Hollywood again thinking: Me too, this time. This is the way it happens when it is happening to you.*

Oh boy, I heard Eric Threadcraft saying. I can hardly wait to get going on this baby. And I said, When do we have to start? And he said, I wish we could start tonight, but that's just it. Looks like I'm going to have to be tied up for at least the rest of the month doing what I still have to do on all that fantastic stuff we laid in today. And I do mean fantastic, he said. Fabulous. So I'm afraid that's my situation as of now, you guys.

But when I asked how much time we were going to have he said, Plenty of time. No sweat on time as yet. It's just that I really can't afford to let anything intrude on the current stuff in progress. So why don't you just check it out and see what you can come up with for a start. In the meantime, just don't give me any hints until I'm free to turn my undivided attention to them.

Just read the script for the story and make your own musical response to the action, beginning with atmosphere. Just remember it's how you feel about the scene as well as the people in the action that really counts. Don't bother yourself about any of the technical stuff. That's just routine. That's the last thing. Any studio hack can take care of that in his sleep. How many bars here? How many bars there? That's all that is.

So on my way back up into Beverly Hills later on that evening I couldn't keep myself from thinking that my Hollywood gamble was paying off, and that I had reached another landmark. But even so I also realized that I still didn't know what my ultimate destination really was.

XXIX

I read the script in the garage apartment that night and did not bring it into the main house, because I liked the story line and I was already beginning to have a strong sense of the overall atmosphere that the music had to generate, but I wanted to go back over everything scene by scene at least two or more times and then read the novel before talking about it with Jewel Templeton or anyone else.

So all I said about it during breakfast at the poolside the next morning was that Eric Threadcraft had asked me to start playing around with some ideas for a new project that he and Felix Lovejoy had lined up for us as soon as he was done mixing and editing the material that we had finished recording the day before. I didn't say anything about a film score; and she didn't ask for any details, because she wanted to tell me her own news.

I, too, have myself a new project, she said. So what do you think of that, Mr. Studio Pro? And I thought she had finally agreed to make another movie, but it turned out to be a trip to New York to see new Broadway plays.

Studio business, she said. They called me this morning to remind me. I hadn't really forgotten about it, but somehow the dates had slipped up on me. I was thinking in terms of next Tuesday and it's really tomorrow.

Through the weekend, she said, and when she said, Esther and Maurice will be on part time, but if you need them for anything don't hesitate to call on them, I said, If it's all right for me to use the kitchen I'll be just fine on my own, and they can just check by at their leisure.

And she said, That's no problem, I'm sure, since they both like you so much. Believe me, I've never known them to be like this about anybody else, star status notwithstanding.

I pretended to duck behind my forearm as if from a brickbat and said what I said to change the emphasis back to her trip. I said, Hey meanwhile maybe there'll be enough spare time for you to get around to some of the music spots. And she said, That would be a wonderful bonus, but I'm not counting on it. They choreograph every move you are to make on missions like this. It's no junket. Or rather it's their junket not mine.

What a shame, I said, but at least you don't have to feel bad about missing the Bossman Himself. He's out on the road and won't be back for months.

Then when instead of making any mention at all of who was actually going to be where around town during the time she was going to be there, I said I hoped it turned out to be a good trip, she said, Oh I'm certain of that. I'm not really counting on the stage, but there are always the gallery and museum circuit. The fact of the matter is that the people who will have me in tow may be ever so deeply involved in the production and distribution end of this business, but when you come right down to their personal preferences they'll take still pictures on canvases over moving pictures on celluloid any day.

She took off for New York early that next morning, and I stayed in and practiced until midday. Then I drove down to the Pickwick Bookstore on Hollywood Boulevard and found a copy of the novel that the script had been ever so freely adapted from. I wanted to find out how much of the atmosphere evoked by the flow of the author's words on the page had been retained, missed, or deliberately left out by the scriptwriters. Because I was pretty certain that whatever the case, if the author was any good at all his narrative voice as written would of its very nature suggest sound track music as the script as such could not, or at any rate had not. I had not talked to Eric Threadcraft about it yet, but my assumption or working notion was that the sound track should help make the audience feel about the people, the situation and action being projected on the screen the way the storyteller's voice on the page made you go along with how he felt about whatever he was telling you about.

I was almost halfway through the three hundred page novel and was taking a nap on the couch in the drawing room when the phone rang that night. The first play was over and she was back at the Sherry Netherland with a few minutes to spare before changing into what she was going to wear at a party at the Plaza.

The first play was only so-so, which was about all she expected it to be. But even so there was as always nothing like being back in a Broadway audience attending a live performance, because along with everything else you shared with regular New York playgoers, there was also the fact that it put you back in touch with your craft and made you feel not only like an apprentice once more but also as if you were always an apprentice/journeyman no matter how many times you've seen your name up on the much bigger and brighter marquees of the Times Square movie showcase theaters of those days.

Anyway the visit was off to a good start, and was bound to get better no matter how the other two plays turned out. It would be nice to see something that you liked well enough to recommend to the studio of course. But she had agreed to come east not because she herself had any special interest in screen adaptations of Broadway plays. She had always preferred adaptations from books, she said. And I said, I think I know exactly what you mean. But I didn't mention the book I was reading, because I still was not ready to tell her what I was getting into; and that was when she said when you come to New York from Hollywood on any kind of visit it was always like coming back to the seat of empire from one of the far-flung outposts. Then she also went on to say what she said about the red carpet treatment in New York being an absolutely indispensable part of what being in demand in Hollywood added up to.

It was time for her to begin the stroll across Fifth Avenue and Central Park South to the Plaza then, and she remembered that I was going to be working at the Keynote that Thursday night and Saturday night. So she said her next call would be during the daytime, no earlier than late morning and no later than midafternoon, and that unless something urgent came up, probably not until she had seen the third play.

But when she called that Sunday around noontime all she said about the third play, which she had seen Friday night, was that it was okay but not for her. The second play, which she had seen on Thursday, was a musical comedy. It was that and the modern dance program that she had seen that Saturday afternoon and the ballet she saw in the evening that she was looking forward to talking with me about when she came back that Monday afternoon.

There you were, she said. As soon as the downbeat came. You and the Marquis de Chaumienne. And I must say. I really must. What with your off-the-cuff demonstrations of his brilliantly cosmopolitan implications, I will never again listen to music or look at dancing as I once did. At all three performances it was as if he were sitting on one side of me, and you were on the other; and that made me so much more acutely aware of all sorts of missed possibilities that never would have occurred to me before. So I liked just about everything somewhat, if not a whole lot, less than at other times. But it was still a wonderful experience. Because I felt so much more mature and knowing about everything. It was just marvelous.

So you were saying, she said that Monday night as we settled down in the drawing room after dinner. She had come in from the airport and had started right in on what she had to say about the Broadway musical even as she headed for the bathtub, and during the meal I had told her about some of the details I had picked up from Old Pro (and from sources he directed me to) about how the old minstrel shows, ragtime, the cakewalk, the fox trot, the blues, and some of the early so-called syncopated orchestras had influenced the evolution not only of American popular song but also the Broadway musical and so also the Hollywood musical comedy.

The names of such turn of the century and first quarter musicians and performers as Will Marion Cook, Bob Cole, Bert Williams and George Walker, Ford Dabney, and Will Vodery were already somewhat familiar to her because the Marquis de Chaumienne had mentioned them from time to time; and when I said, James Reese Europe, she remembered that he had been the musical director for the famous Vernon and Irene Castle dance team, the forerunners of Fred and Adele Astaire.

When she went on to tell me about how interested the Marquis de Chaumienne also was in American ballroom dance steps as such, I started talking about the way many of the old "how-to" pop song lyrics used to promote new dance fads, and that is how we came to spend the rest of her first evening back from New York with me showing her what I remembered from my childhood on the outskirts of Mobile about how to do such steps as the Strut, the Shuffle, the Black Bottom, the Breakdown, Balling the Jack, the Mess Around, the Georgia Grind, and so on through the Charleston and the Suzie Q to jitter-bugging and the stomp as done elsewhere, even before the Savoy.

XXX

By that next Friday afternoon, I was ready to start trying to find out how many of the little melodic figures, riff sketches, and themes I had come up with could be worked into a first draft. But I decided to put it all aside and spend the weekend making a few pop calls with the bass, while Jewel Templeton was sailing off Catalina Island with the studio people responsible for her trip to New York. I hadn't been into any of the spots in West Los Angeles and out on Central Avenue in several weeks if not a month.

I felt very good about what I had been able to come up with so far, so much so that I was already beginning to speculate about which of the passages would be accepted as is, with the orchestration as indicated. There were some leitmotif riff figures and a few uptempo and slightly cacophonous blues shout choruses to accompany several of the action sequences that I was just about certain that Eric Threadcraft was not going to be able to resist. And by that time I also felt that I was beginning to know enough about him to guess what direction most of the modifications and elaborations he decided to play around with would take. *Yes, yes, yes, I know exactly what you're getting at. Yes, yes, yes. Then he would say, And perhaps also . . . And maybe also . . . And hell, even something like this—or even this. Say you've given us a million options on this thing, fellow.*

As little as I knew about the piano, there was nothing like the keyboard for working up what I was trying to get together, and the Pleyel in the garage apartment was what I hunted and pecked on every morning until midday. Then I would tune the bass and spend at least an hour working out on it until it was time to take a dip in the pool and have lunch.

Sometimes, Jewel Templeton, who always woke up and got started on her various routines before I did, would spend most of the morning in her workshop and then go down to the pool. On other mornings, she would putter around in the garden or with the house plants; and there were also times when I wouldn't hear or see her until she was turning into the driveway from an early shopping trip, sometimes to downtown Hollywood, sometimes to Civic Center, and sometimes to Farmers Market. But that Wednesday she was already at the poolside when I came down to the patio, and that was when she said what she said about the finger exercises I had been zipping through just to keep in shape.

I was listening, she said, and I must say. I really must say. My God, you sound like somebody who was born doing calculus and trigonometry. And I said what I had to start learning to do right after I was born was the Jackrabbit. Because I was born in the briarpatch, I said. And she said, But aren't we all? And isn't it all a matter of idiom? That's what the marquis would say, and he would also say that idiom is a matter of convention, which is basically a matter of how and maybe why you do what you do where you come from. And by the way, to him, that was what the storyteller's traditional opening lines were really about. *And I said absolutely, thinking: Once upon a time in a place perhaps very far away, what came to pass among some people perhaps quite different from us in many ways, nevertheless applies to us in a very fundamental sense indeed.*

I do so hope that I'm doing justice to what the marquis had in mind, she said; because I do so feel that it is precisely the very foundation of that cosmopolitan point of view that he represents so much more casually than anybody I ever met.

In any event, she said—or perhaps I should say at all odds—your briarpatch is somebody else's wilderness or somebody else's highlands or somebody else's bayou lowlands and canebrake and so on and so on. If you know what I mean, she said. And I said, I do, I do, I really think I do. And she said, He would say we were talking about a basic disposition toward adventure and its requirement for improvisation. And believe me, what I just heard was high velocity improvisation indeed. And I said, I think I know exactly what you're getting at, I really do.

Then when I said, But I must tell you, what you heard up there just now was only some offstage stuff, some offstage warmup stuff not actual performance stuff, she shook her head smiling and said, There you go again. You and the marquis. You and the marquis. There's a story, which he corroborated for me, that his standard answer to those who responded to some of his jazz recordings by asking if such musicians could be taught to play the great masters was that he knew many jazz musicians who played the great masters as warmup exercises.

She thought it was a great story and so did I. And I said, the marquis knows his stuff all right, but I also have to confess that I'm not one of those by a long shot. What you heard me doing up there was something I had memorized from Tricky Lou Cartwright in Mobile years before I came to promise anybody that I would try to learn to play that thing myself.

And by the way, I also said, Old Tricks used to call that kind of accelerated warmup routine his Paganini Orini jive, and once I got started running finger exercises one of my goals was to be nimble enough to play note for note all of the figures I could remember him cutting, and in the process I also began making up some of my own. Not that I ever had any notions of ever becoming a pro on that thing, not even a part time pro. All I was trying to do was to see how quickly I could get to be good enough to jam with the combo led by the one who had given it to me.

Paganini Orini? she said. Really? You're kidding. You're pulling my leg. Oh the marquis is going to be completely delighted when I tell him I heard this from you who got it from a Mobile, Alabama, pool shark. Oh when I get you two together. Just you wait, my bright-eyed, nimble-witted, sparkle-fingered friend from the here, there, and elsewhere of road musicians.

El hombre de época, she went on to say and was to repeat from time to time from then on. *Hombre de época.* Do you happen to know what that expression is? she said. And when I nodded remembering my roommate once more who had come upon it in a book by José Ortega y Gasset when he returned for the first term of our sophomore year. That's what the marquis has in mind when he talks about the ideal person that should be the natural product of the American experience, that our schools should be geared to turning out, given the ready accessibility to modern innovations in ever more precise and efficient communication and transportation facilities we enjoy.

Or words to that effect, she said. Then she said, Of course, as far as I'm concerned what it all adds up to is somebody very much like the marquis himself, whose point was precisely that an American would not have to begin with all of the family means and privileges that a European aristocrat such as himself was born to. As a matter of fact, he insists that to be truly representative of the possibilities inherent in the contemporary epoch one must not inherit but achieve one's aristocratic status. Much the same—oh and I do so enjoy telling you this— much the same—although I suspect that fabulous roommate of yours has already realized it—much the same as all of those literally fabulous jazz kings, dukes, counts, earls, and barons have given themselves titles and obligations that they then are expected to live up to.

When I think of the ever expanding implications of some of the very first things he said to me, she was to say and repeat from time to time, sometimes to me but mostly for her own benefit even so. When I suddenly realize how many ramifications some of his most casual remarks have, I can only marvel. And even more marvelous to an American schoolgirl like myself is the fact that he is not like a big time university scholar or deep thinking intellectual type at all.

Which, she went on to say, just goes to show how naive I've been about how things go. After all, what made that circle of people so attractive to me in the first place was that, to me, they were what the world of the international playboy was all about. Then somewhere along the line I became so bedazzled by *haute couture, haute cuisine*, and the glitter of the galas that I lost sight of the obvious. Such people, especially the very richest ones, are seldom less concerned with nuts and bolts than with fun and games.

What I'm only now just beginning to come to terms with, she also said, is something that I really can't say that I didn't already know. Such people don't let their formal education show. Not as such. Not any more than is the case with some of their various other acquisitions.

Some years later I would have said something about education as a matter of collecting ever more highly calibrated tools and devices for your work kit. Because what it all added up to was a phrase I had picked up from Mr. B. Franklin Fisher's Seniors Pregraduation Seminar, in which one of the main discussion topics was "The Aims of Education." What they were about was the knowledge, skills, understanding, awareness, and appreciation to be gained from such subject matter as Language, Mathematics, Science, History, and Religion. But according to Mr. B. Franklin Fisher, of all people, whose doctrine of the ancestral imperatives was not always distinguishable from the Horatio Alger all-American work ethic, what they all added up to was Worthy Use of Leisure Time.

So that's what I told her I had always thought playboys and the international smart set were really about. And she said, Me too, and so they are, in spite of all the emphasis the tabloids put on their self-indulgences and perversities that some are, have been, and probably always will be guilty of. To me whatever else some of them might be, some others are not only the most important patrons of the arts, ranging all the way from the so-called angels who back stage productions to those who establish endowments and those who donate priceless collections that make up the treasures of our great museums.

Everybody knows about their staggeringly expensive jewels and playthings, she said. But who buys more expensive books or more of the better and best books? And where would the most imaginative architects be without them? But so much for my personal theory of the leisure class. You get the point.

That was when she stood up with her finger to her lips and then went up to the dining level and into the kitchen and came back to hand me the bucket with the iced Dom Perignon and went and came back again with a tray on which there were the stemmed glasses and caviar and said what she said about certain things should always be a matter not only of leisure but also of ceremony and celebration.

To which I said, Hey, you know something Miss Lady? This is some pretty deep stuff we're getting into now. But you know something else? It also sounds like an invitation to a dance.

And she said, The dance, Mr. Bright Eyes. Invitation to the dance.

XXXI

Every time Jewel Templeton said what she always liked to say about why she was so pleased that you had come along when you did, all you could do was shake your head and squint your eyes and tighten your lips and look around at nothing in particular.

Not that you doubted her sincerity when she said what she said about how much she was learning from you about music and what she said about how impressed she was with the bright-eyed enthusiasm with which you went about things in general, or even when she kept coupling your name with that of the Marquis de Chaumienne as if to do so were the most natural juxtaposition in the world.

Nor was there any question whatsoever of flattery on the one hand or of all too obvious and all too ofay-eager naiveté on the other. Her praise was nothing if not generous, to be sure, and her frank curiosity was a matter not of naiveté but of a sophisticated self-confidence that on occasion could become downright aristocratic in the exercise of its freedom not to have known already.

As a matter of fact, what your instantaneous, even if not unplayful, reaction was in response to was precisely the ring of sincerity that made what she said add up to being as much a matter of ongoing high expectation and indelible obligation as was the case when Miss Lexine Metcalf used to say, *Who if not you, my splendid young man, my splendid young man? Who if not you?* And earmarked you for Mr. B. Franklin Fisher and the Talented Tenth Early Birds, which was the name of his special accelerated study program for those students considered to be most likely to fulfill the ancestral imperatives.

Apropos of all of which, and in accordance with your own long established conception of the scheme of things, you are not about to allow anything, no matter how genuinely adulatory, the certified glamorous and internationally famous Miss Jewel Templeton said, fake you into forgetting that you, not she, were the apprentice. Because at the same time that she was whatever she was in her own mind and to other people here there and elsewhere as well, in your mind she was no less another one of those good fairy godmothers that you may or may not be lucky enough to encounter in various guises at some point along the meandertale route from Mama, Miss Tee, and Miss Lexine Metcalf, than was Miss Slick McGinness.

Miss Slick McGinness West, I might well have said. Miss Slick McGinness redux, Miss Slick McGinness as of this juncture. But I didn't. Because there was no need to do so. Because what really mattered was not an articulation of the minute particulars of the relationship but rather the com-

patibility that was already there by the time the two of us settled down in the
drawing room after supper that first evening. She had said what she said
about music and had liked my response and that was the beginning and what
followed happened as such things do when one step leads as naturally to the
next as do the also and also choruses in a riff session.

You were who you were to her and she was who she was to you.
And since the fact that the person to person dimension of the relationship, however intimate and however unfrivolous, was only an incidental detail, went without saying, that was all that was necessary.

So whenever she would say what she would say again and again
about what she was not only learning but also coming to terms with
because you were there, all you had to do was turn your head as if from
well meaning but gross exaggeration and then change the subject back
to the point at which her enthusiasm had interrupted you.

It worked every time, and that was how and why the conversations
never became an ongoing exchange of compliments during which you
would have said what you could have said about what she meant to you.
Which was probably all the same to her, since the reason you were there
in the first place was that she was so preoccupied with the Marquis de
Chaumienne, who had convinced her that there was something that she
was supposed not only to represent as a performing artist but also to
embody and exemplify as an American in the contemporary world at
large.

But still and all and still in all and still withal, however else she
saw herself and in whatever other personal terms she defined her relationship to you, such was the perhaps ineluctably mythological nature
of the also and also of things that she was also your fairy-tale godmother in the most functional sense of the word, the undeniably sen-
sual and even incestuous implications of which were already very much
there indeed in Miss Lexine Metcalf's all but disconcerting good looks.

All of which is to say that Jewel Templeton, in spite of the fact that
she never once said anything to me that anybody could possibly inter-
pret as the expression of any kind of authority of status or seniority whatsoever, was my fairy-tale godmother on the scene at that time, even as

Miss Eunice Townsend continued to be the fairy-tale princess in the storybook world of my as yet far from specific aspirations and expectations, and would, I hoped, continue to be so for sometime to come.

It was a gamble to be sure, but no chance taking no adventure and no adventure no hero and no hero no story and no story no storyteller and no storybooks, and no storytellers and story books, no need for compass, maps, and mileage charts since all purpose and action involves risk; and inertia has no destination. Even as entropy has no shape, form, or fashion.

So far Eunice Townsend was still willing to gamble on her expectation that whatever escapades a young part-time journeyman road musician might become involved in during a sojourn in Hollywood or anywhere else in the world of entertainment, for that matter, were likely to be only a part of the also and also of the rights of passage that should help him achieve the personal experience, conditioning, and cosmopolitan outlook that would qualify him for the obligations and expectations of husband and father. Most references to Prince Charming are made with tongue in cheek but the requirement that he and his experience questionable or not be there for damsels in distress and people in need of deliverance is no less urgently expected even so.

In any case her gamble was not a matter of the expectation of puritanic abstinence. Her gratuitously dismissive statement about that was what she said when she said what she said not about being good but being careful. A statement I have never been able to imagine myself making. But then are women ever really as insecure about such things as most men seem to be? Scandalous gossip aside to be sure. And even if it came to that, Miss You-Know-Who would never insist that the passing embarrassment of the deceived wife was as awful as the eradicable disgrace of the cuckold whose status as a father is forever in doubt.

So, the so-called double standard based on the assumption of the absolute equality of male and female options and prerogatives was not an issue for her or even a matter of serious discussion. But for you there was first of all the question of how long you could expect her to extend the amount of time required by the indefinite nature of your postcollegiate apprenticeship and travels.

At present she was still so deeply involved with her own obligations to the ancestral expectations of her hometown sponsors and potential clientele that your continued absence was actually a convenience. But for you it was all a gamble nevertheless. After all, there was also the undeniable matter of that which my old roommate, in the process of applying his notion of the inescapable necessity of taking calculated risks, used to call *the what if*'s that can never be answered until after the fact because they were precisely the ultimate means of measuring the skill, efficiency, and determination underlying good intentions against good fortune. *For yea verily, I say unto you, my dear Vatson, good intention without good fortune availeth naught in this man's league.*

Once upon a time indeed, he also liked to say. *But what about next time? What about this time? What if, my good fellow? What the hell if? That is the question, is it not, stated or not, that is always there, before, during, and after all undertakings. We're talking about the nature of things, to wit, the primordial actuality of things, my worthy fellow. Which brings us by a vicus of recirculation, commodious or not, back to the ultimate notion of entropy itself, does it not? And thereby also to the aboriginal assumption of adventure, without which, needless to say, there can be no story to tell.*

None of which was in direct reference to what you had going on with either Eunice Townsend or Jewel Templeton, neither one of whom he knew. You had mentioned Eunice Townsend in letters from time to time but mostly only casually and in passing. He had never seen her because when she came on campus, he had already transferred to Yale. About Jewel Templeton you had decided at the very outset not to mention her to anybody whomsoever. Not only because of all of the things that were said and signified by Joe States and Ross Peterkin the day after the night in Bel-Air following your first time in the Palladium, but also because to do so might give the impression that you were not yet up to taking such things in stride.

As for what Esther and Maurice made of my relationship to Jewel Templeton I still haven't really figured that out. They simply fell in line with it without ever missing a single beat. I was a young musician on leave of absence from the rhythm section of the world-famous orchestra of the Bossman Himself, and I was there in the studio apartment (also with run of the house) for the time being because I was an essential part of a new project that she had come to be preoccupied with beyond everything else since she came back from her most recent trip to Europe, and that was that. Every now and then she herself would say something about how much they liked and admired me. But for their part I was just simply accepted without any discernible reservation of any kind. No thinly disguised one-upmanship formality on the one hand, and no phony conspiratorial nods and winks on the other. I don't know what she told them about me, but by the end of my first week there, the casualness of our routine interactions was such that all of our verbal exchanges had already taken on a second chorus intimacy. No vamping around the bush. No ever so careful seguing into an unmistakable first chorus. You could begin with the second chorus with or without a vamp or segue and then move on to the out chorus, or skip to the out chorus. Or begin not with the second chorus but with the out chorus.

I never did find out whether they were surprised by the way things turned out with me and Jewel Templeton. If there was any surprise neither one showed any sign of it. Both took my exit almost as casually as they had taken my entrance. Almost but not quite. On my arrival they both shook hands with me and smiled as if to say, We don't know you but we know her, so we also know that you wouldn't be here if you're not somebody special. On my departure they both gave me a tight hug, patted my back, and held my hands as they looked me up and down at arm's length and then turned and left without a word; and I decided that they already knew why I was leaving so suddenly and that it was something they would never discuss with anybody.

XXXII

It was exactly one month after he gave me my copy of the screenplay that Eric Threadcraft left a message for me with the answering service. It was waiting for me when I called in late that Monday afternoon, and I drove over to his house the next morning.

It was nine forty-five when I turned into the yard and he was standing in the door wearing a faded red polo shirt, blue jeans, and rope soled shoes; and he was smoking a dip-bowl meerschaum pipe. He was letting his hair grow long. He pushed it back with one hand, holding the pipe with the other and said, Hi ya, fellow. How are you, really?

And I said, Nothing to me, Mice, as I stepped out of the auto incognito with the manuscript in the briefcase. And he said, It's a hell of a day to be working, as he pushed his hair back again and then shook my hand. I hope you don't mind too much.

The bougainvillea hung down from the overhead trellis. The yard was in full bloom. The sky was almost too bright and blue to look at. I followed him up the stairs to the sundeck and into the studio.

I really hope you don't mind, he said. And I said, Not at all. I was beginning to wonder when you'd call. And he said, This is the first free day I've had.

There was coffee, tea, rolls, and a big bowl of fruit on the sideboard; and he handed me a cup of tea. I skipped the Danish pastry. He poured himself a big ceramic cup of strong black coffee and refilled his pipe. Then he said, Well I certainly hope you've had better luck getting started than I have. I just simply haven't had any time at all. And I said, I don't know, but here it is such as it is. I unzipped the case and when he saw how thick the manuscript was he said, Say, fellow, you've been working. And I said, I started that next morning.

I handed him the lead sheets and he spread them on the piano and stood turning through them, his lips moving, his head nodding, his free hand waving the pipe like a baton. Then as he sat down to the keyboard and went on turning the pages he said, Say you really have been working. And I said, I just thought I'd try to see what I could do. And he said, You've got a whole thing here, fellow. And I said, I had the time. So I just kept on going. And he said, I'll say you did.

He turned back to the first page and sounded my opening chord, sustained it, and then sounded it again. I sat across the room with the shooting script and waited. He played the opening theme three times, studying it carefully, accenting with his head and then tossing his hair away from his forehead. I listened from where I was. And then, when he was ready he moved over and I sat beside him and we started at the beginning again.

He kept nodding to himself and I knew he was pleased and I thought about the Bossman Himself and Old Pro again and wondered what they would think about what I was trying to do. If you didn't have it all working together they would see right through you. They wouldn't knock your hustle, but I didn't want them to have to be nice to me about it. If the Bossman Himself liked it he would say, Hey, that was a pretty little thing you did. And if he liked it Old Pro would probably like it too and would probably say, I heard a couple of nice little tricky things in there, to which I would say, They probably came from you. I just hope I'm not distorting you. But if old Joe States or somebody else started talking about how much money you were making and about all the profitable new contacts you had, they didn't want to talk about the quality of the music at all.

I certainly didn't want anything like that to happen. Anything but that I thought. Not that I was worried about being too commercial for them. None of them would mind that at all as long as you got a few of your special licks in somewhere. Hey you hear my old States up there bootlegging all them old mammy-made riffs in there among all them dollars and cents. Boy, I don't know what's going to happen when them people wise up to the kind of stuff you're trying to put in the game.

Eric Threadcraft stood up, and I slid over to the center of the seat and went on playing, with him reading over my shoulder. Then he began walking back and forth across the room behind me, stopping every now and then to check the score against the shooting script. Then he came and stood in the curve of the piano listening and directing with his eyes closed and I went on plunking until he said, This is good news, fellow. This is great news.

He made another cup of tea for me and poured himself another cup of coffee and refilled his pipe and said, Say listen, man, I feel so good about all this I can't even work on it any more this morning.

I followed him out to the sundeck and saw the terrace and garden again. He pulled at his pipe and squinted against the sky. Then he turned to me and said, Look, fellow, maybe we can get out and take advantage of this fine weather after all. I know that an old smoothie like you always has something lined up, he said winking and pushing his hair back again. And I promised some people I'd come out to Malibu if we finished up here in time.

I had no idea that there would be this much time, he said. I was just hoping that you'd come up with something to get us started, and here we are in business and I haven't written one bar yet. So now let's see what I can come up with. Maybe a day at the beach is just what I need to get me going. Let's see what I can do before we get together again. Say in about a week or so. But meanwhile I think we have something pretty great already, I really do, fellow.

I don't think you realize what you've done, he said walking back and forth again as I got ready to leave. If we had to we could really start rolling tomorrow. All we really have to do is zoom in on the instrumentation a little more tightly.

I went on noodling and doodling around on the keyboard for a while every morning for the rest of that week just for the fun of it. And by the following Wednesday I found myself thinking as if I were back with the band playing for the Bossman Himself and Old Pro again. And that was when I began jotting things down with all of the instrumentation in mind, and that is how I started coming up with full band arrangements all by myself.

The first I did was a getaway stomp for Osceola Menefee, which I called "Seminole" because I wanted an Indian word to go with his first name and also because the Seminole was a legendary railroad line that I remembered tales about along with references to the Piedmont, the Atlantic Coast Line, and the Seaboard from fireside, swing porch, and barbershop tell-me-tale times. So I played around with train whistle riffs for the reed section and Florida palmetto swampland echoes for the trombones; and the solo line for Osceola Menefee's trumpet was based on an old train whistle blues that Luzana Cholly used to strum as he strolled his way up out of the L & N bottom in the twilight on his way to Miss Alzenia Nettleton's cook shop on Buckshaw Mill Road next door to Stranahan's General Merchandise store. I had old Joe States highballing and also taking care of the exhaust piston steam with his cymbals and brushes, and there were also parts for his mallets and the Indian tom-toms that a lot of drummers used in those days when some trap sets also used to include Chinese wood blocks. As for the locomotive arrival and departure bell and the ongoing punctuation, you could leave that open and any good blues oriented piano player would hit it right off, as would also be the case with the way he would share the chomping sound of the drivers with the bass player.

I felt that I had it well enough under control to set it aside by the weekend and when I ran through it again that next Monday morning I still liked it enough to move on to something else, and by noon I settled on one of old Herman Kemble's old gutbucket riffs, which I decided to try to expand into a background gospel shout for the whole band and call "Presiding Elder," because if I could get it right, I'd have old Bloop all set up for one of his surefire church rocking tenor sermons with the trumpets as his choir, the trombones following Fred Gilchrist's soulful call and response lead as his amen corner and the reeds as the organ; and this time the piano would ring church bells, not train bells and also suggest not gothic but down-home stained glass windows.

What I found myself moving on into next was a five-note twelve-bar blues riff that I decided to use as a frame for a string of five solo choruses, each beginning on a two-bar break (followed by a sharp pickup) and lasting twelve bars. The piano would begin things by plunking the riff figure three times over twelve bars of the steady four/four of the rhythm section and moving on to the channel, after which Otis Sheppard would lead off with a getaway train whistle guitar solo to be followed by Scully Pittman with Harmon mute and felt derby, following which would come Big Bloop's street corner woofing tenor, Malachi Moberly's trombone with plunger, and Old Pro on clarinet, which would take it to the ride out.

In a sense it was like routining a jam session, but even so it was also a basic way of composing what was in effect a homegrown equivalent to the European sonata, namely the instrumental, the structure of which is not based on exposition, development, and recapitulation, as is the so-called classical sonata, but rather on a series of choruses of various kinds (most often of either twelve or thirty-two bars each), which function like stanzas or chapters in a narrative.

Now that, as you and that fabulous freshman roommate of yours and my incredible marquis know very well, is what ad-lib theater is so very much about, Jewel Templeton said when I plunked and hummed and described and explained my way through it for her at the piano in the drawing room that night after dinner. I still had not made any mention of Eric Threadcraft's movie assignment because I didn't want her to start thinking about me in that context yet, but the three standard full band arrangements that I had just gotten up represented exactly the sort of workshop examples of the interplay of the arranger's overall control with individual improvisation (and impromptu obbligatos by sections as well) that she found so intriguing about jazz composition.

That was one reason I brought the score sheets along with me when I came down to dinner that night. The main reason I did so that particular night however was that I wanted to have somebody listen as I ran through what I had done. Because I wanted to check out how I felt going through it with somebody listening before I mailed everything off to Old Pro.

When I said what I said about how everybody in the band would already know what the overall voicing was, I also said that the composed parts of each solo were set up in character. And that was when she said it was not unlike growing up and learning how to drive Daddy's car. And I said, Somewhat like that but perhaps even more like learning to ride Daddy's special mount, given the band's long since all but organically conditioned response to his slightest whim and touch.

In other words when you set something up to be played by Ike Ellis, Ted Chandler, Fred Gilchrist, or anybody else in the lineup it was much the same as playing it on the keyboard of an organ designed by the Bossman Himself. The old joke about Joe States sneezing as soon as the bossman's nose began to itch is only a part of it. The other part is that Joe's sneeze just might become an official part of the orchestration, as was also the case with Herman Kemble's bloop, Ted Chandler's belly bellow, and so on.

I mailed all three sketches off to Old Pro in care of the home office in New York that next afternoon, and on Friday of the following week there was a telegram from Detroit that said: Shaking down nicely minor adjustments only before using on Chicago theater date week after next spot for Fred nice touch everybody says big ears check follows hope more where this came from.

XXXIII

Hey, man. Hey, this is great, man, Silas Renfroe said when I called the number he had left with my answering service the night before. Hey, great, just great. Then he said, Say now look here, man, what I was wondering about was if I could get you to help me out on a little out of town gig I got coming up. I was wondering if you could spare from Wednesday through Sunday, coming back by Monday night.

Then going on before I had time to make any response at all he said, Hey, man, I'm talking about Frisco, man. I'm talking about classy stuff, man. I'm talking about a real swanky joint. I'm talking about gourmet spareribs and chitlins à la Waldorf-Astoria, if you know what I mean. I'm talking about The Gray Falcon. Hey, man, I know that something like that is just another one among many in the kind of booking you're used to. But hey, man, I really would appreciate if you can see your way to helping me out.

And I said, Hey, man, I'm weak, man. I'd like to, man. But I have to check with a couple of people and get back to you later on today. Not later than tomorrow morning, I said. And he said, Hey, man. Oh, man. Great, man.

All I had to do was tell Jewel Templeton only as a matter of procedure, because I knew that she herself was all set to go down to La Jolla to visit friends for a few days including the weekend; and also as a matter of procedure I wanted to make sure that Eric Threadcraft and Felix Lovejoy got advance notice just in case they were not counting on my being out of town.

At the end of our opening set at The Gray Falcon up in San Francisco that Thursday night, the management had to limit our encores to seven minutes overall, because by that time the line of the sellout crowd for the second set stretched all the way around the corner; and the early arrivals for the third set were already beginning to form another line on the opposite side of the entrance.

Hey, man, Silas Renfroe began saying as soon as we were far enough into the first set for him to relax enough to look around and realize that there was a full house. Oh, man. Hey, man, is this us? In San Francisco? Hey, man, how am I going to believe some stuff like this? And this is just Thursday. Man, them cats back in L.A. are going to think I've been trying to hand them some kind of old Bay Area fish story, which you didn't really expect them to believe because you didn't really believe it yourself.

But believe it or not, that was the way it was to be right on through the entire weekend, and you also had all day every day all to yourself because the only numbers Silas Renfroe was calling were arrangements of his own that I had already sat in on at the Rumpus Room from time to time and didn't need to rehearse; and on the spot heads on blues changes and such standard surefire pop tunes as "All of Me," "Blue Skies," "Tea for Two," "Sweet Georgia Brown," and the like.

I already knew my way around downtown San Francisco from my first trip there with the band, when I had bought a map and a guidebook and started out at Civic Center and went to Museum of Art and when I came back outside into the hazy sunshine it was midday and I walked along Market Street, and from the sidewalks and the older shops you could tell that you were in an old seaport town even though you were not as near the waterfront as you would have been when you came along Government Street in Mobile or Canal Street in New Orleans.

That time, I had eaten lunch in a snack bar in Union Square and took a cable car up Powell Street to Nob Hill. Then I went to see Chinatown by daylight and came back and spent the rest of the afternoon looking into the shops along Post and Kearney streets and had bought myself a suede jacket in Abercrombie & Fitch and I also stopped in and had I. Magnin ship a silk scarf and a bottle of French cologne to Miss Eunice Townsend back you know where.

When I came back to the hotel nobody in the band was still around, and there were no messages. So I decided to study the map and guidebook and take a nap, and when Joe States woke me up to tell me that we were all going to Fisherman's Wharf for dinner before going to work it was as if he were pulling me away from a San Francisco of earlier banjo plucking ballroom piano times, when the old harbor was a thicket of clipper masts and sails as well as steamer stacks and an endless variety of smaller towing, rowing, and ferrying craft; and everywhere you looked along the gaslit streets teeming with carriages and stagecoaches there were amusement arcades, dance emporiums, music halls, and theaters, which presented everything from minstrels and vaudeville variety acts to Shakespearean and operatic stock company offerings.

The next morning of that first time in the Bay Area I had set out again with the itinerary that I had worked up from the guidebook and map and by the time we pulled out for the trip back east that last week I had gotten around to every site on my checklist. Afterward I had also finished reading Joe States's copy of Herbert Asbury's The Barbary Coast *before we came back to the Great Divide.*

So what I had planned to do during the short stand at The Gray Falcon with Silas Renfroe was to retrace as many of my steps as possible. But after the very first set that Thursday night the club manager brought Elliot Marchand backstage and that was when I was invited to spend the next day at his place.

I remembered his face and voice but not his name until he reminded me that I had been introduced to him by the Bossman Himself and that what the three of us had talked about was ragtime and Harlem stride piano music. Then he said that he had come by because when he read that I was back in town for a few nights he decided to find out if I would like to spend part of whatever free time I had tomorrow checking out his special collection of ragtime piano rolls on his 1912 vintage Steinway eighty-eight-note player piano.

Sounds great to me already, I said. And I also said anytime between breakfast and one hour before show time. And he said, Why not include breakfast? And I said, Why not? So by ten o'clock that Friday morning he had picked me up in his runabout and we were on our way across the Golden Gate Bridge to his place in Sausalito.

Alongside the player piano there was also a 1910 vintage eighty-eight-note upright regular piano. And at one end of the room there was a concert hall grand and at the other there was an old-fashioned country church organ. The two uprights were collector's items from Sedalia, Missouri. The grand was a local heirloom. The church organ had been brought west by a family from Georgia.

His wall to wall collection of records, transcriptions, and air checks was in an adjoining room, which he called the Amen Corner and which was where he usually spent most of his listening time. But which we were not to settle into until later that afternoon.

We spent the rest of the morning playing rolls by Scott Joplin, James Scott, Luckey Roberts, Jelly Roll Morton, and James P. Johnson; and when we were called for lunch we were joined on the terrace by Elliot Marchand's wife, Kimberly, who had just driven back from a committee meeting at the museum in Civic Center.

My guess was that like her husband she was in her middle to late forties but there was no gray in her sandy shoulder length mane and she had very friendly hazel eyes, and I was not surprised when I found out later on that she was one of the best dressed women in San Francisco.

I was also to find out that she spent thousands of dollars every year to help poets and painters and that the two of them also under-wrote art exhibitions as well as dance groups and music and dance per-formances on campuses and also in public concert halls. It was also sometime later on that I came to realize that the two of them helped to finance the publication of some of the noncommercial journals of the arts that I saw in their library that afternoon.

She shared her husband's enthusiasm for ragtime and stride piano music but the first thing she wanted to talk to me about during lunch that afternoon was what it was like to work that close to the Bossman Himself, which she said she hoped would not be a drag for me to go back over yet again; and I said, Not me, and told her how it had come about. And she said my account was entirely consistent with her con-ception of his creative genius.

When Elliot Marchand brought the conversation back around to Harlem stride piano music his wife also wanted to know what details about the menus and recipes typical of the old rent party spreads had passed along to me by people of that generation. And that led to ques-tions about eating your way across the country in a road band. That was when the three of us began to realize that we were becoming newly found food friends as well as music friends and that was why they drove me back into town early enough to change clothes and have dinner at one of their favorite restaurants before show time. And when they came backstage after the first set to say good-bye they made me promise to notify them of my next trip to San Francisco in advance so that they could take me for a tour of the vineyards in Napa Valley.

Silas Renfroe pulled back into Hollywood early that next afternoon and I had him let me out at Sunset and Fairfax and took a taxi. When I gave the driver the address he looked at my instrument and suit bag and said You play up that way much? and I said, I guess you could say that. I don't know what he thought was in the overnight bag, probably something to go with my act.

Beverly Hills, he said. They have some wild parties up in here, and you musicians get to see it all up close. Say now that's something, that's really something. You could learn a lot of fancy tricks up in this neck of the woods.

Hey here we go right here, my man, I said. And he said, Well all right. This is going to be a good one I can tell. And I said, Keep the change. And he said, Hey, yeah, well thanks old buddy, and good luck and remember, see no evil, hear no evil, speak no evil, but I don't have to tell you. And I don't have to tell you to keep tabs on the kitty either.

Jewel Templeton was still in La Jolla and Maurice was taking the day off so the only one at home was Esther and she was getting ready to leave on an errand to downtown L.A. when I arrived. I decided to stay in and raid the pantry and read some more about San Francisco as I waited for the call I expected from La Jolla. And I also decided not to get in touch with Eric Threadcraft until that next morning.

XXXIV

When I couldn't get Eric Threadcraft on the telephone by that next afternoon, I called Felix Lovejoy, and as soon as you heard his voice you could tell that things were going much better than he had ever let himself even hope they would. Not that he didn't have high horizons of aspiration, but his immediate expectations were always based on practical considerations rather than wishful thinking.

There's that man, he said as he always did when he had good news. How was the trip, old buddy? I've been waiting to hear from you since last night. Eric is in Europe. Things are happening, my man. Fantastic things. Uptempo and splitting. I mean really, I mean quantum leaps. Incredible! Looks like we're just about in there, good buddy. And I do mean there.

And when I said, Hey I'm listening, man, so hey lift the veil, man, he said, Not over the phone. You free tonight? And I said, Nothing yet. And he said, So let me buy you a fancy dinner and clue you in. And I said, That's all right with me. And he said, About eight. And I said, Fine. And he said, Benvenuto's okay with you? And I said, So long as it's your money, man. And he said, Correction. Corporation money, man. See you between eight and eight-thirty.

You could always depend on him to be on time, so when I came through the door at Benvenuto's at exactly eight he was already there leaning on the piano holding a drink and listening to Curtis Howard, who was working as a single at that time and who when he saw Felix Lovejoy and me nodding at each other segued into a few bars of the intermission band call riff of the Bossman Himself and winked at me and then went on to the next chorus of his cocktail lounge variations on "Dream a Little Dream of Me."

On the way through the main dining room, which was already two-thirds full, I saw several people I knew by sight and one couple waved for me to join them at their table and when I indicated that I was already with somebody they smiled, applauded silently, and blew kisses as I followed Felix Lovejoy and the maître d' on out to the terrace.

From our table you could see the lights and the traffic along Sunset Boulevard, and across the busy intersection was Schwab's famous drug store. And I could also see all the way to the curve of Crescent Heights Boulevard, where I had parked the auto incognito. It was his treat and choice of restaurant so I said I would go along with his recommendations from the menu and we began by sharing an order of clams Vasto style (Arselle alla maniera di Vasto), and he suggested that I try the quail en polenta and for himself he selected rabbit gourmet style (lepre alla maniera dell ghiottone), which he was to insist that I sample and there was also a huge green salad for the two of us.

We talked about San Francisco until the clams were served. Then he turned to the business at hand, and that was when he said what he said about the corporation, which he said was primarily a moneymaking proposition, but which would be no less effective as a device for career development, because it would stand for high quality as well as something very much in demand.

Because that's what this town works on, getting to something that is in demand. So why not us? My job will be to make it us.

Okay. So we're already beginning to be a team, right? So now we become a corporation, which stands for professional teamwork. Professionally organized and programmed teamwork that adds up to big time production under one made-up name that we promote into a brand name with its own trademark. If you know what I mean. Whatever name we finally choose, which as you and I know could really just simply be Eric Threadcraft, as in Eric Threadcraft, Inc., because as of now that's what our first buyers are going to think whatever name we choose stands for anyway. Because he's already perceived as up and coming. But

Eric doesn't feel that would be fair to you given how he feels about your creative input and editorial say-so. And I agree. But on the other hand he also had to admit that coupling your name with his at this stage of the game would not add anything to his market value. So we decided to go along with long established Hollywood practice and propose a screen name and what he came up with for a start was Youngblood, Inc. Ernest Youngblood, Inc. Ernest Youngblood of Maestro Music, Inc. Which is not bad when you consider the riff he's playing on that Ernest Hemingway crack about maestro that you're always pulling on him.

Inside, Curtis Howard was playing around with "Three Little Words." Across the street at Schwab's Drug Store clusters of young and hopeful actors, writers, studio technicians stood around talking near some convertibles and motorcycles at the curb, some around the entrance and along the showcases in both directions. As I looked at them, the first thing they reminded me of was the autumn of my sophomore year and how it was when you came along the walk from the clock tower and the music hall at the upper end of the campus to the block where the Varsity Drag was. Then what came back to mind were the drug store blocks as you saw them in the early evening as the band bus made its way from town to town and coast to coast. *Soda fountain U.S.A.*, I thought. Mostly with the same movie magazines along with whatever else in the line of pop fare.

As I said, Felix Lovejoy said, It's only a proposition. So it depends on the agreement of the parties concerned, and naturally that depends on how you really feel about the overall thing at the very outset. Hey, but wait a minute, he said, I said this was supposed to be a money proposition and here I am about to get the cart before the horse. The basic proposition is the split. And what we're proposing is fifty, thirty, twenty for Eric, you, and me in that order.

You don't have to answer now. All I'm supposed to be doing is giving you something to think about. That's what Eric had in mind and as I know you fully understand, the only reason he's not here doing this himself is this European thing, which happened so fast all he had time to do was get on over there.

This is just to alert you to what looks to us like a more professional way of handling the kind of really big time stuff we're beginning to get into. No more freelancing. We'd like to be able to deal in corporate terms. It carries a bigger impact when you talk with a corporate budget in the equation.

I said I would think about it. And he said I wish I could tell you when Eric is going to be able to make it back. But right now he really doesn't know how long this Paris, Rome thing is going to take. He just knows it's worth the time, and he will clue us in as soon as he gets back because that is most likely to be the sort of thing that he wants a corporate setup to handle.

I said okay. I said, But don't forget this music scene is something that I'm just into for the time being. Not that I have a definite cutoff point in mind yet, I said. But I don't see myself as being in for the long haul either. Not as a full time professional, I said. And he said, We'll see about that, good buddy. We'll see about that. We'll cross that bridge when we come to it.

Then as we slapped palms outside on the sidewalk before I headed for the auto incognito, he said, Got any club dates? And I said, There's always the Keynote on weekends. And he said, Whenever you want to line up something else just let me know. Eric and I are always good for local spots in this part of town. Just give a buzz.

And I said, You bet.

XXXV

I came cruising along West Adams and turned into Crenshaw and the first thing I saw when I pulled into the parking lot behind the Home Plate (as in down-home plate and home cooking) was Gaynelle Whitlow's robin's egg blue convertible. I came through the restaurant and saw her sitting in the bar.

She was alone in a booth near the jukebox, and I recognized the medium tempo instrumental blues that I had made with Radio Red not long after I began freelancing. I had a copy of it along with everything else I had recorded, but that was my first experience of walking in and hearing myself thumping in a place like that. She looked up and saw me and waved. She was wearing dark glasses and her hair was swept up and her earrings were large hoops of brass. I went toward her walking deliberately out of time with myself on the jukebox.

Hey, where you been, home boy, she said. And I said, Across town. I gave her an exaggerated show biz kiss on each cheek and stood back and looked her up and down and she pretended to ignore me. Then she cut her eyes at me with her hands on her hips, and then she smiled and said, Somebody said you were still out here. What you been doing with your cute down-home self around this big old ultrafrantic hick town?

Making records and trying to learn how to scratch out a few charts, I said. And she said, Well good. Well nice. Well fine. Sit down. And I slid into the booth beside her. She was sipping a margarita, which she let me taste, and I ordered one for myself and another one for her.

The jukebox played on, and beyond the music you could hear that hum and buzz of the other conversations and the sound of clinking flatware that all dining rooms seem to have in common. I looked around but I didn't see anybody I knew.

Hey, you seen Ross Peterkin? I asked. And she said, Not lately. I think he must be down around Acapulco or somewhere like that. He's got himself some new thing going. And the last time I saw him he was doing a lot of talking about a boat, so I figured he and whoever she is must be down there somewhere cruising around. You know that Ross.

Somebody played another number by Radio Red, and there I was again dragging the beat so that the atmosphere would be honky tonk cozy enough to suggest a down-home menu. There was a piano, bass, and drum opening and when we hit the second chorus she stopped talking and started snapping her fingers soundlessly, moving her head and shoulders ever so slightly, and humming the background accents. Then there was a break, then the other sections came in and faded away for the vocal.

Ray Red, she said. Old crazy Ray Red. He may be full of stuff but he can sure get down with some good old good time blues when he wants to. And when I said, You see him around anywhere? she said, Not over this way. I think they're still out at that place off Central. And when I said, What about Silas Renfroe? she said, I saw him the other day. He told me about that great gig you all had up in San Francisco. I don't think they're in the Rumpus Room. You playing over somewhere this way tonight?

I shook my head slowly from side to side looking at her until she spoke again. Which is when she said, So what are you doing over in this neck of the woods? Looking for some of your kinfolks? And I said, Looking for you. And she said, You guys. She said, You guys in that band. And when I said, I'm not in that band anymore, she said, Don't make no difference. She said, You were in there long enough.

I don't know what you're talking about, I said. Then I said, I was just cruising around hoping I would run into you. And here you are the very first one I see. And she said, See there. There you go. You know where I live and I distinctly remember giving you my phone number, because everybody ain't so lucky. To which I said, Yeah baby, but I didn't know whether or not you would remember me. And she said, Look you can't help it can you? Once you've been around with that band and all them thugs you're ruined for life.

I really don't know what you're talking about, I said. And she looked at me laughing. And while I was trying to look puzzled, the waiter came back and I ordered another round of drinks. There was a jump number playing on the jukebox then and she started snapping her fingers again, her head tilted, her big earrings dangling, her leg brushing time against mine under the table. I thought about that night at the Vineyard. But I didn't say anything.

So you got out there and forgot all about me, huh, she said. And I said, You know better than that. And she said, Ways and actions, that's what I go by. Ways and actions. And forgetting myself I said, You know something very special I remember about you? And she said, Tell me anything. Boy, you didn't think about the likes of me until you walked in here just now and saw me.

Your hands, I said.

My what?

Your hands, I said. You have hands like a princess. And you know something else? You've got a lot of regal stuff going anyway. Elegant stuff.

And she said, So now you're going to try to pull some of that fay boy stuff on me too, huh? Or is that just some of that college boy stuff? And I said, You know better than that, baby. And that's when she said, Well you know I heard all that. All that African queen stuff, all that Coptic princess jive. Hey you know something else? I'm so regal I'm supposed to be a regal fritillary.

A regal what-illary? I said. And she held her unlit cigarette out at an angle turning her hand and tapping it on the ashtray with her fore-finger. A regal fritillary, she said and she pointed to the pin she was wearing. It was shaped like a butterfly.

I was going with this fay cat from out at Caltech. He was an archi-tect but he also had this freakish thing about butterflies. Sometimes we would be driving somewhere in the country and this big hairy butt clown would stop the car and grab that little goddamn fancy net that was always on the backseat and take off across the field like he had bees at his bottom or something. You know what that butterfly stuff is called, I said. And she said, some crossword puzzle sounding name. And when I said, Lepidopterology, she said, No better for him.

Then she said, He also had a freakish thing going for Billie Holiday and you know flesh and blood singers and dancers, no clothes on. I don't know, maybe his papa snuck up to the Cotton Club one night and came home and got his mama pregnant on the afterbeat. Anyway one night he was taking me to eat at this place out on the Strip and he kept saying, They'll think you're an exotic entertainer. You know you really could be from the Middle East. And I finally said, I don't want them to think that. I want them to think you're a rich businessman and I'm your secretary, like in *Esquire* magazine. He never did get that. I bet you every time he remembers me he thinks I want to be a dumb blonde. Some fay boys. I'm telling you, home boy. Almost as bad as some boot cats I know.

Hey, it sure is good to see you, I said, hooking my arm in hers. And as I looked at her cutting her eyes at me like that again, I knew that she was also pleased to see me. Then she said what she said.

Tell me anything, she said, half pouting half smiling. You know. Down-home girl. Way out here all by herself. Green. You know what I mean. A well-stacked country girl, frantic, and cute enough so we don't have to hide her, but not in the class with them sophisticated Fisk and Spelman girls, them Bennett College cuties, them Howard hincties. You know what I mean. Big time musician, girls all across the country, schoolgirls begging for your autograph. Blondes and brunettes climbing all over each other trying to get to you. Rich bitches swelling your head. Any old line for the likes of me. If you happen to run into me.

I know you know I know better than that, I said. I was still holding her arm. She held her head back from me. But she had to stretch her eyebrows above her dark glasses to keep from smiling. And I could tell she was having fun playing with me.

I'm the one don't know no better, she said. I'm the one, you know, they got me out of the back country a long time ago, but there's always a chance they ain't got all of the back country out of me yet. And as I tried to snuggle up to her again, I said, Hey what you brought out of the country, baby, is exactly what makes the city the city. She looked at me and shook her head again, making that down-home big mama noise of disapproval with her tongue and teeth.

You really can't help it, that's all there is to it. It's that band. It's that man. Turning all of his little half-smooth children loose on the nation. Then she opened her purse and refreshed her lipstick and said, Come on here, smoothie. And I called the waiter and paid for the drinks.

But hey, wait. Are you sure they don't have you over here looking for people to pick cotton in another one of them Gone with Scarlett O'Hara movies, she said. And I said, No, m'am, not me. No days like that. And she said, You know there really was some little half hip fay boy over here a few months ago trying to get on sometime with all that old stuff about recruiting extras. They used to pull that stuff. Boy, how they used to pull that stuff. But that last clown never did find out that anybody could have scored with them lushes he was getting with all that whiskey he was buying. Girl, I said, talking about that band. You can swap lies with anybody in that band any time.

That's when she said, That's all right about that. So you want to run with me tonight, huh? Boy, if they ever find out that you're out here playing around with Gaynelle Whitlow they'll never let you back in college. They won't even let you into barbers' college. And when I said, That's all right about college—I got their college; she said, Well, you know what I was sitting here getting ready to do when you walked in. I was just getting ready to go home and pull off my shoes and put on a stack of dirty low-down blues and get in the kitchen and cook me a good old home folks meal and sit right down and eat it barefooted. Some hogmeat, some black-eyed peas, some thin corn bread, some finger collards and okra. That's exactly what I'm going to do tonight. So, you still want to run with me? And I said, I just hope I got here in time to get my name in the pot. And she said, and also I also have the fixing for a sweet potato pie. All I've got to do is mix it.

———

We came outside and she saw the auto incognito and stopped in mock surprise and started nodding her head from it to me. I walked on over to it and opened the door and started rolling the windows down. Hey nice, she said. And I said, I'll be right behind you. But still looking the auto incognito up and down, she said, Yeah, very nice, home boy. You're doing all right for yourself out here.

So I said, don't lose me now. And she got into the convertible and backed out and waited and I pulled out into Crenshaw Boulevard and trailed her. We crossed Santa Barbara Avenue and stopped at a supermarket and came on toward Vernon Boulevard. It was almost seven o'clock then and there was the starless twilight sky above the six lane traffic, the neon signs, and the pale street lamps. I drove watching for her turn indicator.

She was living in View Park in those days. I followed her up the hill and along the winding tree-lined street and turned into the driveway behind her. She pulled all the way into the carport and came back toward me, arching her neck and making eyes at the auto incognito again.

So you've got yourself some fancy wheels, she said. And as I got out with the shopping bags, I said, Just something I borrowed. And she said, I thought maybe you were getting ready to start hauling your own little combo around or something. And I said, What kind of old chickenbutt combo? And she said, I don't know. I figured maybe you were getting your own little combo together by now, you being an ambitious college boy and all that. Now if you were still back down the way I might think you just got yourself a little red wagon, a little yellow basket for some of that kind of action. But I know good and well you don't need nothing like that out here.

That was when I told her who the station wagon belonged to and I said I was driving it because she wanted somebody to put some more miles on it and it was just what I needed to get my instrument to and from work. As we came on across the walk to the house I told her about how I met Jewel Templeton at the Keynote. Then I started talking about Eric Threadcraft.

The apartment was on the second floor, and as we came into the living room I saw the black and tan batik draperies and a long low couch and batik pillows. There were also hassocks and three fanback rattan chairs. Two Siamese cats lay curled on a large flokati rug. A snow white Persian padded in from the bedroom and started rubbing itself against her legs, its back arching, its mouth making soft meows.

This is Kitty Boo, she said. And this is Kitty Doo Doo and this is Mr. Skatrosantalango.

The base of the huge lamp on the long, ebony coffee table in front of the couch was a bronze cast of two entwined Hindu dance figures, one male and one female, of course. There were also several busts and torsos of Gaynelle herself on other surfaces around the room. And there were three large oils and a number of expensively framed sketches of her decorating the walls.

Here's this new thing old big butt Gomer put out, she said, holding up the album as she turned on the record player. And I said, I haven't heard old Gomer in months. And she said, And here's old Zonk. And I said, I've met him a couple of times, but I've never played with him. But I did jam with old Gomer one night in Greensboro, North Carolina.

She turned, snapping her fingers to the music, and I followed her through the dining area and into the kitchen. And the first thing she did was make a long cold fruit punch and then she started dinner. And I slid into the padded breakfast nook by the window. She moved about nodding her head to the music. It was dark outside now and beyond the sloping backyard you could see down the hill and out across the lights at the Crenshaw Shopping Center and Linet Park.

So, she said. Jewel Templeton. Is she supposed to be on some kind of music kick or something? And I said, She's got a lot of deep stuff going about the blues. Artistic stuff. Philosophical stuff. And she said, What kind of old philosophical stuff? I thought she was still trying to break into high society. And I said, One of her high society friends is a French marquis who collects all kinds of flesh and blood music.

The phone rang. She answered in the bedroom and while she was talking I had a chance to move around the living room and look at the pictures. In one large oil painting she was a Coptic princess, in another she was an odalisque, and in a third she was a dancer with her breasts bare and her hair done up in a topknot and she was wearing a banana skirt à la Josephine Baker at the Folies Bergère. On most of the drawings and sketches she was either a dancer or a torch singer. There was also a long collage made of light and shadow photographs of her posing nude.

She came back in and saw me looking at the watercolor near the record player. It was titled "Miss Georgia Brown" and it showed her walking along a Harlem sidewalk and in the background there was some abstract design representing the Savoy Ballroom, the Apollo Theatre, and Lenox Avenue north from 135th Street.

How about that stuff! she said smiling and shaking her head. She had changed into a blue gingham dress and as I followed her back into the kitchen I said, So you model some too. And she said, Well in a way, I guess. Somebody's always coming up with some weird idea about what I really look like. A guy named Django did the one you were just looking at. He did some of those little things too. He's always after me to let him sketch me. It's a wonder you haven't run across him by now. He is a real freak about flesh and blood music, she said. And I said, I know about him. I saw him in a studio one night. 7000 Santa Monica. And shaking her head she said, I don't know. Then she started to say something else and stopped and said, I don't know.

I sat looking at her moving about the kitchen in her flat house shoes, her apron nipping her waist like that and suddenly it was almost like seeing old frizzly headed Creola Calloway again, who used to break everyone's heart in Gasoline Point doing that same brown-legged, sweeteyed, sweetmeat, gold-smiling walk, going to the store in her pink bedroom mules, a thin five dollar gold piece on a chain around her left ankle.

She put the pork on, washed and picked greens, made the corn bread, and started mixing the potato pie. She sat on a high chair with the big old fashioned crockery mixing bowl in her lap, her head tilted, her earrings dangling, her cigarette drooping to one side, her eyes squinting against the curling smoke. So that's what you're doing these days, she said. Putting some more miles on it for Jewel Templeton. She kept a straight face and went on creaming the potatoes. And when I said, Hey, is it all right to leave it in the driveway like that? She nodded and smiled and said, They don't call you Schoolboy for nothing, do they? And I said, Joe States started that stuff the day I joined the band. And she said, See there, he knew you were an all-American genius. And I said, He knew I was just coming out into the world and that I had a lot to learn. And she said, A chick like Jewel Templeton can do a lot for you. I know you know that. That's why I know you're smart. Ain't no telling what I could be by now if I had your education. And that Ross Peterkin, he could be an ambassador or something.

She made the piecrust and I watched her put the design around the edge with the fork, remembering Gasoline Point again. Whenever I start thinking about how good old fashioned sweet potato pies can really be, I always found myself remembering how they used to taste on Saturday afternoons at Miss Alzenia Nettleton's cookshop next to Stranahan's store if you got there before they were all gone. And there was also Miss Pauline's cookshop in Gin's Alley, where you could also get the best blackberry pie in season. You could go on and on about Gasoline Point and sweet potato pies. There was Miss Nicey Tompkins, who used to pass our house on her way to Buckshaw Corner balancing one basketful on her head and carrying one basketful in each hand. Then there was Octavia Wilcox, who used to have to make her mix in a big dishpan because Old Buttheaded Tom Wilcox used to lean crosslegged in the kitchen door and eat as many as three before he would move, folding them like apple turnovers as fast as they were cool enough to come out of the pans. And of course there was also Mama. She didn't have to back away from anybody making sweet potato pies either. But she made them only for special occasions like Thanksgiving, Christmas, and church suppers. What she was always making were the best syrup bucket teacakes and ginger bread muffins in the world.

But sweet potato pies, sweet potato pies, sweet potato pies. And then there were sweet potato pones, which were even rarer than fruitcakes used to be. Everybody including Miss Nicey backed away from

Miss Alzenia Nettleton when it came to making sweet potato pones. Not only everybody in Gasoline Point. Everybody in that part of Alabama. After all, not only had she cooked for the governor, but governor's wives still sent for her to come all the way to Montgomery just to make sweet potato pones for one of their fancy banquets.

Hey, you really do kind of go for bad in the kitchen, I said to Gaynelle Whitlow. And she said, Yeah, bad. Ain't no use me trying to deny it. And I said, Spices aside I could tell by the way you move. And she said, I could tell by the way you move too, cutie pie. But you know, like I say. Tell me anything. But what I'm thinking is what I'm thinking about what's happening. Boy, you ain't driving that station wagon around just because Jewel Templeton just found out about flesh and blood music.

That was when she went on telling me what she had started telling me about herself and Hollywood. She was twenty-six years old and had not been married and didn't intend to be. Not any time soon, at any rate. She had been living in California since she was twenty-one. She had left Mississippi on her nineteenth birthday and had spent a year with an aunt in Chicago and sometime with another aunt in Cleveland. Then she had gone to New York and worked in a beauty salon for a year and saved enough money to pay her way out to the West Coast.

She had started out working in a beauty shop on Central Avenue and also taken a clerical course and worked at the Golden State Mutual Insurance Company about six months, after which she had helped to manage a little dress shop. Then, because she also knew how to sew (both of her aunts were seamstresses), she worked in the fitting department of a specialty shop on Wilshire Boulevard, from which she had gone into a fashion designer's establishment in Beverly Hills.

When I asked her if she had ever tried to get into the movies, she said, Believe it or not, and maybe you won't, but I could be in movies. By one means or another. I'll tell you about that sometime. Boy I can tell you some things and with your college education we could write a book.

———

When everything was ready to come off the stove we served our plates and I slid back into the padded nook facing her. She bowed her head and whispered a blessing. Then she picked up her knife and fork and winked at me as her bare feet touched my leg under the table. Then she went on talking.

The first white man I ever got tied up with in my life was a big and I mean big *rich* Hollywood producer, she said. He came in to talk to my boss about some designs we were working on for one of his movies and he saw me and flipped right there in front of everybody. You know how some fay guys start carrying on with all of that two-finger old ooh and aah artistic stuff and get all toted away when they see something they like. He came running up to me with his neck and ears getting all red talking about setting me up for a screen test. And I just looked at him. I had already been out here too long to fall for that kind of bull hype. But he was really gone on me and he kept on calling me and started sending me all kinds of expensive stuff. And I finally started seeing him and I had to quit that job so he set me up in one of those fine apartments that looked like it came right out of his Technicolor movies about the smart set and stuff.

There wasn't a cheap bone in him, and he was really straight about wanting to put me on the screen too, she said. He was always outlining some story and telling me about the part he wanted me to do, and sometimes he used to bring all kinds of fancy costumes by from the studio wardrobe and have me model them while he described scenes that I could wear them in. He had ideas for all kinds of stuff. Night-clubs, harems, slave ships, pirates' coves, Creole balls, South Sea islands. And he was sure enough toted out about that old African queen jungle princess stuff. Wait till I show you some of the wild jewelry he used to bring me. You saw those big paintings in there. He's the one that had them done.

What happened about the movies? I said. And she said, I told him I didn't want to be no actress. I told him if I was going to be in show business I could have been on the stage a long time ago. I got all kinds of show people right in my family. Folks in my family been in some of everything from the medicine shows and the riverboats to the Cotton Club and Paris, France. And I can sing and dance myself and know it. I just ain't going to be no stage entertainer. That's all. You know something? I've been hearing about California and dreaming about coming out here to Los Angeles all my life, but I didn't realize that Hollywood and Los Angeles were in the same place until I got out here. I just didn't. I just didn't care that much about it. I really don't care all that much about the movies. I never did. I used to go and I used to read the magazines just like most of the girls. But I was always more interested in the clothes and the places and the houses and all of that.

So why should I want to try to be an actress? she said as we went to get second servings of everything. There I was in the money and living like that just because I was who I was. Just because I was a fine woman. Just because I was me. You know something I always used to do? I used to walk through all the swankiest stores in town and just look at the chicks who were buying all the best stuff. I used to do that back home. I used to do it in Chicago. I used to do it in Cleveland and I did it in New York. I used to just look at them and wonder who they were. And it was always the same old story. They were just women. Every now and then you might see one that was famous but just every now and then. Most of them that you saw in those places every day were just women with the right kind of man. And it's the same thing out here. And it's the same thing when you look at all them fine houses and apartments. Even in Beverly Hills, most of the people living in all them fine places out there ain't no more famous than me and you.

So what finally happened? I said, not considering the point she had just made until later on. And she said, He had to break it off for his health. After all, he was in his middle fifties and had not had that much of that kind of action before. Naturally he had been playing around with some of his young actresses a little, every now and then. But he was really just a middle-aged family man with a couple of grown-up children. He had everything under control when we started out. He'd come around two or three times a week and sometimes he'd spend the weekend. He'd come by and relax, play his kind of music, and tell me about all kinds of interesting things.

Then something happened and all of a sudden he was getting all frantic on me and starting to act like he just found out what it was made for, and he oversported his constitution. I still don't know whether it was really me or something to do with his work or his home life. But he started spending as much time as he could around me and then he started coming down with all kinds of ailments. I hate to sound country but I really do think rich folks get all kinds of diseases other folks never heard tell of.

We finished the main course of the meal and while the coffee perked, I helped her wash and put away the dishes. Then she took a tray with the pie and dessert plates and coffee cups into the living room and I brought the coffeepot. She was about to go on with the story but when I tasted the slice of potato pie she handed me, I held up my finger and said, Hey, this pie is as good as it looks. You really are some cook. You really are some girl, lady. And she said, I do like to hear that kind of stuff. I guess all women do. But you know something? I really am a bitch in the kitchen. I just flat am. I was just brought up that way. I used to fix one of my good old dinners for old stuff every now and then and knock him dead. And he knows about good cooking from all around the world. I'll just fix some old down-home something every now and then. Not often enough to give him any ideas about having himself a cutie pie who'd double as Aunt Jemima. Anyway the first time he just happened to come in on me fixing it for myself and I didn't make it no better or worse and he kept talking about how good it was smelling. And so that's how that started. And he really was a very sweet guy.

I didn't intend to cut in on you, I said. So what happened? And she said, He had to retire. He was in the hospital for a while and then he decided to move to Italy. She sat silent for a moment picking at what was left of her wedge of pie with her fork. Then she went on. When the time came to go you know what he did? He called me and offered to set me up in my own business. I had mentioned something about having my own little beauty shop or maybe my own style shop one time. And he remembered that. I told him I wasn't ready to start on anything like that yet and he said he was having his lawyer set up a nest egg for it anyway. And I have the papers right over there in that drawer.

We finished the coffee and she took the tray back in the kitchen and came back holding up a plain old fashioned flat pint hip flask of what was obviously a kind of down-home bootleg corn whiskey.

Hey, what's this? I said stretching my eyes. And she said, Boy, I'm on this kick tonight. And she put another stack of records on the turntable and came back and sat on the couch beside me and poured me a single and herself a double and we settled back with the Hammond organ, guitar, bass, and drum quartet playing a walking blues in the background. She sipped her drink and I tasted mine and waited for her to go on.

He was a sweet one, she said. Of course everybody I ever had anything to do with like that was really nice to me. But this guy was just kindhearted. He sure didn't owe me anything after all the other stuff he had given me. You know what I mean? But boy, the next guy. Like I say, they were all nice to me, but I can tell you some pretty funny stuff too. I met this next guy at a party for the guys in the Count Basie band one night. He couldn't dance a little bit. But he was one more fine looking thing. He was in his middle thirties and he had black hair with specks of fresh gray in the temples. In a way he kind of reminds you of a Spanish bullfighter, except that he was a bigger kind of guy and he wasn't built that neat. He was also collegiate looking. He wore those heavy black rimmed college boy eyeglasses and he dressed kind of like you.

He really was one low more no dancing cat, but he kept trying and he kept saying he was having himself the time of his life and it was all because of me and well, you know. So we get out to his place about six o'clock that next morning. And I looked up and there was this great big old delta plantation house sitting up there facing down toward Coldwater Canyon. Big old white columns, honeysuckle vines, mag-

nolia trees, and all. I guess they were honeysuckle and magnolias. I'm
sure they were the nearest thing you could find to the real thing. I bet
you that.

Then when we got inside there were all kinds of old Civil War
stuff everywhere. All kinds of slavery time stuff framed up like art. A
large full length picture of Robert E. Lee with the Confederate flag on
one side and the Virginia flag on the other was the first thing you saw
when you came into the ballroom size living room. And when you
stepped into the dining room there was old Stonewall Jackson. I didn't
say anything. I just kept checking all that stuff. And when you looked
out into the backyard there was all kinds of old corny Stephen Foster
stuff all scattered around. You know, all that old wrought iron stuff and
all them old trees under the care of tree surgeons. The swimming pool
had so many weeping willows drooping around it that it looked like the
Swanee River.

You know what he turned out to be? A rich *and again, I mean very
rich* city boy. And he was on that kick because he really believed he had
missed a big part of the fun of being an American white man because
he hadn't grown up on a plantation down in the good old Deep South
with a lot of us folks surrounding him.

Oh yeah, I know all that old stuff, I said. And then I said, You
know I can still remember how folks used to talk about stuff like that
saying, The first thing some white people do as soon as they get
enough money to pay the rent and start eating regular is go out and
hire a bunch of the *folks* to be around them. And she said, Yeah I know
about that too. But this cat is all tangled up in a way I personally had
never seen before. He had his whole life all tangled up in it. He's supposed to be one of the biggest consulting experts out here for any kind
of production about the South. That's what he got his degrees in. He's
got a whole library full of southern stuff. And right in the middle of it
stretching away from his work desk is a long sand table where he can
lay out any battle needed for a Civil War movie.

What does he look like? I said. Don't tell me he goes around
looking and acting like a Mississippi riverboat gambler on his way to

New Orleans. And she said, No. He isn't that kind of guy at all. Like I said, he's a college looking guy. You know, he's been to Harvard, Yale, and Princeton. And the University of Virginia. And you know something? He'll believe just about anything if he can find enough about it in some books. And he wouldn't believe something he's looking right at, touching, smelling, tasting, or even fucking until he found out what the big book authorities had to say about it. Look. Sometimes he'd start out on some long line of that old unreconstructed moonlight and molasses stuff about what the South was really all about or something like that, and every time I tried to set him straight he would look at me with that little grin like I couldn't possibly know anything about it at all and start talking about what's your authority, what's your source, what's your secondary source, and what's your primary source? And I would say, Man, I'm my own authority. Man, I was born knowing better than all that old stuff you talking about. I said, You talking about where I was bred and born and raised. That's my primary source and common sense is my ultimate authority.

Too bad he didn't grow up around some of us folks, I said. It really might have been good for him. And besides, I looked at her and winked and said, If you're going to mess around with this stuff, best you get started early.

But the main thing about him, she said, ignoring my wink, is that he is really a nice guy. I mean really nice. He doesn't believe in any of that old Jim Crow stuff at all and never has. Let me tell you something. He used to take me almost everywhere. We used to eat all up and down the Strip and across La Cienega and we walked into the first class clubs and have tables as good as any movie stars, and if anybody ever even looked like they wanted to question it he'd turn the place out and pay for it. But wait a minute, what I didn't tell you was that all that old consulting stuff is really just a hobby. He definitely don't need the money. I'm talking about the kind of rich boy that could buy the whole joint just to fire the waiter.

Well, as I was saying, he didn't take any foolishness at all about anything like that. But then when we would get back home, he would always want to try to get one of his old weird games going again. And when I said, What kind of old weird games? She said, Bedroom games. Historical bedroom games.

Well. The first one he pulled he just wanted me to take all my clothes off and stand on a hassock and he would just walk around looking at me stroking his chin and feeling me. Another one he used to like was to come up behind me as soon as I stepped out of all my clothes and tie a maid's apron on me with a hundred dollar bill in each pocket. All kinds of stuff like getting in bed wearing a big wide West Indian straw hat and smoking a long black cigar with a bottle of rum on the floor. Or sometimes it might be a little thing like me letting him tear my panties off. Or me putting on a pair of old fashioned mammy made drawers he got from the studio wardrobe department.

And one night I woke up about three o'clock and there he was trying to handcuff me to the bed, she said. And I said, Hey come on, Gaynelle, not really. Come on. And she said, Why would I lie about something like that? Then she said, He wasn't really trying to start anything rough or anything like that. He was just trying out something he read about or probably had come across in a script he was working on. It wasn't rough. It was really funny to me. I mean funny as hell because the cat was wearing a goddamn patch over one eye. And one silk scarf tied around his head and one around his goddamn waist.

Well what did you finally do about him? I said. And she said, I had to put him down. And I said, What happened? And she said, I don't know. All kinds of weird stuff. In the first place he started getting more and more jealous of my musician friends. Now remember now, after all this cat met me at a band party. I've been knowing band guys ever since Chicago and Cleveland. Some I've been knowing since home before they got with a band. Well you know how you old thugs carry on with all that hugging and kissing and signifying. Man, I suddenly realized that all that old jive time carrying on was scaring the stuffing out of this cat. He'd been reading about some of the old piano players plunking all night and partying all day and he got it all tangled up with all that old historical southern stuff about slavey time stud horse niggers. And

Reconstruction time jellybean gamblers and pimps. And it started backfiring on him and almost drove him crazy. I really thought that he was going to flip his lid. And like I said he was really a nice type of guy.

What happened? One night he came in and started raving about he didn't want no Scarlet Creeper spending the money he was giving me. And when I said, What the hell is a Scarlet Creeper? it turned out to be somebody he had read about in a book about Harlem. And another time he came in asking me about what us folks mean when they say black snake. And when I told him, Hell man, we mean what everybody else mean, he started talking about all them old songs about black snake hanging round my door, black snake creeping in my room, black snake coming in my bed. All that old stuff.

I interrupted and said, Hey I used to know a guy. He used to play all the old black snake songs on the guitar. And boy, I used to like the way he hopped a freight train as much as I liked the way he picked that box. But go on.

Then he really got weird. You know what the last straw was? You won't believe it. You can't believe it. I'm a hip chick. I know it. And I never heard anything like it in all my born days. You know what he did? He offered to give me a twenty-five-thousand-dollar down payment to let him get a baby on me. How about that? He had it all figured out. Not in cash. He was going to give me five thousand cash when he got the results back from the rabbit test and set up twenty thousand in escrow to be paid when I came out of the hospital after the birth. And he was also going to buy me a new convertible and set me up in a house somewhere like on Buckingham Road. You ever heard anything like that in your life? And he wasn't kidding. He offered to go out and get some legal papers drawn up. Well now you know good and well I had to unass the area when he kept coming up with that kind of old stuff, she said.

And when I said, Girl, you know some stuff, she said, Me, I just chalk it all up to experience. I don't know. Sometimes I think I is and sometimes I think I ain't. But you know something? Sometimes I think this cat I'm tied up with now is passing. He knows just a little bit too much. Sometimes I think he keeps me set up like this just so he won't have to be homesick for Dixieland. I really do. He's out of town on a business trip now, but I really wouldn't be a bit surprised if he's really down home visiting some of his flesh and blood kinfolks.

You really think he might be pulling some stuff like that? I said. And she said, It keeps crossing my mind. Every now and then a little something will happen. Not that he's raising all that much extra hell and getting all greedy and acting like it's going out of style. But you know, every now and then he really does remind me of one of them high yaller boys, half with it and half running from it.

I said, Like I said, girl. You sure do know some curious stuff. I said, Girl, you could get in there and trade choruses in any key and any tempo with the one and only Miss superhip Shari herself. And she said, The one and only Miss Shari who? And when I said, Zaad, she said, Oh her. Then she said, Did she really jive that horny stud out of it every night for a thousand and one nights in a row and him being a certified sheik with a whole harem full of so many of the best looking and best stacked chicks that he could afford to kill one every night just because he didn't want anybody else to have any of what he had been with?

And I said, Not really. I said, The idea was to keep him coming back every night because she had something more to offer than just her body. And she said, Okay, yeah, I can dig that. So she had some geisha jive going for her. And I said, She sure did. And with her it was a matter of life or death.

Then I said, Because the thing was not to keep him from doing it but to avoid the gorilla reaction to detumescence. I said, You know what they say about the gorilla? They say once that somich blows his stack, shoots his wad, busts his balls, he's through with the female and is subject to kick her ass out as if she (not he!) were an empty carton.

And that was when I also said, As for Scheherazade preserving her cherry, it turns out that at the end of that thousand and one nights she and old King Shahryar had begotten three boy children, one walking, one crawling, and one sucking. And she said, See there. Look at that. Boy you're something. Boy you're deep. Boy they don't call you Schoolboy for nothing.

When we went to bed she started kidding me about Jewel Templeton again, and all I could do was take it and squirm and wait for her mood to change. And when it did she said, Okay, I just wanted to see if you let that big name bitch go to your head. Some guys do, she said. Some guys act like it's the greatest thing in the world to look up there and see all that stuff all spread out against that big screen and be able to say that they been next to it. Like what is that? Plenty of guys and I mean plenty are willing to pay all kinds of alimony and shit for the rest of their lives. Especially the ones that didn't do anything with it when they had it.

Boy these people, she said laughing. Then she said, So you got the big head about that famous bitch? And I said, No, ma'am, not me. And she said, Now you gonna lay up here and try to tell me that Jewel Templeton is just another piece of well stacked meat to you? All right now, all right now, all right now. And I said, I didn't say that. And you know it.

And she said, Well okay. Because I was just about to say that driving her station wagon around must be giving you something even worse than the big head. Because if there's one thing I know it's you flesh and blood cats and that's another thing I have against fay chicks. They always spoiling you. Ain't no flesh and blood woman going to be spoiling you like that. Unless it's some kitchen mechanic and she ain't going to take but so much of you either. And there are plenty brown-skin cuties like you walking around wearing all kinds of switchblade and razor tattoos to prove it. I bet you that's exactly how your old boss-man got that cute little scar on his cheek. I bet you fifty dollars he made some bat salty and she went upside his pretty head. You can't tell me much that I don't already know about flesh and blood, she said.

Then she said, So tell me about it. And I said, About what? And she said, About all this stuff you got going with the famous Miss Almighty Jewel Templeton. And I said, Well now, you also have to admit that she is also one more fine looking woman fame or no fame. And she said, I'm not talking about that. She said, I wouldn't try to take anything away from her looks. Yeah she's fine. But good looking women come a dime a dozen and you know it. And you also know good and well you're used to seeing even better looking chicks than her hang around the bandstand every night all across the country. Better looking, better built. Both younger and older. And easier. But not famous. Me, I don't care anything about all that myself. I'm just trying to find out whether you got the big head. And I said, Well I'm not going to say her name doesn't have anything to do with it because I know you know better. But I do say it's not really the main thing.

And she said, I know, I know. I'm just teasing you. Ain't no big deal. I don't know. Maybe it's because I'm surprised at how pleased I am to see you again after all this time. So you really took me at my word that next morning at the Vineyard, didn't you. You showed me, didn't you. Jewel Templeton. Not bad, home boy. Not bad. Even for a college boy.

Then she said, But there I go teasing you again. But I really am glad to see you, home boy. But you got to prove you're not lying when you said what you said. So, come on over here and show me how much you missed me all that time up in the hills. And I said, If you say so. *And then there was only the two of us again as in you and me and me and you equals us and we were doing what we were doing which was what we had been doing plus what we were then doing which was what I was doing within that which she was doing and beyond the bed, the room, and that part of Los Angeles Hollywood was far away and there was all that which I was going to be doing plus that which I had already done and I thought this is what I shall have done.*

What woke me up that next morning was her saying, Hey is that daylight out there? Don't tell me that's daylight out there. That can't be daylight this quick, she said. I just closed my eyes three minutes ago. I don't believe this, she said. And when I opened my eyes I saw that the darkness was gone and that the time was six o'clock plus. *California, hey California.*

Now I know good and well the famous Miss Pink Nippled, Pink Toed, Mane-Tossing Jewel Templeton ain't about to be keeping you that busy, she said. She got her famous face to worry about. Them pale tailed chicks come out of a night like that with telltale splotches and stripes all over them.

You could see all around the room. The air was damp. But not as aromatic and chilly as it was in Beverly Hills. You were in California all right but this was not Hollywood and Beverly Hills and Bel-Air. This was Los Angeles, West Los Angeles, and Baldwin Hills and View Park territory. I pulled the spread up and closed my eyes again as she was saying, I know you know better than to be expecting this kind of old carrying on every time you just happen to come over this way Mr. Schoolboy Wonder. But I'm just telling you up front because I don't want you to be getting no wrong ideas about anything. You know what I mean. Because if I don't know about you flesh and blood cats when it comes to this kind of fooling around I don't know nothing about nothing.

And I also know all about how some of you all act when you're around them fay bitches. I know exactly how some of you all go around putting on all them classy airs and pulling all that old ooh la la hype. And then come around us and act like all they know what to say is, Come on baby. And all they expect to do is not go somewhere looking at fancy pictures and listen to high class music and stuff, but just to do that and eat and sleep. You hear what I'm saying? Like somebody like the likes of us ain't even intelligent enough to want to get the news on TV. And I said, You want to get the news on TV? You want me to turn it on? And she said, I'm not talking about you personally. She said, I'm just talking, boy.

But you know good and well them fay broads ain't going to let you lay up like this all the time even when they are rich enough to be keeping you. And they don't even have their hair to worry about. This sweaty mess is going to cost me money to get untangled, boy, she said. And I said, All chicks worry about their looks. I said, All chicks spend money on their hair these days. All sharp chicks, that is, I said. And she said, okay, smarty.

She got up at seven-fifteen and made coffee and fed the cats. And then she got up again at a quarter of nine and I dozed back off and when I woke up hearing the radio I was also smelling bacon and eggs. It was nine-fifteen and on my way to the bathroom I heard her talking to the cats.

We sat in the breakfast nook, me in my fancy shorts and her wearing a shorty short peignoir. She had done her hair up in pin curls, which she had covered with a silk scarf that she wore like a turban. There were grits, bacon, eggs, and hot biscuits; and as we ate you could see the morning mist lifting outside; and the windows of the houses stretching away down the hill were beginning to glitter although the sky was still streaked with haze that was going to become part of the late morning smog.

And don't be expecting this kind of brownskin service every time either, she said smiling at me. She looked almost as good in the morning with her face freshly washed and without makeup as she did all dressed up and out zipping around town in her convertible.

I know Jewel Templeton can serve you squab on toast every morning, she was saying. But just remember I did all this with my own two hands. Just remember that. Cotton field princess fingers and all, Mr. College Boy.

She poured herself another cup of coffee and lit a cigarette and looked out of the window. On the radio there was a program of show music. I watched the sky clearing beyond Linet Park. And when I looked at her again she was yawning. She saw me looking at her and almost blushed. I never was to see her really blush. And I never was to see her really angry either. She was always signifying about something and I still haven't figured out how much she was signifying at me and how much was really meant for herself.

The music played on and I followed each melody remembering most of the words without humming them. Then the one playing was "Blossoms on Broadway," which was somebody's radio theme during my freshman year in college when my roommate and I always kept up to date with what was happening in show business, not only by going to the periodicals room to read the entertainment section of the *New*

York Times and the *New York Herald Tribune*, but also by reading the copies of *Stage* magazine passed on to us by young Associate Professor H. Carlton Poindexter from Hamilton College and Howard University and the University of Chicago. He was the one in whose class we both studied Introduction to Ideas and Forms in Literature, and he was also the one who was to become the faculty equivalent of my best of all possible roommates when my roommate transferred to Yale, even as he was already the college extension of Mr. B. Franklin Fisher.

Boy, I heard Gaynelle Whitlow saying then, I must be out of my head or something, messing around here, playing around with my birthright like this. And I said, Is that what they call it now? And she said, That's what I call it. And in imitation of the jive line that I knew she would spot as coming from the Bossman Himself, I said, I never argue with beautiful people. Not in the morning, I said. Not on a beautiful morning like this. Not in such delightful circumstances as these. And she let me get away with it and said, Naturally. I don't blame you. Look at you. Just look at you. You should be ashamed of yourself, she said. And I said, Aw come on, baby. And realized how it sounded as soon as I said it. But she let me get away with that too and said, Boy, what am I going to do about you? And I said, You'll think of something.

When I got ready to go that afternoon, she decided to trail me as far as Crenshaw and Adams and we stopped at the Home Plate to have a quick one for the road. And she said, Call me sometime. Like the last time, she said. You know. Anytime for me. Sometime when you get around to it. Sometime when you think you might be coming over in this part of town again.

One day when you wake up with them old down-home back alley blues again, she said. And I said, Come on, Gaynelle. It's not like that and you know it. And she said, Yes it is too. And ain't nothing wrong with it. Ain't nothing in the world wrong with knowing where to go to find something good for what ails you. I'm just letting you know you're welcome to give me a buzz sometime when you don't have anything better to do.

And I said, Why are you talking like that? And she said, Like what? And I said, Like that. And she said, Me, as far as I'm concerned, I'm just glad to know you. And I said, Now see there, here you come again. And she smiled and said, One of these days I'll probably be happy just to say I used to know you. And I said, Okay, okay, okay, but me, I'm just as happy as I can be just to say I know you right now.

Then she said, Yeah but I'm talking about you're on your way somewhere to be somebody important. And when I said, Everybody is somebody important, she said, I know all about that. I told *you* about that already. I told you about me and show business. I made up my mind about that a long time ago. Before I left Mississippi. I used to read all them movie magazines just like everybody else. But all the other girls were dreaming about being stars and seeing their names up in lights. And what I was dreaming about was mostly the clothes and the houses and stuff like that. But you know what I really want? I just want to live good and know a few fine people in different walks of life as friends along the way. That's me just like what you out there in the professional world trying to find out what you really want to do is you.

When we came back outside she walked over to the auto incognito with me, and when I started the motor she said, Be sure not to give my regards to Miss Jewel Templeton. But I do wish her well, because I wish you well, honey boy. And that's also why I got to say this. Boy, you be careful over there now. There is a lot of big money invested in that chick and I know you know as well as I do that it don't take much to make some of them people nervous, and I mean very nervous.

XXXVI

All Jewel Templeton said on the telephone just before dusk that Monday of what turned out to be the last week I was to spend in Southern California for several years was that she was glad that I was already there and that she was on her way. But the sound of her voice gave you the impression that there was a problem of some sort that she wanted to tell you about as soon as she could get through the rush hour traffic along Sunset Strip.

So when she finally came in almost forty-five minutes later I was surprised, because she seemed every bit as unruffled as she usually was; and she said what she said as if what she had in mind didn't have anything to do with any problem, only a quick shift into uptempo for a few measures before settling into another groove.

That was why when she told me what she told me later on I suddenly realized that I had actually stopped thinking of her as an actress. Not that you ever really forgot that she was a movie star. Maybe because it was as if a movie star was somebody who practiced the art or craft of make-believe only when there were locations, sets, lights, cameras, crews, and a director. Otherwise movie stars spend most of their time trying to be free to be whoever they really and truly were, warts and all! Whereas it seemed to me that it was not at all unusual for actors and actresses of the theater to approach real life situations as if they were scenes in a play. Anyway it was easy enough for me to forget that Jewel Templeton was, after all, first of all, or rather along with everything else, an actress because there was hardly anything theatrical about the person that I had come to think I knew as well as I did.

Not that anything would have turned out any better or worse if I had been aware of the whole story at the time. And besides what the way she said what she said really amounted to was pretty much the same old fake-out that long trusted good friends are forever using to set up a surprise party. When

you look back, the subterfuge although not entirely untrue is also transparent
but not at the time of the come on.

What she did when she came in that evening in Beverly Hills was make me a proposition that we both knew I could hardly refuse. The first thing she said was what she said about being held up in traffic. Then she said, So this is what's up. But then with just the right touch of feedback twinkle in her voice as well as her eye, she said, Speaking of the ever so definitive matter of improvisation the existential implications of as I have or think I have come to understand it from you and the marquis, how flexible are your various projects and contractual obligations as of now? Or perhaps I should say how portable?

And when I said, As flexible and portable as almost always, which I hope is enough, she said, Does that by chance also mean that you have a current passport? And I said, It just so happens it does. I said, Not that I've ever used it yet. But that's one of those professional personnel details that Milo the Navigator sees to it that you take care of right away, even while you're only a temporary replacement in that band.

And she said, I thought as much, because as little as I knew about that part of the world of music before I met the marquis I always knew that the Bossman Himself like Louis Armstrong was an international American force. Then came the proposition that you knew you were not only expected to accept or decline immediately but also be ready to act upon in a matter of several days at most.

She said, How would you like to join me on an expense free trip to Europe for an unspecified number of weeks or maybe months? And I said, Very much. Then I said, What part of Europe? And she said, the South of France, arriving Nice Saturday you by way of a change in New York and me from business matters in Paris after other aspects of the same in Milan.

I leave tomorrow night, she said, And we meet in Nice Saturday. All I have to do is call the travel agency in the morning and your kit will be delivered here before noon. So what I was hoping was that all you have to do is pack a bag or so and make a few phone calls. There's cash on hand for all incidentals between now and Saturday and some to spare. Oh yes, just in case you're wondering, it's studio money all of it. So as you will see everything is strictly first class.

Oh this is fine, she said then. Just fine. As I hoped it would be, she said, and now I must zip up to Esther and get together what I need for two conference stops before setting down in Nice. The Côte d'Azur is to be sure no problem. Not for people from these parts. But let me go so there will be time for a brief toodle-oo until Saturday.

You couldn't keep yourself from wondering what it all was really about, but once she had presented it as a game of improvisation at the very outset, you couldn't start asking for explanations and the usual routine details without running the very likely risk of creating the devastatingly scandalous impression that you were hesitant about committing yourself to a spur of the moment situation that was after all obviously only a real life equivalent of the jam session.

She had said where and she had said when and if she had wanted you to know any of the specifics of wherefore at this time she would have told you that too. So to ask why could easily imply that you actually had doubts about her intentions. *Which was not the case at all. Quite the contrary. You had no reason whatsoever not to go along with anything she was so eager to share with you precisely as fairy tale aunts in whatever disguise have always done. Who have become guardian angels when necessary but never wicked witches. Not so far at any rate. And whoever else ever took such sheer delight in springing surprises. Who themselves were nothing if not surprises in the first place.*

So what I settled for was the immediately credible possibility that what she had taken advantage of some studio project to set up was a trip that would include meeting the Marquis de Chaumienne perhaps as much as a surprise for him as for me. Not that I didn't cross my fingers, but further questions were *out* of the question because there was also the totally unnecessary risk of being a spoilsport.

Which is why it was not until we had been in the South of France for a week and a half that I finally found out that the slight edge of agitation that I had thought I heard as soon as her voice came over the telephone that afternoon was actually only a bit of not quite controlled excitement involved in the elaborate game of one-upmanship she had worked out and was on her way home to spring on me.

Not that it had taken me that long to ask about it, because I never would have done that. Not me. Not about anything that had to do with studio transactions and policies. If she brought it up, fine. Otherwise no mention. Maybe if she had been in production during my time there, things would have been different. But that was not to be.

What brought the sound of her voice on the telephone back to mind that many days later was her response to what I said about not going back to Hollywood when she went, because the time had come for me to move on into the also and also of whatever else I had to find out about myself and about what I was going to do about which of the inescapable ancestral imperatives.

That was what I had been getting myself ready to tell her for several weeks, and then we were already where we were, and I had already gone through what you go through whenever you have to pack up to move on, but as soon as I drew my breath to say it I suddenly realized that she not only already knew what I had in mind but had also already known it long enough to plan the open-ended junket we were on. Something she had long since planned to do for and with me before I myself either went to rejoin the band or decided not to put off going east to graduate school any longer—or before she herself came across a script she liked and became caught up in the all-consuming details of her next production.

I went ahead and said what I said, which was only enough to make the point I wanted to make about the never stated but never ending obligations that come with the endlessly bountiful hospitality of storybook guardian aunts. And that was when she said what she said about fairy tale aunts existing only in the self-made world of storybook princes.

Apropos of all of which, she was also to say, as we made our way down to the surf after lunch and siesta that afternoon: Tinsel Town,

Tinsel Town, Tinsel Town. That's Hollywood, to be sure. But if you believe that there is less make-believe in the South of France or any- where else than is concocted in those studio sound and special effects stages and all of those far-flung "location" picnics you are most assuredly and totally mistaken.

Of course there's make-believe and there's also make-believe, she said, as we spread the towels on the stony sand, and the difference is a matter of taste, which is, as the marquis points out, much the same with life and the arts as with cuisine, that is to say, *a sense of the optimum quality, proportion and processing of the ingredients in the recipe.*

So put that into your big brown oracular goddess of a bass fiddle and pluck away my bright eyed nimble fingered road musician, she said as I sprinted ahead to the damp sand and water's edge thinking, *This many miles beyond Chickasabogue Bridge and the canebreaks and the bayou, this many more miles along the way.*

Three

THE CRAFTSMAN

XXXVII

A few years later on there would be the Great Circle Route from Los Angeles International nonstop over the pole. But at the time that I left California to meet Jewel Templeton in Nice, you didn't really feel that you were actually on your way to Europe from anyplace in the United States until you finally took off from Idlewild International in New York and headed out across the Atlantic on a trajectory that was pretty much the same as the one that took Lindbergh and *The Spirit of St. Louis* to Le Bourget back when I was in the seventh grade.

So my first transatlantic passage by air began by also being my first cross-country flight all the way from the Pacific Coast to the eastern shores of the early colonials, traversing the legendary deserts and the Bad Lands, the Great Divide, the Great Plains, the Mississippi Delta, and the foothills of the Pennsylvania Appalachians at speeds beyond any super express train and at altitudes that made falcons and eagles seem earthbound.

Also in those days as was likewise the case back during the high times of the transoceanic liners, when the ports of embarkation had to be reached by road or rail, the stopover in New York gave you what was not only a two-part journey but in effect was also two distinctly separate journeys altogether, each with its own significantly specific objectives. Because as incidental as the first part was to the second it was no less a destination as such than a junction, even so.

New York, New York, I said as the flight pulled on away from El Segundo and beyond the Sierras. *Back to the Apple yet again*, I said, realizing even as I did that I would be there in a matter of only hours and minutes this time. By super streamlined train it was a matter of days. By road band bus it was a matter of at least several weeks of one night stands and theater dates at best.

From Mobile back when New York was as much the Philamayork of fireside and swing porch yarn spinners as an actual point of arrival on a timetable, you took the L & N northbound to Montgomery and changed to the eastbound West Point route to Atlanta, from which the southern took you on out of Georgia and through South and North Carolina and Virginia and into Washington, the border town of Dixieland and the transfer point for the Pennsylvania Railroad and the last six hours it took to get through Maryland, Delaware, the state of Pennsylvania, and New Jersey and into Penn Station at 33rd Street and Seventh Avenue.

The trip from Mobile by train was also a matter of perhaps three days at most (with fair connections). And the thing about it in those days was that most of it took you through what had become of the old Confederacy, most of which (largely because of the notorious Hayes-Tilden Compromise of 1877) was not only far from being reconstructed in accordance with the Thirteenth, Fourteenth, and Fifteenth amendments, but still in violently reactionary defiance thereto.

Mobile, to be sure, was also a part of the old Confederate South, but even so you never thought of Mobile as being a Civil War town as Montgomery, Atlanta, and Richmond were. Montgomery was where old Jeff Davis was sworn in to lead the seesesh against Lincoln and the Union to defend to the death their freedom to own slaves. Atlanta was Sherman, Sherman, Sherman, and the wages of rebel yells. And of course Richmond was the actual wartime capital of the ever so arrogant but ill-fated C.S.A. from which Jeff Davis had to flee once Grant did what he did to Lee. But Mobile as I grew up knowing it was always somehow different. On the one hand it was nothing if not loyal to the southern cause, and the Battle of Mobile Bay was a very important Civil War event, indeed, coming as it did after the fall of New Orleans. So there was no shortage of C.S.A. monuments and Confederate flags.

But on the other hand along with forever advertising itself as a

City of Five Flags (Spanish, English, French, Confederate, and American), it was not only an international seaport into which ships and seamen came from all over the world, it was consequently also a place with downtown streets and side streets along which it was perfectly natural to find yourself among people representing so many of the languages and customs and even costumes of so many of the lands that Miss Lexine Metcalf's Windows on the World bulletin board made you realize what classrooms were also about.

Eastbound by air from Los Angeles International it was at times somewhat as if you were cruising above a sand table mock-up of a physical (not political) map of the Zone of the Interior U.S.A. Not that you could actually see very much except when the altitude and visibility were such that the pilot would announce over the speaker system that you were approaching this or that landmark on the right or left. But even so your ongoing reaction to the flight was that of a map reader superimposing overlays of political boundary lines and historic sights over natural earth shapes and features.

Along with all of which there were the recurring times when you nodded off and woke up again feeling the way you felt because as soon as you realized that you were still airborne, there was the also and also and elsewhere and elsewhere of moving on once more, and each time you checked your watch and closed your eyes again thinking, *Yes, very much the same as if alone on horseback with saddle pack, even so. Very much the same, indeed, for you and who if not you will go where you will go. Riding, riding, riding through the night through the day, riding, riding.*

I said, I come from Alabama. I said, This many miles from the spyglass tree and the also and also of the train whistle guitars of Gasoline Point and the saw mill bottoms on the outskirts of Mobile north of the bay and the coast of the Gulf of Mexico. This time by way of California, hey California. This many months after the elsewhere and elsewhere of road band bus routes. I said, This time after the first time since the campus of being in one town long enough to become used to not being used to being there. Which was pretty much the same as I realized that I had come to feel about the campus that spring as commencement time approached. Then on the road with the band you became used to not being used to being in the same place for more than a week or so at most. Which is why that is also what I said when old Ike Ellis said what he said about me being a quick study on the bandstand and also a quick study of life on the road. I said, Hey man, I'm just getting used to not being used to this stuff out here just as I'm getting used to not being on the campus anymore or back down in Mobile anymore. And he said, Hey man, that's deep, college boy. They don't call you Schoolboy for nothing. That's psychological. That's very psychological.

In New York I checked into Hotel Theresa and headed straight down to midtown to the Libraire de France off Fifth Avenue on the promenade to Rockefeller Plaza and bought the latest editions of the Michelin and Blue guidebooks to the Côte d'Azur, Provence, Burgundy, and Paris. I had taken French at Mobile County Training School as well as in college, but that was also when I picked up a copy of the beginner's exercise book that I was later to use at Alliance Française.

Then I walked up Fifth Avenue to 53rd Street and went to the Museum of Modern Art mainly to revisit the permanent collection, especially what there was of Cézanne, Matisse, Braque, Picasso (*Ma Jolie, Woman in the Mirror, and Guernica*), Léger, Klee, Miró, Mondrian, Modigliani, and so on, in those days, the first two catalogs of which I still have.

There was also time to go to a special current exhibition of architectural design. Then afterward, I took the bus down to Greenwich Village to see a few of the writers and artists that I had kept in touch with since my times in New York with the band, and the first one I called invited three others to meet us at a cozy place off Sheridan Square where they treated me to a light early dinner and we talked until I had to leave to get uptown in time to pop in on musician friends working in spots along Seventh and Lenox avenues on my way to catch the first set at the Savoy Ballroom.

My New York stopover agenda for the next day included an early start for revisits to at least three of the landmarks that I had preselected from my ever handy old Federal Writers' Project guide to the city and environs (which I still have and which is mostly long since not up to date but which continues to become more and more important as a historical document of the period during which it was published).

From Jewel Templeton's collection of Phaidon volumes on the great masters I had also preselected what I wanted to see during a mid-day page-flipping-tempo visit to the Metropolitan Museum, from which I went on uptown and arrived at Sugar Hill on time for my pre-Idlewild visit with Royal Highness who pointedly reminded me of what he had already been telling me about his travels across the water; and also said, Now this is what I have to say: Boy, ain't no telling what I would have come back from over there in them parts with if I had been the kind of schoolboy you had sense and guts enough to become, young soldier. And don't miss my point about coming back. Because that's the main point of going over there in the first place. Don't ever forget that. All some splibs talk about when they tell about being over there is how free they felt from these old color line problems over here. And that's important. That's very important. But frankly, between me and you, young soldier, I can't name one refugee splib that's putting out anything even in the class with this homegrown stuff we turn out a dime a dozen. Let alone being out of sight of us because of all the advantages that they're supposed to enjoy by being over there. Not a single one. And you know why? Because it takes more than just being somewhere away from all this old cracker mess we got over here. So you can't put all the blame on them jaspers.

Of course now, if you want to become a brownskin Frenchman or refugee or some other kind of foreigner over there, that's your personal business because after all it's your life. But now, as for me, I just want to be the goddamnedest world-beatingest American I can get to be, because that's my birthright. Hell, young soldier, I know Josephine Baker, Sam Wooding, and Spencer Williams and most of the rest of them, and some of them might even have their French papers, but they're still foreigners to them Frenchmen as crazy about them as them Frenchmen supposed to be. And what they do is still something foreign from over here. Don't care how much them Europeans like it.

But hell, I'm satisfied that you're already on to what that's all about. So the main thing I'm hoping about you is that you will go on over there and see and learn about as much as you can. Because my point is you don't know enough about the world until you learn some more about it the way they've been dealing with it from over there down through the ages. Look at them Japs. Look at them Chinamen. They got some stuff that goes all the way back to ancient times too. And they know good and well that it all counts for more when you're tied in with all that stuff you're headed for.

But like I say. I'm satisfied that you know what my point is. So go on over there and find out as much as you can firsthand about all that stuff you already been reading about and studying up on in school. Then come on back over here and see what you can do with it.

Which reminds me of one more thing I'm counting on you for, young soldier. Whenever it come down to the point of being a splib dealing with them jaspers, don't ever forget that the main thing about this country we got over here is that so much of it is still a matter of unfinished business. Don't ever forget that. And don't forget who told it to you. Me, an old broken down entertainer. Maybe you're one of the ones that realized this rock bottom point from school. But don't nobody practice it better than splibs in show business. Take old Louis Armstrong. When old Louis puts his mark on a tune them jaspers find out that's what this country's music is supposed to be like. Don't care what they say in them conservatories. But hell, I don't have to tell you. The bossman and Old Pro and them got you branded from now on regardless of what you brought out of school.

That was the only mention of me and the band and the Bossman Himself during the whole visit. And that was the way I let things stand.

XXXVIII

When the flight to France finally taxied out to its takeoff runway and climbed to the assigned elevation and leveled off into its cruising speed I adjusted my seat to the coziest position for reading and pulled out the map, guide, and language workbook; but what I found myself thinking about was all of the first fireside and swing porch talk about the AEF troop transport crossings from Newport News, Virginia, to Brest on the Normandy coast back when Uncle Sam joined John Bull on the Western Front in the world war against Germany and the Kaiser (a.k.a. Old Kaiser Bill, he of the piked helmet, satanic mustache, and shriveled hand), *which was that many years before I found out where over there was because I can also remember hearing war songs and also talk about submarines and submarine chasers before I was yet school age and you didn't have to know about maps and geography until you reached the third grade.*

By which time it was as if I had known Soldier Boy Crawford from as far back as I can remember either the fireside or the swing porch. But the fact of the matter was that the way he used to tell about it that many years afterward made it all seem as if you had been over there in the trenches and at the outdoor cafés, in the country wine cellars, over there tramping in hobnail boots, eating hardtack and drinking cognac, over there talking parlez-vous, voulez-vous *zig zig.*

Old Soldier Boy Crawford, who talked French as much with his eyes, shoulders, and fingers as with his voice and lips, saying sand meal killing my trees easy to Paris, with his fingers articulating the syllables as if on a guitar (which come to think of it he couldn't even play). Old Soldier Boy Crawford, whose Parisian experiences as related in Papa Gumbo Willie McWorthy's barbershop were even better than any of the stories I had overheard about Storyville and Algiers down in New Orleans or about the Barbary Coast of San

Francisco; and whose notorious and long since dog-eared deck of French post-cards of positions for doing it (including sixty-nine a.k.a. reverse ninety-six) Little Buddy Marshall was finally to find a way to borrow for our ever so casual but hardly calm perusal from time to time. In much the same manner as he used to borrow Mr. Big Buddy Marshall's .38 Smith & Wesson six-shooter every now and then for one another of our derring-do capers.

Old Soldier Boy Crawford. There was his France and his Paris, and then after Miss Lexine Metcalf and the earlier times of Charlemagne and Roland, which were followed by the even earlier times of Julius Caesar when it was not yet France but the Gaul of the first of two years of Latin conjugations and declensions that made first year French easier than it would have been without them. Meanwhile along with the movies and no less than the Wild West pulp magazines there were the Three Musketeers and D'Artagnan that many school years before the Paris of the Champs Élysées, the Arc de Triomphe, the Eiffel Tower, and then Montmartre and Montparnasse.

Sometimes it was as if the France of Mr. B. Franklin Fisher began with Louis XIV and then brought forth Jean-Jacques Rousseau whose writings including The Social Contract *helped to bring about the American war of independence and constitutional democracy thirteen years ahead of the French Revolution and the Declaration of the Rights of Man. And other times it was as if it had all happened so that a schoolboy genius like Napoleon Bonaparte could rise from the obscurity of Corsica to establish France as a supreme international military power and Paris as the most cosmopolitan of all cities.*

What my good old best of all possible roommates had in mind when he sketched the design for the reversible escutcheon that tagged our digs as Atelier 395 was life in the garrets not only of Montmartre, the Belle Époque of the Moulin Rouge out of which came Picasso, Braque, and Matisse, but also of Montparnasse during the postwar period of the so-called lost generation of American artists and writers. And that turned out to be only the beginning. Before midterm test time arrived he had read Helen Waddell's novel about Peter Abelard and Héloïse and passed it on to me. For my benefit he had also read aloud his favorite ballad stanzas from François Villon's Legacy *and* The Testament *and was insisting that I be well into Rabelais'* Gargantua and Pantagruel *before the Christmas holiday break.*

Farce, my good fellow, he was to say time and again whenever Rabelais was the topic, the ridiculous, the hyperbolic, the ludicrous, the downright out-rageous, without which there is no need for mathematical actuality and hence no engineering. Look to your pathetic repeat pathetic categories, my good man. Tragedy represents an engineering failure; comedy and melodrama represent engineering resolutions whereas farce—now there's entropy, old pardner, no less for metaphorical connotation than for factual denotation.

Which brings us to poetry whether in verse prose or drama, which includes the bawdy, robust, tongue-in-cheek and thumb-in-nose Rabelaisian along with the no less earthy but also more elegant world of our very own Ernest Hemingway. Item: the chilly beads of sweat on the bottle of white wine when Jake and Bill take it out of the clear, pebbly bottomed almost icy stream for lunch during that fishing trip in The Sun Also Rises. *Nothing counter-states the vanity of vanity or futility of futility that the book's epigraph is all about. Indeed much goes to show that whenever it was that his Côte d'Azur play pal Gerald Murphy said living well is the best revenge, our boy Heming-way already knew that the indispensable element in living well is elegance.*

Elegance is the best and perhaps even the only revenge against chaos, my good old trail buddy, he said. And the key to elegance is play. As who knows bet-ter than our fun-seeking verbal jeweler the intrinsic importance of the play repeat play of light and shadow and also sheen, sparkle, glitter, and twinkle? If you miss that and the verbal and auditory equivalents to it, such as conno-tation in words and overtones, chords and so on in music, shame on you, my good man. You might as well be a stone, or a particle or wave. Because we're talking about the quality and potential range of human consciousness, my fel-low sojourner.

But back to Rabelais, mon semblable, mon frère. *You're going to be hard put to come up with anyone who better understood the basic function of slapstick and slapdash in this matter of forming meaning. Back to the vul-garity and popularity of the commedia dell'arte. But even so, your* Gargan-tua and Pantagruel *is no less notorious for its scholarly sophistication than for its irrepressible exuberance and its unflagging zest for fun and games. But then is it not written that Rabelais was "a monk by convenience, a doctor of medicine by instinct and choice, an editor by disinterested zeal and, finally, a writer because the medium of literature alone allowed him to express his infinite exuberance."*

That was the way such sessions almost always went during those two sine qua non, yes, sine qua non years that he was there. And then when he went on to the Yale School of Architecture, no new roommate turned up for my next year but from that midsummer before my junior year on through to graduation there was Mr. (associate professor but not yet doctor) Carlton Poindexter of the English Department who was already the faculty member that my roommate and I had identified most closely with from our very first Monday morning in English 101. Not only because he was already so obviously a big league college professor before he was yet thirty but mainly because of all of the current books and magazines on the shelves and the conference table in his office that looked out across the unclosed quadrangle to the library and the gymnasium with a parking area for the tennis court and the alumni bowl in between.

The current books and magazines along with the photographs and travel posters of textbook places as well as the color reproductions of contemporary art around the walls made him seem accessible to me and my roommate to a degree that was not even thinkable to me in connection with anybody on the faculty or staff back at Mobile County Training School. Nor was I yet as ready for it as I began to be as soon as I realized that I was in college and on my own without any hope of any financial support from any relatives anywhere. Which is also why I was ready to do what I did that summer. Because by that time I had not only taken two of his electives along with the two courses required by the prospectus, my roommate and I had also been asking him all of those historical and literary questions and also borrowing books from his office that were not directly related to any subject matter that he was teaching on any level. Meanwhile for his part he had also begun passing along things for us to read, not as teacher to student but as fellow enthusiasts, albeit somewhat less advanced. Nor could anything have been more flattering than the fact that he seemed to take it for granted that our extracurricular preoccupation would not intrude upon our required assignments in any other classes.

So from that summer on to graduation, he was the one who was there as my official faculty adviser and also as the nearest thing to a replacement for my roommate, whom he knew how much I missed because he missed him very *much himself. Not for the same reason to be sure. But, given his sincerity as a teacher, perhaps not much less acutely even so. In any case, even as the two of us reminisced about him during the week before my commencement it was still as if his absence was only temporary. He was still my legendary roommate and still his most legendary of all pupils although his major field was architecture.*

As for Carlton Poindexter himself, the difference between his authority and that of Mr. B. Franklin Fisher was especially significant to me at that time. Mr. B. Franklin Fisher's authority was that of a headmaster whereas one of the most striking things about Carlton Poindexter was how tentative he was about what the subject matter he knew so much about added up to in the workaday world at large.

Not that Mr. B. Franklin Fisher was ever dogmatic about literal application but his world of secondary education was the realm of pragmatic fundamentals, the world of carefully monitored drill sessions and the elements of grammar, mathematics, science, and the precise documentation of historical events and geographical relationships.

Which was entirely consistent with the all too obvious fact that at Mobile County Training School it was almost always as if the highest premium was placed on meeting the precise standards of eligibility required by the occupations and professions that added up to social, economic, and political betterment as such. Nor could anything have been more consistent with community expectations, not only in general and in accordance with conventional ancestral imperatives that book learning was assumed to be about, but also with the specifics of what they had expected from him in the first place.

I can remember them talking and speculating about him all that summer before he came. It was also the summer before I was to be in the third grade and carry my books strapped onto my wide First Year Geography instead of a primer grade book satchel, and everywhere you went sooner or later somebody would mention something about the coming school year and the fact that there was going to be a new principal. There were sermons and prayers about it at church and discussions and arguments about it in Papa Gumbo Willie McWorthy's barbershop, and you heard no end of gratuitously avuncular signifying about what he was going to be like as you moved around the neighborhood and during swing porch visiting time at home.

They tell me that new principal, that Professor B. Franklin Fisher is supposed to be rolling in town the day before Labor Day, and they say he is a natural born pistol. They say he has a way of just cutting his eyes in the direction of any kind of naughtiness that'll make these young rascals and freshtails straighten up as fast as cracking a whip; and they also say he got a tongue that can take the hide off of a Hog Bayou alligator.

"Lift Every Voice" was already a school bell song along with "My Country 'Tis of Thee" and "Oh, Say Can You See," but when he arrived that Monday morning it also became the anthem that specifically evoked the ancestral imperatives of the Talented Tenth. From then on it was also a school bell song that resonated as if surrounded by stained glass windows. That was a very special day indeed.

We were all there waiting, students, a number of parents, welcoming committees from civic groups as well as churches; and at five minutes before the last bell, the Ford bringing them, Mr. Hayes, who was driving, Miss Duval and Miss Lexine Metcalf, turned in and rumbled across the cattle-guard and came flivvering on up the drive with two carloads of faculty of staff people following.

Mr. Hayes got out first. He was wearing surveyor's boots and britches, and he was carrying a tricorn folded flag, and on the chain around his neck there was a whistle, which he blew and began lining everybody up parents and all for the Pledge of Allegiance ceremony. Then he marched us all to the entrance to the Assembly Room, and everybody was thinking that he was the one, until we got inside and found out who was going to speak.

He was standing at the podium wearing a dark blue hand tailored suit, and as soon as people saw him we could tell by the look on their faces that most of them were either mumbling or wondering is that him? That boy? Is that boy the man? Because what he looked like was a boy evangelist. The other teachers except Mr. Hayes who was standing at parade rest in back of the room and Miss Duval who was at the piano, were seated on the stage looking not unlike the evangelical chorus that they in fact turned out to be.

The music Miss Duval had been playing for us to get in step with as we came up to the landing to march into the assembly and find our seats and stand waiting by was a very fancy strutting New Orleans march called "High Society." But I guessed that the first number that we were going to have to sing together was "Lift Every Voice" because it was already the sound that went with school bell times and classroom smells, but that was the first time it also made you feel like being in church, which is exactly what Mr. B. Franklin Fisher wanted, and somehow even before he opened his mouth to say the first words you knew he was about to begin a sermon. And the first thing he said was that he was beginning an old time revival meeting that was going to last for nine months.

I've come here to these notorious sawmill outskirts of the historic and legendary seaport town of Mobile, Alabama, he began in a voice that was nothing if not that of a boy evangelist, to revive the spirit that that song from the turn of the century was composed to generate. It was first performed by schoolchildren such as you as a part of a celebration of Abraham Lincoln's birthday. But for me it is song of songs. For Mobile County Training School it is to be by my decree the clarion call to excellence.

The spirit of the extended revival meeting which I have come to conduct for this student body is the same that motivated and sustained the fugitive slave on the Underground Railroad, Harriet Tubman, Frederick Douglass, the nonpareil nobility of the magnificent volunteers in young Colonel Shaw's Massachusetts 54th. It was what motivated bondage-born Booker Washington to service and uplift as freeborn white youths were inspired to wealth and status by the books of Horatio Alger.

Who knows perhaps the grounds of our campus like those of some of our outstanding universities, colleges, and normal and industrial institutes were once a part of a plantation that our forefathers were bound to. Well true or not, it is in effect another kind of plantation with another sort of overseer. And I intend to raise my kind of crops on it. Yes, I come here to raise crops that will supply this town with the civic nourishment it hungers and thirsts for: Instead of catch as catch can common laborers, expert technicians and artisans who will prosper by putting brains and skill into the common occupations of life; crops of dedicated professionals with certification second to none and along with everything else in every walk of life our people need leadership, leadership, leadership, the potential for which may even now be fermenting in the most lawless and backward seeming corners down in Meaher's Hummock.

Apropos of all of which there was also to be that assembly session that I remember from the term in which I was in the ninth grade. He began nam-ing famous leaders and their historical achievements and calling them our appropriate ancestors and he singled out old Elzee Owens and said, Citizen Tom Paine and when old crazy Willy Lee Berry whispered what he whispered to old Elzee about being put in the dozens the assembly which usually lasted from ten to ten-thirty each Wednesday went on until three o'clock with only a twenty minute break at one o'clock.

The dozens, he said. Stand up Willy Lee Berry. So now you're wonder-ing how I heard you. Well, I got twenty-twenty vision as well as absolute pitch, so I didn't have to hear you. All I needed was to see you lean over and I didn't even have to read your lips. The dozens. Boy, I'll tell you something about the dozens. Boy, we were already in the dozens generations before we were born. Boy, they brought the flesh and blood ancestors of our people over here in chains in 1619. Boy, I'm not up here talking about bedsprings and berry thickets. I'm trying to tell you something about history and responsibility. I'm talking about you and your obligations to yourself and your allegiance to the principles on which the United States of America is founded.

If you call that playing the dozens, then I'm going to be playing the dozens with you from now on. All of you. Every last one of you. Boy, Tom Paine is precisely the great-great-great-granddaddy that suits the signifying you seem to think you're already qualified to whisper while your principal is addressing the junior high school student body. Citizen Tom Paine, yes, Citi-zen Tom Paine. Boy, I forbid you to put your number eleven feet on these grounds that we are in the process of hallowing until you read enough about his life and work to explain why I match you with him. And I'm going to be right here waiting for you at seven-thirty tomorrow morning. We'll all be here at seven-thirty and when we've heard from you we'll hear from your good friend Elzee Owens.

Then before Elzee Owens could figure out whether he also was supposed to stand up, the voice from the podium went on to say, In fact, I don't think we should slight any one of you, if you know what I mean. I mean I'm going to be standing right here pointing my finger and ready to pat my foot if it takes the rest of the week for every last one of you to testify. I mean I am herewith promulgating my grandfather clause. The Mobile County Train-

ing School corollary to the grandfather clause, effective as if of tomorrow morning at seven-thirty and appertaining to everybody in the seventh, eighth, and ninth grades. Your homeroom teachers will be right up here on the stage with me tomorrow morning and when they call your name you will answer by giving the ancestor you've chosen for emulation. You may change to someone else later as your aspirations come more and more into focus as you advance to graduation, but the ones you select for this exercise had better be suitable. Duplication of choices will be permitted but your reasons must be yours and yours alone. And please don't let me catch you using anybody's name in vain.

At that time I had my own reason for wanting to say Benjamin Franklin, but I knew very well you could never get away with that. And nobody would ever let you live it down. So I said what I said about Frederick Douglass as fugitive slave and said, For the time being.

That was the instantly legendary Mr. B. Franklin Fisher who had come not only in response to the official call of the school board and community elders but also as answer to the old folks' prayers down through the generations. And yet this was also the selfsame Mr. B. Franklin Fisher who said what he said when I won the award I won in the tenth grade: Note bene, note bene, note bene. *Every time some bright-eyed pupil like this comes out of the sawmill bottoms of Gasoline Point and makes straight A's in Latin 1 and 2, not only because he studies his lesson as required but also because he likes the history and the stories that he's able to translate, we are witnessing yet another personification of hope for the survival of the human proposition as such.*

But then who if not he was the one who said what he was to say when he presented me my diploma and announced the college scholarship award. Everybody stood up and applauded and he said, We expect special things from this one. He said, All we ask of this one is that he try to the best of his God given ability and considerable potential.

And even as I said, I promise that I will always do my best, I was not at all unaware of the ever growing number of previous Mobile County Training School graduates who were already declaring their eternal gratitude to him because the vocational guidance he had literally forced them to follow had been so specific.

I said, I promise. I said I promise that I will always do my best and he nodded smiling his satisfaction as he led the audience in the applause that lasted until I got back to my place among the other members of the graduating class. I said, I promise. Which is also what I had already told Miss Lexine Metcalf when she said what she said that many terms earlier when she said, You will go where you will go and you will do what you will do, my splendid young man. Because, who if not you, my splendid young man? Whatever it is, my splendid young man. And who if not you is to say?

I said what I said because I was also talking to Miss Lexine Metcalf, Miss Tee, and Mama, who were also smiling and applauding, and when I found Mama and Miss Tee on the way out and handed Mama my diploma, which she handed to Miss Tee, they looked at each other and began shaking their heads, and then they put their arms around me and started laughing and crying at the same time.

Then when I went on over to say good-bye to Miss Lexine Metcalf, who was going up to New England for the summer, she put both hands (instead of her magic wand blackboard pointer) on my shoulders and held me at arm's length, moving her fairy-tale face up and down in A-plus approval. And I said what I said again and said good-bye and when I looked back to wave one last time I could tell that she had just dabbed her eyes with the dainty handkerchief that she switched to the other hand before waving back.

When I promised what I promised Mr. B. Franklin Fisher as he handed me my Mobile County Training School diploma, it was good enough for him for all of his primary emphasis on career specific vocational guidance, just as it had been already good enough for Mama and Miss Tee long before Miss Lexine Metcalf was to say, There is at yet no telling what a young man of your caliber and potential can make of yourself once you decide what it is you want to be.

The word (for a while) on Mr. B. Franklin Fisher among career experts of a decade later on would have been that he had either discovered or in any case had decided that you were inner-directed not other-directed. But by that time Mr. Carlton Poindexter had already said what he said along with his congratulations on your graduation from college. He would talk about graduate course content but never about personal vocations. All he said that day was, Now you will see what you see and you will make of it what you can.

The also and also of the ongoing transatlantic flight sound was always there as if it were what your sense of the stream of time consciousness itself was. But at the point that you also became aware of the intrusion of the preliminary intercom static and then the buzz within which the voice of the pilot announcing that the coastline of Europe would be visible in less than five minutes, you realized that you had fallen asleep thinking about Mobile County Training School and that you were now heading into sunrise over the province of Normandy. *And I said, This many miles from Mobile Bay. I said, This many miles along the way.*

What I also realized the instant I turned my wrist to check my watch (because I was thinking of the early risers in the towns and countrysides that we would soon be flying over), was that we were now heading into a time zone that was five hours earlier than the Eastern Standard Time of New York, which was three hours earlier than the Pacific Standard Time of Los Angeles and Beverly Hills. When you were that close to Europe you were also that close to the prime meridian, which was the zone of Greenwich Mean Time, the mean that was the basis for universal time.

The South of France, like Paris, would be one hour earlier than Greenwich Mean Time, which is also the time zone of London.

XXXIX

The villa was on a hill above Juan-les-Pins and the sea, and beyond the pines, the palms, and the terra cotta rooftops along the slope you could see sails and the long white streaks from the speedboats cutting back and forth on the blue water as the clear Mediterranean sky stretched away to the south toward Corsica, Sardinia, and North Africa; and on the distant horizon from time to time you could see the sails of larger craft and also the deluxe cabin cruisers. Sometimes there was a long white yacht with festive flags and sometimes there were also the ocean liners and freighters that came in that close because they were en route to Nice and Villefranche.

Beyond Alpes-de-Haute-Provence were the Alpes-Maritimes, which came all the way down to the coast at Monte Carlo, on the other side of which was Menton and the beginning of the Italian Riviera. Northeast beyond the Maritimes was the Italian region of the Piedmont. It was only five hundred kilometers from that part of Italy to the Swiss border, and fewer than six hundred kilometers across Switzerland by way of Berne to the Rhine and Germany. North beyond the French Alps and Haute-Savoie was Geneva. *You were that close to all of that then and you could say all the way from the seat by the map stand, eight thousand miles from the U.S.A.*

There was a grand piano in the long high beamed drawing room where soirees and parties were held, but I used the Danish spinet in the studio on the second floor, and through the wide window which opened out onto the balcony overlooking the vegetable garden and what was left of an old sandstone wall, you could see the mountains again. These were the Pré-Alpes de Grasse.

There was also a balcony outside the great bedroom where we slept, and from there you could see the traffic along Avenue Guy de Maupassant and the flags along Promenade du Soleil; and with the binoculars you could survey the beach and the surf and watch the water skiers. You could also see the casino and the curve of the cape beyond which was Antibes.

From the dining terrace above the tropical gardens you could see west along the dense and teeming shore toward Cap-de la-Croisette and Cannes; that was the route past the Massif de l'Estérel to Saint-Tropez, above which was the Massif des Maures and beyond which was the rugged route to Marseilles, north from which was Provence. Southwest beyond Montpelier, Narbonne, and Perpignan was Spain.

When you looked toward Antibes it was as if you were looking due east, but the actual direction of the coastline at that point was northeast. You couldn't see very far looking that way from where I was because of the trees, but the Hôtel de Ville was only two kilometers away and going there was like going into the old town from the suburbs. But actually you were not aware of crossing any town line at all.

On the way to the Musée Grimaldi on the bicycle I passed Place Charles-de-Gaulle, circled through Rue de la République, and strolled pushing the bike through the market. Then I found my way through the narrow streets to the sea and came pedaling along Promenade du front de Mer. The museum was an old château with a square tower, and close by was an old church and not far away was the old harbor. There were white breakers and the curving shoreline of the Baie des Anges. And then there were the blue-green mountains against the pale sky above Cagnes-sur-Mer.

I locked the bicycle and went inside and bought my ticket. In the lobby I was still aware of the bright, blue high afternoon sky and the mountains, and I can also remember how you could still feel the nearness of the sea. I looked at the floor plan. The main thing about the museum was the special collection of paintings and ceramics by Pablo Picasso, but there was also a permanent exhibition of historical documents, maps, pictures, and regional antiques, which I decided to look at first.

I had been reading about Antibes in the travel guide before breakfast that morning and I had also checked the maps and looked at the pictures in the travel brochures. In a way I guess I've always been a student of geography and history. I've always been a student of just about everything. Old Joe States, he didn't know how right he was when he nicknamed me Schoolboy. Or did he? You never can tell about old road musicians. Especially if they're from Alabama by way of the T.O.B.A. circuit and have been swapping that many lies in that many wayside inns for that many years.

In any case I knew that Antibes was the old port town of Antipoles, which went all the way back to the time of the ancient

Greek sea merchants. Nice was also an old Grecian port. Its original name was Nike, which meant Victory. The original name for Marseilles was Massailia and then it was Massilia. I didn't remember what that meant but it always used to make me think about Marsala, which was a wine, and that made me think about the wine trade but I also knew that Marsala was in Sicily and I guess that it had also been a Grecian settlement. I knew that Marseilles went all the way back to the Phoenician sailors.

I also knew that southern France had been a part of the Roman Empire. I had known about that since junior high school where *Gallia omnes in partes tres* was *divisa*. In ninth grade declensions nominative, genitive, accusative, dative, ablative, and very very vocative under Miss Kellogg the Conjugator. And in the tenth grade there was still more Julius Caesar and Gallic Wars, which had begun with the Helvetians who lived in Switzerland. And there was also Cicero who called upon Catiline, oh Catiline in oratorical accents to be used in assembly programs. And Virgil told about Aeneas and Dido when North Africa was known as Carthage, while algebra moved on toward what Mr. B. Franklin Fisher called the quixotic windmill country of quadratic equations and springtime adventures in quest of cube roots.

I was thinking about all of that then and I don't remember what I saw representing the Middle Ages but something made me remember Roland and Oliver fighting for Charlemagne in Spain in fifth grade. That was adventures in literature. Switzerland was adventures in geography like the dikes and the wooden shoes of Holland. The French Revolution was adventures in world history like the Battle of Waterloo and also the campaigns of Alexander the Great, Hannibal, and Scipio Africanus.

There was a special exhibit on Napoleon. He had landed in Antibes in 1794 and had returned from exile in Elba by way of Golfe Juan in 1815. He came in the eleventh grade along with first year French for some including me and first year Spanish for others. But he was in another classroom which was the homeroom where I was an all around student and a four letter athlete with never a thought of ever becoming a musician of any kind to say nothing of going on the road with the big league band that was the champion of all big league bands, but I did prefer Duke Ellington to the Duke of Wellington even then and not only did I get away with ad-libbing "It Don't Mean a Thing if It Ain't Got That Swing" in my cleanup rebuttal that time in the city-wide debate finals against Frederick Douglass High School, I brought the house down dignitaries and all and won the trophy for M.C.T.S. and went around tipping on Sugar Hill patent leather until the track season began.

I came outside and saw the sea from the terrace and walked through the garden looking at the sculpture and there were some of the largest storage urns I had ever seen. There were also fragments of ancient columns and sections of bas-reliefs from some of the local ruins. Some of the urns that had been brought up from the bottom of the old harbor had once been used in the wine and olive oil trade. Some of them were almost five feet high. They were now used for decoration and as planters.

The garden was in full bloom. The bright flowers moved sparkling in the keen salty breeze and the warm sunshine. I sat on the thick wall, which had been a part of the ramparts of the old fortification, and looked at the gulls circling and swooping over the glistening water. Then I looked back across the promenade toward the beaches and the point of the Plateau de la Garoupe, which I guessed had been an invasion point since ancient times.

I went back inside and looked at the paintings and drawings remembering what I had seen in California and what I had been reading about in the guide books and the library at the villa. Picasso was like the Bossman Himself. He could do everything any other painter could do and do it better, and there were all kinds of other things that he could do that nobody else would even try. Joe States used to swear that the Bossman Himself could even make a business report sound better than the next best musician sounds with lyrics. He probably would have said that Picasso could stain a wall with a stream of you know what better than the next best painter. For my money he could.

There was always somebody like that. It was always worth more of my money to see Sugar Ray Robinson working out on the speed bag than I would pay to see a lot of other good fighters win a title by knockout. It was worth the price of a World Series ticket to see Willie Mays warming up in any baseball park, or even on a sandlot; and I would trade a touchdown in the Rose Bowl by almost anybody else just to see Jim Brown run signals. As for the Bossman Himself, he could sit at a piano better than most musicians could play it. The band always played better with him there even when he didn't do anything but sit there and point and make faces.

At one end of the grand salon there was a large triptych of a satyr, a faun, and a centaur with a trident. All three panels were very simple black and white drawings on a white background and they looked like enlarged sketches from a book on Greek mythology. But as soon as you saw them where they were you realized that all of that was also a part of the life you saw around you every day on the Mediterranean. You didn't have to think about it. All you had to do was be there and look at it after seeing the plage at Juan-les-Pins.

At the other end of the same room there was a painting of Ulysses and the Sirens, and through the door you could see related paintings and sketches on the walls ahead. There were also still-life studies that showed some of the local fruit and regional seafood. The reclining figures were also local. So were the sailors. One sailor was eating sea urchins. One was yawning. Another was dozing. All of that went with the old harbor. And later on I read about another related painting called *Night Fishing at Antibes*, which I was to see again when I got back to New York. That was that afternoon at the Museum of Modern Art where I was playing in the garden with Eddie Larkin's pickup group and during the intermission I found it on the third floor landing and on the way back down to the garden Eddie Larkin kept saying, *Night Fishing at Antibes*. I like the way that makes you think about Rock Skipping at the Blue Note. You dig? Makes you think about a beach in

France, makes me think about a club in Chicago. Man if you were getting to more of them in France than I was getting to in Chicago, you were getting to a lot of them.

I remember the design stylized from sea urchins in picture after picture. They were used very much as riffs were used in music. I had never seen so many sea urchins before in my life. I grew up in a seaport town and I don't remember ever even being aware of such a thing until I went to college. I don't remember knowing about them in California, not even in San Francisco. I was too busy with yellowtails, flounders, and sand dabs in California. I didn't even get around to albacore. In Gasoline Point I was too busy crabbing and shrimping for gumbo. And the standard fish were croakers and catfish. Channel cats came from Mobile River and mudcats came from Chickasabogue Creek.

I tasted sea urchins for the first time the day after Jewel Templeton and I arrived. We stopped at a seafood stand near the beach and she ordered them and the vendor could tell that I didn't really know what they were and she showed me what part to eat. And when I tasted it and nodded smiling, she said, Now you're on the Côte d'Azur, *monsieur*. Now you are truly there. That night I had côte de veau de la crème and the next day we drove all the way to Toulon's for my introduction to bouillabaisse.

I liked the paintings, and as I moved from room to room I also liked the way everything blended into the remodeled interior of the fine old castle. So much so that before I was even halfway along I had already decided to come back again as soon as possible. It was too much to take in on one visit anyway. All you could really do was find out what was there and pick out what you wanted to see the next time.

I also liked seeing the other visitors and hearing that many languages spoken everywhere you went, all day, every day. That was something else that was part of being on the Côte d'Azur. I had played in some fine casinos all over the United States and I knew a lot of beautiful beaches, but none of them compared to the South of France. They had their points. They had the sand and the water but people were forever getting fed up with them over one holiday weekend because of other people. But creeps, jerks, bandits, thieves, and other criminals have always swarmed all over the Côte d'Azur and they haven't ruined it yet. Not for me. But maybe I'm just a down-home high school boy after all. I really don't know. But there is such a thing as style and class in places just as there is style and class in say singers and boxers, and Miami Beach doesn't have it. Las Vegas doesn't have it. Monte Carlo does.

A tall distinguished looking middle aged man and two slightly younger looking women came in and stood looking at the painting called *Joie de Vivre*. The man, who was deeply tanned and had a neatly trimmed sun bleached mustache, was wearing a cruising cap, a blue double-breasted blazer with white shorts, and was carrying a camera and a swagger stick. The women were wearing straw hats. One was wearing a sheer red and white polka dot dress. She looked like an Italian. The other, who looked French, was wearing a gray and yellow candy striped blouse with a white finely pleated skirt. Both were carrying straw bags. All three were wearing espadrilles.

They stood talking softly in English and French. The man was explaining the composition in English using the swagger stick as a pointer. The way he moved it made me think about a conductor waving a baton. He had a British accent and he had the kind of vibrato that went with London town houses and country manors. I guessed that he had his own private art collection, his own racing stable (or maybe it was polo ponies), his own yacht, and maybe his own plane. That was an old bandstand game we used to play in all of the swanky nightclubs. Somebody, say old Malachi Moberly, would pick out a ringside party while he was at the solo mike and when he was laying out he would ask somebody in the rhythm section what kind of whiskey was being served and sometimes the answer was big steel whiskey or oil well whiskey or automobile whiskey department store whiskey and so on. Old Otis Sheppard used to look at the way certain girls were dressed and the way they acted when the waiter was there and classified them as rich bitch stuff, expense account stuff, pay raise stuff, big chance stuff, and so on down to wide-eyed stuff and meal ticket stuff.

Regardez, regardez, the French woman was pointing to one of the fauns in the picture, *comme* Picasso *à* something something too fast for my textbook French at that time. *C'est mignon* something something something something in machine gun staccato.

The other woman answered in Italian as I had guessed she would and the French speaking woman caught her breath twice, batting her eyes, and I suddenly realized that she was not gasping but was saying, *ah oui, oui* as in oh yes, yes. *Mais définitivement.*

Tu sais, the man said to her as I moved on away. *Eh bien,* the great painters of the Renaissance. *Habituellement, ils ont* something something. Not only the faces. Most of the background landscapes.

I moved on toward the ceramics and the pottery. That was what Jewel Templeton was excited about during that time. She had been reading everything she could find about it all that week and she had been to see it three times already although she had been coming to the Musée Grimaldi for years. I liked it too. I had my own reasons and I also knew what hers were, and when I got back up to the villa late that afternoon she was waiting to go for a drive before dinner, and the museum was the main thing she wanted to talk about. And the first thing I said was, That Picasso. He's together. He's got it all going.

We were passing through Golfe Juan, and she knew that I knew we were that close to Picasso's villa because she had pointed it out and told me about all that the day after we arrived. She looked at me and smiled behind her new Italian dark glasses. Her hair looked like a shampoo ad. We drove on through Cannes.

When she asked me what I liked most I said, The bullfight dishes and the female jugs and bottles, looking at her looking at the road. At the intersection she decided to take the route through the back country of Estérel to Fréjus and Saint-Raphaël and come back along the sea. Still looking at the road she reached one hand into her bag and took out a purple headband. She put it around her neck like an elastic collar and then lifted the front end over her face and swept it back to keep her hair from blowing in the wind.

———

And I also see what you mean, I said. And she said, About my food thing. And shook her head and then said, It's incredible. It's absolutely incredible. And I said, I thought it was the most natural thing in the world. And she said, That's just it. All this time and all of a sudden I realize that. What was I thinking about before?

We zipped on through the town of Mandelieu. I looked it up on a carte Michelin. It was twenty plus kilometers from Fréjus and well on our way up into the rugged green Massif. The sun was still high but at that altitude the temperature was already beginning to be cool.

What was I thinking about all that time? she said shaking her head again. And I said, All of the things that all of those wild forms and figures make you think about. That's enough to make you forget all about the fact that what you're looking at is pottery.

And she said, Maybe you're right but you didn't. And I said, Maybe because I was already clued in. Otherwise I might have been thinking about beach toys or something. Mexico or something. Pueblo or something like that. And she said, Maybe you're right. Then she said, You remember the "Ode on a Grecian Urn"? I'm sure you read that poem in college. And I said, In English 104, 5, or 6. Ideas and Forms. One, 2, and 3 were Freshman Composition.

Maybe it was something like that, she said thinking about it. After all it's not really pottery anymore. It's not really decorated utensils. It's art based on decorated utensils.

She thought about it again. She was always thinking something out. It never embarrassed her to let you know when she didn't understand something. She would ask you about anything if she thought she could get the information she wanted. She never minded starting out sounding stupid because once she learned whatever it was that she didn't know before she had it from then on. Maybe it was because she was that good looking and that famous she didn't have to be already hip to everything. That was also the way certain rich people were. They were so rich and powerful that they didn't have to prove that they were also smart. Once upon a time there were aristocrats who didn't even read. They didn't need to. There were plenty of people to read for them. Her good looks made her an aristocrat of sorts. And she was smart too. But she didn't confuse it with being hip.

She drove on looking at the road and then she said, I've always had this thing. I've always had this big thing about buying my kitchen stuff at the hardware store and the restaurant supplier. We were zooming along through the hills then, the motor echoing in the trees and gorges. She took the curves with ease. She enjoyed driving in terrain like that. Sometimes she did it for relaxation and sometimes that was the way she memorized new parts. I had read that in a magazine in college. According to the articles she did it alone then, late at night and early in the morning on 101A north from Santa Monica, on 66 east toward San Bernardino, and on 60 and 111 to Palm Springs. She was not really the same person I read about. I was not really the same person either. In a way I was. In a way you always are. When she was not there she was almost always Jewel Templeton, especially at first. More than later. When she was there she was who and what she and the relationship was about.

I took the map from the glove compartment again and located Mont Vinaigre. We came on through the Col de Roche Noir. And I pinpointed the Tour de Mer and the Pagoda. And then there was the old Roman town of Fréjus. I saw the ruins of the aqueduct and we came on through the gate that was left from the old fortified wall and circled by the ruins of the ancient theater and arena. But we didn't stop that time and we headed back along Route N98.

We were on the Côte de l'Estérel then, where the blue water crashed and foamed white against the rugged red rocks, and some of the backwash looked like it had been stained with fresh blood. I had seen the California coast south from Monterey and Carmel and that was something too, but I had never seen rocks that made reefs and miniature bays and islands and natural swimming pools like these. At some points the pools were so still and clear, and the jagged escarpments were so sharp that you could look down and see all the way to the bottom even that late in the day. On our left was the Massif de l'Estérel against the westward sky.

She drove toward Miramar, Théoule, and La Napoule-Plage. She had seen all of that many times. And every now and then she would pronounce the name of the town we were going through. Anthéor, Pic du Cap Roux, Clanaque de Maubois.

She drove on and the next thing she said was, But this pottery thing. Suddenly it is the most fascinating thing in the whole world. I don't really remember what I said to that if I said anything. Maybe I just nodded or touched her without taking my eyes from the sea.

Present company excepted, of course, she said watching the serpentine road and patting me there at the same time. I put the map away and we came on back toward Cannes, the incoming breakers foaming phosphorescent on the beaches in the twilight and in a few minutes the streetlights twinkling like stars.

I'm going to buy some of it, she said finally. That's what I'm buying this time.

The next morning we drove up to Vallauris. And I saw the workshops and the kilns and we watched the craftsmen. There were also vineyards and olive groves on the outskirts of town and everywhere you went there was also the odor of the flowers that were grown and distilled for the perfume industry, the focal point of which was Grasse. We saw where the special potter's clay came from and I found out that Vallauris had always been mainly a pottery town. Its earthenware utensils had been used all along the Mediterranean for centuries.

See what I mean? Jewel Templeton said. In the old days it was like pots and pans from the hardware store. And I said, That's exactly what I was thinking. I said I was thinking about tinware. I was also thinking about galvanized water buckets and washtubs and cast iron skillets; and I remembered a tinware repairman who used to come onto our street from Gin's Alley carrying two charcoal furnaces, which I used to think looked like railroad lanterns, who used to call himself the tinware man, the inware man. Inwamp! Inwamp man!! He also called himself the devil's disciple. And if you called him a tinkerer and said, Inwamp or inowamp he would chase you with a red hot soldering iron. Sometimes when you followed him around too long he would suddenly whirl on you brandishing it like Satan's pitchfork. And if you pointed your finger at him it was as bad as playing the dozens.

The people from Gasoline Point, Alabama, used baked clayware. They also used crockery churns for making buttermilk and sometimes they used them to ferment wine in. Most of the time it was blackberry wine and muscadine wine, but sometimes they also used elderberries and wild cherries. You could get drunk from eating too many of the kind of wild cherries that grew in Gasoline Point. Old Cateye Gander Gallagher once fell out of a tree doing that.

Now they put frames around it, Jewel Templeton was saying. I nodded and she went on and I was looking at the black pine smoke moving skyward from the kilns. It rose above the pink tile roofs and the trees and faded away in the upper air. I looked at the horizon. There was no view back down to the sea. They frame out the connections, she said. But I still don't see how I missed it all this time. I never missed it with porcelain.

We stopped in Place Centrale and looked at the statue of the man carrying a young sheep. And she told me about it. But from the rear he looked like a saxophone player taking a solo as you see him from where I stand by the piano. All he needed was to have his toes pointed in a little more like Herman Kemble. But he could almost rock as he was. Maybe he was taking a sweet solo. Maybe he was cooling it because he had it all in his fingers, all in his head and fingers like so many ofay musicians. Maybe he was trying to riff like Charlie Parker. Maybe he was the man with the yardbird horn. Too bad Picasso didn't get onto the blues as he got onto African sculpture. He would have had a ball just sketching old Louis. He could have done all kinds of harlequin things with Dizzy Gillespie, the crown prince of arabesque. Too bad he never made the Harlem scene not to mention the cross country scene with the Bossman Himself.

The statue was called *L'Homme au Mouton* and from the front he looked like a businessman carrying a sheep. There was something about that which made me think about Old Pro. Not that there was any physical resemblance. Maybe it was the neatness of his hips. There was something about the neatness of Old Pro's trousers that went with the spotless way he copied out his manuscripts. There was something about the statue's neck and shoulders that made me think of trumpet players. There is almost always something military about the way most trumpet players hold their shoulders, especially when they're playing as a section. When they solo you get something else. You get a lot of things you don't even see in the dance groups. I wish Picasso knew all about that. Then he could do musicians as the Greeks once did athletes. He could do them on plates like his bullfight plates. And they could be chitlin plates, I thought. He could have a blues period to go with his blue period and then he could have a Kansas City period and maybe an uptown downbeat period that would really cause a downtown uproar. I wonder if Picasso would go for down-home cooking.

I didn't say anything about any of that and Jewel Templeton must have thought that I was still thinking about the statue and she called it the dignified banker with the billy goat and I said, Left holding the billy goat without horns and she said, Passing out billy goats without horns.

We headed back down the hill toward Golfe Juan and then there was the sea again. She pulled off the road and we sat looking at it beyond the palms. The damp breeze stirred the leaves on the hillside. The rooftops shimmered under the open sky. The sun, like the vegetation, was tropical again, but you could still smell the lavender and jasmin from Vallauris.

As soon as I heard her voice, I knew that she was changing the subject from pottery to something else. She was excited about pottery. She was suddenly solemn about what she was thinking about now. I tried to be as casual about it as possible and waited for her to go on. And she said, I don't know when I've been so happy. Really happy. Not with success, not in triumph, just plain happy.

I was having a good time too. I was having the time of my life. But somehow or other I did not think of myself as being happy, and there was something about the way she said she was that was suddenly almost like an embarrassing confession. It was as if I was not yet old enough. Happiness was something I was still getting ready for as I was still getting ready for life with Miss You Know Who. So what she said made me suddenly aware of the difference between her age and mine. She was not really old but she was that much older than I was. She was as old as most of my teachers had been. She was as old as Mr. B. Franklin Fisher himself. She was older than Carlton Poindexter. But that still didn't make her very old and I didn't really have to remember that because I had never actually forgotten it. It only made me feel very young. It made me feel almost too young to know what I was really doing there. It made me remember how many young men my age were still in school. Well so was I.

And now I'm going to tell you something else, she was saying then. Now I'm going to tell you a big, fat secret.

I looked at the palms and the sea. I was sitting with my legs crossed and my fingers clasped together around my knees. Then she was looking at me again and I wondered if she had changed her mind about what she was going to say. Because she reached out and touched my wrist, her hand covering my watch. I unclasped my fingers and put my arms around her shoulders.

Then what she said was, I never say things like that anymore, absolutely never. Every time I say I'm happy about something, I get frightened. I look back over my shoulder. I cross my fingers. I can't help it. Maybe it's just show biz superstition.

I held her and looked at the Mediterranean and thought about the day I had decided to extend my stay with the band. And then I was thinking about the day I decided to stay in California. I wondered what was going to happen next, but I was really too busy to think about it. Too much was happening now. I was too busy keeping time every day, me and my almost middle twenties years and my bull fiddle from Miss Hortense Hightower and my bright-eyed curiosity.

So much depends on luck, she was saying. So much depends on chance.

XL

O n the way along Autoroute Estérel-Côte d'Azur from Biot, where we had spent the afternoon making the rounds of all of the pottery works on the list she had made, she began telling me about her maiden trip to the South of France on her delayed honeymoon eighteen months and three productions into her first marriage.

Speaking of fairy-tale dreams come true, she said as we zoomed on in the direction of Nice to the intersection with Route N7, which would take us back toward Antibes and the turnoff to the hills above Juan-les-Pins, my first time in these incredible parts was as the saying goes nothing if not precisely that. And more. Because at the very same time it was also an excursion into all of those historic moments and events that you are only very vaguely aware of before, but that our Baedeker, Michelin, and Blue guides were forever referring to. And don't forget. The groom himself was an art director. So dressing up and making the scene in Monte Carlo was great young movie celebrity fun, but when we went up to Èze and La Turbie he threatened to try his hand at writing a historical novel, because of a sudden urge to sub-merge himself in the study of the manners, architecture, and costume of those times. He didn't follow through on the novel, but his enthusi-asm was real, and he did get a chance to apply his researches as a designer on a couple of class B costume productions. Nothing on the scale of Cecil B. DeMille, but he had fun.

I must say, she said, you couldn't have picked a better traveling companion. It was a fairy-tale episode all right. But not kid stuff by any means. He was not really Prince Charming. Being slightly older and representing that much highly professional authority, he was some-what more like a bachelor king who marries one of the slightly younger not entirely naive but not quite yet cosmopolitan ladies of the court, if you know what I mean. Anyway that honeymoon was, as you like to say, storybook stuff for a midwestern schoolgirl type like me.

The trips to Europe she had made with her family during her childhood had been tours of such major cities as Paris, Rome, Milan, Venice, Vienna, Berlin, Copenhagen, Amsterdam, and London, during which she had seen the countryside mostly en route between stops on the itinerary prepared for her father by his travel agent. But the honeymoon was a matter of deluxe and completely casual serendipity, which made his ever expanding scholarly inquisitiveness even more exciting to her undiminished schoolgirl curiosity than it already was when she was attracted to him in the first place.

Up to that time she had said whatever she had said about him ever so casually and almost always as if only incidentally and also as if referring to something I already knew anyway—and I reacted in kind and related it to what I had read about him in the magazines and trade papers. But after dinner that night she went on reminiscing about that part of her life, and that was when she finally got around to telling what she wanted me to know about what he had meant to her.

Speaking of self-made men, she said, he qualifies on all counts. Then she said, When I told the Marquis de Chaumienne the story that I'm about to tell you, he said the matter of personal identity is not at all the same in America as it is in Europe, and his very first example was a story that F. Scott Fitzgerald told in *The Great Gatsby*, which I had read as a Jazz Age novel about status seeking but which he described as a novel about passing. He knew very well that to almost all Americans passing meant mulattoes crossing the color line to be accepted as white people. But *his* point was white people passing as whiter people, if you will pardon the expression. Anyway I reread it, and there was that self-improvement routine right out of Horatio Alger and all.

But Mark Howell, *né* Marcus Aurelius Howell, from that little town down in Arkansas, she said, saying his name to me for the first time, was no Jay Gatsby.

I got the marquis' point all right, she said. But unlike Jay Gatsby,

Mark Howell would have seen straight through Daisy Buchanan. Mark agrees with Fitzgerald that the very rich are different and he also liked Ernest Hemingway's quip that it was because they have more money. But Mark himself was about living well being the best revenge.

Mark Howell had hitchhiked his way from Arkansas out to California the summer following his graduation from the local technical school with a diploma in carpentry and woodworking and had found a job with a scenery construction crew; and in six years he had completed enough academic as well as laboratory courses in architectural history and design and in film technology to be well into a career as an all around production technician, as ready with specific details about the geographical and historical background of the story in production as he was handy with on the spot technological adjustments.

When the two of them met at a producer's party, he had been in California eight years and his reputation as a highly regarded art director was such that it attracted a higher level of publicity for their courtship and marriage than her bright very promising new star status. Her publicity was about glamor. His was about taste and class, which gave him an edge in local social circles that she enjoyed rather than resented. After all, some reporters scored his class as a conquest for her glamor.

When I met him, she said, he was just enough older than I was so that it was easy to feel very close to him and defer to him at the same time. Naturally I was very much impressed by his position and his authority with studio bigwigs but he himself was much more concerned with his personal development than with his career per se. He told me his story quite candidly. No games, and without the slightest impulse to impress. He was much too serious about himself to misrepresent his past.

He described his Arkansas background as being redneck, hillbilly, and white trash. And why should he not? After all look at what he was making of himself. You were listening to somebody who had used the accessibility of the movie industry's fantastic collection of international experts in just about everything to perhaps an even greater and certainly no less immediately personal advantage than your ideal Ivy League student uses his venerable professors. Or so I'd like to think at any rate.

In any case, his reputation as a classy guy was no hype. It was something he earned and something I think he understood better than Jay Gatsby, and F. Scott Fitzgerald too, for that matter. He certainly knew more about what to make of Hollywood than Fitzgerald did.

But you know something? As I told the marquis, for my money Fitzgerald, for all his fame and the impression he made in certain New York and academic literary circles, never really outgrew being the wide-eyed overeager young man from the provinces come to seek his fortune in the big city. If you know what I mean, she said. And as I said I did I was thinking about that subsequent generation of immigrant boys out of the Lower East Side and Brooklyn, who went to C.C.N.Y. and to the 42nd Street library, the Metropolitan Museum of Art, the Madison Avenue and 57th Street galleries, somehow came by cheap seats in Carnegie Hall and the Metropolitan Opera, and who hung out in Greenwich Village. But I did not say anything about that because I wanted to hear what else she was going to say about Mark Howell.

And that was when she told me what she told me about how it had begun. Each already knew who the other was when they were introduced at the producer's party, but that was the first time they had actually seen each other in person. He was not as strikingly handsome as Hollywood matinee idol types go, but he was good looking enough in his tastefully cut clothes, and when he smiled, the sincerity of his eyes matched the warmth of his voice, which might have been that of a professor in the liberal arts department of a Big Ten university. So even as they shook hands she realized that she was hoping that they would stroll and chat for a while before the evening was over.

Being of the theater, she said, smiling in anticipation of my mock shock at her all too deliberate stock company of theater, and therefore having a more professional interest in twentieth century theories and experiments in production design than the usual starlet, I decided to ask him if he had any personal contact with Robert Edmond Jones who was at U.C.L.A., and you couldn't have picked a better topic. Except for several brief separations for one or the other to chat with old associates and acquaintances, we spent the rest of the evening talking about such pioneers as Max Reinhardt, Norman Bel Geddes, Jo Mielziner, and Lee Simonson among others, and a week later we began dating.

She didn't go on to talk about their life together, since she had already referred to that ever so matter of factly all along, and I had already seen her photo collection and fan magazine files, which is also where I came across what I know about her other two husbands to each of whom she was married only briefly (six months and eleven months) and neither of whom she ever mentioned to me by name. Somewhat (I couldn't help cracking to myself) as if they had been miscast leading men in two mercifully forgotten class B movies.

Nor did she ever say anything at all about why she and Mark Howell had not had any children during their seven apparently enjoyable and certainly unstormy years togethePr. Nor did I ever mention anything about that either. But since Mark Howell for his part had gone on to become the father of two children by his second and only other wife, I simply assumed that studio control of the private affairs of performers at that time was such that production schedules represented a higher priority than family development; and that the momentum of her approach to stardom had not permitted time out for childbearing.

So, for the time being at any rate, she had chosen career enhancement over motherhood, and if she had any regrets she never mentioned them, or said anything to suggest them. Not that she placed her career above everything else, but only that at that time she did not feel that she was far enough into it to run the risk of not moving beyond the threshold.

As she went on talking about the honeymoon almost as if it were something that had happened only months ago, you got the impression that Mark Howell was not only somebody that she still admired and respected as much as she ever had, but he was also somebody with whom her relationship was still no less cordial for being altogether less intimate. *Which I said was great, because I was thinking it must be a great satisfaction to be able to change a choice without having to regret having made it in the first place. And when she said there was nothing to regret about her choice about Mark Howell because there had never been anything about him that was misleading and that neither could she bring herself to regret her choice of a career over a relationship with him, I said, I see what you mean because I really thought I did, given the schoolboy promises I had made as much to myself as to the expectations of anybody else, beginning back even in the preschool times of Mama and Miss Tee before Miss Lexine Metcalf and Mr. B. Franklin Fisher.*

But even so I crossed my fingers as I always found myself doing whenever something for whatever reason made me so sharply aware once more of the also and also of Miss You Know Who back down you know where as if meanwhile back in Homeric Ithaca that many ages before medieval castles with fairy-tale princesses. Not that you had to be reminded from time to time any more than Odysseus himself had to be, whose fingers were already crossed for the duration of the ten years of the Trojan War before the ten that as every schoolboy should know included Calypso, the Sirens, and Circe.

XLI

I don't have to tell you that this is not good-bye, do I, Mr. Brown Eyes, she said when the time came. We know very well that this is only for the time being, however extended it may turn out to be. You know that as well as I do, she said, perhaps even better. Then she said, After all, it's you not me who got us into this fairy-tale-aunt business. So you know very well that fairy-tale aunts never say good-bye, don't you, Mr. Brown Eyes. They will always be there, won't they?

I had decided to go to New York by way of Paris. She was going straight back to Hollywood, stopping in New York for only as long as it took to change planes. I was taking the autobus route up through Provence and Burgundy so that I could stop off in Avignon, Lyons, Mâcon, Dijon, and maybe Vézelay.

As for myself, she said, trying to keep her eyes from twinkling, What I had in mind when I came back from Saint-Moritz was finding myself a trail guide for an expedition into a territory that I had been made to feel that unless I could not only come to terms with but could relate to no less than to apple pie that I was neither as American nor as cosmopolitan as I thought I was by way of becoming.

That was what I had in mind when I saw and heard you at The Keynote, she said, and then not minding the twinkle in her eye she also said, Not that I remember having had any objections to finding one that I just might also be tempted to share a bedroll with from time to time. But that by my reckoning is a pretty far piece from being a bed-able fairy-tale aunt, young pardner.

But as we say in the trade, it was not a part that I was out there looking for but when it turned up I couldn't imagine myself turning it down. In strictly professional terms, the wicked witch, as any agent will tell you, is almost always the juicier part for your career. But in the personal world of private fantasy the good fairy is really the one you always wanted to grow up to be, beginning all the way back with the very first cradle rocking bedtime stories you ever heard.

On the other hand, I said, I guess I fell into that trail guide role pretty fast myself, native overtones and all. And she said, Well what I was actually thinking in terms of was the idiomatic rather than the native implications. But I must admit that it does carry all too American overtones of the forest primeval and the westward movement nor can I deny that the marquis is almost literally a white hunter of sorts.

A French Denys Finch-Hatton, no less—if you know what I mean, she said. And I said, I think so. Because after my roommate and I read Hemingway's *Green Hills of Africa*, "The Short Happy Life of Francis Macomber," and "The Snows of Kilimanjaro," we had also read Isak Dinesen, *née* Karen, who became Baroness Karen Blixen. Denys Finch-Hatton, no two-finger Swahili expert, he, I said. And no Stephen Foster either, I said.

And she said, All the same, Mr. Brown Eyes. All the same. I'm beginning to miss you already.

We were standing that close together again then, and there was that all too familiar catch in her breath that made you close your eyes because you did not need to look into hers, and before I could think of saying what I was only going to mumble anyway, she put two fingers to my lips and said, Storybook, history book, or clay book, who wouldn't miss such a well brought up young man of parts as you? Just look at you this very minute. Always the completely charming proportion of ever so tentative but undeniable naughtiness and irresistible enthusiasm. No wonder you became such a wonderful bass player in such a short time.

We were already beginning to do what came next as you do it when there are only that many days left before you wave so long for the time being. So I didn't say anything about such upbringing that I had come by beginning with Deljean McCray, Trudie Tolliver, Miss Evelyn Kirkwood that many boyhood years before Miss Slick McGinnis. As for Hortense Hightower and the bass fiddle, I was absolutely certain that I had neither said nor implied anything that could be mistaken about that, but I did like the notion that the gift suggested that Hortense Hightower had my number on all counts.

It had all turned out as if scheduled. When I came back up to the villa from an informal workout in Juan-les-Pins with a group of French musicians, some local and some down from Paris, the news she was waiting to tell me about was that by noon she had finished reading and rereading a new script that she had found not only suitable but also so actually exciting that she had already agreed to go back to Hollywood within a week or ten days because she wanted to be in on all of the preliminary production conferences. She had already agreed to the studio proposal, which included approval of the director plus input on all story line revisions and final editing.

I won't bore you with the current version, she said but I will say that as of two readings it is very much the sort of thing that I've been looking for ever since coming under the influence of the marquis. In any case I'm eager to find out what I can do about this sparkling daughters and muddy waters of the upper and lower Mississippi business that he has made me so conscious of, and if I bring it off you will deserve much of the credit. And if I don't bring it off, I'm going to insist on as much remedial work as your circumstances will permit. But I must say, I really do think I'm on to something, Mr. Bright Eyes. We shall see. We shall see. We shall see. Won't we, Mr. Bright Eyes?

That was that Monday, and she already knew that I was all set for a place to stay during my stopover in Paris. So all she said about checking out of the villa was soon maybe very soon. But no rush, because there were still a few details in the contract to be cleared up and finalized over there and also a very personal matter that she was still hoping to take care of over here before pulling out this time.

So, as it says in the song, she said, Soon maybe not tomorrow but soon. Or better still, she then went on to whisper as if into a hand-held after hours microphone, *not now, not now, not now. I'll tell you when.* And I said, I'm with you, sweet mama. I'm with you. Then with the back of my hand to my mouth in a mock stage aside I said, No torch singer this one. Not this mane tossing sparkling daughter from the upper waters of the Big Muddy.

To which she said, Oh but aren't you ever the bright-eyed one. Then she said, But seriously. And that was when she said what she said about my having come over to the Côte d'Azur as if on a split second segue and thereby earning the luxury of going back stateside by way of Paris as if on one of the ever so many totally casual seeming modulations she had come to think in terms of after listening to me practicing and playing on records, especially along with the Bossman Himself plus Joe States and Otis Sheppard.

I was all set for Paris because through music loving artists and literary friends in Greenwich Village I was in contact with an American couple who was spending eighteen months in Europe with the Hôtel de Londres on Rue Bonaparte in Saint-Germain-des-Prés as a base of operation as they had been doing from time to time for more than a decade. All I had to do was get in touch with them twenty-four hours in advance of my estimated time of arrival.

Meanwhile it was easy enough to go on doing what you had been doing on the Côte D'Azur where, after all, there was always more of the same along with something even better. But as soon as Jewel Templeton said what she said about the latest script, everything suddenly became a matter of vamping in stoptime to the out chorus. No rush, to be sure, but no more lollygagging either.

Then when I pulled in from Cannes that Thursday afternoon the personal call that she had been waiting for had come through, and she had decided when we would be pulling out. But first she wanted to tell me what the call was about, and she said, Of course you know who's arriving Nice just in the nick of time. And I said, Who else but. And she said, It's touchdown and takeoff but we meet for dinner tomorrow night, early dinner followed by need I say what somewhere, maybe some little informal spot where they will insist that you take a turn.

If you don't mind of course, she said. And I said, Okay by me, I said. I know more places between Antibes and Cannes than between Nice and Monte Carlo but whichever, since all it takes is a word from him anywhere in these parts. And she said, This is all so wonderful. She said, I can't tell you how much it all means to me to have things turn out like this, and I do so hope that it's going to be as much fun for you as I'm absolutely sure it's going to be for him. And for me too of course, she said. And when I said, Hey why not, she said, Okay, okay, okay, okay, I know, I know, I know, I know. But it's still something that you might find yourself going along with more as a favor to me than because you really feel like joining in on your own impulse.

And I said, I know what you mean. I said, I know exactly what you mean, but hey, I'm expecting to have a ball. And that is also when I said, After all without him not. Repeat not. I said, without him none of this. No him, no you and me. No us.

And hey, I also said, look at all the fun I'm going to be having up there pretending that I'm not checking on how you're responding to the riffs I'm sneaking in there just because I know you're going to realize that I'm signifying about us.

Which made her smile and shake her head as I knew she would. Then she said, But aren't you the sly one. And I said, Not me. That's my old roommate. I'm supposed to be the nimble one. I'm the one from the briar patch and the candlestick. He, not me, was Reynard the Fox long before I came up with that stuff about Dr. Faustus during our freshman year. Which only led everybody else to turn him back into Reynard the Fox in a disguise of the snake in the grass. Not because he was really snake-sneaky but because he was almost always so offhanded that it was as if he were downright sly and tricky.

The main thing the marquis wanted me to talk to him about during dinner at the outdoor restaurant he took us to in Cannes that Friday night was the time I spent playing with the band and when I told him how it had all come about through Hortense Hightower he said, *Formidable, merveilleux, incroyable!* Directly out of college and into the very center of the pulse of that incomparable orchestration. One had the immediate impression that you were realizing if not a childhood dream of your own, then certainly one derived from dedicated parents.

Which reminded me once more of the fact that nobody had ever set any specific goals for me. Nobody. Not Mama and/or Papa or

Uncle Jerome. Not Miss Tee. And neither Miss Lexine Metcalf, nor Mr. B. Franklin Fisher himself, who was known not only as a fisher of men but also as a molder of men and women commensurate with ancestral imperatives not only of Frederick Douglass and Harriet Tubman in America but also of heroes and heroines in the storybook world at large.

But I didn't say anything at all about any of that. I said, Not me. I said, I didn't realize that I could do what I did until the time came. I said, I never thought anything at all about becoming a musician of any kind, certainly not a professional musician. As much as I've always taken for granted that it was an indispensable part of my life, after all cradle songs and oop-de-doodle bounces were already there before songs became fairy tales.

I said, All I can say is that as far as I was concerned the way that band played music was the way I had come to think about music. I said, What I heard when I heard that band was not only the sound that went with the way things looked and felt but also the sound of how I already felt about things. It was the sound equivalent of whispering to yourself. *The sound not only of my blues bedeviled situation, I said, but also of my aspirations, my fears and frustrations, and my celebrations and exhilarations.*

I said, Once you were in the middle of all that it was not a matter of being able to play through anything that was put in front of you. Nobody expected you to be able to do that. The kind of musicianship they wanted in that position at that time did not begin with technical virtuosity as such. It began with what you heard or thought you heard or wanted to hear. As was also the case with painters and writers. They don't begin by being able to zip through exercises of all kinds of examples. They begin by evolving their own conception of writing or painting and then they have to develop the technique to bring it off.

That was the principle Joe States had in mind when he told me that the band was a bunch of homemade all-stars. We don't hire them, Schoolboy, we make them. Of course, now special talent and/or manifest genius is another matter. We know what to do with it, and we can't stand to let it go to waste or be misdirected. Hell, we don't really need it, but if we happen across it we create a need for it. First the Bossman spots the possibilities. Then there's Old Pro with the necessary touch-ups. And then we see if he can get by the old trickmaster himself.

In my case, Marquis, I said, it was not only like the rabbit in the briar patch, it was also almost like the rabbit in the pet shop. And he said, I can't begin to tell you what this means to me, and I do hope that my how do you say it amateur curiosity is not going to interfere with your appetite or be bad for your digestion, because the cuisine here is really quite good. And I said, Not at all. I said, I really don't mind one bit.

Because I really didn't. I hadn't expected his questions to be any-thing like those of an entertainment page reporter, and they weren't. They were completely consistent with everything I had been told about him. And I could also tell from the very tone of his voice that he had taken at face value what Jewel Templeton had said about me, beginning with the fact that my nickname in the band was Schoolboy.

I really don't mind at all, I said. I've been looking forward to this ever since I first heard about you. And he said, I must tell you. I made reservations here because I know you grew up in the Gulf Coast seafood area of Alabama, and I'm counting on the superb seafood cui-sine here to offset the banality of my hyperenthusiasm about all of this.

And I said, Hey, no days like that. Not from you. And Jewel Tem-pleton said, We're in for a treat, Mr. Bright Eyes. Nothing but nothing can possibly spoil anything the marquis orders anywhere. If we were in Texas I would want him to choose the chili joint. And speaking of seafood, if we were in Spain, you could be sure whose paella choice I'd follow.

They both said that I'd never forget the langouste thermidor and I haven't. We were a party of three for the evening. The marquise was flying in from Italy that next afternoon and along with her would be two couples who were looking forward to meeting Jewel Templeton when we joined the marquis again at the bullfights in the old Roman arena in Nîmes that Sunday afternoon.

During dinner I also agreed to spend several hours between mid-

morning and midafternoon listening to old radio air checks and transcriptions that the marquis had brought along from his collection hoping that I could not only supply missing and garbled titles and explain
puzzling ones but could also identify some of the soloists that he didn't
recognize or was uncertain about.

When we stopped in at the Vieux Colombier in Juan-les-Pins later on
that night, and I was invited to join the house combo for a set, I suggested that we play whatever the marquis wanted to hear, and everybody agreed and he made three requests, which was all you needed for
a generous set in the totally informal atmosphere of a club like that.
After all, since the primary emphasis was on the quality of the improvisation you could extend one number for the entire duration of the set
if the response made you feel like going on and on. As the marquis
knew very well. But he had his own reasons and the musicians were
very pleased with each choice.

The first was "Indiana" (Back Home Again in). The second was
"Sweet Georgia Brown," and for the third he wanted us to run as many
riff ensemble and solo choruses on any twelve-bar blues progression in
any key or keys of our choice as would take us to the end of the set.

So I kicked off "Indiana" as a medium uptempo Kansas City jump tune,
which got an immediate bravo from him. Because as anticipated, he was to say
shaking my hand and clasping me to him when I finally made my way back
to the table after two reprises of blues out chorus, what you did changed home-
spun nostalgia into a cosmopolitan celebration of arrival. And that was when
he also said, I must tell you. One day when I'm in America again I must do
something that has been on my agenda for years. A small thing perhaps but
very personal to me in my fascination with Americana. So many brownskin
jazz bands have such marvelously jubilant arrangements on such an obvi-
ously, how do you say it, ofay standard, that I would just like to see what I can
make of their response as I sit listening in a predominantly ofay audience in
an Indiana Hoosier town like Fort Wayne, Muncie, or even some suburb of
Indianapolis, for instance. I don't know. Perhaps they take it simply as

expertly ingratiating entertainment for white folks not unlike the blackface minstrels of the old times. But given such music I suspect their response is a matter of much more complexity than that. Here are these troubadours who are just dropping by en route to somewhere else and they make the place sound more enticing than any native Hoosier ever has. You can't help wondering what they make of it. The arrangement you played in the band makes it sound like a state anthem. On the recordings of Count Basie's radio broadcasts from the Famous Door it sounds like the perfect place for a holiday romp. And there are the Lester Young combo recordings that make you feel as if you are somewhere being caressed by an elegant lullaby.

Then he said, "Sweet Georgia Brown" was a different matter altogether. With "Indiana" you could have missed, especially with a combo of musicians not native to the idiomatic nuances of jazz, who may alas actually be charmed by the standard version precisely because it strikes them as being as American as a Norman Rockwell cover for The Saturday Evening Post. *But with "Sweet Georgia Brown" you couldn't possibly miss. It can only be a syncopated rhapsody. She is as earthy as she is elegant.*

And when I said what I said about the appropriate tempo of her ineluctable down-home plus uptown modality and he said what he said about Anna Livia Plurabelle, I didn't say what I could have said about Deljean McCray and Charlene Wingate and Creola Calloway and Miss Slick McGinnis, all I did was snap my fingers on the beat and tilt my earlobe on the afterbeat. And he said, Voilà, voilà, voilà. *There you are. Even the pulse of it is idiomatic. That is what is so difficult to come by over here. And without it your authenticity is questionable no matter how competent your musicianship.*

I said, As for your request for a blues based wrap-up. By the time we got to that point, the right groove was no problem at all. And he said, So I noticed and so I had hoped. And incidentally, I can't thank you enough for the totally unexpected pleasure of being granted the privilege of making those requests.

I waved to the musicians, and they all came to the table to say good-bye, and when the three of us were outside again the marquis reminded me of the audio research project scheduled for the next morning and also made sure that the details of our Sunday rendezvous in Nîmes were all clear. Then he began shaking his head again as he had been doing from time to time throughout the session.

I must say, he said holding my hand once more, you inspired them and kept their exhilaration under excellent control at the same time. So they exceeded their technical competence. They, how do you say it, outdid themselves. Then he also said, So you must concede this much to the French. We may appropriate here and there but nothing is also more French than our genuine appreciation and respect for the idiomatic wherever we find it. Yes, we borrow and enrich ourselves thereby, but not only do we remember the source we also return to it time after time for replenishment.

XLII

A t ten o'clock that Saturday morning I met the marquis in front of the music store at the street number in Cannes that he had given me during dinner, and we spent three hours listening to old air checks and radio broadcast transcriptions that he had brought along from the main part of his comprehensive library of recordings, which he kept in his archives in Paris. Incidentally, most of the impressive collection that Jewel Templeton had seen in Saint-Moritz was only his portable selection of vacation duplicates.

The playback equipment in the back room audio workshop was available to him for as long as he needed it over the weekend, but he had brought only twenty items because his time in the vicinity was even more limited than my own had become. He was flying back to Eastern Europe on Monday. I was heading for Paris by midweek.

We didn't need the services of the resident technician because the marquis himself was fully qualified to operate the system we were to use. So we settled in immediately and by noon we had played through all twenty selections, repeating whatever passages I needed to hear again and again, and I was able to come up with answers for fifteen, which he said was at least twice as many as he had allowed himself to hope for.

But of course, he would say as I supplied title after title and identified soloist after soloist. But of course. And he was especially pleased whenever I could also name a well known popular song that the selection in question was a takeoff on, as was the case with one of the band's unnamed getaway shouts that I told him was another one of our many versions of "Please Don't Talk About Me (When I'm Gone)" that so far as I knew was still in the book each with its own call code in the bossman's piano vamp system.

And so it is, he said shaking his head and nodding agreement as I hummed snatches from three examples. And so it is. *Bien sure, bien sure, bien sure!* And furthermore what we have is not simply three variations on the same melody, what we have for the band's functional intents and purposes are that many entirely different compositions. But then such is the nature not only of this music but also of the act of aesthetic creation in general. That what really counts is the treatment. It is not the raw material as such but the treatment that adds up to the aesthetic statement that we perceive as the work of art.

But yes, he said again then, *bien sure*. That is why it is as it is with this magnificent man. Given his ultraspecial sensibility it is as if it is all the same with him. A melody from a highly chic Broadway musical is no less a piece of raw material to be reprocessed than is a folk ditty. I mean really. Indeed, I find myself very much in accord with those who suggest that Tin Pan Alley has been a major source of raw material for jazz musicians ever since the band backed vocals that Louis Armstrong recorded several years after the Hot Fives and Hot Sevens.

That is also when he said what he said about Louis Armstrong's singing being no less a revolutionary influence on contemporary music than his trumpet. Then in the time left, we listened to four of the most recent Armstrong releases available at the counter out front, and after each one he said, Bravo, bravo, bravo. *Voilà, voilà, voilà. Comme il est formidable.* But it is always there, is it not? He is definitive, no question about it.

And on the way along the sidewalk where the cars were parked he said, Speaking of idiomatic nuance, the problem for most outsiders, by which I mean those not native to it, is very complex indeed. First there is the matter of authenticity. Ooh la la, what could be more difficult? It is precisely the same as with speaking a foreign language. There is always the problem of the telltale foreign accent, which the natives almost never miss and which immediately destroys the illusion for them, because their instantaneous response is that of detrimental empathy. If you know what I mean. It is precisely the same as occurs in the theater whenever something happens to make the audience iden-tify emotionally with the actor's stage problem rather than his make-believe situation in the story. A very serious matter indeed, he said, which reminds me of a chat about singers and the basic blues that I had with your bossman some years ago in Paris. He knew very well what I was getting at; and how could I ever forget what he said: that the tim-bre, vibrato, and pulse were no less matters of idiomatic authenticity than slurring and mispronouncing the words *correctly!*

A very serious matter indeed, he said again as we came to where the cars were parked. Then he looked at his watch and held up his hand to indicate that there was still plenty of time for him to drive to the airport in Nice before the marquise landed. Then he said, Another problem is that all too often the outsider's fascination with the idiomatic is likely to be the same as with the exotic.

If you see the connection, he said. All too often it is a matter of escape, rejection, or even full blown rebellion and revolution, or in any case a matter of being deliberately unconventional. Whereas when you are native to the idiom you're simply being conventional if you see what I mean. Your basic objective is to measure up and then maybe excel and in some cases also exceed.

It is not at all a matter of rebellion or revolution or even counter-statement or anything of that sort, he said. Not really. It is, on the con-

trary, a very urgent matter of mastering the fundamentals of an established or, yes, traditional local way of doing something. Basically, you
play the blues the way you play the blues because that is the way people among whom you grew up conditioned you to hear and play the
blues—without, by the way, denying either your individuality or even
personal idiosyncrasy. Such, as I see it, is the nature of the source of
idiomatic authenticity. The effect on outsiders may well be tanta-
mount to revolutionary innovation. But it is not all a matter of experi-
mental trial and error to insiders.

And yet, he also went on to say as he settled himself into his convertible. And yet. It is through the impact that it makes in the larger,
richer, and more complex context of the outside world, is it not, that the
vernacular achieves universality. Otherwise it remains provincial as is
the case in language in the matter of regional dialect, shop talk, or slang.

As for myself, he said turning on the motor and gunning it but
not very loudly and then letting it idle, As for myself, I insist that your
wonderful American music is anything but the folk art of a subculture.
It is the music that I find to be the very embodiment of the rhythms
and disjunctures along with the sonorities and cacophonies of our
epoch. And one day we must discuss the profound significance of its
being extended into the world at large by those to whom it is indige-
nous as compared with the efforts of very gifted and well-intentioned
appropriators.

Until tomorrow then, my marvelous young friend, he said pulling off. Until tomorrow.

That Sunday afternoon Jewel Templeton and I met the marquis and
his party for lunch at the Cheval Blanc, which was directly across the
thickly shaded plaza from the partially restored ruins of the ancient
Roman arena where the bullfights were held. According to the travel
guides this Spanish ritual became a local event back in the middle of
the nineteenth century. Before that the Visigoths, who came after the
Romans, turned the old stone structure into a fortress with a moat,
ramparts, and towers, later removed.

The other guests were two very elegant fiftyish-looking Italian wives, whose husbands were to join them at the Chaumienne château in Médoc when the marquis returned from Eastern Europe two weeks later. I hadn't decided whether I would still be in Paris or somewhere else in Europe by that time or already in New York, but Jewel Templeton would definitely be back at work in Hollywood.

I didn't have any idea of why the marquis was going wherever he was en route to and I didn't ask Jewel Templeton anything about it because she was the one who had made me realize back at the very beginning of our relationship that you never ask such people any direct questions whatever about their personal involvement in business or political matters not to mention international relations. And she said if they themselves volunteered information about such matters it was almost always more likely to be some sort of cover story than anything factual. In such matters it was as if everything involved espionage and intrigue she had said shaking her head knowingly. But that's the way it is, believe me.

The trip to the bullfight was really the fulfillment of a promise to the Italians year before last in Cortina. The marquis had insisted on being the one to introduce them to it because he wanted to make sure that they responded to it not as a barbaric spectacle or gruesome sport such as the Romans had built the arena to stage but as a profound ceremonial Spanish reenactment of the condition of mankind. The Roman arena was a secular place, he began by reminding the Italians, but to the Spanish the bullfight was about very sacred matters indeed.

Jewel Templeton had been invited to come along and bring me not only as a means of adding that much more time to our all too brief encounter, but also because the marquis knew that she was someone who for a number of years had attended bullfights in Spain and in Mexico as well. I had known about that all along because it was something else that dated back to her first husband, through whom as the marquis also knew she had come to have personal acquaintanceships with several well known matadors on both sides of the Atlantic.

As for myself, I hadn't seen my first actual bullfight until Joe States and Ross Peterkin took me down to Tijuana one Sunday during my first trip to California. But before that there were the movies and then in college there was Ernest Hemingway with *The Sun Also Rises*, *Death in the Afternoon*, and "The Undefeated," which my roommate and I had gone through in my sophomore year along with all of the other Hemingway stories and articles you could find in current and back issues of magazines.

When we came to our seats in the arena, the marquise sat between me and Jewel Templeton, and the marquis sat between their two guests and began explaining the structure and sequence of what was about to begin. Jewel Templeton brought the marquise up to date on the current status of the forthcoming production that was taking her back to Hollywood. Then when she also mentioned that I was going to make at least a short stopover in Paris on the way back to New York the marquise said, Yes I know, and opened her purse and handed me an embossed memo card with a list of people to call, places to visit, and things to do and said, As many as time will allow or as many as you fancy. As for the people, Yves is absolutely certain that all will be delighted to be in touch even if you only have time for a call. All being aficionados of your music, speak English, somewhat amusingly to you in some instances, but you would have no problem understanding them.

At the sound of the bugle I looked over at the marquis and nodded and he held up his hand and nodded back smiling. Then he leaned over and picked up his binoculars and settled himself again. His two guests also smiled across at me and then sat forward looking down into the arena, and I got the impression that they were confident that they had been adequately briefed on the minimum essentials of the five acts within which the three classic *tercios* must be accomplished with each of the two bulls that each of the three matadors would have to take on.

So all I expected the marquis to do once the action got under way was to identify specific passes and comment on the quality of their execution from time to time. Otherwise he would hold off on his commentary and evaluation until after each matador had dispatched his second bull. After all it was not a matter of converting the Italians, or even of overcoming any anticipated squeamishness about the blood-shed. They were simply uninitiated, not skeptical. They were curious but not at all naive. To them it was only a matter of close-range on-the-scene orientation.

I myself knew what to expect in each of the five acts because I remembered what I had read about them when Joe States had set up the trip down to Tijuana. I had bought an illustrated book at the Pick-wick Book Store on Hollywood Boulevard not far from Grauman's Chinese Theatre, and I still have it along with six others that I picked up over the years.

It was during dinner in Aix-en-Provence that night that the marquis said what he said about bullfighting and playing the blues. As we sipped our apéritifs Jewel Templeton was telling the Italians about how she, like so many other Americans, had grown up thinking of matadors as daredevils who took unnecessary risks just for the thrill it gave the bloodthirsty spectators, who callously accepted the fact that the bull would still be slaughtered even if he won the contest. It was not until her first husband persuaded her to read *Death in the Afternoon* on her first trip to Spain that she came to appreciate how interwoven the cer-emony of the man and the bull was with the Spanish approach to things. Before that trip she had not realized that the corrida was more ceremonial than spectacular, much more a matter of existential pro-fundity than of festive amusement. Before that she had also shared much of the American view of Hemingway as a tough guy. In Spain she had come to realize that machismo was not a matter of aggressive arro-gance but of a disposition to confront unfavorable odds. The world of the bullfighter was a world of fear. Machismo was not a matter of dis-playing force. It was a matter of overcoming fear with grace and style as well as with skill.

Speaking of your Ernest Hemingway, the marquis said when Jewel Templeton finished her account of her initiation, I think I under-stand why it was F. Scott Fitzgerald that your journalists and social historians most often mention when they refer to the American high times of the 1920s as the Jazz Age. But in my view it is Hemingway whose work is actually closest not only to jazz but also the underlying blues that make the best jazz a possibility. Even when the material at hand is really a thirty-two-bar popular song chorus. Fitzgerald may evoke the twenties decade in a reportorial sense much the same as leafing through illustrations in old stacks of magazines of the period.

Which reminded me that the Ernest Hemingway whose stories and articles had become such a very special part of what my old roommate used to call the goods that I had come by during my first year in college, was not a part of the New York speakeasy scene of the decade following the Prohibition amendment in 1919 as Fitzgerald, who had published *This Side of Paradise* in 1919 and followed it with *The Beautiful and the Damned* and *The Great Gatsby*, came to be. After the war Hemingway had returned to Paris to cover Europe as a foreign correspondent and to begin his career as a writer of serious fiction. It was during this period of apprenticeship that he came to realize that what he learned from the bullfight as ritual was directly applicable to the art of fiction, both in terms of style and of fundamental content.

We were at a rectangular table, with the marquis at one end and the marquise at the other. I was on his right with Jewel Templeton on my right with the two Italian guests facing us across the center decoration. When we finished our *pastis*, the marquis suggested Tavel because we were in Provence and also because we were having a quick supper not a full French dinner. *Then when the waiter left with our orders and the women began to chat among themselves, he turned to me and said, I find much in the bullfight that is entirely consistent with the existential implication of the blues when fully orchestrated. First there is the bull, which is nothing if not the blues made visible, the blues in the flesh, destruction on the hoof, chaos personified, the symbol of all dragons and monsters, in a word, anarchy! Then there's the matador in his suit of lights with his myrtle wreath of a pigtail. He's nothing if not, as Thomas Mann put it, "life's delicate child" who must survive not by his strength and power, but by his flexibility, his wit, and his style. Is not that very much the same as the musician who must contend with the blues? For all of the power that the percussion and the incredibly high notes that your music is noted for, it is the musician's elegant improvisations, especially on the brink, that I find so basically relevant to the disjunctures of contemporary life.*

XLIII

E arly that next Wednesday morning Jewel Templeton drove me down to Cannes, and I shipped the bass directly to Paris by railway express. Then we came on to the autobus station, and I checked in my luggage for the trip to my stopover in Avignon and came back outside, and we sat in the open Jaguar until boarding time, and that was where we finally said what we said instead of actually saying good-bye.

She had picked up a copy of the Paris edition of the *New York Herald Tribune* for me while I was inside, and after skimming quickly through it she refolded it and handed it to me. Then as we sat saying nothing for a few minutes, it was almost as if I had slipped all the way back to the day Miss Slick McGinnis gave me my high school graduation and going away present. It was Miss Lexine Metcalf who not unlike Miss Tee, had always said You will go where you must go. But when graduation time came you could also tell that the ever so slick Miss Slick McGinnis, who herself was forever coming and going, was also more preoccupied with anticipation than the separation at hand.

As so now was Jewel Templeton sitting thigh to thigh in the Jaguar outside the autobus station in Cannes that many years later and that many miles away from Mobile Bay, Mobile River, Three Mile Creek, and the Chickasabogue who looked at me and then looked ahead through the windshield again and said, So have fun doing Paris on your own and all of my very very special good-fairy best wishes or whatever for whatever you decide when you get back to New York.

And I said, And all the best to you back on the Coast and also in the box offices border to border. And remember: no better for such reviewers as don't even get the most obvious point of the effort but presume to grade the outcome. And she said, You said it, Mr. Bright Eyes. You said it. No better for plus than for minus and by the way the moneychangers have already declared themselves certain of fat profits regardless of reviews. Not that such matters concern me at this stage of the game. I think you know very well what concerns me at this stage of the game.

After all, she also said then, you're the one. Not me. As excited as I am about the possibilities of this new thing, it's still mostly a matter of going back to the same line of work with a keener perception of nuance and a new resolve. Not that I'm not as pleased as I can reasonably expect to be. But when I think of all of the options that you still have coming I literally tingle for you.

So anyway you have fun doing Paris, she said again. And I have no doubt whatsoever that you will. After all, who now comes to town? Not just another one of those small town sports from the provinces such as Balzac sent there as Eugène de Rastignac in *Le Père Goriot* and as Lucien de Rubempré *né* Chardon in *Lost Illusions*. Or such as Flaubert sent as Frédéric Moreau in *L'Education sentimentale*. No, this time it is who else if not *le vrai lapin agile*, if you pardon my midwestern high school French, from the Alabama briar patch by way of here there and elsewhere.

We sat saying nothing then, and I remembered what she had said one time when we were talking about the all-American elementary schoolboy and schoolgirl in us all. *She had said, Even now I am still almost as much the schoolgirl as I ever was. Incidentally I do not say that motherhood is not for me but I do keep on saying not yet. And that is when she*

also said, Alas it may very well be as Edna St. Vincent Millay declares in that
poem when she says whether or not we find what we are seeking is idle biolog-
ically speaking.

Maybe so, she said, maybe so. But what counts with the schoolgirl in me
and the schoolboy in you is how we feel about things. What counts is that we
are seeking whatever we are seeking. And I had said, In other words it may
also be as Lord Raglan the Fourth Earl of Fritzhugh suggests in his book
about the origins of civilization when he points out that the most natural
state of human existence may be a state of low savagery. But even so, if there
is always entropy, there is also always the ineluctable modality of the per-
ceivable.

To which I was later to add what I also came to understand about the
incessant interaction of imaginative exaltation (or self-delusion) and ever
impending banalization as I continued to try to come to terms with the ever
more comprehensive implications of the Mobile County Training School doc-
trine of the ancestral imperatives, which amounted to nothing less than the
human proposition itself.

When I turned to kiss her and go because it was time to move to
the boarding line, there was her voice vibrating that close again and
her saying, I really must thank you once more for being so wonderful
with the marquis, who thinks you're just fantastic. Oh, it was as if I had
used my magic movie star wand to conjure up a golden brown storybook prince who was by way of becoming the very embodiment of
what the music you play is all about.

Oh, I very much doubt that anybody from *Burke's Peerage* or the
Almanac de Gotha could match your impact on him. As for myself there
you were once more as you were the night I accosted you as you stood
at the curb outside The Keynote with your arm around the neck and
shoulders of that rich toned earth brown earth mother of a bass fiddle
looking for all the world as if you had just alighted from a foam flecked
steed. Oh, I must say, she said.

And I said, And now it is my time to thank you for arranging me
to have such a very special one-on-one personal encounter with a truly
contemporary cosmopolitan who is as much to the manner as to the

manor born. Who, I could have added, like other sophisticated Europeans almost always apt to strike Americans such as ourselves as being
casually insightful rather than academically or even intellectually
brilliant.

I could also have pointed out that in any case there was seldom if
ever any trace of the schoolboy and schoolgirl left in sophisticated
Europeans once they were grown up, as if they had just simply evolved
as organically as a plant evolves into what it is cultivated to become but
I didn't say anything else because she had clicked on the ignition.

And now you must go, she said, not looking at me again and also
as if to say, We shall see what we shall see as you go wherever you must
go to do whatever you must do. Then as I turned and headed for the
departure gate I heard the Jaguar pull away, but I didn't look back until
I was sure it was out of sight.

XLIV

On the way out of Provence and into Burgundy by way of the
Côtes du Rhône and Saône, I began thinking about the band
again, not only because I was on a cross-country bus trip again and
suddenly missed being a part of the lineup as I hadn't had time to miss
it when I stayed behind in Hollywood, but also because of a train of
thought that my exchanges with the Marquis de Chaumienne over the
weekend had started. And there was also the matter of my forthcoming
functional identity as a musician among musicians in Paris.

After finishing the Paris *Herald Tribune* I spent most of my waking time between Cannes and Avignon tracing the route in the Michelin guide and reading, mostly about the old days of Cézanne but also about Van Gogh and Gauguin in the pocket sized booklet on the beginnings of contemporary art that Jewel Templeton had picked up for me to browse through. I had already been playing around for some time with the notion that Louis Armstrong's influence on the music most representative of our time was comparable to Cézanne's influence on contemporary painting, and as I thought about it again that afternoon with Mont St. Victoire in the distance I suddenly realized that I had missed a chance to mention it to the Marquis de Chaumienne, but I was pretty certain that he would have agreed with the analogy.

The side trips out from Avignon were strictly all-American schoolboy stuff. So at Pont du Gard, as had also been the case with Arles and Nîmes, you were back to the illustrations in your ninth and tenth grade Latin textbook. At such points as Les Baux-de-Provence, Gordes, and Roussillon you were back in your first and second year French language, literature, and culture textbooks once more.

At one turn during the guided tour through the Palais des Papes I became aware again of how impressed I had once been with what Frederick Douglass had been able to make of what he saw there on his journey through that part of Europe in the mid-1880s.

His ruminations about the headquarters of the popes being at once a palace and a prison, with halls of judgment, halls of inquisition, halls of torture, and halls of banquet, like the remarks he also made about the Roman arenas in Nîmes and Arles, had struck me as being very wise observations about the contradictions that are as much a part of the universal condition (or fate) of mankind as everything else.

But even as I considered this as noteworthy evidence of how far this magnificent ex-slave omni-American ancestor of mine had transcended the intellectual restrictions of racial provincialism, I couldn't keep myself from also remembering that alas this same Frederick Douglass, himself a mulatto, now traveling with a white wife, had then gone on to Egypt and in effect claimed a special kinship with the ruins of ancient Egypt, not as a part of his natural inheritance as a human heir of all the ages, but as a darker skinned American some of whose foreparents were captives from West not East Africa.

Nor are matters helped when Douglass goes on to say that his trip to Egypt had "an ethnological purpose in the pursuit of which I hoped to turn my visit to some account in combatting American prejudice against the darker races of mankind, and at the same time to raise colored people somewhat in their own estimation and thus stimulate them to higher endeavors."

Because I had long since come to revere his magnificent ancestral status as much for his wisdom and intellectual sophistication as for his courage, I had come to assume that Frederick Douglass's conception of the human proposition underlying the American promise was more profound than such pathetic defensiveness reveals. Feeling an urgent need to prove to Union, the abolitionists, and the Confederacy alike that downtrodden slaves are able, ready, and eager to fight for their liberation was another matter altogether.

Not that my disappointment amounted to a major disenchantment. As far as I was concerned Frederick Douglass was still the unsurpassed embodiment of *Homo americanus,* warts and all. And with the autobus rolling on beyond Montelimar and Valence toward the next night's stopover in Macon it was almost as if you were seeing the countryside from your old seat in the band bus with Joe States (whose take on the ancient Egyptians I definitely preferred to the implications of Frederick Douglass as I understood them at that time) nodding across the aisle from me once more.

Egyptians? Come on, man. But I will say this much for them. They were some great undertakers. And they left some pretty conspicuous tombs. If you go for such things, which I don't. Man, just look at them frozen butt friezes or whatever you call them and stuff. Man, them people ain't swinging. They ain't stomping cute. And what kind of old stiff-kneed shuffling is that? Man, them goddamn people always look to me like they're on their way to a funeral. And when I think of all them goodies them frigging pharaohs took to them tombs with them instead of parceling that stuff out among all them hungry survivors.

In all events whatever you inherited from ancient Egypt you had to come by like everybody else, not because of any special kind of kinship whatsoever. As for ancestral antecedents, elsewhere on the vast and ever so demographically varied continent of Africa Joe States was pretty much on the case on that too. Not that it was a matter that ever seemed to concern him very much. *Africa? Africa? Africa? Let's be realistic, home boy. This band is a class act. We don't play no music for no rusty-toed clod busters dragging and whirling around for no chief. Man, we don't even want to look out there and see some somitch that need his shoes shined and his pants pressed.*

Africa? Africa? Africa? Hey, that's all right with me about the great-granddaddy of my drums and the grandmammy of the mellow brown in my complexion and all the little cousins of the kinks in my hair. This music ain't got nothing to do with sending no messages to some chief across the river somewhere over yonder. This music we play is about going somewhere and getting on some time in the United States of America.

Man, what I'm laying down for these thugs in this outfit is strictly stateside stuff and mostly down-home stuff to boot. Man, by the time I came along the granddaddies of my drums were them honky-tonk guitar players strumming their driving rods under them fret-fingered train whistle guitar blues in tempos all the way from slow dragging locals and switch engines all the way up through express and highballing express to limited express. Boy, I was already way into all of that I don't know how many years before I put my trap set into a cotton sack and hit the L & N northbound.

As the autobus made its way through Vienne bringing back more recollections of textbook illustrations from Mobile County Training School classrooms and settled into the stretch that would take us on beyond Lyons, I began thinking again about how the marquis was to the manor and manner of the château born, and about how Jewel Templeton and I and most other Americans were born wherever and however we were born to be reborn on campuses. *Certainly the most basic of all things about universal free public education in the United States is that for all its widespread and longstanding entanglement with racial segregation it is predicated on the completely democratic assumption that individual develop-ment, self-realization, and self-fulfillment is a matter of inspiring learning contexts not of one's family background and certainly not a matter of one's ancient racial forebears. So assumed Miss Lexine Metcalf and Mr. B. Franklin Fisher, neither of whom ever confused race with culture. Windows on the world indeed. Windows on basic patterns and idiomatic variations in human behavior.*

Joe States Joe States Joe States, I kept thinking as the Paris bound auto-bus pulled on away from Dijon heading for Avallon and the swing over to Vézelay before continuing on to a turn through Auxerre. *Joe States Joe States Joe States, Uncles Bud, Doc, Ned, and Remus as same height big brother in bespoke tailoring second to none.* Everbody's main man was the Bossman Himself to be sure. And everybody's undisputed master craftsman of musical nuts and bolts second only to the unfathomable genius of the main man himself was who else but Old Pro. But even so, who else but Joe States was the band's self elected and unanimously approved elder statesman? *Who said, me and you, Schoolboy. Get to me fast. You may be just what this band needs at this stage of the game.*

Listen, Schoolboy, he kept repeating during my first month or so in the band, this stuff we play for this band is not just music. This stuff is life, School-boy. Life! LIFE. Man, I mean I'm not just talking about cutting some dots. Man, I'm talking about making them dots mean something.

Being a member of this outfit is not just a matter of being an expert in cutting some weird dots, Schoolboy. When you come right down to it what I'm talking about is having your little story to add to the bossman's big story. And don't ever forget that this is a dance band, whatever else it might be. It's the bossman's stories with all of our little chapters in there that make people want to move something.

You know what we're always up there trying to do when we're out there on them concert and stage variety tours? Trying our best to make everybody

down there in them orchestra rows and over them boxes and up in them bal-
cony tiers wish they could get up and get out on the floor and dance.

One of the first things you found out as soon as you came on to
the stand to play your debut dance set with the band was that Joe States
was the one who always made sure that you were keeping close tab on
how the couples out on the floor were responding. Your job was not
just a matter of being good enough to fit in with the rhythm section he
said, it was also really a matter of helping the bossman please them
people out there trying to get on some time.

The bass player is not just some kind of picture frame or pedestal,
Schoolboy, he said. The bass is always there to lay that indispensable
foundation for the ongoing stories. Them pistons and drivers got to
have a track under them. And that was when he also insisted that what
you did in every bar could also be just as personal as what the featured
horn men did in their solos and fills.

Hey man, my motto for this band is let's get them dancers first, he
always used to say. Even when they're lying in bed listening to the
radio. Even if they're all entwined together somewhere out there in
lovers' lane. You keep them dancers happy and you ain't got nothing to
worry about because they'll be coming back. Like I told the bossman
back when we were just starting out. I said, We got to make people
want to dance that think they can't dance. And know what he said? He
said, You can dance with a lot of things other than your feet.

So naturally, Joe States was the one who said what he said that
night in that ever so classy country club in the suburb of that midwestern town that I won't name because the band always has been and still
is so popular there. Hey like I said, Schoolboy, this stuff we put out is
supposed to make people want to do things, but man, sometimes I also
wonder. Man, sometimes some people go into action before they get
the message. Now here I am making damn sure this band puts this hall
in a groove that's hip deep, and just look at what some of them people
out there doing. Man, goddamn. Man, I declare. Man, but what can I
tell you except there it is again.

But what the hell, he also said two numbers later. We got them up and out there trying and having themselves a hell of a good time in the process. So there you go, Schoolboy. We do what we can. And if they didn't like what we're about we wouldn't be here.

Then as we file offstage after the first set there was somebody behind me saying Just keep thumping, Schoolboy. Just keep thumping. And I didn't recognize who it was at first because I hadn't been in the band very long yet, and when I looked back I was surprised because it was Fred Gilchrist, the first trombone man, who was called the Silent Partner not only because he took so few spotlight solos but also and perhaps mainly because he did not talk very much to anybody about anything whatsoever.

Just keep thumping that bull fiddle, Schoolboy, he said again backstage. Man, I used to think I'd never get used to some of the stuff people do out there. Man, sometimes I used to have a hard time just trying to keep a straight face instead of laughing or frowning. But then I realized something. Man, we got them people doing their best to try to get with it.

That was only a few weeks after Joe States had introduced me to the band as a newcomer at that rehearsal in Cincinnati that first morning. His smile and handshake had made me feel as welcome as everybody else's had and he had also stopped by the booth to shake hands again when Joe States had taken me out to see some of Cincinnati that first evening. But that night between sets was the first time he ever said anything to me person to person. And he never actually brought up the topic again, but every now and then when we were playing another dance in a similar place somewhere and he saw me looking back at the trombone section he would nod his head toward the dance floor and wink.

The scenic route to Paris from the South of France by way of Provence and Burgundy was not through Flaubert country, to be sure. Flaubert's native territory was Rouen and environs in the northern province of Normandy. But regional differences notwithstanding, it was Flaubert's famous remark about peasant life that kept coming to mind as the bus made its way through the small towns and smaller settlements and on past the vineyards and farms and rolling pasturelands along the Côtes du Rhône and then the Saône with what I took to be the hunt country in the distance.

As a matter of fact the legendary pronouncement that I hadn't heard since the night Eric Threadcraft kept repeating it as we drove back across town from a jam session out on Central Avenue to take the Hollywood Freeway to the Sunset Boulevard exit, popped into my head the very first time the bus made a rest stop that was long enough for a short visit to an open air market.

Ils sont dans le vrai, ils sont dans le vrai, ils sont dans le vrai, Eric Threadcraft had kept repeating as much to himself as to me. And I told him that was the first time I had heard anybody actually say it since my old roommate and I used to play around with its implications as early on as the first term of our sophomore year. *Then my roommate and I had become more impressed with what William Empson had pointed out about how sophisticated artists and intellectuals used pastoral (or the glorification of peasant life) as a literary device or rhetorical strategy to depict "an inversion of values" by representing peasant life as being richer in the basic virtues of humanity than aristocratic refinement and elegance!*

So I said, Hey man, he was talking about country folks. I said, he was talking about peasants. I said, Man, you got to watch that "blisses of the commonplace" jive, if you know what I mean. I said, Hey man, don't go sentimental on me.

And he said, Not me fellow, not me. He said, I'm not talking about folk music. I'm talking about Kansas City four/four. I'm talking about not losing touch with the fundamentals. As Count Basie never does. As the Bossman Himself never, but never, never has and never, never will. Hey, fellow, I'm talking about keeping the flame.

So then I said, Maybe that was what old Flaubert was really talking about too. And you know good and well that I'm all for it. But man, don't ever forget that the hometown expectations that made me the schoolboy that I became are about raising the horizons of aspiration of the so-called common man. *What was important to the folks in my home-town was not that you could have a good time among the so-called common people of Gasoline Point on the outskirts of Mobile, Alabama, but that such a place could produce people of extraordinary potential and achievement.*

After the stopover in Dijon during which there was a side trip back to the vineyards of Nuits-Saint-Georges, Clos-Vougeot, and Gevrey-Chambertin that had been passed up after stops at Poligny-Montrachet, Meursault, and Pommard on the way to Beaune, I finished the travel books about the dukes of Burgundy and France in the Middle Ages.

Then on the way to Auxerre after Avallon and the side trip to Vézelay (where references to Bernard of Clairvaux and Richard the Lion Heart took you back to the Crusades) I wished for something to read about storybook castles, knights, and troubadours. But when you pulled on through Joigny and headed for Villeneuve and Sens, it was as if you were already approaching the outskirts of Paris.

So I took out the Michelin and Hallewag city maps of Paris (both of which showed the key landmarks in three dimensional drawings that looked like the cutouts on Miss Lexine Metcalf's third grade sand table) because even as we rolled on past the turnoffs to Fontainebleau and Corbeil and Senlis, *I was thinking first the banlieues and then the arrondissements and thinking when you see the Eiffel Tower and the Seine you're there.*

XLV

When you came out on to the narrow sidewalk in front of what was the Hôtel de Londres on Rue Bonaparte in those days, you were facing a grilled entrance to a courtyard of the École des Beaux-Arts, which meant that you were in the Latin Quarter. So when you turned right and went to the corner *tabac* to get the newspaper, directly across Quai Malaquais and the Seine was the Louvre, and the French Institute was in the block on your right.

On your left along Quai Voltaire was Pont du Carrousel, which led to the gateway through the courtyard of the Louvre by way of the Arc de Triomphe du Carrousel, which you could see was in a straight line with the center walk of the Jardin des Tuileries, the Obélisque in the Place de la Concorde, the Avenue des Champs-Élysées, and the Arc de Triomphe in the Place de l'Étoile.

From the exit on the other side of the courtyard of the Louvre, you crossed the Rue de Rivoli, Rue Saint-Honoré, and you were on Avenue de l'Opéra, at the other end of which only a few blocks away was the Paris Opéra itself, a stroll to which would take you past Brentano's Bookstore, the Grand Hotel, and the Café de la Paix. Then when you crossed Boulevard des Capucines you were not only at Place de l'Opéra but also Rue Aubert and at Hotel Scribe and the legendary Paris office of American Express.

Across Boulevard Haussmann directly behind the Opéra were Les Galeries Lafayette and Au Printemps, the two most famous department stores in Paris. That was as far as I went on my first exploration of the Right Bank. But when I had to go back to use the American Express exchange service a few days later I went on as far as Gare Saint-Lazare and came back by way of Madeleine, the Place de la Concorde, and Quai d'Orsay.

When you turned left from Hôtel de Londres, Rue Bonaparte led to Église Saint-Germain-des-Prés, which was the name not only of the small square but also of that whole quarter of Paris, and its main thoroughfare was Boulevard Saint-Germain. Across the square from the church were the sidewalk tables of Café des Deux Magots, across the street on the other side of which was Café de Flore, across the boulevard was Brasserie Lipp. These were all literary checkpoints, and the main checkpoint for American musicians, not only in Saint-Germain-des-Prés, at that time was the Vieux Colombier, which was a downstairs club in the same building as the Café des Deux Magots.

If you took Boulevard Saint-Germain to Rue de Tournon and turned right you came to Place de l'Odéon, Shakespeare and Company bookstore, and Palais Luxembourg, in which there was a gallery that I knew about from reading Hemingway and there was also the Odéon branch of the Comédie Française; and beyond the Palais was the Jardin du Luxembourg, which took you all the way to the Place de l'Observatoire beyond the intersection of Boulevard Saint-Michel and Boulevard du Montparnasse.

I turned right and headed along Boulevard du Montparnasse for Boulevard Raspail and the Dôme, the Rotonde, the Select, and the Coupole, cafés I had read about in *The Sun Also Rises*. I had a beer in the Select and studied the map and guidebook and decided that I would come back through Luxembourg Gardens again the next morning and turn left along Boulevard Saint-Michel and visit the Panthéon and the Sorbonne on the way to Notre Dame and then browse my way through the book stalls and go on along the quais past Île de la Cité back to the French Institute and Rue Bonaparte once more.

It was also in the Select that I decided that on the day following the trip down Boulevard Saint-Michel and back along the Left Bank from Notre Dame, I would find out how to take the bus to Montmartre and then another bus across to Étoile and walk on over to Palais du Trocadéro, Palais de Chaillot, and the Musée de l'Homme. Then from there you could go on across the Seine to the Eiffel Tower or there was the Musée Nationale d'Art Moderne on the way back along Avenue New York at the crossover to Quai d'Orsay.

When I left the Select I went back to the Hôtel de Londres by strolling along Boulevard Raspail to Rue de Rennes, which took you directly to Saint-Germain-des-Prés. Then after a nap I took a shower and changed clothes and ate at the nearest bistro on Rue Jacob. Then I headed across Pont du Carrousel to my first encounter with the ladies along Boulevard des Madeleine and Boulevard des Capucines.

Not because I actually expected anything more fancy or exotic than what you had already been initiated into as an apprentice road musician in those days, and certainly not after having spent as much time as I had spent freelancing around Hollywood. But really because it was something that I had fantasized about ever since I had been ever so subtly permitted to contrive to overhear the capers Soldier Boy Crawford and other AEF veterans reminisce about in Papa Gumbo Willie McWorthy's barbershop.

It was not at all a matter of curiosity, exploration, and revelation for me as it had been for old Soldier Boy Crawford and the other doughboys who after all were still as oblivious to the existence of the *Kama Sutra* and the *Perfumed Garden* for instance (as I was not by the time I had finished junior high school) as they were of Miss Lexine Metcalf's bulletin board and sand table peoples of many lands. No, with me it was really a matter of personal verification of the actual texture of the also and also of the fable and the flesh.

And as you turned off Avenue de l'Opéra, there they were, walking that walk and talking that talk that made all the difference in the world. And on my way back to Pont du Carrousel and Hôtel de Londres afterward, I was to tell myself that what made it worthwhile and worth doing again had as much to do with the idiomatic nuances of Parisian French as only they spoke it and with Parisian perfume as only they wore and projected it (not without the faintest pleasant hint of bistro garlic and bistro carafe wine withal) as with any unconventional range and specifics of the choreography as such.

As a matter of fact such was the tone and tempo of the one to one intimacy that was so instantaneously generated during my first and second evenings that as much as I had also picked up over the years about how there were always pimps keeping tabs on the streetwalkers with the same authority as house madams had over their ladies, I forgot all about that part of it much the same as you forget about the proscenium, the footlights, and the director as soon as the curtain opens on the stage set. And not only was such the case the first two times, but even as I spotted the signal as my choice of the evening passed a corner bar on my next exploration, it made no more difference than when you passed the stage manager in the wings on your way into the action on stage.

There were also the ladies of the sidewalks near Gare Saint-Lazare and also of Montmartre and the kikis of Montparnasse and such also was the also and also of the "parlors" on your checklist that even as each madam began her all knowing smile the schoolboy in you stepped into the plushest pleasure domes of the *flâneurs* and grand horizontals not only of the Belle Époque but also of Balzac's Paris of fifty years earlier.

Meanwhile there was also the also and also of all the other reasons you were stopping over in Paris en route to New York. Which in addition to guidebook tours on your own also included mornings or afternoons and sometimes whole days in the Louvre, the Orangerie, Musée Nationale d'Art Moderne, and the Musée de l'Homme. Along with which there was also not only the also and also of the contacts with fellow countrymen on the scene, made available by backstage friends in New York, but also those chance encounters that sometimes turn out to be even more memorable than some of the key items on your carefully prepared agenda.

By the end of that first week I had also started checking out what was happening in jazz clubs around town, beginning with the Vieux Colombier in Saint-Germain-des-Prés because it was only a few blocks away from Hôtel de Londres and also because I was already as familiar as I was with the Vieux Colombier in Juan-les-Pins.

The one in Juan-les-Pins was on the beach on your right as you pull out heading for Antibes. The one in Saint-Germain-des-Prés turned out to be somewhat smaller than I had imagined because of its reputation among musicians. But there was no reason to doubt that it was one of the most important clubs of its kind in all of Paris at that time.

Another not very far away spot on my list was Chez Inez (Cavanaugh) over near the Sorbonne, and after that there were several other now mostly forgotten ones in and around the Latin Quarter. Then when you cross over to the Right Bank and made your way on up to nighttime Montmartre you were entering the part of Paris in which American entertainers and jazz musicians had become *all the rage* back during the heyday of Place Pigalle and all of the other hot spots you grew up hearing and reading about in stories about Josephine Baker, Bricktop, Frisco, Spencer Williams, Sidney Bechet, and the one and only Royal Highness.

The Montmartre that I had visited by day was what was left of one ever so bright-eyed schoolboy's Belle Époque world not of musicians as such but of the entertainment provided in places like the Moulin Rouge by such legendary night creatures as Yvette Guilbert, Jane Avril, and La Goulue among others, and celebrated by Toulouse-Lautrec and Édouard Manet, among others.

Nor was there very much of what you had imagined of the heyday in what you came across in nighttime Montmartre. But it was still very much the capital of Parisian nightlife, and as such was second to no other such district in the Western world. After all, entertainers like Josephine Baker were still around and so were Bricktop and Frisco as were musicians like Sidney Bechet and a number of others including Don Byas and Kenny Clarke. But as far as I was concerned the best sets that I heard while I was in Paris at that time were not in any club including Vieux Colombier but during concerts in auditoriums like Salle Pleyel in the Palais de Chaillot and during the dances I went to in Salle Wagram because some group on tour from the States was booked there.

Not that the state of American music in Paris was really a matter of any urgent concern to me at that time, because as completely involved with music as I had been between the time that I went on the road with the Bossman Himself and the day I left Hollywood, I was not stopping over in Paris as a journeyman bass fiddle player or even as a part time semipro freelancer. I knew very well the chances were that I would be spotted and invited to do guest shots from time to time by somebody who recognized me from the context of the band, and I didn't mind obliging. Not only because it provided an easy way to choose new friends, but sometimes it could also lead to a little extra chicken change, not that I was looking for it.

Incidentally unlike a lot of horn men and guitar and chin fiddle men, who perhaps more often than not used to take their instruments along with them when they made their rounds in those days, I didn't take my fiddle into any club in Paris until after I had been asked to fill a request on the current bass man's instrument and had then been invited back. Actually the only time I ever took my instrument along when I was making the rounds anywhere was when I left the band and was getting started as a freelance newcomer around Los Angeles. And the main reason that I could bring myself to do so then was that having the use of Jewel Templeton's auto incognito made having it at hand seem so casually incidental. After all the last impression you wanted to create anywhere was that you were expecting or hoping to be invited to join in.

Anyway, although I didn't really mind being recognized being flattered and applauded, I had not come to town to enhance my reputation as a promising young musician. As useful as such an identity was especially in Paris, I was there only for a stopover for essentially the same reasons that I would have spent the summer and only the summer there between college and graduate school if I had been able to afford to do so at the time that I had gone on the road with the Bossman Himself as temporary replacement for Shag Philips.

Not that being in Paris at long last was no more (or any less) of a schoolboy's dream come true than it ever was when I was in college. But by the time I actually arrived, there was also the also and also of my recent personal encounter with the Marquis de Chaumienne, whose catalytic impact on me had already become no less than his undeniably crucial influence on Jewel Templeton through whom indeed his effect on my conception of coming to terms with my functional definition of my personal identity and universal whereabouts had already begun during that first morning when she told me what she told me about meeting him in Saint-Moritz.

So in a sense it was very much as if the actuality of being in Paris was so consistent with all of your longtime anticipations made you somehow almost restless to complete your visit and so have it as an accomplished dimension of the firsthand personal experience that was an indispensable part of the equipment in your existential tool kit (*and thus also a part of the back home practice sessions you so often find yourself all but yearning for as if precisely because things are turning out so well for you elsewhere*).

Not that I ever seriously or even tentatively considered shortening my checklist. But even so, what the also and also of the day to day patina of Paris at firsthand clearly stimulated beyond all else was an irrepressible urge to be back stateside getting on with what was to come next, whatever it was.

Which was a reaction that turns out to be much closer to how Jewel Templeton came to feel about her trips to Europe as soon as she entered the charmed circle of the Marquis de Chaumienne and his cosmopolitan friends than to how any of my idiomatic cousins among the Americans I met in Paris felt about being there.

Ezel Adams, for instance, an after hours piano player from the outskirts of Chattanooga by way of Pittsburgh, uptown Manhattan, and Greenwich Village piano bars, who was rooming in a pension in Saint-Germain-des-Prés when I was there, and who said, Hey, what about this Paris, man, and said, Man, this is the life, and said, Man, every time I wake and realize that this is where I really am I have to pinch myself to prove that I am really here in the flesh and blood and not just dreaming.

I had heard him play two sets at the Vieux Colombier, and I had also seen him come in with friends during my second guest shot in there, and we had nodded and smiled and made the high sign to each other each time. But we didn't actually meet each other until he came over and introduced himself while I was sipping a *citron presse* at a sidewalk table of Le Petit Mabillon on Boulevard Saint-Germain several blocks away from the Café des Deux Magots in the direction of Café Tournon.

Hey, what say there, my man, he said, sounding down home and uptown at the same time, I just wanted to tell you how much I enjoyed your gig the other night. That was some nice stuff you laid on them, man. Nice, nice. Very nice. And they picked up on it too. And I said, Hey, thanks, man, and nodded for him to join me, and said, Man, I was in there when you laid some stuff on them yourself, remember? I said, Man, there they were with all their ever so Parisian and international chicness and you eased them right on out into the back alley and had them responding as if it was the most natural place in the world to be.

And he said, Hey, man, that's this Paris for you. Ain't nothing like it. Man, this goddamn Paris, France, is the place I been heading for all of my born days. Now I'm not saying I always knew it or anything like that. I heard enough about it to want to see for myself and when I got here that was it for me.

When I told him that I was there only for a stopover, he said, What a pity and a shame. So, when I told him that my limitation was self-imposed all he could do at first was shake his head and say, Hey, come on, man, you expect me to believe that? And I realized that he just might be thinking that I was trying to cover up the fact that I was either short on funds or uncertain about my chances of making a living in Paris as a musician.

Whatever he actually thought, the first thing he said when he introduced me to Calvin Curtis at Café Tournon a few days later was, Man, this cat is incredible. Man, this cat is on his way back stateside on his own timetable when he could gig around over here for no telling how much longer if he wanted to. And Calvin Curtis, who was knocking around Europe as a reporter and features writer from Chicago said, Man, what for? And when I said, Unfinished business, man, he said, Come on, man. Or do you mean that you got yourself a big fat surefire deal waiting that you just don't want to string out any longer? And I said, Hey, man, what can I tell you? I'm just here to touch a few bases before getting on back to the matter of some very important unfinished business. That doesn't mean that I'm not already planning to come back from time to time. It just means I'm not sticking around but for so long this time. And he said, Hey, man, it's your call. It's just that a lot of home boys over here wish they had the option to stick around that you musicians have. And I said, I think I know what you mean man, I really do.

And that's when I also said, Listen, man, what they like is American musicians playing American music. Our kind of American music. Don't forget that. Man, I don't know anything about them wanting American musicians to become French musicians. Or American writers to become French writers. If you're an American musician and you move to France they still expect you to play music in an idiom that is authentically American.

Then I also said, And as for painters, man, ain't nobody in the world more crazy about Paris than American painters and sculptors have mostly been over the years. But I don't know any instances where the French have ever sent for any of them as they send for our kind of American musicians.

And he said, You got a point there, my man. You got a deep point. I can tell that you really have been thinking about all this stuff. I really mean it. In fact, I'm beginning to wish you'd stick around a while longer just because you're so different to talk to, my man.

Danny Dennison, a writer from New York, was also somebody I had exchanged nods and waves with in Vieux Colombier before we said hello and had a drink together at Le Petit Mabillon. I was to get the impression that he had become much more involved with my kind of music and musicians as such since coming to Paris than he had ever been back in New York. He had grown up in the very heart of Harlem, but his was the Harlem of church folks rather than the Harlem of bars, nightclubs, and ballrooms. The clubs and bars he had come to frequent when he grew up were those where certain writers and artists hung out in Greenwich Village. In any case, I remember him as identifying much more intimately with folk and hot mama blues and the earthier forms of down-home church music than with jazzing, swinging, stomping, riffing, grooving, bopping, and so on. Although he was anything but square and could get up to date with it on the dance floor if the occasion called for it.

To each his own is what I always say, he said in response to being told of my self limited stopover status. To each his own. He flourished his Gauloise *bleue* cigarette, his instantly friendly "smart cookie" eyes twinkling playfully. Or as they say over here, *Chacun selon son goût.* Or in my case, *selon sa faim.* Because in my case, it was truly a matter of life and death. No two ways about it, baby. When it really hit me. When I could no longer deny what those awful people over there really had in store for me it was a matter of hauling my black ass out of there, pronto.

Some stay and submit. Some stay and contend. And believe me when I say I honor and celebrate them because I really do. But these nevertheless are such personal matters. Whatever they saw there must have inspired or indeed fired them on. But what I came to see was myself being consumed whole soul and body—*soul before body!* Many bodies survive through street smarts, but the survival of one's soul is another matter altogether. The existence of my soul depends on me being a writer and I could not become a writer in that place. It was as if it were against the law. Against the law for us, I mean.

He always referred to himself as being black, which I took to be a matter of principle or policy, because he was in fact only a slightly darker shade of brown than Ezel Adams whose hair texture before processing was also pretty much the same as his. He was also shorter and slighter than Ezel Adams who was about five feet eleven and weighed about one-eighty and had a slight paunch that is not unusual in piano players even before they are thirty.

Also, unlike Ezel Adams, who dressed like the well-tailored after hours piano player that he was, and who did a version of the patent leather avenue limp walk that gave the impression that he was wearing house shoes even on the bandstand, Danny Dennison's clothes and carriage made him seem as much a part of the world of ballet and modern dancers in New York as the world of writers and artists in Saint-Germain-des-Prés.

Calvin Curtis was a not quite high yaller northern city schoolboy type that some down-home folks regarded as being a bit too concerned with proper speech and bearing. But as far as I was concerned the main thing about him was his preoccupation with academically certified conventional standards of excellence, whether in personal appearance or professional performance. And I found myself thinking that he would have made a much better military officer or say airline pilot, than a newspaper reporter and features writer he had become at that time. Precisely because he would have derived far more personal satisfaction from proving that he could measure up to the most stringent professional standards than he seemed to be getting from trying to express his personal point of view of things in his published articles.

We didn't talk about vocational choices although my own choice was what was very much on my mind at the time. But whenever something brings him back to mind I can still see the look of personally achieved security on the face of the air force officer or airline pilot as he and glamorous guests are seated at a ringside table in one of the exclusive clubs that I used to play in. (Incidentally it would not be the uniformity of the uniforms that he may or may not wear to the nightspot that attracted him but rather the challenge of sartorial perfection required by the air force and the airlines.)

I met the painter Roland Howard Beasley one afternoon at Montparnasse when I happened to be sitting close enough to his table to overhear him referring to Royal Highness as if to a longtime acquaintance. He and his companion, who turned out to be a college English professor and poet on a traveling fellowship, were talking about old vaudeville performers who were always in and out of the old Lafayette Theatre, the Harlem Opera House, and the Alhambra when he was growing up on 135th Street off Seventh Avenue.

There were not many people in the Coupole during that part of that midweek afternoon. So you could hear what conversations at nearby tables were about without really paying any specific attention. But when I realized that Royal Highness was being mentioned I stopped reading what I was reading, and when I heard Roland Beasley referring to him as Daddy Royal, I decided to introduce myself to him on the way out; and the three of us left together and at Boulevard Raspail, Roland Beasley and I promised to meet at the Closerie des Lilas that next afternoon.

When I got there he was waiting by the statue of Marshal Ney and on the way inside he began telling me that he was going to be on his way back to New York in several weeks when the term of the special courses in contemporary French culture and philosophy he was taking at the Sorbonne would be over. He had hoped to extend his stay in France a few weeks longer but he was also looking forward to getting back to his studio.

Man, what can I say? he said as we waited for our drinks. You can't beat this goddamn Paris, especially if you're a painter, but it ain't home, if you know what I mean. And you being a musician I'm pretty sure you do, because you know there's all the difference in the world between playing music for people over here and doing it for folks back home.

Because, he went on as we tasted our drinks, it is a matter of making up the music for them. Because you're making it up out of something that you and that audience over there share so much of. That's where you start. Then if you go on and get good enough you just might also turn some of what you come up with into something that people all over can relate to. And by that I mean as if it's the most natural thing in the world of here and now and maybe for some time to come.

The fact of the matter is, he was to say later on, that I came over here to find out as much as I can about how these people came up with all this stuff that's so fantastic and so much a natural seeming part of everyday life in the workaday world. And how much of it I need for the express purpose of doing my own thing with my own stuff. So you know what? I guess that makes me one of the truest sons of that bunch that

Malcolm Cowley wrote about in *Exile's Return*. Man, as I'm sure you know, that bunch was over here loving every minute of it. But their best stuff was about being Americans if not about the United States itself.

And remembering reading Cowley's book at my favorite table in the main reading room of the library during the fall of my senior year in college (with tennis balls plopping back and forth outside but with my best of all possible roommates not there to discuss such things with anymore) I said, Hey, man, you know it too. Hey, too much, man. I said, Man, you *know* something. *Because there we were sitting in the very same Closerie des Lilas where Hemingway had come up with some of his back home four/four prose (derived in part from the style sheet of the* Kansas City Star) *that in its own way was as idiomatic, valid, reliable, and comprehensive as the "St. Louis Blues."*

I stuck out my hand because I was absolutely certain that he knew what I was thinking, and as we slapped and snatched palms, he smiled and then laughed with his tongue between his teeth like a schoolboy, and his eyes became moist, as I was to find that they always did when he was especially pleased about the way something connected with something else. It was the same prankish schoolboy chuckle that I was to see when things were going well in his studio when I visited him in New York time after time during the years that followed. And I decided that it was as if a joke was being played on the complexity of actuality. As if the joke was the means by which form was achieved from the actuality of the undefined.

Anyway, my man, and I do mean my man, my brand new cousin, he said, wiping his eyes that afternoon in Paris that many years ago. As much as I really would like to stick around a little while longer and also zip back through some of the places I've taken in, that is why I got to be getting on back across the pond to my little old dinky woodshed and see what I can come up with. Hemingway could do it over here and other places too. But man, as much as I love it none of them cats knocked as many people out overseas as old Louis Armstrong and the Bossman Himself.

My woodshed and my launching pad, man, he said, because what old Louis and the bossman make me realize, when I listen to them over

here, is that when you talk about achieving universality in the arts
you're talking about something that is really a matter of interconti-
nental ballistics, my man. When you listen to that stuff over here you
keep thinking about where you know old Louis and the bossman are
coming from back home.

As for me and Daddy Royal, he finally said several afternoons later
when we met at Brasserie Lipp as we had agreed to do, Johnny Hud-
gins, the comedian, was there first. But Daddy Royal became one of
my main uncles. By which I mean along with being the headliner he
was for everybody else I got close enough to him for him to become
the same kind of uncle as Uncles Bud, Doc, Ned, Remus, and Zack, if
you know what I mean and I'm sure you do, home boy.

And I said, Down-home boy. Which makes us idiomatic cousins,
I said. And he said, Idiomatic. You said it, man. So let's keep in touch,
cousin. And I said, By all means, thinking this is also what the also and
also of being in Paris can add up to.

XLVI

---

*Z*one of the interior, I began thinking again as the plane settled
into its cruising speed en route from Le Bourget to New York.
*Zone of the interior from border to border and coast to coast (plus twelve) of
the continental limits of the United States, which began with a gradual settlement of the lucky thirteen aboriginal colonies that somehow and anyhow*

came to predicate a nation that was a new kind of nation on the principles underlying their declaration of independence from the England of King George III.

That was the precise phrase become poetic notion that had popped to mind again on the way back to the hotel from dinner with Roland Beasley at the Mediterranée in Place de l'Odéon the night before. We had spent most of the meal talking about what I later came to think of as the vernacular imperative in the creative process. But we had also spent some of the evening questioning the depth and scope of the sense of alienation that so many of the idiomatic relatives we had met in Paris were forever talking about. So when we said so long, and he went along Rue Monsieur-le-Prince and I came on to Boulevard Saint-Germain and headed for Rue Bonaparte, that was what I was thinking about again and I said, As for me, it's back to the zone of the interior.

Which was part of the terminology I remembered from the junior high school textbook for physical geography and so already knew when I came to political geography and political science. But which over the years had also come to have as much to do with the natural human resources definitive to national character as do such Department of the Interior concerns as roads and bridges and waterways and mineral deposits and parks and wildlife have to do with national subsistence.

Not to mention the exercise of national power in international affairs, which include matters that you were to become increasingly aware of your personal involvement with as you advanced from the geographical descriptions of elementary and intermediate school studies to the awareness of historical causes and effects that high school and college courses and professional monographs were so much about.

The original out of doors benchmark and mercator projection school map triangulation point of all of which was the chinaberry spyglass tree in the front yard of that sawmill quarters shotgun house in Gasoline Point on the L & N Railroad outskirts of Mobile, Alabama, from which the North Pole was due north beyond the Chickasabogue horizon and Nashville, Tennessee, and Louisville, Kentucky, and

Cincinnati, Ohio, and Chicago, Illinois. Which made Philamayork north by east up the Southern and Seaboard route to the Pennsylvania Railroad. So San Francisco, California, and Seattle, Washington, were north by west as the eagle flies, whereas Los Angeles, California, was west to the Pacific from New Orleans through the deserts and plains and across the mountains. Due south beyond Mobile Bay and the Gulf Coast was the old Spanish Main of the historical romances followed by the boy blue adventure stories about derring-do and the seven seas.

Zone of the interior, zone of the interior, zone of the interior, I said as I let the seat all the way back to the reclining position and closed my eyes. What the Marquis de Chaumienne may or may not have known was that you for one could have become as instantaneously nostalgic about the Mobile and Gulf Coast environs of the Alabama that was the well-spring of all of my sky blue aspirations when I heard "Back Home Again in Indiana" (for all its Hoosier connotations!) as when I heard "On Mobile Bay" or "Stars Fell on Alabama."

Nor could "The Star-Spangled Banner" take you more deeply, if as deeply, into your own personal zone of the interior than Louis Armstrong's rendition of "Sleepy Time Down South" always did. What "The Star-Spangled Banner" was most likely to take you back to were those Mobile County Training School flagpole ceremonies and assembly room periods that were so much a part of what being an all-American schoolboy was also about. As did "My Country 'Tis of Thee" and "America the Beautiful." Whereas Louis Armstrong's instrumental version of "Sleepy Time Down South" took you all the way back to the coziness of the chimney corner chair on winter nights and the breeziness of swing porch steps on summer evenings back in those ever so wee preschoolboy years when the yarn spinning used to begin as early as twilight time.

Return of the native born, I thought once more as the tires of the landing gear finally screeched, skipped, and settled ever so gently down onto the runway, and as we headed for the taxi lane and our parking berth, you felt the way you felt because you were rearriving in North America for the first time ever. *Commodious, vicus of recirculation, indeed,* I reminded myself remembering the very first globe I ever saw and which Sunday school boy that I also was at that time I thought represented the whole universe above which was heaven and everlasting bliss and below which was hell and eternally infernal damnation.

Remembering also how it revolved on its tilted polar axis and how because of its position with reference to the sun, its revolutions made the difference between the nights and days that add up to weeks and months and years and so on to ages on the one hand and on the other hand could be subdivided into hours and minutes and even split seconds. Then later on there was also the equally important matter of the earth's orbit around the sun, which accounted for the seasons.

Which is why it was that even as I made my way through customs, I had already decided what I wanted to try to get set up to do in New York during the next fall term. And I had also already estimated that I could complete all of the advanced arrangements for matriculation and lodging in ten days or less. After which I would be heading south for the outskirts of Mobile. But only after the commuter flight from Atlanta to central Alabama by way of Montgomery at long last for the also and also of the reunion in the home place of Eunice Townsend.

Apropos of all of which was also the also and also of the encounter I had with a long forgotten hometown boy during the last three days of the stopover, who said what he said about his own obligations, aspirations, and expectations and who also said what he said about the way things turned out for him that Wednesday night.

1.

when I came out of the IRT subway on the uptown exit between Seventh Avenue and Broadway, I stopped at the newsstand and bought the

Times, the *News*, and the *Post* and waited for the light to change looking at the traffic flowing along Broadway toward Times Square. The sidewalks were already thick with late morning sightseers and theater district people, performers with makeup kits, dancers with their rehearsal togs in shoulder bags, entertainment producer and agent types with briefcases.

across Broadway in the same block as Jack Dempsey's restaurant, which was a midtown sporting scene landmark in those days, there was the usual cluster of musicians on the corner near the Turf Club eatery and the Brill Building in which there were booking offices as well as rehearsal studios, and I was suddenly homesick again for my schoolboy status in the band, which I knew was doing one-nighters in the Midwest. I hadn't seen the Bossman Himself since California. I hadn't heard from Joe States since his letter responding to my card from Juan-les-Pins.

when I looked up Broadway toward Columbus Circle I checked my watch against the clock on the Mutual of New York insurance building and remembered that Carnegie Hall was on the southeast corner of 57th Street and Seventh Avenue. The traffic light was green again then, but as I started to cross the street a cab pulled up to the curb and I recognized the young man getting out as soon as the door opened although I hadn't seen him since he left Gasoline Point back when I was still in high school.

it all came back in a flash. He had gone to Chicago and I don't remember hearing or even thinking about him since I left town for college. He stood waiting while his companion closed the door and paid the fare. Then the two of them turned and started toward the newsstand. They were a perfect match for size and also seemed about the same age. Both were wearing gray turtleneck sweaters and identical safari jackets and tan water repellent porkpie golf hats, brims down.

hey, you're Marvin, I said. Marvin Upshaw!

and he saw me then and turned and came toward me calling my name as easily as I had called his. The last time I saw him he was fifteen. Now he was six feet tall and weighed at least one hundred and seventy pounds.

man, what you doing way up here, this far away from the L & N Railroad and the cypress swamp bottom? he said. And I said, Man, just dogging around, just dogging around. And he said, Hey, this is one of my old homeys, man. And as his companion, whose name was Ben Rutledge and who I could somehow tell was also a down-home boy although not a hometown boy, shook hands, he (Marvin Upshaw) said, Man, this is a hell of a long ways from Hog Bayou. Man, this is a thousand miles beyond Chickasabogue Bridge and Hog Bayou. Man, they don't have no fishhead stew up here.

and I said, Man, that's not what they told me. Man, they told me you can get that stuff anywhere these days and they were not lying because I had some of the best I ever tasted down in southern France. They called it bouillabaisse over there but they can't fool me, not about that kind of stuff. Which is not to say that they can't lay some of the greatest dishes in the world on you, I said. Man, they declare that that is the original gettin' place for fishhead stew, I said.

and he said, Hey, man, you too? Man, it didn't take me no time at all to find out that you can get black-eyed peas and collard greens in Chicago just like on the outskirts of Mobile, Alabama. And I'm talking about along with all that big city stuff to boot. Ben knows what I'm talking about. I know I don't have to tell you he's one of us. He's not a city, but he's a statie. Ben's from the Ham, man. And Ben Rutledge said, Bessmer.

and when I said, One of my very best older friends is from the Ham, thinking of Joe States, he winked and said, And I bet he intends to stay away from there too. I sure do. I intend to stay as far away as I can get. And the reason I ain't no further than I am now is that I really do believe the world is round so I'm subject to come around to it again if I go any further.

hey, Marvin Upshaw said, let's have a quick sip of something if you've got a couple of minutes. We have a few. Where you headed? And I said, Pork Chop Eddies. And he said, Too many people in there I don't want to have to talk to today.

so we stopped at the snack bar on the corner and they ordered hot tea with lemon and I ordered the same, but with sugar and remembered the two of us in Gasoline Point. He had never been one of my cut buddies, but at one time Little Buddy Marshall and I had been very friendly with him, and sometimes the three of us used to turn up at the same time to hang around to eavesdrop on the man among men conversations in Papa Gumbo Willie McWorthy's barbershop when old Cateyed Gander Gallagher the gallinipper had a shoeshine stand there, inside in the winter and out on the porch in the summer. And sometimes we also used to stand out on the sidewalks together waiting for the girls to come out of Alzenia Nettleton's cook shop at twilight on Saturday nights.

when he and his family moved up north to Chicago I knew about it, but only because I heard about it, and I didn't really miss him very much because he had dropped out of school and gotten a job first as a delivery boy for Stranahan's store and then in downtown Mobile, and all we had been doing the last year or so was waving and nodding at each other as we passed on the street. I don't remember anything that we actually stopped and talked about during that time.

from where we sat you could see across 50th Street and Broadway to the huge Roulette Records billboard. As I sipped my tea, he said, So, are you still into baseball as much as you and old Little Buddy Marshall used to be? You still walking in the footsteps of old Gator Gus? And I said, Man, I haven't played baseball since high school. And he said, Is that so? I was already gone before then. But that's right, I remember all that now. You were one of the smart ones in school. Man, me, I found out what that thing was about and that was the end of school.

and Ben Rutledge said, Man, that was the end of school for a lot of cats I know, including me. You know what I told them? I said, I got your conjugation. I told them, Man, while y'all conjugating all them verbs for class, me, I'm going to be doing my kind of conjugation even in the grass, if ain't nowhere else handy. And Marvin Upshaw said, Man, the goddamn grass is exactly where I started, playing hide and seek.

but now him, he said looking at Ben Rutledge but indicating me with his thumb. He was out there digging his toes in the grass, not just on picnics, but anywhere else just like he's one of the gang and all the time he was sneaking off not just conjugating them verbs for class but reading every book he could get his hands on.

and when I said, Hey, man, they had girls in school too, he said, Man, I forgot all about them. Man, I guess I must have thought them girls up in Tin Top Alley and places like that were the only ones doing it. Man, I never thought about schoolgirls like that. Man, if I had known then what I found out later about how hip them girls were by the time they got to college I probably would have gone on and got myself a goddamn Ph.D. by now. Man, all that ladylike neatness, deportment, and punctuality turned me off, man.

and when I said, What about Miss Lexine Metcalf? he said, Man, I was scared of that woman. Man, he said shaking his head in schoolboy bewilderment that many years later, I was scared to even think about Miss Lexine Metcalf.

and I said, Man, I never have been scared of anybody that good looking. Man, I couldn't keep myself from dreaming about her like I also used to dream about old Creola. And he said, Old Creola Calloway, Yeah. Everybody used to dream about old Creola. But that Miss Lexine Metcalf. Man, that was a mean and evil woman.

and I said, Not if you got her lessons.

which I damn sure didn't ever do, he said. Man, that woman was so mean and evil, she was downright ugly to me. Like them evil women in them nightmare movies. Man, as far as I was concerned Miss Lexine Metcalf was as ugly as any bear in the bottoms. Man, every time she crossed my mind, all I could see was that classroom and them blackboard problems, maps, and shit like that.

but hey, man, he said then looking at me with down-home affection and approval, what you been doing with yourself? I can see you've been doing all right whatever it is.

and I said, Man, you won't believe it and don't ask me to explain it. Man, I went on and finished high school and college and since then I've been knocking around as a musician. And now I'm right at the point where I'm about to decide what I'm going to do next.

that was when I told him about how I happened to go with the band and about being in Hollywood and about going to Europe. I didn't mention Jewel Templeton. But I did name some of the records I had made with the band. And he said, Hey, that's big league stuff, Scooter. Man, that is sure enough incredible. Man, when I think of you back when we were kids, what I remember didn't have nothing at all to do with being a musician. I mean what comes to my mind is school and sports. Man, I remember you being as crazy about sports especially baseball as about school. And here you come helping Joe States and Otis Sheppard lay down stuff for Herman Kemble and Scully Pittman to the specifications of the Bossman Himself.

Malachi Mobes, Ben Rutledge said, Mister Chandler, Ike Ellis, Osceola Menefee. Man, you turn up with a musical instrument around them thugs and ain't ready you'll get mugged not out in no back alley. Right up there in the spotlight! And Marvin Upshaw said, I can't get over this. But now that you're telling me what you're telling me I do remember that you did used to hang around Papa Gladstone's jump band even when they were just rehearsing. But a lot of baseball players were like that about music, just because they were so hip and so smooth with the chicks on the dance floor. But you, man, you were always such a schoolboy, I figured you were all set on being a doctor or lawyer or somebody who was going to break some new ground and open some doors in politics and stuff. Or maybe get into something sociological. Or maybe philosophical. Man, I never would have thought you'd be a musician of any kind, let alone a big league musician.

and I said, Man, me neither. Man, I just woke up one morning and I was on my way into the greatest band there ever was. And he said, Now that you tell me, I really shouldn't be surprised because you always did have that reputation for picking up on things. So now that I think about it, I bet you just automatically memorize every last note played by every last member of Papa Gladstone's band.

then for the benefit of Ben Rutledge he said, Old Papa Gladness. Man, the dances he used to play at the Boommenunion. The old Boommen's Union Hall Ballroom. The men who used to work in the log boom feeding time up the chute to the log carriage in the sawmills. Gasoline Point was a sawmill outskirts of Mobile long before they built the Gulf Refinery tank yards there.

it was part of a seaport area too, I said, with dry docks and a waterfront and longshoremen and all that with ships coming from all over the world. And Ben Rutledge said, Naturally we knew about Mobile being a banana and coconut town up in the Ham. And I said, And a railroad town too.

then Marvin Upshaw said, But old Papa Glad. He always did have a big league band. Did any of them big name bands mess with him except to try to steal away some of his musicians? Man, Papa Glad and them fools would tear you up. Tell them cats a band was coming through from somewhere up north and they'd start licking their chops before the word was out of your mouth.

we laughed remembering and then I said, What about you, Marvin? You used to try to box. And he said, Man, I'm still trying. And I looked at his face and hands more closely. Some prizefighters are really show biz personalities. They wear show biz clothes and have their hair taken care of like nightclub entertainers. But he looked like a cleanly scrubbed and massaged college athlete, a shifty halfback or a fancy dribbling basketball playmaker back in the days before it was unusual for basketball stars to be only six feet tall. Ben Rutledge was his trainer. You hardly noticed the scars on their faces and neither had cauliflower ears.

all I could say was that I had been out of touch with the fight game for a longer time than I realized. And he said, I fight under the name of Maddox. Then he said, I'm in this thing this Friday night. And Ben Rutledge said, It's in there, pointing to the newspaper at my elbow. And I said, Hey, let me see and opened the *Times* to the sports section. And there were waist-length bare-knuckled pictures of him and a fighter named Buddy McDaniels. The caption was, TITLE QUEST. The winner of the match at the Garden Friday night between contenders Marvin Maddox and Buddy McDaniels (a.k.a. Buddy Mack) will be the next challenger for the light-heavyweight crown currently worn by Freddie Hopkins. Queried as he broke camp in New Jersey yesterday, the ever cordial Maddox, who skips rope to Duke Ellington's "Mainstem" and whose graceful intercollegiate bearing belies the lethal power of his hands, admitted that he would be gunning for a quick KO and the odds are tipping in favor of his explosive right, which has dispatched his last three opponents within five rounds. Buddy Mack would say only that he was in excellent condition and expected—

there was Marvin Upshaw's voice again then, Hey, maybe you'd like to come, he was saying. And I said, You know something? I just might try to do that. And he said, Be my guest, and nudged Ben Rutledge, who reached into his bag and took out a breast pocket billfold and handed me a ringside ticket. And Marvin Upshaw said, Old home boy and all. Man, I haven't run across anybody from down the way since I don't know when.

we finished our tea and came on back out to the sidewalk again, then, and I said, Marvin Upshaw. Old badass Marvin Upshaw from Stranahan's Lane, which folks used to think was haunted because that was where Bea Ella Thornhill killed Beau Beau Weaver. You remember that? Ripped his bowels open with a switchblade. *Bea Ella with a switchblade!*

and he said, Man, I used to have to walk that lane to get home at night. But speaking of remembering Stranahan's Lane, how about that time when you went upside my head about them marbles. Then smiling at me ducking behind my elbow, he told Ben Rutledge, He tore me up.

and I said, Man, I forgot that. Man, I forgot all about that as soon as I saw how fast you were outgrowing me. Man, you just shot up overnight and I never did catch up.

that was when he said, Come on back to the dressing room afterward. Ben will let you in. And we shook hands, and as he turned to head for Eighth Avenue he said, Win, lose, or draw.

2.

he was wearing purple trunks and from the third row inside seat I could see the expression on his face as he danced up and down in his corner, touching his gloves together, his feet barely leaving the canvas, his head cocked to one side, the blue and gold robe draped around his shoulders. He looked ready and confident but I felt myself becoming tense. It was always easier for me to sweat out something I myself was getting ready to do than to watch as somebody else's time came nearer and nearer. When it was me, I was always busy thinking about what I was going to do, but when it was somebody else (whose side I was on) my best wishes were always mixed with misgivings.

around me amid the mounting excitement there was the uptempo but detached and comfortable banter of sports reporters and old ringside hands. I looked across the ring at Buddy McDaniels, who stood shifting his feet out and back, his arms hanging casually at his side. And I wondered if he were moving his bandaged fingers inside his glove and that made me remember the Bossman Himself moving his fingers as he stood waiting to come on stage from the wings. He was wearing black and gold trunks, which made me remember the Bama State Hornets basketball team, many of whose games used to be followed by a dance played by the Bama State Collegians, the best college dance band ever. He rotated first one shoulder and then the other and then turned to his corner and began to do a slow shuffle, facing but probably not really seeing the dim rows of spectators.

when I looked across at Marvin Upshaw again, he seemed unconcerned enough, but I had never seen him fight as a professional and I didn't know what to expect. The last time I had seen him in a prize ring he was fighting in junior weight preliminaries and battle royals, and I had no idea that he had any serious notions about becoming a full time boxer. He was just old badass Marvin Upshaw from Stranahan's Lane who, come to think of it, sometimes did stand around going through symbolic motions of Jack Johnson's old notorious uppercut much the same as he used to imitate James Cagney hitching his waist with his elbows. As I looked at Buddy Mack and realized that he was probably one of Jack Johnson's boys too I remembered Royal Highness talking about himself and Jack Johnson and I also remembered my homemade cement sack punching bag under the chinaberry tree in the front yard of our old shotgun house on Dodge Mill Road, and then I also realized that even as I practiced my Jack Johnson moves I was wearing my money ball pitcher's blue baseball cap because I was also one of Gater Gus's boys.

then I remembered becoming an all around high school athlete. Plus lead-off orator and clean-up debater because I had also become one of Mr. B. Franklin Fisher's Early Bird boys headed for college, where my good old best of all possible roommates used to say, Yea, verily I say unto you my good fellow, such is the nature of true, which is to say functional ancestry that necessity is the mother of fathers. It's a matter of choice my good fellow, he always liked to say. It is a matter of incentive and depth of personal motivation—a matter of horizons of aspiration.

while the two fighters surrounded by their handlers continued their warmup routines, neither looking in the direction of the other, in the row in front of me the sports reporters went on comparing notes. I listened to them sizing up things according to the latest inside dope and it sounded mostly like the same old stuff sports reporters usually talk. I didn't read sports columns very much anymore. They're almost as bad as jazz columns. But not quite. Sportswriters know at least as much about the sporting event they cover as do most sports spectators, and their predictions are either borne out by the final score or they're not. Many jazz journalists, on the other hand, often write as if they have earned an authority that qualifies them to pronounce final decisions on the outcome of a jazz endeavor so much so that without knowing what a given jazz musician is trying to do (what raw material he's trying to stylize into aesthetic statement) too many jazz journalists presume to report and assess the outcome.

as I looked around the ringside I thought about the sportswriters dead and alive that I still liked. I still liked A. J. Liebling and Ring Lardner and Red Smith and some of the ones on *Sports Illustrated* when it was new. There were also famous sportswriters who couldn't tell the players without a scorecard, but at least they knew whether they were looking at baseball, basketball, football, tennis, track, golf, or boxing. The distance of jazz journalists from flesh and blood musicians was mostly such that they obviously relied on scorecards. In any case they were usually accurate about the names of the musicians that they bested in their perpetual game of one-upmanship.

the radio and TV crews were already on the airways with up to the minute prefight details, and as the cameramen focused on the preparations in the ring I thought about sports announcers and disc jockeys. There was no comparison. There was no way in the world for sports announcers to ignore athletic champions and record holders the way disc jockeys (and some ideological jazz journalists) ignore living master musicians in favor of the latest bad taste.

there was the ring announcer then and then the referee took over and the two sides were in the center of the ring, the fighters finally looking at each other when they touched gloves. Then they were back in their corners and then the gong sounded and they moved toward each other.

and as I leaned forward watching Marvin Upshaw I remembered what I had read about in the prefight buildup. I liked his stance and I was also watching reflexes, and as soon as the first punches were exchanged I could see that his hands were as fast as they had been reported to be. And he moved his feet like a welterweight. Buddy McDaniels was also fast and no less shifty. It was not easy to hit him and when you did he could take it, and he counterpunched so sharply and followed up so naturally that you forgot who actually started the exchange.

but Marvin Upshaw had his own bag of tricks, and the next time he led he knew exactly what to do. He jabbed, slipped a counterpunch, got his cross in, followed it with a right, and kept the initiative, forcing

Buddy McDaniels backward. There was applause then and I felt easier about him in spite of myself.

he got the best two out the next three exchanges, and looked good in the clinches, and near the end of the round he scored on a combination that caught Buddy McDaniels by surprise and brought cheers from the crowd. Buddy McDaniels was not hurt but when the bell rang he knew that he had lost the round.

the second round began with Buddy McDaniels moving in, and I got a chance to see how good Marvin Upshaw was when he was forced to be on the defensive. He could block, roll, sidestep, counterpunch, and I especially liked the way he scored moving away. He did not try to take the initiative back until the round was half over and then he finished toe to toe and I thought he evened things up, but I wasn't sure enough not to feel a twinge of uneasiness.

they stepped up the pace in the third round and it seemed to me that Marvin Upshaw still had the edge and he was snapping and jabbing and increasing his lead all the time. But you could also see that he was not really trying to win on points. He was scoring effectively but he was really looking for an opening. Neither had tried a big punch yet.

at first Buddy McDaniels was going for the body, but near the end of the round he shifted and got in a sharp snapping left to the face and Marvin Upshaw tied him up in a clinch. But as they were separated, he got in two left jabs, which he followed with a hard right and a left hook that left a gash. And when the round ended, Marvin Upshaw's right eye was beginning to close.

they stopped the bleeding and put cold compresses on the swelling, and when round four began I knew that the exploratory phase was over. The pace picked up and the punches were harder. Buddy McDaniels switched back to the body attack but he got caught with a neatly executed combination and had to clinch, and when they broke there was a cut under his left eye.

they're gunning now, one of the sportswriters near me said. And the one next to him said, Smoking. Which was an old term I associated with the great Sugar Ray Robinson. Smoking, man, smoking. Man, these dudes can smoke.

which reminded me that whereas sportswriters not unlike jazz journalists have been picking jive language from athletes and musicians for years, athletes were now beginning to use sportscasters' lingo as a part of their idiom—for interview effect in any case. They now talk about holding their focus and concentration and developing a very fine ball club and so on, in accents straight out of the broadcast booths and editorial rooms.

this is anybody's fight, a third sportswriter said. And there was another tit for tat exchange of snapping lefts and Buddy McDaniels backed away with a cut under his eye and before he could get set, a right jolted his head back and I knew he was hurt. The crowd was in an uproar then, and I must have relaxed, or somebody must have jumped up and down in front of me, because the next thing I saw was Marvin Upshaw's knees buckling and Buddy McDaniels, one eye swollen shut, moving in on him.

the bell saved him. I watched them working on him in the corner and they had him on his feet before the fifth round again. Buddy McDaniels sat on his stool until the gong sounded. And then he moved in swinging. He knew he had him then and he was out to win big, to increase his bargaining power for the championship fight he was now next in line for.

but he couldn't knock him off his feet. The referee stopped it after a minute and forty-five seconds. It was nine-thirty.

3.

as I made my way toward the dressing room I was trying to think of what I was going to say. But when I got there and finally got inside, he was already in the shower. The doctor still wearing a stethoscope was talking to the handlers, who were waiting at the rubdown table. The manager stood off in the corner with two men I guessed were either his assistants or his business associates. I waited just inside the door near Ben Rutledge. Everybody was standing around in clusters, but nobody was saying anything about the fight. The manager was talking about airline tickets. The two handlers were telling the doctor about a forth-coming golf tournament.

he saw me and waved as soon as he came out of the shower. So all I had to do was wave back. I didn't have to say anything. He was cut and bruised and his left eye was still swollen but he looked as much like a getaway halfback as when I recognized him on Broadway. He had been banged up in that last round, but looking at him toweling himself you couldn't tell whether he had just won or lost.

hey, stick around, he said as he moved over to the rubdown table, I promised I'd bring you home with me. He put on his shorts and sat on the table and the doctor checked him over again. And then while one of the handlers worked on his face, the other gave him a massage. And when they were finished he sat up with one towel draped over his head and another around his shoulders and they let the reporters and photographers in.

he looked like a prizefighter again then, and as the photographers' lights began flashing I remembered Gasoline Point once more and how much I used to like the way the sports pages used to feature the faces of prizefighters and baseball players as cutouts on a white background.

there was always something about that which went with trophies and medals and citations with seals and ribbons. Sometimes a sports page cartoonist would sketch a crown at a jaunty angle on the head of the cutout of the champion and then sketch the rest of his body in miniature, one foot forward, gloves in position.

it was a great fight, man, a reporter said as they crowded around the table. And he said, Thanks, I hope everyone got their money's worth. And then he said, Man, the biggest drag is when they come out saying it was dull. And somebody said, Not this fight, Marvin. Never a dull split second with you in there. And he said, Well, I sure hope not. And when someone said, How do you feel, Marvin? he said, Surprised, shaking his head. And then he said, And hungry. And somebody said, Good sign, Marvin, good sign.

he took the edge, someone else said, but he couldn't put you away. So do you think he ever had a chance to throw his Sunday punch? And Marvin Upshaw said, Man, I honestly don't know. But I would say he must have got in most of the rest of the days of the week.

did he hurt you?

not really, but maybe I was too numb to know it. However, I won't deny that my feelings were hurt when I realized they were stopping it.

when did you begin to realize that you were in trouble?

when they stopped it and held up his hand.

not until then?

man, I was pretty busy up there before then. Or at least I thought I was.

what do you think of his chances with the champ?

he's a pretty rugged boy.

what are your own plans, Marv?

to get back in the top running as soon as possible, the manager said cutting in. That's all for now, fellows. Let's give him a rest. Thanks for coming by to see us. We really appreciate you not forgetting us on a night like this.

when we came outside most of the crowd was gone. The traffic along the avenue was normal again and as we stood waiting for Ben Rutledge, I looked up at the stars twinkling beyond the lights of the Manhattan skyscrapers and thought about the New York of the Hollywood cops and robbers melodramas and drawing room comedies of my early and middle teen years.

the dark aviator glasses that Marvin Upshaw was wearing covered most of the Band-Aid under his left eye. He turned up the collar of his trench coat and stood with his hands in his pockets. Behind us were the huge placards announcing the matchup of the two leading contenders for the light-heavyweight championship.

man, Estelle is really looking forward to meeting you, he said. I was telling her about you being a college boy and all that. She went to college for a while, too. And I said, You've been married five years. And he said, Six. They got it wrong in the paper. Man, I won the middleweight Golden Gloves, got married, and turned pro all in about eighteen months' time. And was on my way to being a father too. I'm actually a little older than you, but not as old as old gallinipper.

a black Cadillac with Ben Rutledge at the steering wheel pulled up to the curb then and we headed up Eighth Avenue the three of us sitting in the front seat listening to the radio. We were on our way to 730 Riverside Drive, which was at the end of West 155th Street overlooking the Hudson to Palisades Amusement Park. But at 58th Street they decided to take the long way around through Central Park. So we circled the statue of Christopher Columbus and passed through the portals at 59th Street where Eighth Avenue became Central Park West.

the record playing on the radio was a series of long-winded empty-headed fancy-fingered solos strung together by a piano pretending that what was being played was not the changes to "Please Don't Talk About Me (When I'm Gone)." It was all very hip, and each soloist knew exactly what he was doing because he knew precisely whose gimmicks he was stealing. And so did I. And the chase choruses went on and on and then finally as we came on toward the 72nd Street exit to the east side and the cross route to the west, there was a commercial.

they decided to continue on up to the 110th and Seventh Avenue exit and cross on over to Riverside Drive from there, and when the next number came it was the Bossman Himself. He was playing low register piano in unison with the bass with Joe States answering their call with his ride cymbal. They did sixteen. Then the piano called in the trombones and the whole band fell in growling and sounding almost sadly yearning at the same time.

hey, yeah, Marvin Upshaw said snapping his fingers and tilting his head to the right in time with the big stomping bass. Hey, is that you on that record?

not that one, I said. Because it was Scratchy McFatrick and he had it thumping. That's since my time, I said, missing them more than I could have brought myself to admit.

that's a good one, man, he said. And Ben Rutledge said, Listen to that goddamn Herman Kemble cutting them dots. And now here come old Wayman Ridgeway. That's when Marvin Upshaw said, I've got to get some of those records with you on them. And I said, I'll get some to you. And he said, You in there with the Bossman Himself. Boy, can't nobody say you ain't no big league musician. That smooth talking somitch has been the champion ever since I can remember.

ever since anybody can remember, Ben Rutledge said. Man, all that old jiveass bullshit is just to put people off because what he's hiding is the fact that he is as much an outright genius as any raving mad scientist you ever saw in any of them late-night movies.

and that was when Marvin Upshaw said what he said, as if he had forgotten that anybody else was present. Now that somitch is always in there winning because ain't nobody yet come up with nothing that he ain't got an answer for.

we were on the upper end of the park then and you could see the reflections of the lights in Harlem through the trees as you curved downhill and around the outdoor swimming pool and lake area. But instead of bearing a right and going up Lenox Avenue we went left to the Seventh Avenue exit. And nobody said anything about music or anything else until Ben Rutledge let us out in front of the apartment building.

man, this old lady of mine is a natural born stone fox, Marvin Upshaw said as the elevator started upward. If I do say so myself, man. He had buzzed the apartment as we came through the lobby and when we stepped out on the eighth floor she was waiting in the open door across the hall. She was wearing blue slacks and a gray V neck cashmere sweater with the sleeves pushed up and with a purple silk scarf knotted cowboy style. And I said, You said it, man.

we were there then and you were that close to that copper-brown,

satin-smooth skin and her dimples went with the way the fullness of
her hips matched the thinness of her waistline. The way her shade of
brown skin complemented the glossy sheen of her jet black bangs and
ponytail suggested down-home black Creek Indian relatives rather
than the taste of curry sauce.

as she said, Estelle, and we shook hands and stepped inside the
apartment, there was an after hours cocktail lounge organ, drums, and
tenor sax combo recording of an ever so soft blues shout thumping
ever so cozily on the sound system, the controls for which I spotted at
the other end of the living room near the dining area. I didn't know
whose group was playing it but I liked it. I also liked the apartment.

hey, sonny boy, Estelle said putting her hands on her hips and
pretending to frown as she looked her husband up and down, You look
like you went out somewhere and got into a fight or something. She
kissed him then and Marvin Upshaw said, imitating Louis Armstrong,
You hear this stuff, man? You see what Papa Gumbo and them were
talking about when they used to be talking about them old battle-axes,
bears, and barracudas? Man, he went on, You come home after a hard
day's work and the very first thing you run into is some old bossy lady
ready to turn salty on you.

boot chicks, man, he said as she gave him another squeeze and
then a shove and headed for the kitchen.

she was born and raised in Savannah and had gone to Spelman for
two years before her family moved to Chicago, where she began taking
professional classes in music and drama and decided to go in for show
business. She had been a nightclub entertainer in the Chicago area for
several years when she met Marvin Upshaw and decided that they
would be good for each other and also good parents.

man, I might as well tell you this too, Marvin Upshaw said, I'm all
signed up with one of the sneakiest broads you ever came across. *Man,
she was there tonight. She was there, man.* She was sitting way back up in
there somewhere with them goddamn spyglasses. He pointed to the
binoculars case on the shelf near the record player and said, That's supposed to be part of her racetrack equipment, but man, she was right up

there zeroed in and trying to help me duck all that shit that somitch was throwing at me.

she came out of the kitchen and went into the dining area, and that was when I noticed that table places were already set up for three. The record player was still going with the same extended blues romp, which by that time I realized was intended to last an entire set and which I decided to pick up at a record shop before leaving town. But even so I couldn't help wondering if we wouldn't have been listening to Ellington's "Mainstem" if Marvin Upshaw had won.

you never know when she might be there, he said as she went to get Virgin Marys for the two of them sour mash on the rocks as a down-home gesture of welcome back stateside for me. Sometimes, he said, it's all straight and she'll be right there at ringside, but sometimes she'll be talking about promising to go somewhere to play cards, which takes care of having to bring in a baby-sitter and then she'll sneak up there somewhere with them glasses.

he shook his head and pretended that her concern added up to an unnecessary burden, but he couldn't quite hide the fact that he was as pleased as he could be because she tried so hard to hide whatever anxiety she may or may not have about any given fight. Sometimes she stayed away or pretended to stay away because she suspected he was too sure of himself, and sometimes she was there in the third row hoping that her presence would give him the additional confidence that she was afraid he very much needed.

you never know, man, he said. Then she came back with the drinks, flirting with him with her eyes and her walk and taking me into their orbit of affection with her smile. He said, Like I told you, home boy, she's a natural born stone fox. And I said, Hey, man, you remember that old one on the piano rolls when we were way back down in grade school? And he nodded and together we said, If you've never been vamped by brownskin, you've never been vamped at all.

and he said, Old Scooter, the same old Scooter. Always did have that special birthmark for remembering everything like a flesh and blood dictionary. No, wait a minute, like a walking encyclopedia of universal information. What did I tell you? Didn't I tell you that this cat is something else? That's what I remembered after all these years as soon as I realized who you were when you hailed me down on Broadway the other day.

you had to be flattered, but what coming up with James P. Johnson's old ragtime piano roll had also brought back to my mind was the fact that I was all set to go by and visit Royal Highness that next afternoon.

but Marvin Upshaw went on telling his wife about the old days. Old Scooter, he said as she moved back and forth between the dining room and kitchen, He always was one that was staying in school and also keeping tabs on all of that old street corner and honky-tonk jook joint jive at the same time. Without any of them bell ringing roll book wardens over at old man B. Franklin Fisher's county farm ever catching on. Old Scooter, he said. That's how deep you already were. Even back then. Like I say, psychological, philosophical.

all I could do was shake my head and laugh at his impression of me as I was that many years ago. Then as if he suddenly remembered that he himself was now the father of a little boy who would be scooting about on his own terms more and more every day, he said, What about Wendell? And his wife, who was just about ready for us to come to the table, said, He's okay. No sweat. I told him it wasn't your night.

he already knows that you don't win them all, he said. But he thinks you should always try. He's going to be the world's champion jet pilot or spaceman or something plus a TV detective. When he retires from being the world's champion shortstop after setting the record for double plays.

at the table my place was the one that faced the window and I could see the traffic lights along Riverside Drive and the Henry Hudson Parkway. And I guessed that if you moved close enough to look north from the window you could see at least the New Jersey side of the George Washington Bridge.

it was a down-home meal of baked rabbit with all the trimmings including sweet potatoes, turnips, and thin golden brown slices of corn bread. And as we sat down he said, Well it's about time. Man, this woman may be as ugly as homemade sin, but she sure can cook. That's one thing you got to give her. She can play natural dozens with a mixing bowl. Man, that'd be the last thing you ever thought about if you saw her on the stage, but man, this foxy lady can make a frying pan talk down-home talk with some of the best I can remember.

hey, you better let him taste some of this stuff first, honey, she said. After all, he's not just another hungry Alabama prizefighter. He's a big time musician. He's used to all kinds of good eating and all kinds of places that I'm not so sure we're going to be able to afford when you get to be champion. Light-heavyweight champion. Maybe heavyweight—

man, he said cutting in before she could finish, I'm telling you she's right up there with Miss Alzenia Nettleton and Aunt Nicey Tompkins. And as soon as I took my first mouthful I said, He's not bragging. He's just telling it like it is. And I stood up and said, My compliments to the chef, who gets four stars in my Michelin any day.

we started talking about restaurants then and neither one of them said anything else about the fight until we finished eating and were back in the drawing room area and she put on another blues organ combo record. We sat keeping time, me on the couch, him on the overstuffed leather chair, and her on a hassock with a cup of coffee on a stool beside her. We were just sitting listening together like that and I had decided that I would say good night in ten minutes.

but as soon as the combo hit the groove on the third number I saw him drop his head and begin staring at his hands. And she must have seen it at the same time because she stood up and went over and sat on his lap and put his arms around her and kissed him.

you had him, she said. He's good. Very good. But you can take him and you had him. I don't know what got into you. And he said, Me neither. He said, I thought I had him too. And when she said, I knew you had him, he said, Maybe that's what happened.

then very casually she said, How do you feel? And he said, Right now I feel fine. I really do. I started my left and it got all tangled up in a bunch of cobwebs. And before I could get it free and shoot my right the fight was all over.

still ever so casually she ever so gently touched the tape under his eye and said, How about this? And he said, Nothing to it. And when she said, That had me a little worried, he said, I figured that and that's why I got him back double. He cuts a lot easier than I do. But when she said, But seeing you getting carved up bothers me more than seeing you go down, he said, Maybe that's because you ain't never seen me not get up. And she said, That's true. I've been spared that so far. But I still don't like nobody carving on that pretty face.

she started kidding him again, then and he started talking like Louis Armstrong once more and I got up to leave. And she brought me my hat and at the elevator he said, Sure is good to come across an old home boy, Scooter. And don't forget, me and Ben Rutledge will be driving you to the airport Monday morning. Call me Sunday night.

XLVII

So it's back down home from up the country for you, hey, Scooter? Marvin Upshaw said as Ben Rutledge pulled on through the tollbooth between the Triborough Bridge and the Hellgate span to Long Island en route to LaGuardia and my flight to Alabama by way of Atlanta. On our right across the East River as we merged with the traffic coming down from the Bronx, there was that view of the Manhattan skyline that suddenly gave me a pang that I later realized always came back whenever I took that route on my way out of the New York area by air.

Back from up the country and elsewhere as well, he said. And I said what I said then because I had already been thinking about what I was going to be saying and repeating when I rearrived in Gasoline Point from central Alabama and begin making the old rounds to Stranahan's store, Papa Gumbo Willie McWorthy's barbershop, Miss Alzenia Nettleton's cook shop, all on Buckshaw Mill Road now become the U.S. 90 approach to Cochran Bridge, and then on up to Shade's across from the old Boommen's Union Hall Ballroom up on Green's Avenue and also on over to the Mobile County Training School campus once more. I said, Back down the way from up the beanstalk.

I said, Back down the beanstalk that the chinaberry tree became, thinking: and Miss Lexine Metcalf's magic wand Windows on the World continued.

And Marvin Upshaw said, See what I mean? What did I tell you? Didn't I tell you that this cat has always been something else ever since I first knew him when we were kids in knee pants? Man, I remember you up there in that chinaberry tree using your cupped hands as make-believe binoculars and sometimes a long cardboard wrapping paper tube for a pilot's spyglass. Up there boxing the compass, man. And I'm not just talking about just some Boy Scout woodcraft stuff, man. This little rascal was already geographical even back then.

Old Scooter, he said. Man, me and old Ben here were talking about you yesterday and on the way over to pick you up just now. Old Scooter. Back down to Gasoline Point from points north and elsewhere.

And I said, Back to touch base before heading out again. I didn't do so after college. I joined the band in Cincinnati to pick up some cash I had to have to go with my graduate school scholarship, and one thing has led to another and another up to now. So now, I said, crossing my fingers, I got to go back and find out if I can pick up on some of the matters that have been on hold all this time, if you know what I mean.

And he said, I can guess. And man, if she's anything like that stone fox I lucked out with, which I have good reason to believe she could be, because I remember you and Charlene Wingate just like I remember you and that chinaberry tree and old Little Buddy Marshall. Take her with you this time. Maybe you don't know it yet, but you need her, man.

And I said, She was still in school when I graduated and there were also some hometown strings attached to her college scholarship, but she's supposed to be beyond all that by now. So what it really comes down to at this point is whether I get the benefit of the doubt, I said. And he said, Man, if she's the one, you will. And that's all you need.

We were out at LaGuardia in plenty of time for me to check in and also have breakfast with them in a concourse snack bar, and when we came on through the cafeteria line and found a table, he said, Man, I wouldn't take nothing for running into somebody from down home like this, especially somebody like you, Scooter. Because you remembered that I didn't have enough sense to want to hang on in school and get up there and be one of old man B. Franklin Fisher's Talented Tenth Early Bird boys like you did, and you were from even deeper down in the sawmill and L & N Railroad bottoms than any of us. But once I got up to Chicago and saw all them skyscrapers and plate glass windows and glittering lights, the bulbs in my dumbass head started lighting up and I got my stupidass ass back in school.

I earned myself a trade certificate first and along with it I also got the message of what schooling is truly all about if you really want to do something with your life. So that's when I made up my mind and went on back and got in night school and got my high school diploma. Because by that time I was saying to myself, Hell I could be my own kind of Early Bird. I told myself, If you buckle down and get to be good enough at doing something that amounts to something you can be somebody folks would be just as proud of as any other kind of Early Bird.

So that's my story, Scooter. And one of these days I hope to make old Mobile proud to claim me just like Chicago is going to be doing before I'm through. Man, like me and Estelle have already started telling Wendell, Whatever you do, if you do it with enough class, you can make your ancestors smile in their graves.

And I said, Hey, man, they smile in their graves whenever a contender sets his sights on the championship. I said, man, they start smiling in their graves the very minute they realize that you realize that nothing less than your personal best is good enough. I said, But man, what makes them turn over in their graves is a promising apprentice and journeyman who becomes a qualified but contented craftsman among other craftsman instead of a contender to be reckoned with in the realm of mastercraftsmanship.

Man, I said as we headed for the departure gate, That's why I'm still trying to figure out what it is that I'd be best at trying to do.

And Marvin Upshaw said, Hey, look, Scooter, I'm just going to say this for what it's worth coming from somebody like me that's been out of Gasoline Point all these many years and wasn't ever all that close to you back then. And man, this ain't just because you told me you're coming back up to go to graduate school either.

Man, he went on then, My guess is that it's bound to be something psychological or philosophical because look, Scooter, just about everybody in Gasoline Point have always been knowing that something like that is what you have been about. Just like home folks can tell when somebody else is all about growing up to be a preacher or something. See, now that's how me and you are different. What I got is an undeniable obligation to try to be champion. But that's not a calling. That's just my obligation to do my best whatever it is I'm into. But a calling is for the rest of your life.

Like the Bossman Himself, Ben Rutledge said as I took my place in line with my boarding pass ready; and Marvin Upshaw said, That's exactly what I'm talking about. Man, when you told me you went straight out of college and into that band, I was really surprised at first. But then it hit me. Man, the Bossman Himself ain't the bossman just for nothing. He knew exactly what he was doing when he hired you right out of college with no professional experience and didn't even major in music.

Like wham, man, he said. And that's also the way it hit me too. So there you were, up there helping him and Joe States and old sportyotie Otis Sheppard keep the beat and hold the time frame and boot the accents for that band of all-star musical thugs. Man, that's got to mean that he spotted something philosophical about you that you yourself didn't know you had yet, home boy.

And that was when Ben Rutledge got in the last word before we slapped and snatched palms and I headed for the gate. Man, he said, talking about philosophical. Man, it's exactly when that stuff of his hits that groove whether it's in a dance hall or anywhere else and that somitch starts siccing old Bloop and old Sir Wayman Ridgeway and old chickenbutt Ike Ellis and bootybutt Scully Pittman, the Gold Dust Twins, and old Malachi and that nasty talking plunger or any of them other laid-back ass-ripping tigers on you and you start snapping your fingers (and not just patting your feet) because your insides are already dancing, that's when he's laying his heaviest philosophical stuff on you. Man, but I don't have to tell you that that's when that stuff is really deep. What I'm talking about is some stuff just as deep as anything that ever made folks shout in church.

The also and also of all of which is also why, airborne and southbound to Alabama by way of Atlanta once more, I settled all the way back in my seat next to the window remembering yet again what Mr. B. Franklin Fisher always used to reiterate so strongly in his Principal's Farewell Remarks at the close of every commencement ceremony. As soon as he came to the part that you knew was going to be about faring forth, you knew he was also going to remind one and all once again that, along with literacy, the most important portable equipment that your MCTS diploma certified amounted to a compass, a spyglass for microscopic as well as long-distance inspection, skill with pencil and paper, and a knapsack for the other minimal personals. But no maps and mileage charts and timetables. Because pioneer pathfinders, trailblazers, early settlers, and frontiersmen must of necessity shoot their own azimuths, select their own triangulation points, and establish their own often tentative benchmarks.

So then with a smoothly droning Delta Air Lines jet cruising on southward above and beyond Maryland and Washington and on over Virginia and the Carolinas, there was also the also and also of my personal accountability to the ancestral imperatives again. *Not to the people of Gasoline Point, I said to myself. Not as such at any rate, I said. To the imperatives as such, I said. Your own azimuths, triangulation points, and benchmarks, indeed, I said. What are the expectations of a brownskin boy from the outskirts of Mobile, Alabama, when it comes to basic questions of the human proposition and the expansion and elevation of horizons of human aspiration? No less than is expected of any other boys elsewhere.*

Then there was the pilot's voice back on the intercom again announcing that the flight would soon be entering the Atlanta area approach and landing pattern, and I felt the way I felt because there was only that much more time before I would be back home again from college after that many years. *But only for the time being. Home again, home again, in again, out again. And do you come back bearing the Golden Fleece? The golden apples? The magic jewels? The magic wand? You do not. As Odysseus, most masterful of voyagers, did not. What he brought was that which he had acquired in experience in due course of his meandering: perhaps more pragmatic insight into his own identity and a deeper appreciation of chance, probability, and just plain lucking out. As for magic keys, are they not always a matter of the cryptographic information you acquire about combinations?*

The estimated time of arrival of the flight from Atlanta was only a matter of approximately thirty minutes once you take off and turn into your designated heading, and what I will probably always remember about that leg of the journey home is not so much what I was thinking as what I was wishing. *Rover boy, rover boy, where have you not been? Not yet to any castle with the true princess therein.*

Then, when the light propeller-driven short-range commuter craft touched down at last in central Alabama and came rumbling on along the taxiway to the two-story tri-city airport hangar where Eunice Townsend was waiting thinking whatever she was thinking, I uncrossed my fingers and crossed them again.

ABOUT THE AUTHOR

Albert Murray is the author of seven previous works, including the novels *Train Whistle Guitar* and *The Spyglass Tree* (which, together with *The Seven League Boots*, form a trilogy about the maturation of a young American in the first half of the twentieth century). He lives in New York.